MW00826572

OVERLOAD FLUX

CENTRAL GALACTIC CONCORDANCE BOOK 1

BY CAROL VAN NATTA

CHAVANCH
PRESS

WWW.CHAVANCH.COM

ORLAND PARK PUBLIC LIBRARY

Van Natta,
Carol

OVERLOAD FLUX
Copyright © 2014 Carol Van Natta
First Ebook Published October 2014
Published by Chavanch Press, LLC
ISBN: 978-0-9831741-4-1

ALL RIGHTS RESERVED. Except for use in any review, this literary work may not be reproduced in whole or in part by any means, including electronic or photographic, in whole or in part, without express written permission of the author.

All characters, places, and events in this book are the pure invention of the author; they are fictitious and have been used factiously, and are not to be construed as real. Any resemblance to actual persons living or dead, actual events, locales, or organizations is strictly coincidental.

Cover design by Gene Mollica Studio
Edited by Shelley Holloway
Author website: Author.CarolVanNatta.com

DESCRIPTION

* * * * *

The only vaccine for a deadly galaxy-wide pandemic is missing ... and the only ones who may be able to find it are a powerful talent on the verge of a meltdown, and a security specialist hiding her extraordinary skills in a menial job.

Brilliant investigator Luka Foxe must act fast if he's going to save the civilized planets of the Central Galactic Concordance. For as a pandemic sweeps across the galaxy, someone is stealing the vaccine. To make matters worse, Luka's hidden mental talents are out of control, leaving him barely able to function in the midst of violence and a rising body count. The convoluted trail leads to a corrupt pharma industry and the possibility of an illegal, planet-sized laboratory. In the face of increasing threats, he must rely on an enigmatic, lethal woman who has secrets of her own.

Mairwen Morganthur hides extraordinary skills under the guise of a dull night-shift guard. The last thing she wants is to provide personal security for a nova-hot investigator, or to be plunged into a murky case involving sabotage, treachery, and the military covert operations division that would love to discover she's still alive. Worse, she knows that two more deaths won't bother their enemies one bit. Their only hope for survival is to share their darkest secrets. With everything in their universe at stake, can they learn to trust one another?

* * * * *

"Overload Flux is a brilliant, suspenseful tale that will keep readers captivated from beginning to end." ~ S.E. Smith, New York Times & USA TODAY Bestselling Author of The Alliance series

* 2014 SFR Galaxy Award Winner *
* 2015 National Excellence in Romance Fiction Award Finalist *

CHAPTER 1

THEIR FOOTSTEPS ECHOED in an empty corridor of Rekoria's planetary spaceport. Mairwen Morganthur caught herself touching the outside of her coat pocket that held the wirekey, and ruthlessly controlled herself to keep her uneasiness at bay. Though neither man she accompanied down the tall, wide corridor had said so, she had the feeling they didn't want to be discovered doing whatever it was they were about to do.

Motion-sensor lighting triggered as they approached each segment. At ninety-four minutes before midnight, the noisy passenger area of the spaceport had been as busy as ever, but the commercial shipping section where they now walked was deserted. Trending galactic headlines and bright vids flashed silently on the continuous overhead displays along the corridors, creating constantly changing lights and shadows. It could have been worse; in the passenger section, the animated displays took up entire walls.

She walked two paces behind the two men, like any average, incurious security guard, and kept her expression blank. Her company uniform and long topcoat passed as conservative corporate wear at a casual glance. As long as no one noticed her heavy boots, she wasn't likely to draw unwanted attention to their group.

Personal security detail wasn't her usual assignment. While she did usually work nights, it was mostly as a solo guard or security systems monitor at large industrial complexes in marginal sections of town. This was supposed to be her night off.

She hoped the only reason she'd been chosen for tonight's activities was because she was a name on a La Plata Security Division "night-shift available" list of dozens, and not because she'd stood out in some way. She'd been careful to stay unremarkable. This was the first time in months she'd allowed herself to open her extraordinary senses even a little, noting and cataloging the distant sounds of automation and the stale scents of people. She shouldn't be doing it now, but the increasing tension of the two men she was accompanying was contagious.

The older man, Velasco, about her height, was entertained by the flashy wall displays in a variety of languages, and softly repeated the words that caught his attention. He again switched the padded strap of the large forensic kit he was carrying to his other shoulder. Lukasz Foxe, taller than Velasco by a dozen centimeters, stood straighter and carried two bags slung over his right shoulder, a smaller hardcase and a larger curved bag, and had a winter greatcoat over his left arm. He was leaner and clearly in better shape than Velasco. So far, Foxe hadn't said much.

When she'd received her orders from dispatch to check out a company vehicle, pick up the wirekey and a forensic kit for Foxe from the office, then pick up Velasco from a restaurant and take him to the spaceport, she had assumed she would then remain with the company vehicle while Velasco did… whatever it was he was here to do. Instead, for reasons unknown to her, Velasco had told her to come with him to collect Foxe from the gate of an incoming interstellar ship. The need for her presence certainly wasn't for her company or conversation, because once they'd entered the brightly lit spaceport, Velasco had all but ignored her. She was relieved. From what she remembered from meeting him once at a company event, he had nothing worth saying.

She'd never met Foxe before tonight. Dispatch's orders had included his company photo, which didn't do him justice. Even though he was obviously tired, he was handsome, with light brown skin and wide, angular cheekbones, and wore his casual business clothes with more style than Velasco's ultra-trendy but unflattering suit.

She was already familiar with Lukasz Foxe's name. She'd memorized most of the Investigation Division's investigator names and titles so she'd know whom to avoid. She didn't want the possible attention that came from being in the orbit of a blue-hot company star. She didn't know what a High Court-certified forensic reconstruction specialist did, but she had the feeling she was about to find out.

She hadn't quite figured out what Velasco's role was. From something he'd said in the first burst of jabbering he'd subjected her to as she drove him to the spaceport, he was with the Security Division of La Plata, but assigned to Investigation. She'd mostly tuned him out for the rest of the trip, choosing instead to focus on traffic, which wasn't well automated, day or night. Etonver city drivers were allowed to disable vehicle autopilots, and mostly did, making for bad ground traffic, twenty-five hours a day.

The spaceport corridor split, and they turned toward the section with commercial interior warehouses. When they rounded a corner to the left, Velasco pointed halfway down the hall to a large cargo bay door of opaque flexglass. The logo said "Centaurus Transport" in huge letters. A smaller, human-sized door farther down to the left had the same logo. The two men stopped in front of the bay entryway, and Foxe looked to Velasco.

"Anything from the Port Police?"

One of the benefits of working for a security company was official access codes for police bands. Foxe's first order after arriving had been to tell Velasco to monitor the frequency from his percomp. It had been Mairwen's first clue they were expecting trouble.

Velasco activated the company-issued percomp he wore strapped to his wrist. It was a more recent model than hers; night shift tended to get refurbished leftovers. Tech Division had been nagging her to surrender her clunky hardware for an update.

"Nothing," Velasco said after a moment. Mairwen got the impression he hadn't been paying attention to it until asked. Fortunately, his assessment was accurate. Even though she hadn't been ordered to do so, she'd been monitoring the same frequency via live audio sent to the earwire adhered to her jawline, and had heard only two routine communications in the last eleven minutes.

Mairwen was becoming increasingly resentful at being kept off the net as far as what she was being dragged into. She had no idea why investigators from her company were going to the warehouse office or what they expected to find, other than something that would need a forensic kit. Meaning it was more than a simple slice by interstellar jackers or some ground-based theft crew. But she couldn't ask without drawing unwanted attention to herself, so she stayed quiet. It was one of the few times she'd ever wished she was a telepath. Most telepaths she'd ever met were under the thumb of the Citizen Protection Service, and she knew the steep price of that all too well.

The door frames of the transport company entryways had visible security monitoring devices in the form of flat camera eyes that looked glossy and new. She angled herself away from them, not knowing their peripheral range. If they were like the industrial versions she was familiar with, they'd only be triggered when the doors opened, but better safe than sorry. She considered whether or not a simple security guard would notice the cameras or think to point them out. Probably not, she decided.

Foxe checked the elegant, transparent percomp he wore on the back of his hand. "Still no pings."

He sighed and ran his fingers through his dark, wavy hair, making it look even more unruly than it already did.

"Let's go in." He didn't look happy to be there. Mairwen sympathized.

Velasco held out his hand toward her expectantly, and Mairwen slipped the wirekey from her pocket and gave it to him. As he fumbled with the lock on the smaller door, she took a couple of steps back from both men and the camera eyes, toward the center of the corridor. She opened her senses wider to check that they were still alone.

Sounds came from the electric hum of lights, the pulse of the air circulators, and the whine of automated grav sleds. Somewhere inside the warehouse, a loose vent rattled intermittently. There were scents of lubricant, petroplastic, paper dust, and humans, mostly hours and days old except for the strong new scents of Velasco and Foxe. Velasco smelled of too many cosmetics, synthetic fabric, fruity alcohol, and meat, probably steak. Foxe smelled of wool from his coat and a natural buttery, subtle exotic wood scent that was incongruous in a spaceport. Velasco's scent was boring, but Foxe's was… interesting, almost intense. She caught herself just in time from stepping closer to breathe in more of it. *Very bad idea,* her cautious brain told her.

Velasco couldn't get the wirekey to work on the small door, so he tried the cargo bay door. It lifted swiftly and quietly.

She was immediately assaulted with the unexpected stench of blood, bile, bowels, and recent death as colder air billowed out from the warehouse. She slammed closed her suddenly overloaded senses, blinked away involuntary eye moisture, and smoothed her face to hide her reaction. She was glad neither man had been watching her. They didn't appear to notice anything amiss, but she couldn't tell what normal people could smell. She focused on Foxe to see if he expected this magnitude of trouble, and thought he didn't. It wasn't likely to make him any happier to be there.

When they stepped in through the bay door, bright overhead lights in the warehouse blinked on. She hung back momentarily, thinking of standing guard in the corridor, but concluded the Port Police would consider her equally involved if she was outside or inside with Velasco and Foxe. She followed them in, tucking her face into the shadow of her high, wide collar as she passed the cameras. Velasco closed the bay door behind them and inexplicably handed her the wirekey again instead of keeping it. Probably he didn't want to be caught with it. She put it back in her pocket without comment.

Mairwen looked around for more security devices but saw none. She'd have liked the time for a more careful examination.

Before them were several disarrayed rows of waist-high palletized crates. Foxe and Velasco walked roughly parallel paths through them. They passed a line of grav sleds into a more open area. She followed Foxe's route and stepped to his left, stopping when they did.

She hadn't seen a lot of underground spaceport warehouses, but she imagined this one looked and smelled like any other. Except for the mute evidence of a wholesale robbery by a sloppy crew in a hurry. That, and the two dead bodies in a pool of congealing blood on the floor. From the smells, which she couldn't totally block even with her senses practically zeroed, the bodies were only a few hours old.

Velasco's shock caused him to inattentively drop the forensic kit with a crash, missing his own foot by centimeters. Foxe stared at the bodies for six or seven seconds, then turned toward her and focused on some point above and behind her to her left. He didn't look squeamish or nauseated like Velasco did, but he was paler than before. His jaw was tight and his breathing was shallow, like he was wishing he didn't have to breathe at all.

"Shit... shit... shit," Velasco muttered, mesmerized by the horrific aftermath of violence in front of him. He swallowed hard.

Foxe gave Mairwen a quick, assessing look, which she met with equanimity. He nodded minutely, perhaps relieved that he didn't have to deal with incipient hysteria from her, too. He turned his head to focus on his associate.

"Velasco, check the rest of the warehouse for doors and offices. Tell me what you find."

"What? Oh, yeah, okay," said Velasco, almost stumbling over the forensic kit at his feet. "I'll see if there's an evac map or something so we'll know what... Shit, is that more blood?" He leapt away from a black smudge and looked at the bottom of his shoe, then skirted away toward the wall and disappeared down a row of shelves. "Why don't they have auto lights... Oh, finally... It's a mess back here..." His voice trailed off as he all but ran away. Babbling seemed to be his method of coping with stress.

Foxe turned toward Mairwen again and activated his percomp. His earwire was probably as unobtrusively elegant as the unit. Investigation Division stars rated much better tech than night-shift guards. At least all the La Plata company percomps were encrypted for traffic and location, so a later net dump by the Port Police wouldn't be traceable to any of them.

"I'm at the warehouse. It's been sliced, and Leo and Adina are dead." His tone was flat, but his face showed a depth of emotion not expressed in his words. "I'll do what reconstruction I can before the police get here. I'll ping after." He disconnected. Whoever got that message wasn't going to be happy tonight, either.

His knowing the murder victims explained some of the look of distress in his hazel eyes, the look that said what he'd seen had been etched in his memory with acid.

He studied the nearby stacks of crates, as if memorizing them, then put his luggage on top of one stack and pulled on his greatcoat against the chill of the warehouse. He retrieved the forensic kit from the floor and set it on another stack of crates and opened it.

Velasco returned from his task and stopped near the suspended work surface along one wall. He looked up toward the lights, clearly avoiding the less pleasant things on the floor.

"There's a regular door in the back, and an office, and a full fresher. The alarm was tripped back there, or at least that's where it's blinking. There's nothing else, uh, like that." He tilted his head toward the bodies. He looked bilious. He turned away and picked up a stylus, as if to examine it, but dropped it on the floor. He retrieved it, but in trying to avoid looking at the rest of the floor, he bumped into the work surface hard enough to set it swaying.

Foxe happened to be facing Mairwen's direction again, so she saw him wince before he smoothed his face and turned to Velasco. "Why don't you go watch the back doors and monitor the Port Police chatter?" Though phrased as a suggestion, it was unmistakably an order.

Velasco had the grace to look faintly embarrassed as he headed toward the back. Mairwen had taken him to be older, though with decent bodyshop work, he could have been nearing civilian retirement age at 130, and no one would know it. His unprofessional behavior, regardless of whether or not he'd known the victims, made him seem absurdly young and inexperienced. Odd that he was paired with Foxe.

Foxe began pulling instruments from the forensic kit. It was obvious he knew exactly where in the kit to find each item he wanted. So as not to disturb him, she stood still where she was. She turned down the volume of the Port Police frequency on her percomp so she could listen for changes in audible rhythms from outside the warehouse. If the police weren't using their net, she hoped her senses might at least give her an early warning.

The tripped alarm, evident from the security system's blinking lights, should have brought a response within minutes, but the Port Police were infamously slow in handling incidents that didn't involve passengers. It made her antsy not knowing how long the alarm had been signaling, but there was nothing she could do about it. She focused her gaze forward and used her peripheral vision to watch Foxe work.

From what she could tell, the instruments he used were for detailed measurements or capturing images, like the cloud of little flying 3D cameras he was directing now. They resembled the nuisance flying adbots that increasingly swarmed retail shoppers and tourists throughout the galaxy, but Foxe's had camera eyes instead of holo projectors. She had the vague notion that crime scene investigation involved taking samples, but she'd never seen a reconstruction specialist in action. They weren't common, and Foxe was touted as an expert, which was undoubtedly why La Plata's Investigation Division had hired him. La Plata Security and Investigation specialized in providing the best, and set their fees accordingly.

He moved economically and gracefully as he worked, but it was still eating up the minutes. He was looking everywhere except the bodies, but his tense expression as he looked at her, which was increasingly often, said they were all he was thinking about. She supposed she might be affected, too, if they were her friends, but she didn't have any, so she could only speculate.

He hadn't said more than three sentences to her since she introduced herself at the gate, so his request now almost startled her.

"Morganthur? We're on borrowed time. Can you do something with their office comps, and still monitor the Port Police band?"

She didn't think he'd noticed when she'd adjusted her percomp. She made a mental note to be more careful around him.

He sounded tired and hurting, although she couldn't have said how she knew. A moment of uncharacteristic empathy made her want to help him, instead of act fog-a-mirror dumb like she ordinarily would have. Like she had for the past four years.

"Clone, take, or flatten?" she asked. Admitting to some comp skills was probably safe enough.

His eyes widened and an eyebrow raised, and she had the impression he was actually paying attention to her for the first time that night. She disciplined an impulse to flinch at the surprising force of his regard.

"Clone, preferably without leaving a trace."

To her relief, the connection broke when his gaze left her. He opened the small hardcase he'd brought with him, which turned out to be another forensic kit. He pulled out a clonewire and handed it to her.

She went to a large terminal on a nearby mobile table and inserted the clonewire. The wire was fast and the cloneware was glossy. It only took a few moments to breach the warehouse's barely adequate internal security and get their entire data hypercube. Centaurus Transport must trust its employees a lot more than the average company, she thought. On a whim, she found and cloned the security module while she was at it, noting with wry amusement that the warehouse was scheduled to have the new door cameras operational later that week. More worryingly, she discovered the intruder alarm had been tripped more than two hours ago.

Four minutes later, she disconnected the clonewire and wordlessly handed it to Foxe. She was unexpectedly… aware of his proximity, so she backed away fast to return toward her self-appointed post near the crates. His voice stopped her.

"I need your help."

He looked toward the direction that Velasco had gone, then back to her. His expression and tone said he really hated having to ask. "If you can handle it, I need you to search the bodies quickly, and tell me what you find."

He'd given her an out, but the despairing, almost haunted look that shadowed his warm hazel eyes and tense mouth were more than she could stand. For whatever reason, he couldn't handle it right then, and she knew she could. She knew death from way back.

"Gloves?" she asked. She didn't want to leave her biometrics around for the sniffers that even incompetent police typically used. She removed her topcoat rather than chance trailing it in body fluids. The warehouse felt cold but not unbearable.

He handed her a pair of microskins from his kit. She smoothed them on as she looked more closely at the bodies. They were about a meter apart, both wearing black civilian clothes and light coats. The dark-skinned woman would have been tall and imposing in life. One of her long legs lay across the lighter-skinned man's feet. His body was curled in a fetal position, so it was hard to judge, but she guessed him to be considerably shorter than the woman. She crouched between the bodies, balancing on the balls of her feet to avoid the combined pool of blood and less-pleasant fluids that had leaked after death. Her boots would leave a distinctive print if she wasn't careful.

"What are you looking for?" she asked.

The corpses were starting to stink, so she cut off her awareness of it. There were other scents nearby, besides Foxe's, but too degraded to be of any interest, except a couple of hours-old human scents and maybe a hint of something medicinal. She cut off her awareness of those, too, dismayed that she had so unthinkingly and easily allowed them to register in the first place.

"Tell me what's in their pockets, anything unusual about their clothes. Anything you notice about their injuries," he said. Although he was turned away, she thought he might be watching her with his peripheral vision. He still looked pale, almost traumatized. "If you have to move anything, try to put it back like you found it, so it doesn't screw up the official investigation too much." His tone implied he didn't think much of the Port Police's ability to notice things like that. Given their reputation and lack of response so far, she had to agree.   ·

She started with the man first. Foxe had called him Leo, and she finally put it together with the last name of Balkovsky that she remembered from the Investigation Division. He was the source of most of the blood and stench, and now that she was close, she could see why.

"A broken-handled forceblade is stuck in the man's left pelvic bone. The forceblade is large, maybe twenty-five centimeters. The strike came from right to left through his pelvis and intestines. He bled out." If the handle hadn't failed, the forceblade would have finished cutting the man in half and spilled more of his fried entrails. He'd died with an anguished look on his ash-white face.

Perhaps that was part of why Foxe couldn't look at the bodies. In her peripheral vision, she saw him shiver as if even his winter coat couldn't keep him warm.

She gently probed the body with her gloved fingers and searched the clothing, while avoiding the blood and tissue, and described what she found. Foxe had her clone the gory wrist percomp but leave it and the earwire on the body, as well as the ankle gun, jewelry, and a couple of wirekeys. When he told her to take and bag a joyhouse souvenir token, she did as he asked, but a hint of puzzlement must have shown on her face.

"It's a percomp. Leo liked hiding things in plain sight." He kept his eyes focused on hers, so she could see the effort it was taking to maintain composure, and his strong jaw pulsed once. It was like seeing someone unexpectedly naked.

She shifted her focus to the woman, Adina, whose body was lying on its right side, legs twisted unnaturally. She was feeling the pressure of time and worked quickly. "Holsters empty... pockets too. They were searched."

"Why do you say that?" he asked.

She started to show him, but he'd retreated to his resolute stare away from the scene. "Pockets partially pulled out."

"But not Leo's?"

"No." She continued her examination. "Blunt impacts on the left shoulder... Left elbow feels broken... Knuckles are bruised and broken... Percomp like yours on her left hand." She leaned in and looked at it more closely and saw the characteristic distortion pattern and pinpoint blood spots on the nearby skin. "De-rezzed. Probably a mister." Misters were small hand weapons that could temporarily paralyze or render unconscious. They were illegal in most places, but not in Etonver, where almost anything could be openly carried or concealed.

"A mister?" he asked.

Mairwen could have kicked herself. Dull security guards wouldn't know what mister damage looked like. But she'd already opened her mouth, so she might as well go on. "Two shots, maybe more. Left arm, neck."

"Misters aren't usually fatal."

She gently lifted the lapel and collar of the woman's singed flatcoat to look underneath. "No, but a forceblade through the heart is." The singed entry wound was unmistakable. The bottom half of the coat had soaked up most of the leaking blood.

She saw the hint of a tattoo on the woman's neck and pushed aside the shirt collar to see the rest of it, and the skulljack behind the ear she expected to find. Now the woman's bruised hand and broken elbow made sense.

"She did some damage to her attackers after the man—Leo—went down. Ex-Jumpers are hard to kill."

Jumpers were the military's elite special forces under the Citizen Protection Service. Unsurprisingly, both La Plata's divisions employed a large number of military veterans.

She made one more discovery. Under the woman's body, obscured by the blood-logged coat, were three identical, sealed packages of what looked like medical capsules, labeled with obscure identification codes and symbols. They were the source of the medicinal scent she'd caught a whiff of earlier. She shut down her sense of smell yet again, perturbed by how often that evening she'd been lured into breaking her own rules about using her extraordinary senses.

"Three squibs under her, maybe pharma or blackmarket chem samples," she told him.

"Bag them." She used her right forearm knife to lever each sample up and slide it into the bag he held open for her. She re-sheathed the flat blade and used her glove-protected fingertip to gently smear nearby blood around to obscure the shape of the void the packages had left.

She started to ask if he needed anything else from the bodies, but momentarily froze when she realized the rhythm of sounds from the corridor outside had just changed. Wheels on plascrete, the click of motion-sensor lights blinking on, human voices. Very likely the Port Police. If she said nothing, and the police entered the warehouse before checking in, she and her co-workers would be caught in a locked room with two murder victims.

Foxe noticed her hesitation and focused his eyes on hers. "What?"

Unable to come up with a plausible excuse, she gave him the truth. "I thought I heard something." It sounded lame. She looked toward the bay door they'd used twenty-three minutes before.

He considered her words a moment, then put the evidence bag in his kit and started rapidly closing it up. "I think we've pushed our luck far enough. We'll go out the back way with Velasco."

She quickly stripped off the gloves inside out and put them in her pants pocket, then grabbed her topcoat and the large kit he'd just finished sealing and slung its strap over her shoulder. He picked up his luggage and hustled toward the back of the warehouse. She kept pace right behind him through the jungle of shelves to where Velasco was standing. She was now glad he'd given her the wirekey earlier, because it meant they wouldn't lose valuable seconds waiting for Velasco to produce it. As she edged in front of Foxe and headed straight for the door, voicecomm from the Port Police band sounded in her earwire.

"*Base two, six thirty at Centaurus Transport bay side. No visible breach. Harris is downloading the keycode now. Sitrep in ten.*"

Velasco heard it, too. "Shit, the police are out front. They're getting the key now."

"We're done. Let's go," said Foxe.

Mairwen used the wirekey to open the door in the hope it wouldn't trigger another alarm. She calculated they had maybe ten seconds before the police entered at the other end of the warehouse. They'd be as unpleasantly surprised by the bodies as Foxe and Velasco had been. All in all, no one was going to be happy that night.

Once Foxe and Velasco were through the door, she sealed it and put the wirekey in her pocket, while turning up her senses to make sure more company wasn't coming. Foxe seemed all right, but Velasco's shallow breathing and fast heart rate said he was headed toward panic again.

She took the lead to get them walking fast down the corridor to get Velasco to put some of his adrenalin to good use. She heard a distant grav sled coming their way. She looked for and found the corridor split and led them into the side hall. She wanted to avoid triggering the motion sensors for the hallway lights, so she slowed to a stop after a few steps, as if adjusting the shoulder strap.

Velasco's breathing was heavy, but he seemed to be in better control of himself now. Foxe took the opportunity to call up a holo map of the spaceport on his percomp. She was relieved because it meant he could plot their path away from trouble and out of the spaceport. She'd already planned multiple escape routes the moment she'd learned the warehouse's location, but that wasn't the kind of initiative exhibited by unambitious night-shift guards.

"Cart coming," warned Foxe. Thankfully, his hearing was good enough to notice it. She felt him step close behind her. His unique, exotic scent teased her senses before she ruthlessly blocked it. What the hell was wrong with her?

Foxe's fingers brushed her arm. "Wait until it goes by," he said. Velasco nodded. She nodded, too, but stepped away because she didn't want Foxe touching her again. She put her coat on and sealed it, wishing it was lined with flexin armor.

Even when he was quiet, the pressure of his breath and the resonance of his voice rumbled in her ears, provoking a desire to hear more. *Very bad idea,* the cautious part of her brain told her. She dulled all her senses to practically comatose levels. Her inexplicable and uncontrollable awareness of him was an unwelcome distraction, and dangerous. If the universe loved her, after tonight, she'd go back to her safe routine and never cross his trail again.

CHAPTER 2

LUKA FOXE SLUMPED in the company vehicle's well-padded back seat and huddled in his greatcoat while rubbing his throbbing left temple. The cold was in his bones again. He was grateful he didn't have to drive, because even at one in the morning, Etonver traffic was horrible. He'd have liked to blame the double full moons, but Etonver traffic was notoriously bad all 388 days of the year.

He was deeply tired and stressed. Re-certifying his expert credential at High Court on Concordance Prime hadn't been a vacation, and the last few hours had been a *klústérfökk*. The incompatibility of ship schedules and local times on two planets meant his body clock was haywire. He didn't sleep well on small starships. He didn't appreciate cramming five hours of reconstruction into twenty minutes. He didn't like dodging the police. And he didn't reconstruct murder scenes any more. Especially when one of the victims had been his best friend.

The vivid impression of the bodies of his colleagues Adina Schmidt and Leo Balkovsky was still acid sharp. It had only taken seconds for the phantasms of how it could have happened to ooze up and contaminate his mind with bile. Even though he'd looked away quickly, he'd already seen and memorized too much. The talent-driven visions of possibilities had twisted his train of thought, until he could hardly think of anything else.

It hadn't always been that way. When he'd worked as a civilian for planetary police and military criminal investigation units, his hidden minder talent to see a crime scene and imagine the scenarios that fit had been useful. Involuntarily triggered by evidence of violence, but manageable. His final case changed everything. He'd hoped time and disuse would have made his talent easier to handle, but tonight proved that, if anything, his wayward ability was just as strong, and his ability to control it weaker.

As tempting as it was just to doze, he needed to organize the data and send a preliminary report now, because he expected to flatline for at least eight hours once he got home. The only bright spot of the night was Morganthur. She'd been much more useful than his nominal assistant, Velasco. He was glad they'd dropped Velasco off first.

"Assistant" was maybe too strong a word. La Plata policy required its investigators to have partners, but no one else had the background to help him, and he was accustomed to working alone. They might have let the policy slide, except for his tendency to lose all track of time and space when he was deep in a reconstruction, even without using his talent. La Plata solved both problems by assigning him a personal security detail out of the Security Division. His assistant accompanied him, drove him places, provided another set of hands, and kept track of things. He'd gone through several of them. The latest was Velasco, who was comparatively reliable and affable, but talked a lot, was distracted by women, and was prone to fidgeting with anything nearby, including evidence.

Luka hadn't really noticed the difference until tonight, when Morganthur had stood quietly still for fifteen minutes straight. At the end, when the violent visions of what had happened to his friends in the warehouse were practically blinding him, she'd been a living, steady anchor to reality, even if she didn't know it.

That she'd been both unperturbed and competent in searching the bodies was a small miracle. Velasco would have thrown up on them.

Luka encrypted his findings and the data clones Morganthur had retrieved and transmitted them to Seshulla Zheer's attention. The net connection was secure, but it never hurt to use added security with sensitive data. He guessed Zheer, the president of the company, was now his boss until she found a replacement for Leo.

Luka had never wanted a lead role, at least not until he regained control of his talent, and not while Leo enjoyed leading. Luka was numb now, as if he'd applied a slap-patch anesthetic to his emotions, but he knew the heartache would come. He was fluxed and wrung out at the same time. He swung his long legs across the seat and leaned back in the corner, trying to think of other things.

Movement up front from Morganthur caught his eye. He'd initially taken her for ex-military, but she was too slight to be an ex-Jumper, and her movements were too unconventionally fluid for regular military standards. Her almost translucent pale skin, arctic-lake blue eyes, and spiked blonde hair should have been dulled by the gray and black of her company uniform and coat, but weren't.

Now that he had time to think about it, she was an enigma. She clearly had some intelligence behind the bland stolidity she wore like flexin armor. His other wayward talent, the one that let—or forced—him to see the essence of a person was curiously quiet around her.

And maybe he was too tired to think straight, and maybe he shouldn't be imagining intelligence or mystery in a woman he'd only met two hours ago.

Just as his eyelids were drooping, he was surprised by a live ping from Zheer. He kept it earwire-only, rather than bring up the visual holo on his percomp.

"*Where are you?*"

"On the way home. I sent the data already." His voice sounded as tired as he felt.

"*It's already being analyzed. Stop at the office first and see me. LANR says you're close.*"

LANR was the nickname for the planetwide Location and Navigation Reconnaissance system. Businesses paid to use it to track their commercial ground, water, and air vehicles anywhere on the planet surface. Up until that moment, Luka had thought it was a good idea.

"It can't wait?" He couldn't keep the reluctance out of his tone.

"*No, but I'll make it quick. You need to get any samples in custody, anyway.*"

He started to say there hadn't been time to collect any, but then he remembered the unidentified squibs.

"Fine," he said, and disconnected. "Morganthur, we have to stop by the office first."

She nodded and changed lanes. She said nothing the rest of the trip, for which he was grateful.

* * * * *

The executive suite of La Plata's president was palatial, designed to simultaneously impress visitors and make them comfortable. Mairwen had never been there before and didn't want to be there now. She suppressed the uncharacteristic urge to fidget.

The meeting shouldn't have involved her, and yet there she was, becoming a known name and face to the company president. Foxe wasn't helping.

"Getting the warehouse's security cube was Morganthur's idea," he said, pointing her direction.

Zheer reflexively glanced at her with a slightly raised eyebrow. Mairwen kept her expression blank.

"Well done," Zheer said, then returned her gaze to Foxe. "The analyst on call sent preliminary data trends to your display."

La Plata needed to hire a better photographer, because Zheer's official picture didn't do her any more justice than Foxe's had. Zheer's patrician features, deep black hair, and slanted eyes spoke of an Oriental heritage, and she had an undercurrent of strength. Her age was impossible to gauge. Despite the late hour, she was dressed as if for a board meeting.

Although Mairwen sat and listened politely, underneath she was irritated. She didn't care that Juno Viszla Casualty, La Plata's insurance company client, was trying to get out of paying more claims from Centaurus Transport. She didn't need to know that the murder victims, Balkovsky and Schmidt, had been looking into a series of thefts, or that they'd notified Zheer earlier that night they were investigating a fresh break-in at the warehouse. Foxe and Zheer should have let Mairwen wait with the vehicle so she could take Foxe home, then get back to her ordinary life. The life where low-level uniformed security guards worked the graveyard shift, and didn't have meetings in plush executive offices that smelled of expensive coffee, leather, and a hint of smoke.

Mairwen was glad Foxe was looking less distressed than he had in the warehouse. It made it easier to be annoyed with him now. At least he had the good sense not to talk about how she'd helped search the bodies, or that she knew what forceblades could do, or what mister wounds looked like. Her background records were as average and boring as she could make them, and she couldn't afford the chance that someone smart might notice the discrepancy between her life on paper and her real life. Someone like Foxe, whose keen intuition was off the charts.

Even though he was plainly exhausted and distracted, he'd quickly seen a pattern in the thefts that suggested the real targets were Loyduk Pharma vaccine shipments, not the shipping company itself. She wouldn't be the least surprised if Foxe turned out to be a minder, some rare type that the Citizen Protection Service hadn't yet found a way to exploit. Which made him all the more dangerous, beyond the fact that her physical and sensory awareness of him hadn't faded. She needed to get away from him soon.

Zheer opened her display, then gave Foxe a measured look.

"I'm making you the lead for this. I know you don't like working murder cases, but you were damn good at them. We just lost two top-notch investigators. La Plata will be picking up the tab for the murder investigation for now, but I'll work on getting Juno Vizla Casualty to pay for it. Hand off or subcontract your other cases. I want you on this full time."

Foxe's expression darkened, and Mairwen thought he might be about to object. Apparently so did Zheer, because she stood up and leaned in toward him, fists on the desk. "No arguments, Luka. I am beyond angry at whoever killed my friends and yours, or had it done. Go find them for us."

After a moment, Foxe nodded, his reluctance plain. "Is that all?"

"For now," she said, seemingly unperturbed by his icy tone. "Go home and get some rest."

She waved toward the door, signaling the end of the meeting. Foxe stood and grabbed his greatcoat, and Mairwen followed suit. She watched him surreptitiously, wondering how he was taking Zheer's hardnosed attitude, which was less considerate of a star employee than Mairwen would have expected. More than anything, he looked stunned.

She slung the strap of his small forensic kit over her shoulder as he grabbed his travel bag. He nodded thanks, but she wasn't doing it for him. The faster he left the executive suite and the sooner she got him home, the faster she'd be out of sight and forgotten.

The rest of Mairwen's night didn't go any better than it started. After driving Foxe to his townhouse and returning the vehicle to the office, she discovered the company garage was closed, as it was occasionally. Her neighborhood wasn't safe for new-looking vehicles, even with upgraded security features, so she parked it near the office. Dispatch told her they had no orders on what she should do for the rest of her shift, so she took the metro home, where she cleaned her apartment, tried to read but couldn't focus, and did reps on her force isolation exerciser until the garage reopened at seven.

She parked the vehicle in an available stacker slot, then pinged dispatch that she was signing out. They pinged her back promptly with an order to report to her supervisor before leaving.

Malamig's office was on the first floor, near the La Plata building's back entrance. He was only just hanging up his coat when she arrived.

"Sit. What did you do last night?" His expression was mild, but his tone had an unexpected note of hostility. He sat at his immaculately arranged desk and aligned a cup of hot coffee with the edge of his deskcomp.

"Should I file a report?" she asked. Her usual assignments required shift activity reports, so perhaps he was displeased because she hadn't submitted one.

"If Investigation Division wants one, they can request it through proper channels. It's bad enough I have to special bill them so your salary doesn't come out of *my* budget. Who did you talk to? I want to know why Investigation asked for you without going through me."

Good question, she thought, but if Malamig didn't know, she doubted she'd ever learn the answer. She shrugged. "Dispatch sent orders."

"Yeah, I've already had a little chat with them." His narrowed eyes and thinned lips told her dispatch probably hadn't enjoyed the exchange. He leaned back and crossed his arms. His chair creaked as he rocked.

"Company policy says I have to give you a compensatory day off, so I'll have to take you off your current assignment."

"I'll waive—" she began, but he interrupted.

"Too late; I've already changed the roster." The creaking stopped, and he gave her a smug, almost taunting smile. "Next time Investigation calls you, maybe you'll think to check with me first."

Mairwen gathered his intent was to punish her for her part in what he perceived as a challenge to his authority, regardless of her blamelessness, and was using company policy as his weapon. Before she could answer, he leaned forward in his chair, feet stomping flat on the floor. "And don't get any ideas of working for Foxe or Investigation Division, either. I say who goes, and it won't be you ever again."

That was the best thing he could have told her. She almost smiled. "Understood."

He looked nonplussed by her response, as if he'd been expecting an argument, maybe even hoping for one. She'd heard rumors he enjoyed exercising power over his subordinates, but she hadn't experienced it until today. She presumed it would soon blow over and he'd go back to ignoring her. To most of the night-shift employees, he was just a name on procedure memos.

He waved her away dismissively as he woke his deskcomp. "You can go. I'll have dispatch ping you when I find a new assignment for you."

She left his office and started to leave the building, then changed her mind. Since she was already there, with unexpected free time, she went to the Tech Division on the second floor and surrendered her percomp for updating. They loaned her a thincomp and told her to come back at eleven.

Since she didn't have a vehicle, there was no point taking the forty-minute metro ride home, only to have to turn around and come back almost immediately. She'd get home and to bed later than usual, but she didn't usually need much sleep.

With no office of her own, she cooled her heels in the employee lounge area and got caught up on some administrative work. She even wrote a shift report on the previous night, in case Malamig changed his mind. She didn't want anything unusual in official records, so she phrased it to imply her role had been little more than chauffeur and door guard.

Fifty minutes later, a co-worker she remembered from previous assignments and more recent company meetings came in. The woman had a fruit cube and spoon in hand and plopped on the well-worn but durable couch. Beva Rienville, if Mairwen remembered the last name right, was a breezy, generously built woman with smooth chocolate skin and a lilting accent that Mairwen recognized as a French variant. Beva was the most congenial, sociable person Mairwen had ever met on the night shift, or anywhere else, for that matter. Beva insisted on using first names immediately whenever she met anyone.

"Mairwen Morganthur! *Comment vas?* How are you? Don't see you in the office much, at least during daylight hours."

Clearly Beva had a better social memory than Mairwen, who needed sensory cues, usually scent or sound, to remember people's names. Keeping her extraordinary senses dulled to near unconscious levels had its disadvantages.

"No," agreed Mairwen.

"Still like working in the field?"

At Mairwen's nod, Beva smiled. "Good for you. I never looked good in the uniform like you do, and I got tired of them forgetting I was even on the planet. Besides, my wife wanted me home on time, and I missed our kids. And now I'm up for a promotion." She took a bite of yellow fruit. "Mind you, office work has its downside. Tech is upgrading the network, and half the time, we may as well have dumb kiosks at our desks." She rolled her eyes. "Hard to get work done when you can't get to your work, *savez?* Know what I mean?"

"Yes," said Mairwen. Should she say something else? She'd never gotten the hang of chatting.

"Does it smell like sour coconut in here to you?"

"I have a poor sense of smell," said Mairwen, a lie she'd told so often she almost believed it herself.

"Probably Junnila's breakfast curry again. And speaking of deadly," she said with a smile at her own joke, "did you see in the news where the NVP pandemic might be hitting Rekoria in the next couple of months? If it does, I'm not coming into the office again until they find a frellin' cure. They can fire my *grand cul*. No job is worth the chance one of my co-workers might bring it in for 'show and share.'"

Mairwen couldn't think of anything to say to that, but Beva didn't seem to mind. She continued her meandering conversational monologue another nine minutes, content with Mairwen's willingness to listen and respond occasionally.

After Beva left, Mairwen spent some time reading intergalactic news, which she'd been lax in keeping up with because it never changed much. The Central Galactic Concordance now had 506 member planets, and three new frontier planet candidates. Concordance Command Space Division was again cracking down on jack crews who preyed on space freighters, stations, and spaceports. A sensational non-fiction publication about a horrific crime last year continued to break sales records. A Citizen Protection Service proposal to require a round of additional minder skills testing for all citizens at age twenty-one was voted down by the High Council. A representative for the Concordance Ministry of Health assured the public that a vaccine against NVP 70 was one of their top priorities, and the public mustn't panic.

Mairwen snorted at that last item. If Beva's declaration was anything to go by, the ministry was trying to load ground cargo on a ship that had already gone interstellar transit.

Unaccustomed to sitting for long, Mairwen killed more time by taking a walk around the block twice, despite the blustery autumn wind. She regretted that her uniform and boots weren't appropriate attire for using the company gym or going for a short run.

When she finally traded the thincomp for her updated percomp near lunchtime, Tech apologized for how long it had taken, what with network contractors under foot and getting in everyone's way. She stuffed the percomp in her topcoat pocket and headed downstairs to the northeast exit, which was closer to the neighborhood metro station. If she was lucky, she'd be home and in bed in an hour.

She heard her name called just as she got to the door. She suppressed a sigh as she turned and walked back down the hall to where Malamig stood outside his office door.

He was glaring at her, red-faced. "Did you tell Investigation Division that you were available?"

This was not good. "No, I did not."

Malamig looked taken aback by the strength of her denial. "Well, somebody did. They want you again tomorrow. Day shift security detail for Foxe." His resentment was palpable.

She was sorely tempted to refuse the assignment, but doing so would give Malamig something to use against her later, and maybe even cause Foxe to come looking for her.

"Where and when?" She knew it'd been a colossal mistake to feel sorry for Foxe and help him last night. Nothing good ever came from good deeds.

"Check your percomp," Malamig huffed. "They copied you on the order directly." Another breach in protocol, apparently. He poked a crooked finger toward her face. "Don't get used to this. You haven't earned it. Security Division is the financial engine of this company. Investigation has no right to poach my staff."

He dismissed her and slammed his office door shut.

Late that evening, after a few hours' sleep and a longer run than she'd planned because she needed it, Mairwen paced in her small apartment. She was full of resentment and other, less easily identifiable emotions. She regretted that she didn't need as much sleep as other people, because it gave her time to brood.

She hoped Malamig got what he wanted. He was a hidebound jerk, but he managed the Security Division schedule and assignments well, and he usually ignored her. Besides, if he got the director's position that he'd reportedly been bragging that he was toplisted for, he'd no longer be her problem.

Foxe was another matter. To quote a saying she'd once heard, he was nine yards of trouble.

Eleven hours from now, she was to check out a company vehicle and meet Foxe at the office, then accompany him wherever he wanted to go. She didn't want to be his company. She didn't even want to be in enclosed spaces with him, where the sounds and scents of him were too intense. He was dangerously smart and dangerously... tempting. She'd caught herself entertaining idle thoughts of how it would feel to touch his skin, or what his mouth would taste like. It was an involuntary and inconvenient hormonal response to his presence. She'd seen it in others, and read about it, but it was the first time she'd experienced anything like it herself.

She supposed she should be grateful to regain that small bit of normality. It had been four years since she escaped from the Citizen Protection Service, but they'd had nineteen years to burn out most of her humanity. They'd given her the ability and knowledge to survive and succeed in the harshest of conditions, but no useful skills to do ordinary, civilized things, such as have a friendly conversation. Much less how to navigate attraction.

Exasperation coursed through her. She'd only spent a combined total of about three hours with Luka Foxe, but thanks to her suddenly runaway senses, she already knew the cadence of his walk, the timbre of his voice, the smell of his soap. She liked that he had a brain and knew how to use it, but it made her vulnerable to his powerful intuition. If anyone could uncover her secrets, he could, and it would likely get her killed.

Since her sex drive was going to wake from the dead whether she wanted it to or not, why couldn't it have picked a nice, stupid person?

The only safe course, she finally decided, was to do the job asked of her but nothing more. Foxe would conclude she was useless to him and send her back to the Security Division. Malamig would be happy to get his way, and Mairwen could go back to the safe, quiet anonymity of the night shift, and forget how proximity to Foxe made her feel.

Chapter 3

LUKA HADN'T EXPECTED to be back at the planetary spaceport quite so soon, and not in the middle of a workday. The huge port was teeming with crowds of people, some in a hurry to get somewhere, some doing their jobs, some waiting. He'd never cared for crowds, and especially not since his talent had flared. More than half the people were carrying one or more weapons in holsters, rigs, sheaths, and pockets, which he still wasn't used to even after a year of living in Etonver. The city didn't even require biometric safeties on any of them.

His eventual destination was the food court commons, the public place where the informant wanted to meet. The unlooked-for informant that Zheer had sent him to meet, in Leo Balkovsky's place.

For now, he stood on the pedestrian bridge above to get the lay of the land. Morganthur stood quietly to the side and a couple of paces behind him, as had been her habit so far. Her dark green civilian suit, a long jacket over a buttoned shirt and pants, didn't fit perfectly, so she probably bought it set-sized instead of from an autotailor. He wondered if she didn't have the money or didn't care. At least it and her light overcoat concealed any weapons she might be carrying besides the wrist knife he'd seen at the warehouse. Her expression and body stance were neutral, but he had the feeling she was very aware of her surroundings.

He hadn't planned on bringing Morganthur today, except he'd been in a bloody-minded mood the day before. He'd mostly forgotten about her after the dead-of-night meeting when Zheer had forced him into leading the case. He owed Zheer for giving him a job and working around his... eccentricities. If he really wanted off the hook, he'd have to tell her the truth about his talent, and he wasn't willing to take the chance that she'd consider him impaired. The case was too important to give to anyone else. Zheer knew he'd been a lead investigator before, and had the record to prove it. La Plata's top investigator had been Leo Balkovsky, a mid-level finder who made it out of the Minder Corps of the Citizen Protection Service more or less sane, but he'd been gutted like a fish in the Centaurus warehouse. Luka missed Leo's good-natured teasing and confident leadership with painful intensity.

After what had happened at the warehouse, Luka hadn't slept well and had gone into work early. He'd been too restless to work in his office, so he'd decamped to a nearby conference room, as he sometimes did when he needed room to pace. Vengeance fantasies kept infiltrating his rational thought processes, and the movement helped him stay focused. He'd heard Velasco looking for him, but hadn't been in the mood to deal with him. Then he'd heard another voice, and it became apparent that Velasco had run into Malamig, the scheduling manager from Security Division. Luka wouldn't have eavesdropped if he hadn't heard his own name.

"…pick Morganthur to drive me and Foxe last night?" asked Velasco.

"Don't ask me," replied Malamig with evident antipathy. "Investigation Division chose her from *my* roster. Something about availability and location. Why, did she screw up?"

"No, she didn't do anything except drive and stand around. Wouldn't talk to either of us. Typical graveyard shifter—no social skills whatsoever." He snorted. "Once I saw her in the light, I remembered meeting her a few months ago. Tall, skinny blondes with little titties aren't my type." Some men remembered women's names, faces, or jobs; Velasco remembered their bodies. "I mean, Foxe is weird and all, but he's got nothing on her. Dekkil says she always carries two or three knives."

"She's stupid, and she doesn't know how to cooperate," said Malamig with vitriol. Luka wondered what she'd done to piss off her boss. Perhaps she'd turned him down for sex. If so, Luka's estimation of her taste rose a couple of notches.

"You better be careful," continued Malamig. "She might be willing to spread for Foxe to get *your* job, and then you'll be back in patrol doing shift work again."

Velasco laughed. "I'm not worried. Foxe is oblivious to women, and even if he wasn't, I doubt he goes for zero-witted or hostile."

The conversation had ended a minute later, with Malamig headed back to his office and Velasco leaving for parts unknown.

If they hadn't mentioned Morganthur's name, Luka would never have guessed they'd been talking about the same quiet, unexpectedly competent woman who'd helped him in the warehouse. Even if she was uncooperative or hostile, which he highly doubted, she'd been immediately more useful than Velasco. He didn't care what either Velasco or Malamig thought of him personally, but oddly, he'd found himself annoyed on Morganthur's behalf.

So Luka had given in to malicious impulse and sent a request to Zheer for Morganthur to accompany him the next day to the meeting. An informant with information about the case just dropping in from the sky still felt entirely too convenient. He firmly told himself he'd asked for Morganthur because he hated to see good talent to go waste, and definitely not because, for the first time in a couple of years, he was attracted to someone—a lithe, cheetah-slim woman with hidden depths.

"Ten minutes."

Her low-pitched, slightly raspy voice brought him back to the present. He'd asked her to give him a countdown at five-minute intervals, in case he got distracted by his talent or violent memories. He hadn't, but only because he'd been distracted by thinking about her. He gave himself a mental shake to focus on the job at hand.

"Showtime, I guess."

He was still bothered by this meeting. Even if his talent was unpredictable, his intuition was as good as ever, and it was pulsing warning pings.

They rode the moving stairs to the floor below and threaded through the thinning lunchtime crowd to the prearranged meeting place under the giant clock. It displayed galactic coordinated date and time, local time, and similar data for a dozen popular destination cities on Rekoria and other planets. The murmurs of dozens of languages made a sea of sound. Luka snagged an abandoned tray so he wouldn't look out of place and found an empty table. Morganthur had already drifted away, making their connection less obvious. The informant knew what he looked like, so all he had to do was wait to be found.

It didn't take long. An older, round-faced, olive-skinned woman with gray-streaked black hair, wearing the uniform of a spaceport maintenance worker, slipped into the chair opposite his. She was trying to play it cool, but her eyes darted around too often.

"Lukasz Foxe?" She mangled the pronunciation of his first name. Most people did.

When he nodded, she said, "I'm Sandy Green."

Almost certainly not her name, but he understood her caution.

"Call me Luka. Pleased to meet you," he said, not as warmly as he'd intended. He was liking this situation less and less. It felt like a setup, although he didn't know who the target was. "I understand you have some data you're willing to share?"

Green pushed her hair back behind her ear in a nervous gesture. "Do you work with Balkovsky? He's who I talked to."

"He's unavailable at the moment." If she didn't know Leo was dead, Luka wasn't going to be the one to tell her. "Your message said you wanted to talk immediately. You're moving soon?"

"I'm being transferred," she said, and her flat tone hinted she wasn't happy about it. She leaned closer and said more quietly, "Look, Balkovsky promised me a reward if I told him who's been after Centaurus Transport."

Luka showed more surprise than he felt. Greed was so dependable. "This is the first I've heard of it. I'd have to run it by the office."

"*Carajo*, don't you people even talk to one another?" Green's expression hardened in annoyance.

Luka made a placating gesture. "If your information is good, I think we can work something out. How much did you have in mind?"

She named a figure that raised his eyebrows. Small ocean yachts could be bought for less.

"I'm the one taking a chance here," she said defensively. "He'll kill me if he finds out I'm talking to you."

She painted a picture of a man with a grudge because Centaurus Transport's poor service had cost him his business, his home, and eventually his family. She was saying all the right things, but Luka thought it felt too easy, too believable. On the other hand, it could be true and he could be twisting himself with patterns that didn't exist. He wasn't a finder like Leo, able to extrapolate truths from unconnected, random data.

Hell, this was why he'd resigned his Concordance Command commission and left criminal investigation. Before last year, he could have focused his talent on her to get a sense of whether or not to trust her. Then he'd forced his talent to burn bright to catch a predator. It had nearly cost him his own life, and now he couldn't make it stop. He could see a lot more and deeper, but once he started, his own thoughts got swamped and he drowned.

A stark memory of Leo, curled like a child in death, rocked Luka. If he didn't take a chance, he'd never get justice for his friend. Maybe with so many people nearby, he'd be able to use them like a white noise generator to counter the input from his talent.

For the first time in months, he hesitantly tried to see the essence of the woman in front of him. His initial impression was that Green was sincere and worried, maybe with a thread of vengeance, but there was an unexpected layer under it, and it was nothing he recognized. It was almost like looking at pieces of a mosaic without being able to see the whole, and seeing the whole was the core of his talent. He'd never felt anything like it, and didn't want to now or ever again. His stomach turned leaden.

Needing to get away from the disturbing fractures in her, he dragged his focus to the young man at the next table. It helped some, but now he was starting to sense the man, and cold visions started to form around the details that told stories of the possible. In growing desperation, he looked around as casually as he could. His eyes lighted on Morganthur, who was leaning one shoulder against the pillar of the huge clock, looking like a bored passenger with time to kill. He focused his talent on her, keeping her in his peripheral vision as he looked down at his hands resting on the table.

To his relief, the images in his mind began to mist away and his talent cooled. For whatever reason, focusing on someone he knew, however slightly, was helping him regain control. He returned his gaze to the woman in front of him, while still keeping Morganthur in his sight as his talent quieted. Green had stopped talking, and he quickly replayed in his head her last few words, something about being scared of the vengeful man who had nothing to lose. She was fidgeting nervously with the beads of her necklace-style percomp.

He opened his mouth to speak reassuringly, but movement from Morganthur caught his attention. She'd straightened up and gone from being still to... not still. It was subtle, but if he had to describe it, he'd say she was looking antsy. It reminded him of how she'd looked in the warehouse when she'd thought she'd heard something, and turned out to be right. Even though the food court was large and open, he was suddenly feeling claustrophobic.

That was enough for him. He stood up, and Green did, too, though with obvious reluctance.

"I don't blame you for being cautious," he told her, not meeting her eyes. "You deserve the reward you were promised, so don't give me the man's name right now or my boss might think he doesn't need to pay you." He handed her a La Plata comm card. "I'll do what I can on my end, so ping me tomorrow." He didn't care if she thought he was rude, but he had to get away.

He strode quickly toward the moving stairs with the pace of someone running late. To his relief, his talent quieted fully as the distance increased. On the stairs, he turned to check the local time on the big clock, giving him the chance to confirm that Morganthur wasn't far behind him. She was seemingly focused on her percomp, but the immobility of her shoulders said she was still on alert. At the bridge level, he threaded himself in and between clumps of people until he got to a safe vantage point from the pedestrian bridge. Keeping his face in shadow, he looked at the food court to see if Green was still there. She was, though she was now closer to the clock pillar.

He felt Morganthur's approach behind him without having to look. "What now?" she asked softly. He was grateful not to have to explain his actions to her. Velasco would have been on his twentieth question by then.

"We watch Green," he said. "Too many inconsistencies."

Once he'd gotten away from the woman, away from the threat of losing control, he'd had the chance to consider why his intuition was giving off warnings. Mostly little things, like her uniform had been too new, her makeup too expertly applied, her English accent too precise, and her percomp too delicate and expensive for a maintenance worker. The story about a vengeful man sounded like the plot from a tri-D detective drama. Not to mention that nauseating fracturing of her that he'd sensed, though his talent wasn't exactly reliable these days.

Morganthur stepped forward and leaned her elbows on the railing. Though she was looking down at the food court, she looked like she was lost in thought, not really seeing anything.

After only a minute, one man, clearly a mercenary even when seen from a distance, approached Green, and two other mercs converged on her from two other directions. Green talked, the merc nodded and talked, Green shrugged, the merc talked more. Her body language said she knew the man and wasn't afraid of him. Green walked away, and the first merc said something to the other two that had them heading in the same direction Luka and Morganthur had taken, toward the moving stairs. Luka had to force himself to keep in mind the possibility that Green had hired the mercs to protect her, not target him.

He was startled out of his thoughts by Morganthur, who had turned to look at him. "I need to run an errand." Her expression was unreadable. He suddenly realized he hadn't given a thought to how her schedule had been disrupted because of him, and he felt guilty for not asking.

"Sure, go ahead. We're done here." He looked at his percomp for the time. "I'll catch a flitter. That should get me back in time to do some running on an actual planet for a change."

She nodded and strode off, but into the port instead of toward the exit. Out of curiosity, he'd have liked to see where she was going, but decided it wouldn't be prudent to chance running into the two mercs who'd headed for the moving stairs.

He lucked out and snagged a piloted flitter to take him back to the office, above the horrendous traffic. La Plata could damn well eat the cost. He paid extra to engage the privacy field, then used his percomp to live-ping Zheer with a quick report of the meeting and Green's subsequent interaction with the mercs, including the reward request and his suspicion that it was a false lead.

His intuition still said the Loyduk Pharma vaccine was the target, not the shipping company. "If someone had the right distribution lanes," he told Zheer, "they could sell a pandemic vaccine for triple or quadruple the price of retail, especially if the theft created the shortage in the first place."

"I think you're on the right track," she said. "By the way, you have an appointment tomorrow at an independent testing lab to get those samples from the warehouse analyzed." The live holo of Zheer temporarily faded as it was washed out by the bright autumn sun. "This is getting serious, Luka. From now on, I don't want you going anywhere without security."

"What do you mean by 'anywhere'? Off hours, too?" The thought of spending hours on end with Velasco had him grinding his teeth.

"Anywhere, as in working, eating, shopping, running, rescuing abandoned pet-trade creatures, or whatever you do. And think twice about going anywhere with crowds. I'm not taking any more chances with my people."

Luka sighed. "Fine, but I approve the personnel." He knew from her tone that Zheer wouldn't budge any further on the issue. "Anything else?"

"Yes," she said. "I was thinking of assigning Morganthur for your personal security detail rotation." At his frown, she added, "Your choice, of course. Her record is clean, and she's got basic skills and experience, but Malamig, her supervisor says she's stupid, difficult, and out of her depth. He made a formal complaint to my office about Investigation Division stealing his staff."

Luka laughed. "You know you live for petty office politics, Seshulla."

"Bite me," she said with mock irritability.

Luka laughed again. "I'll accept her. She's got the social skills of a cactus, but she's a better driver than Velasco, and she's definitely not stupid. She's observant, too." He described how she'd seen the mercs coming in the food court long before he would have, and how her early alert had given them time to watch the mercs interact with the informant.

"My one-eyed, deaf great-grandmother would have seen them before you did," Zheer said. "That's part of why I'm assigning you continuous detail for this case. Once you get focused on your work, a heavy hauler could crash into the building and you'd never notice."

"Bite me," said Luka.

Zheer laughed as she ended the call.

He wasn't looking forward to a constant parade of company. He liked time alone, and he needed it when his talent muddled his thought processes. Velasco was barely tolerable, and Luka hadn't been impressed with other Security Division employees Malamig had sent before.

On the other hand, spending more time with Morganthur wouldn't be half bad. From what he had seen, her observational skills were on par with a scanning telepath. That night at the warehouse, she'd probably saved them from an uncomfortable night with the police, and after seeing her today, he suspected it might have been more than luck.

His hot mess of a talent went blessedly cool around her, and he had no idea why, but he wanted to find out. He made a mental note to ask Zheer to confirm that Morganthur's security background check had actually been done. His experience with her so far said she was much more interesting than her record suggested.

* * * * *

In between avoiding the worst of Etonver's inevitable traffic congestion areas, Mairwen berated herself all the way from the spaceport to the La Plata campus to return the company vehicle. She'd been firmly in the "do your job, nothing more" mindset from the moment she'd picked up Foxe, right up until her senses told her the mercs were converging. Or perhaps earlier, when she'd thought Foxe had been in some kind of trouble during his conversation with the woman called Green, and the distressed, almost haunted look was coming back to his face. In any case, Foxe had somehow read her when she'd sensed the threat and it was good they evaded what might have become a problem.

Unfortunately, she hadn't stopped there.

From the bridge, when Foxe had said there were too many

inconsistencies, she hadn't been able to resist the temptation to find out if he was right. She'd turned up her senses to listen to the conversation between Green and the merc leader. She was four years out of practice, and it had been a challenge to filter out the cacophony of light, sound, scent, and sensation, and to hear only the voices she was interested in. She'd gotten lucky with acoustics and the merc leader's naturally resonant voice, or she'd have missed half of it.

Green explained to the merc leader that she'd signaled when it became clear that Foxe wasn't biting, then Foxe had left abruptly for no reason she could tell. The merc leader asked where Foxe had gone, and Green shrugged. The merc leader told her and the other two mercs they were done for the day, and he'd report in.

Even then, Mairwen couldn't leave well enough alone. After she'd gotten free of Foxe, she'd ghost-shadowed the merc leader through the port. Her blandly corporate clothes and the crowds made it low risk, she'd rationalized. She'd ruthlessly suppressed this part of herself for a long time, even made herself forget she knew how, so it was unsettling how easily it came back to her, and how good it felt. Still, she caught herself making small mistakes that might have cost her in a higher-risk hunt, such as not taking smaller reflective surfaces into account where he could have seen her if he'd been looking.

The merc leader ended up at a bank of pixcons. She didn't know why he bothered with a secure connection when anyone nearby, even with normal senses, could overhear his side of the conversation, conducted in spoken standard English, no less. Eavesdropping yielded nothing until the end, when he'd mentioned payment from Loyduk Pharma. The makers of the vaccine being stolen.

Her first impulse had been to tell Foxe, but her cautious, rational brain that had kept her well hidden the past four years crushed the idea immediately. She'd have to tell him how she got the information, and she couldn't do that. Security guards who showed initiative or extraordinary skills got noticed, and that would be the first step in a trail that would inevitably lead to her exposure and death. Or if the universe was really malicious, her recapture and reconditioning.

Foxe would have to find the connection on his own. He probably would, anyway, as smart as he was. It would just take him longer.

Her day did not improve when she got back to La Plata. Malamig ordered her to report to his office the moment she arrived. She wasn't used to having to interact with him, or anyone else, on a daily basis. She was very ready to return to the comfortable solitude of the graveyard shift.

He'd obviously had drinks with lunch, because the smell of garlic and grain-based alcohol was unavoidable. He was seething, and his rural English Isles accent became more pronounced as he ordered her to sit.

"You've been assigned to Foxe as one of his security assistants for his 'special project,' by direct order of the company president."

Clearly both Malamig and the universe were highly displeased with her. Malamig was likely feeling threatened by the loss of his authority, and she was a convenient target. The universe had no excuse.

He told her tersely that she and the others assisting Foxe were being assigned company vehicles and pre-authorized use of a company flitter, which not even Malamig had.

Mairwen didn't want a special assignment or a vehicle; she wanted to be left alone. It was safer than being around Foxe and his sharp intellect and even sharper curiosity. Something of her reluctance must have broken through her usually neutral exterior.

"Is there a problem?" he asked, obviously hoping she'd give him an excuse to sandbag the Investigation Division.

She grasped for something he'd believe. "What about a contract?"

"If you want to renegotiate your contract, you'll have to ask your new pal Foxe, because I'm sure as shit not doing it for you." His upper lip twitched in disdain. "What's this special project, anyway?"

She ignored his question. Malamig's ignorance wasn't her problem. By now, even the janitorial staff knew.

Her silence must have goaded him.

"You just don't understand the concept of loyalty, do you?" he hissed. "When you need a new assignment from me after they dump you, you'll be wishin' you did. Are you really that stupid, or just a stubborn bitch?"

Mairwen assumed it was a rhetorical question and waited for him to say something pertinent. He dismissed her with a snarl.

While she was apprehensive about the visibility of working with Foxe, and the disturbing temptation he represented, at least he was vastly easier to put up with than Malamig, who'd grown considerably less tolerable in a very short time. She went in search of her new boss.

CHAPTER 4

HILDREE FANNAR, WHOSE comm card currently proclaimed her to be an independent security risk consultant, firmly told herself it wasn't good business to kneecap the client's representative. Even imbeciles like Tamanun Harado, Loyduk Pharma's vice president of Market Assurance, which was corp-speak for their competitor spying and sabotage division. Other pharma companies she'd worked for had similar positions, though they usually had "strategy" or "intelligence" in the title, neither of which would ever apply to Harado. He'd made insane decisions from the start and gone downhill from then, so she was being paid very highly by Loyduk's security director to take care of Harado's "little problem." Office politics sometimes created lucrative business opportunities for people in Hildree's line of work.

Her own generous paycheck notwithstanding, Loyduk had a reputation of being stingy, and too many of Harado's actions reflected it. Unfortunately, she'd been ordered to take direction from Harado, the instigator of all the troubles in the first place.

Now she sat attentively in the splashy top-floor-view suite and pasted a look of supportive interest on her face as he finished reading his report out loud, word for frecking word, with self-congratulatory asides as he went along. The same report he'd sent to corporate; the same report he knew she'd already read. His nasal, singsong tenor voice was grating, especially when he spoke Mandarin, and his delivery was that of someone reading to a dimwitted six-year-old. He finally got to the end of it and asked if she had any questions.

She was sorely tempted to ask why his parents had let him live and who he had blackmail holos on that allowed him to keep his job. Instead, she asked, "What was this 'special operative' you got from your silent partner supposed to do, exactly?" She decided to keep the conversation in English, though she spoke Mandarin fluently. She wanted the flexibility that could be blamed on translation errors.

She assumed the silent partner had connections to the chems and alterants blackmarket, although it was equally likely the government's covert operations organization, the Citizen Protection Service, was involved. They had their fingers in a lot of pies, especially in the pharmaceutical industry. In her experience, the industry was a cutthroat, sleazy tangle of duplicity, corruption, and greed. Fortunately, it gave her many more options.

"Since *your* leaker had already vanished, we needed to give La Plata somewhere else to look besides Loyduk," he said defensively. Hildree barely suppressed rolling her eyes. Based only on the fact that she'd discovered the leak in his organization, he'd been desperately trying to give her ownership of the missing employee and probable whistleblower who'd been the origin point of the whole mess. He tried for an affronted look. "It's not my fault the operative didn't sell it."

"Of course not," Hildree agreed in her best sympathetic tone. She wondered with sudden alarm if the delusional pinhead was thinking he could have done better "selling it," and if she'd have to talk him out of personally playing spy. On the bright side, maybe it would get him killed.

When the theft crew reported the presence of "mercs" in the warehouse, Harado had panicked and ordered the "mercs" killed immediately—then panicked again when the victims turned out to be investigators from a respected security company—and had the crew set up the scene to look like a robbery. The kills had been sloppy, and the crew had forgotten to cleanse the comps and search one of the bodies, so it was a fuckup already.

Hildree didn't blame the crew, who were professional thieves, not professional killers. She blamed Harado, who would no doubt see nothing wrong in asking plumbers to fix the electrical system while they were there, as long as it saved money.

Harado, as was his habit when his decisions went horribly wrong, tried to shift the blame, this time to the crew for overzealousness, and her for not giving him good advice. He was making a shambles of the whole project, and unfortunately, she was stuck with him.

Loyduk Pharma's claim to fame was a group of ramper drugs, designed to improve human strength and reaction times, and highly popular with athletes and military-type personnel. Too bad they didn't make smart pills for their executives.

She looked at her percomp and gave a show of surprise. "Oh my, look at the time. I'll miss the ship if don't get in the lane." She stood and picked up her coat. "I'll contact you once I'm on Rekoria." For whatever reason, Rekoria, and specifically Etonver, had become the convergence for the project, so she'd manipulated Harado into ordering her to go there.

"Yes, you do that, and I'll give you instructions." Harado was back in delusion mode, imagining she wouldn't make a move without him.

Letting the imbecile drone on had served the purpose of distracting him from giving her orders immediately, meaning she'd have more latitude to take more effective remedial action on her own. At least she now knew who La Plata's new lead investigator was, and not to underestimate him. Fortunately, she'd already found a nice hook into La Plata's organization, and planned to use it wisely. If she was lucky, she could neutralize the whistleblower and clean up the few loose ends before ever having to check in with Harado. He'd try to take credit, of course, but she'd make sure her client knew who was really responsible for the success.

CHAPTER 5

GROUND TRAFFIC THROUGHOUT Etonver was legendarily bad, and Luka counted himself lucky that the current traffic snarl was so far making them only thirty minutes late for the afternoon appointment with the independent testing lab Zheer had found. They couldn't fly a flitter into the restricted medical district air space near the lab, so they were stuck dealing with the chaos on the streets.

He was glad he'd chosen to sit up front with Morganthur. He often lost his temper in traffic, and her imperturbability at the stop-and-go progress made it less annoying to him. Her light overcoat, in boring company gray, hid a navy corporate suit, identical in cut to the green one she'd worn to the spaceport. He had the impression she valued practicality over style. He wouldn't call her peaceful to be around, because he was too intrigued by her, but she was somehow calming. She was also the quietest person he'd ever met.

"Morganthur, when they assigned you to me, did they tell you not to talk?"

"No." Her voice sounded low and rusty, as if she didn't use it much.

A ground skimmer that was weaving through the lanes came within centimeters of scraping their side panel, but she smoothly adjusted their position to narrowly avoid it.

"Good," he told her. "I'd hate to inhibit your natural garrulousness."

She glanced at him with a raised eyebrow and quirked a corner of her mouth in what may have been a smile, but said nothing.

He laughed, delighted to discover she had a sense of humor. "I get the feeling you don't do this very often."

"Drive?"

"No, have a casual conversation."

"No." An opening in traffic had them going faster for a moment, but it didn't last. Warning horns sounded constantly, but were muted in the quiet vehicle interior.

"Probably because you've been working the night shift and didn't have anyone to talk to. Feel free to practice your conversational skills on me. It'll distract me from obsessing about loose threads." Of course, it wouldn't keep him from being distracted by her instead. At least she wasn't an obsession. Yet.

He couldn't tell from her expression if she was trying to formulate a reply or was simply focused on traffic. After a long silence, she said, "I'm bad with words."

"That's what practice is for. Pretty soon, we'll have you up to fifteen or twenty words at a time, maybe even two or three sentences in a row."

In between lane changes, she glanced at him as if she was unsure if he was serious or not. Finally she said, "Loose threads?"

It was the first time she'd initiated conversation, so he didn't mind that it was about work. It was a start.

"The fact that Green never called for the reward. Why the losses are mostly the NVP 70 vaccine made by Loyduk Pharma. Why Balkovsky and Schmidt were in the warehouse at all. Why a theft crew had two merc-grade forceblades for a simple after-hours slice-and-haul."

"Why didn't they kill Schmidt first?"

The phantasms from his memory stirred uneasily, so he focused on Morganthur more closely. The spiky, asymmetric cut and darker tips of her pale blonde hair suited her strong but striking cheekbones and jawline, he decided. "They tried to, but Balkovsky got in the way. He was protecting her."

Her incredulous look said she thought it unlikely that an ex-Jumper needed protecting.

"He was in love with her, which made him feel protective of her. Her waster's disease was well into stage three, so she was slowing down. He was trying to distract their attackers and give her room to fight. He didn't know two of them had forceblades."

He sighed in frustration at facts that didn't make sense. "I'm not surprised a theft crew had misters, because those are good for derezzing comps and disabling unexpected guards, but forceblades need skill and make for messy kills. Not the usual thief's choice."

"Reconstruction told you all that?" She wasn't exactly accusing him of extrapolating well beyond the actual evidence, but her tone was skeptical.

He realized that it was too *fökking* easy to talk to her, and now he was on dangerous ground. The reconstruction at the warehouse, what little he'd had time for, had only confirmed what his talent had already told him. "Mostly. Leo was a good friend, so I already knew how he felt about Adina, and that he'd have risked anything to keep her safe. She made it out of the service pretty much whole, but the waster's was going to force her into retirement soon enough."

"It's not in your report."

"No, it wasn't relevant to... wait, you read my report?" She nodded, her face serious. None of his current or previous assistants had ever read his reports. Leo used to tease him mercilessly. Even Zheer had probably only skimmed it. "Most people don't bother. They're kind of dry reading for non-specialists."

"I've read worse."

He snorted. "Really? Name one."

"The most recent Etonver traffic study."

He laughed out loud. "Good lord, why did you read that?" He thought a moment. "Oh, I get it. Driving for me. Has it helped?"

She shrugged a shoulder. "Too soon to tell."

"What other hobbies do you have besides reading odd things?"

The look she gave him said she wasn't sure why he wanted to know, or that she wanted to answer. Finally she said, "I run."

Yet another reason he was glad to have met her. "Would you go running with me? Velasco and Alhamsi won't." He smiled at her hopefully.

Traffic forced their vehicle to a standstill. The dashboard display gave them an estimated delay countdown from Etonver's traffic control system in Arabic numerals and Chinese characters.

She gave him a long, assessing look, then looked forward again. "Yes."

He was inordinately pleased. Even Leo, his only real friend in Etonver, had refused to do that.

The independent testing lab was in a medical building, one of several on the block. After Luka gave the lab custody of the packaged squibs from the warehouse, he and Morganthur went to meet with a pharmaceutical researcher named Dr. Eglatine Tewisham. Luka had arranged the meeting to get an expert's view of the pharmaceutical industry, because Luka's intuition said it was a key to understanding the case.

Tewisham turned out to be a big-boned, furry man with red hair who looked more like a frontier farmer than a scientist, but his stylish clothes were expensively hand-tailored and his standard English accent was distinctively posh, maybe even Albion Prime posh.

Luka introduced Morganthur as his assistant, then wondered why he'd never introduced Velasco in similar situations. Maybe because Tewisham's eyes kept returning appreciatively to Morganthur. Which was an idiotic reason, because Luka was pretty sure he wouldn't care if Tewisham was interested in Velasco.

Tewisham invited them to sit, then launched into a rapid-fire lecture on the background of how pharmaceuticals were developed, produced, and distributed, a process that turned out to be much more convoluted than Luka had imagined.

"It's a matter of liabilities and loopholes," said Tewisham. "The pharma industry as a whole is obscenely profitable, so as you might imagine, competition is fierce. Pharmas prefer not to pay damages if their latest wonder cure turns out to be worse than the disease, so they've learnt to take advantage of every corporate ownership loophole in Concordance and planetary law they can find. Plus they've invented some new dodges that are still being tested in the courts."

Tewisham stood and began striding back and forth, as if he were on the dais in front of a university lecture hall full of D-level students, instead of in a corporate researcher's office full of displays, holos, and stacks of real paper.

"No one company owns more than a part of the process, so if the problem turns out to be, for example, harmful side effects, only the development company can be sued, not the production, distribution, or marketing companies." Tewisham's path took him closer to Morganthur's chair. "Unless you can prove someone's in bed with someone else." He winked saucily at her. Her bland expression didn't change.

"Couldn't you sue the owners of all the companies?" asked Luka.

"Certainly, if you could find them and prove the relationship. Legally, the companies are independently owned and directed. Only shortsighted or greedy companies try to save money by keeping more than one function in-house. Profits to the real owners are funneled through silent partnerships, subcontracts, royalty payments and licenses, shell corporations, and so forth. Do you recall a popular drug called Pelderammodox? It was an antiemetic, used to treat nausea, that rendered long-term users sterile. It devastated sperm counts and destroyed female ova altogether."

Luka nodded. "Top galactic news trend for months."

"Just so. The pharma development company was unwound in the first year, and the production company was next, but twenty years later,

Concordance prosecutors are still uncovering individual owners to this day. That was for a high-profile case. If the problem is less damaging, perhaps turning your hair the same delightful shade of blonde that Mairwen—may I call you that?—wears to such advantage, even the hungriest of lawyers will look for easier commissions."

Tewisham seemed surprised when his flirting got no visible response from Morganthur. He was probably used to seducing women with his accent alone. Luka was mildly pleased he could tell she found Tewisham's overtures tedious.

An idea sparked in Luka's mind. "What about counterfeits?"

"Ah, now you're sailing in blackmarket seas. Most drugs can be back-engineered or cloned, eventually. Rival companies do it regularly. It's generally only a matter of time, and not much time, before they begin eroding profits. The costs to trace the clone back to the blackmarketer's temporary laboratory are prohibitive. Consequently, pharmas flood the market with new product as quickly as possible to skim the profits, then drop the price to make it less profitable for rivals and blackmarketers to undercut them. It's an arms race, really—the faster to market, the higher the profits. I'd wager every pharma company in existence has a blackmarket mole or two."

"What if the clone is bad, and causes the bad side effect?"

Tewisham plopped himself in his chair and steepled his fingers. It looked like a practiced gesture.

"Nobody wins. It's hardly worth the original producer's expense of recalling the drug, because the damage is done." He gave them both a wicked, piratical grin. "Sadly, greedy and sloppy blackmarketers crop up every year."

"You approve of blackmarketers?" Luka asked in surprise.

"They're the only real check we have on pharma companies. The expansion of galactic civilization has given us millions more chances to encounter or evolve new diseases, and the pharma industry has blossomed. Pharmas are monstrously profitable as is, and they expend a great deal to avoid regulation and accountability. If pharmas had no competition, imagine where we'd be."

On their way out of the building, Luka detoured to the lab and asked them to add amino origin tracing to the array of tests he'd ordered. The clone idea was worth pursuing, if only to rule it out.

The only thing worse than Etonver ground traffic was Etonver parking, which explained why they had to walk six blocks to where they'd left the vehicle. Fortunately, pleasant fall days were one of the compensations for living in Etonver.

Despite the relief of being able to stretch his legs, Luka's thoughts were chaotic. He'd been off balance ever since coming back to Rekoria, and he still hadn't gotten a full night's sleep. He couldn't stop thinking about the patterns and possibilities that fit the too few facts they had. He had no objectivity left to work on a murder case in which one of the victims had been a good friend.

It had been Leo who'd convinced Seshulla Zheer that La Plata needed a reconstruction specialist in the first place. Luka had a large number of casual acquaintances across the galaxy, but few friends. Sooner or later, his obsessiveness, intuition, and hidden talents made most people uneasy or angry. Leo was one of the few who took them in stride, and more than that, respected and valued them.

Luka knew he wouldn't be good for anything unless he regained some equilibrium. Maybe a long run after work would help him find it.

They turned a corner, and he wished he hadn't been distracted by his upcoming meeting on the way in, because then the presence of a Citizen Protection Service minder treatment clinic would have been less of a shock. There was a sameness about the look of the clinic, like all the other CPS clinics he'd ever seen or been in on other planets. But it was the distinctive smell that got him, a kind of smoldering-medicinal-plastic miasma that drifted out over the walkway. Almost as bad as the cheap potato-mash alcohol his father favored. The rest of his thoughts fell apart as dark and bitter memories came tumbling like sharp rocks swept in by floodwaters.

* * * * *

Mairwen was puzzled when Foxe slowed to a stop on the sidewalk in front of the local CPS minder clinic. She was almost getting used to his sudden changes in focus. She waited for him to turn and explain, but he was staring at the door with unseeing eyes. His expression reminded her of the haunted look from the warehouse and in the spaceport, though not as vivid.

Not knowing what else to do, she simply stood with him, keeping watch to make sure he wouldn't be a casualty of some inattentive pedestrian. After a long passage of seconds, an obnoxiously loud vehicle horn caused him to startle and wake from his trance. She waited, keeping an eye on him as he found his bearings and noticed where he was.

"Sorry, I..." he said, and then hesitated. He slanted a long look at her, then focused on the pavement. "Old, bad memories."

"It's okay," she said softly. She had more than her share of her own, just buried deeper at the moment.

He took a slow, deep breath, then started walking again, faster than before. Once they were past the clinic, some of the tension left his face, but not his shoulders or his gait. She didn't expect an explanation, so she was surprised when he spoke, his voice low and flat.

"My mother was a high-level telepath in the Citizen Protection Service, recruited right after second testing, but she didn't do well on the enhancement drugs. After she left the service on disability, my *fökking* father refused to take her to the treatment clinic because he thought it was her own fault for getting addicted. As if the CPS had given her a choice. He believed she should be able to kick the addiction if she really wanted to." He took a ragged breath. "When I was nine or ten, I started going with her to the clinic when he wouldn't. Toward the end, I had to jump school to take her while he was at work or he'd stop us." The fingers of his left hand curled. "He got violent when he couldn't control things."

Mairwen had the feeling he didn't talk about this often, and she had no words for him. When the CPS had gotten their hooks into her, she'd lost everything at once, not by centimeters and days and bruises at a time.

At the next crosswalk, she gave into impulse and stepped closer to him than usual and briefly brushed his hand with her fingers. She hoped he would understand it as a gesture of comfort. To her astonishment, though he didn't look at her, he threaded his fingers through hers and gave her hand a gentle squeeze before letting go. She was equally astonished with herself. She didn't like physical contact with anyone, but with him, not only had she initiated it, she realized she liked the feel of his skin on hers. *Danger,* hissed her cautious brain.

As she walked beside him in silence, she experienced a curious sense of emptiness in her chest, almost painful. It wasn't external, because she'd already opened her senses to take in Foxe and their surroundings, and she'd have felt it sooner. She resolutely set it aside as something to think about later. He was too vulnerable to see to his own safety at the moment. Even if she didn't know how to ease his pain, or didn't know if it was even possible, she could at least keep her senses open and extended for him.

That was why she knew there was a disturbance between them and their destination. Traffic was slowing. She heard people's feet slowing and the excited murmuring of voices, and smelled fuel, burned lubricant, and hot metal.

Rounding the corner proved her senses right. A chaotic accident involving a public transport and a traffic column was blocking the far lane on the next block. Emergency responders began arriving on foot, pushing through the offloading passengers and milling spectators. At least the injured were fortunate to be in a medical district. If she and Foxe could get to the parking structure quickly, they had a chance to get out before the street became impassible. Unfortunately, they'd have to push through the crowds to do it.

She looked at Foxe and was grateful to see that he'd regained most of his customary alertness. He apparently saw the same options she did. "Let's take our chances with the horde." Even as he spoke, a damaged lamppost toppled to the ground, adding to the chaos.

She nodded and fell into step beside but one step behind him, evaluating possible threats as they entered into her sphere of influence. Providing close-in personal security was an unaccustomed use of her skills.

They were about halfway to their goal, just coming up on a garish chems and alterants shop, when their already bad luck took a nosedive. Something was happening in the shop, something noisy and violent, something they needed to avoid. She grabbed Foxe's coat sleeve to pull him to the side and around, but they were hemmed in by people and walls and the fallen lamppost. The sound of crashing glass told her they were out of time, so she turned to face the trouble and dropped into full-tracker mode.

Time *slowed...*

A halo of iridescent glass shards showered out from the shop window. A monstrously huge woman, the tallest and most muscular Mairwen had ever seen, burst through it in an explosion of forward motion.

Her clothes and skin art proclaimed her a hardcore merc, and her grotesquely overbuilt musculature screamed blackmarket ramper. Her face was a kabuki mask mix of berserk rage and gleeful insanity, the result of one too many bad drugs and backstreet bodyshop mods.

A few hundred milliseconds dragged by before two burly men from the shop came through the opening in pursuit. The berserker broke the first man's neck as her feet hit the glascrete. She ripped the throat out of the second with her other hand. The unlucky pedestrian who'd been passing by died almost as easily when his head smashed like a melon into the wall. The bodies were still falling when a quicker-thinking woman to the left drew her projectile gun and shot, but the berserker didn't even notice the shoulder wound as she bellowed and tore the shooter's arm off with a terrifying laugh.

Mairwen knew none of her knives would penetrate berserker's bulging muscle mass very far, so she scanned the crowd for visible weapons. Finally the universe deigned to favor her, because the man two paces from her, who clearly had more money than sense, was carrying a holstered, non-safetied Davydov plasbeamer, with only a thin strap to keep it in place.

After confirming that no one was noticing her, except maybe Foxe, which she couldn't help, she glided low over to the rich man and relieved him of the Davydov, careful to keep her shirt cuff between her skin and the grip. She waited the dozen milliseconds it took to get a clear line of sight and for the berserker to finish turning toward her. She focused her aim on the woman's head and shot twice, then focused on the woman's loud, rapid-fire heartbeat and disintegrated it with a final shot.

Even though the berserker's massive body was dead, it tried to follow through on the last orders it received, but the puppet strings had been cut, and she started to collapse. Mairwen dropped the Davydov on the ground, then pushed and tripped its owner on top of it, careful to thrust his body toward nearby spectators so they'd add to the distraction. She slid back to Foxe's side, trying not to think about the fact that he might have registered her actions.

She breathed deeply and pushed her tracker senses back into a corner of her mind. Time sped up and approached reality. Ten seconds had passed.

She needed to get away, to get Foxe away, before the questions started. Now in realtime, she pulled his sleeve, and he followed behind her as she threaded them quickly through the crowd that was just now reacting to the stunning events.

To Mairwen's relief, Foxe sat in the back seat of the vehicle and said nothing for the entire drive back to the office. She desperately needed the time to choose the answers she'd give him once his brilliant mind found the right questions to ask.

More immediately, she also needed to eat, and soon. Full-tracker mode, even the dozen actual seconds she'd indulged in, came with a price.

She'd reacted on instinct, and although her rational brain was blaring *very bad idea*, she knew she'd do it again to protect Foxe. She had no idea why he was different. He just… was.

The next two days Foxe worked at home, so that's where she, Velasco, and Alhamsi covered the personal security shifts for Foxe's waking hours.

Mairwen thought his open and airy townhouse suited him, though its abundance of pretty morphglass windows and the exposed back courtyard weren't much good for security. There were also no flitter pads anywhere within five kilometers, which explained the assigned vehicles. He kept the townhouse warmer than she was used to, though it wasn't uncomfortable. He'd converted one of its back rooms to a combination office and exercise room, and he spent most of his time there with the door closed.

She didn't know what he did during the other shifts, but during hers, he ran in the late afternoons in a nearby park on a wide, well-designed trail, and she accompanied him. When he wasn't running, he did a lot of reading, pacing and mumbling, and a few domestic chores. Mostly he ignored her.

She always declined his offhand offers of meals, officially because she was on duty, but also because she wanted to avoid opportunities for him to ask her what happened with the berserker in front of the chems shop. He'd trusted her with a private piece of his past, and she didn't want to repay him with evasions and lies.

As it was, she couldn't resist opening her senses around him, indulging in the sounds and sight and unique scent of him. When she ran with him, she was careful to always stay two strides behind him and let him set the pace. He seemed to need running as much as she did.

After he went to bed, she checked in with the external night-shift security guard that La Plata had assigned, which only a week ago might well have been Mairwen. Each night before she left, she stood for a few minutes in the mostly dark living room and listened to him breathe, because it settled something nameless in her.

The night of the berserker incident, she had decided that Foxe deserved her taking her new job seriously, even if it meant exposing more of her unusual skills than was wise. She hadn't expected to find a use for them in the normal, civilized world. She wasn't sure why she experienced the increased sense of duty, but it was undeniable. It felt like a kind of justice to use the skills the CPS had shaped and sharpened to protect instead of destroy.

She'd found a martial arts studio with an open sparring session to test how badly out of practice her personal combat skills were. Running, plus her regular strength and stretch exercise regimen, had kept her fit, but it was exhausting to keep her reaction times normal and to take hits she could have easily avoided. She was sore and sweat-soaked by the time she left, but the workout felt good enough that she planned to add it to her routine. She knew she'd have to avoid the better schools or risk being noticed. Fortunately, nearly every weapons shop in Etonver had an associated studio of some sort, so there were hundreds to choose from.

She knew nothing about Foxe's specialty, so she spent her downtime reading about crime scene reconstruction. His intuition was well suited for his profession, and she wondered how he'd discovered it. He was, surprisingly, the author of a dozen or so technical articles in his field, and was still a certified expert in the interplanetary High Court. He'd presented and testified in hundreds of proceedings.

His last case had been horrific, involving a pair of pedophiles who had kidnapped, abused, and killed dozens of children over several years. The media had dubbed them "the Collectors" because they'd turned a converted commercial interstellar ship into their nightmare playhouse. Foxe's crime scene reconstruction had led to the capture of the pair, but he'd been badly wounded when he'd cornered the one who was trying to escape.

Was she any better than the sadistic twists who collected and killed children? The CPS's procedure and training had made her into a remorseless, deadly machine. In choosing to live, she'd done what they demanded, but she never liked the killing, even when it was deserved. To some, that might be a distinction without a difference, but since escaping the CPS, she hadn't so much as bruised anyone until the berserker, and she'd only done that to protect Foxe.

She would always be a killer, but now it was her choice how, when, and why.

CHAPTER 6

ON MONDAY, FOXE went to the office, so Mairwen began her afternoon shift at La Plata, taking over from Velasco, who complained about having to hang around the office all day instead of just being on call. He implied it was a waste of his considerable skills, but as far as she'd seen, his only skills were blathering on about nothing and staring at women. Fortunately, her small breasts weren't worthy of his attention.

She went to Foxe's office to check in, but he had commandeered the conference room again, where he was reading multiple files on a large display and referring to a holo of a data hypercube. He saw her and smiled, and her breath caught momentarily.

"Morganthur. Good, I was afraid this was your day off."

He waved her toward a chair in the corner, but she declined. Why just a smile from him should affect her was a mystery. It took more effort than it should have to regain control of her awareness of him. She laid her overcoat on the table, then stood at ease near the wall, next to the door. He smiled at her again, as if amused by her presence. This time, she made sure her breathing stayed even.

She expanded her senses to immerse herself in the sounds and scents of the office to set a baseline, so she'd know when something changed. The conference room had a lot of human scents, most of them stale. Velasco's smell clung to the chair in the corner.

She couldn't help but indulge herself in the sounds of Foxe's breathing and his steady heartbeat, and the smells of him. She'd realized just before dawn that morning, when normal people would have been sleeping, that sometime in the past few days, she'd imprinted his exotic, buttery pearwood scent in her memory and could track him anywhere. The CPS had trained her to use the imprint for hunting, so it worried her that her subconscious thought of Foxe as a target. But now the scent of him eased the empty ache in her chest that had never really gone away, so she ignored the voice in her brain that said *very bad idea.*

A few minutes later, he stood up and started pacing, deep in thought. She surreptitiously admired the interplay of his muscles visible beneath his well-tailored clothes as he moved. He stopped suddenly and looked at her.

"I need to check with Zheer first, but we might be going on a little field trip this afternoon on the way home. I'll be right back." He left the conference room, then poked his head back in. "If we're done in time, are you up for a longer run tonight?"

"Yes." She wondered if he'd been keeping the runs short out of consideration for her, but he was gone before she could ask.

She would need to get some food to keep in her apartment after she went off-shift that night. She'd become careless about remembering to eat properly while being just an anonymous night-shift guard with dull senses and a dull mind, and no one to protect but herself.

Foxe came back a few minutes later. "Grab your coat. We're on." He folded the display and made a hasty attempt to reorder the conference room. "The data analysts have been deep-diving in Leo's files. He was working with an informant, all right, but not from the transport company, someone from Loyduk Pharma." He looked at her expectantly.

"The vaccine distributor," she said, and he grinned as if he thought her clever to remember. She regretted she couldn't tell him what she'd overheard at the spaceport.

"Producer and distributor, in fact." His intuition was lighting up, making him as energized as she'd seen him. She followed him down the hall and waited in the doorway of his office as he grabbed his bag and shrugged into his coat. "The analysts found an interesting address here in Etonver. The leaseholder of record doesn't have ties to anything in this case."

"But you think otherwise?"

"Leo did, and so do I. He was a damn good finder, and it's the only untagged data in his files. Hidden in plain sight." That meant nothing to her, but it was clearly significant to Luka.

She exited the building first and scanned their surroundings as she held the door open for him.

The wind was bitingly frigid, making the drafty underground parking area colder than usual. Mairwen opened the vehicle with her palmprint, then pulled on her gloves as she got in. La Plata's vehicles, while armored and secure, were more utilitarian than luxurious, and didn't have heated operating controls. Foxe sat in the front seat next to her and wired the address to the vehicle's navcomp. As she pulled out onto the street and turned north, as the navcomp indicated, she asked, "Do you have an appointment?"

"No. A hunch." He was calling something up on his percomp, but she couldn't see what. She nodded, but he didn't notice.

Even though she'd only known him for a few days, she already knew that when his mind was blazing, he was lost to the outside world. There was no point asking why he felt the need to go now, in person, or what he expected to find.

For once, there were no obstructions to clog traffic, so it only took fifteen minutes to get to their destination, which turned out to be a huge apartment complex with multiple buildings and floors, plus a large vehicle lift and flitter hangar on top. Mairwen thought it looked rather like conjoined university dormitories. Since Etonver had no zoning regulations to speak of, and real estate changed usage and ownership often, the buildings may once have been exactly that.

With guidance from a battered lobby kiosk, she and Foxe rode a lift to the third floor, crossed a bridge to another building, then took a lift up two more floors. The apartment in question, leased to one Vadra Amhur, was all the way to the back of the building at the end of a dead-end hallway.

When they finally found the right hallway, she knew there was trouble. It reeked of day-old death. Even normal senses would have caught it by now if the hallways hadn't been so cold.

She stepped in front of Foxe to stop him. "Security first."

He hesitated, then nodded.

She walked toward the apartment, listening for sounds from any of the other apartments but hearing none. She hoped she was wrong and that the reek came from somewhere else, but it didn't. Beyond the innocuous door that matched all the others were fluids and blood and a corpse. She doubted Foxe would like it.

She walked back to where he stood.

"It smells," she said in a low voice. "Like the warehouse. Should I look?"

"*Fökk,*" he said grimly, running his fingers through his unruly hair once, then again, a resigned look settling on his face. "Do it."

The electronic lock was old and cheap, and someone had already breached it. She slowly nudged the door open a bit, took a second to dial back her olfactory sense so the increased stench that wafted out wouldn't overload her, then opened the door just enough to slip inside. She waited a moment for her vision to compensate for the shadows in the apartment, then found the lighting controls.

Three meters from the entrance, a woman's naked body was zip-tied to an overturned chair. There was blood splatter everywhere. It hadn't been a pleasant death.

Mairwen backed out of the apartment and returned to Foxe.

"It's bad," she said. "Bloody."

He closed his eyes a moment and muttered a curse. He took a deep breath and looked at her. "I have to see."

She let him go in, then closed the apartment door behind them and stepped aside, her eyes on Foxe.

He held himself rigidly still, as if fighting something, but soon the despairing, haunted look she'd seen before started creeping into his expression. After first examining the floor in front of him, he took one careful step closer. He crouched down, maybe to get a better angle to examine the woman's body, then swept his gaze side to side. He lingered over several spots, angling his head at a couple of them, but his gaze drifted back to the body and stalled. He stared as if mesmerized.

Mairwen waited quietly for a minute, watching him closely. He wasn't moving any more, but his breathing was shallow, and she could hear his heartbeat racing. The haunted look had completely overtaken his features. After another minute, she gave into the growing conviction that she needed to do something.

"Foxe?" she asked softly.

He didn't respond.

She said his name again, but he still didn't react. She crouched down in front of him. His eyes were dilated, and tears were streaming down his face. Possibly it was like the old, bad memories, but it reminded her more of a tracker's sensory overload trance, the first step on the road to oblivion. Not knowing what else to do, she gave his shoulder a slight push. He felt stiff.

"Foxe," she said. Nothing.

She took off her glove and put her fingertips on his wet cheek. He didn't react.

She narrowed her focus to just him and flattened her palm on the side of his face. "Foxe... Luka, look at me." She willed him to respond.

Nothing. His skin felt surprisingly cool against her hand. Just as she was wondering if she should maybe ping someone for help, she saw a slow change in his expression. His lost look faded and his focus gelled on her, and his eyes met hers. His full regard rocked her.

769 4222

"Mairwen," he said, as if he was deeply amazed and relieved to see her.

When she would have dropped her hand, he caught it with his own and leaned his face into her palm. "*Bíddu.* Wait. Give me a moment."

The side of his face felt warmer than before, and his dark hair against her fingers felt more wiry than it looked.

He loosened the pressure on her hand, but curled his fingers around hers as he stood. She rose with him.

"You haven't exactly seen me at my best." He squeezed her fingers and let go, then wiped the moisture from his face. He didn't seem to be embarrassed by his tears, which was good, she guessed. She noticed his eyes weren't actually hazel, they were a remarkable mix of blue and green that blended into hazel from a distance. She added the scent of his tears to her imprint of him, and helplessly wondered why even as she did it.

He took a deep breath and let it out slowly. "I need to see the back of the victim and into the kitchen."

He took deliberate, careful steps to the vantage point he was looking for, looking back at her a couple of times as if using her as a reference point. He crouched and did the sweeping scans with his eyes again.

Her hand felt cold, so she put her glove back on. It didn't match the warmth of Foxe's skin, and the emptiness in her chest was back.

Now that he wasn't so close and inundating her senses, she detected the old scents of two other people who'd been in the room recently. She'd have to get closer to the body to know if the scents were of her killers. From the look of the wounds and the faint smell of burned flesh, they'd used a machinist's laserwire for the torture. There was also a mix of scents, predominantly gun oil, graphite, and metal dust, smells she associated with projectile weapons. Mercs or an armed crew, perhaps.

Foxe apparently had seen all he needed and stepped back to her, stopping close enough for her to feel his body heat. "We need to notify the police, but I need a quick look through the rest of the apartment first. Come on."

There wasn't much to see, although once away from the powerful odors of death, Mairwen knew the two people she'd scented earlier had been sleeping in the apartment lately, one in the bedroom and one on the couch.

Back near the front door, Foxe live-pinged Zheer and told her what they'd found. Zheer promised to put the company lawyer on alert in case the police took the impetuous notion to detain or charge them.

Next, he called the police, identified himself as a La Plata investigator, and explained he'd found the body of a woman. He agreed to wait in the

ORLAND PARK PUBLIC LIBRARY

hallway for the police and not touch anything further.

Foxe focused on Mairwen once again. "I'm sorry, but it's going to be a long night."

She had the feeling he wanted to close the distance between them and pull her to him. Or perhaps she was just projecting what she wanted, despite her wary brain hissing *very, very bad idea*.

"Are you all right?" she asked.

"Yes," he replied, as if he was vastly surprised by it. "It's hard to explain, but I want to. I will. Just not now."

She could sympathize with that. She still didn't know what to tell him about what happened with the berserker. A thought occurred to her. "It might be simpler if the police think I'm just a driver."

He gave her a faint smile. "Simple is good."

He scanned the crime scene again, and looked to be in control of whatever had sent him off the deep end before. "Unless they get lucky, it'll take them weeks to figure all this out."

She got the distinct impression he already had.

They left the apartment, pulled the door almost closed, and waited in the hallway as instructed. He sat on the floor and leaned his back against the wall, his elbows resting on his bent knees. He looked cold and drained. She wasn't accustomed to sitting, so she stood and waited, smothering an uncharacteristic impulse to pace. Foxe was a bad influence on her.

Eighteen minutes later, she heard four people walking together in the first corridor from the lift, along with the jangle of metal and creak of leather that spoke of a police officer's uniform.

"Incoming," she said, just loud enough for Foxe to hear.

He gave her a small, knowing smile in recognition of the fact that he hadn't heard anything but knew she had. She gave him a tiny shrug to tell him she didn't care if he knew, then smoothed her face and body to dull impassivity.

* * * * *

Luka handed a fork to Mairwen and invited her to sit at his modest round dining room table. He liked the sound of her first name, he decided. It was nice to like the name of the woman who'd saved him.

The delectable smell of the best Cantonese takeout in town filled the room. That smell was the only thing keeping him from giving in to the chills that inevitably came in the aftermath of a bad incident with his talent. He used his chopsticks to serve himself more steamed rice, then dumped the container of duck and snow peas over it.

"I can't believe you've never eaten this."

"Sheltered life." She sampled a small bite of fried rice. "This is good." She sounded surprised, and took a larger forkful.

He was glad all she wanted was water to drink. He might have been tempted by a good glass of wine, and it never went well with his talent.

The evening with the police had been every bit as long as he'd predicted. It was always interesting, being on the other side of the interview table, but knowing what the police were thinking and recognizing the tactics.

The detectives would have been much happier if they'd found any reason at all to think he had something to do with the woman's death, but he was cooperative, and his alibi was good. He was asked the same questions a half-dozen times by three different people at the scene and again in the interview room at the station house.

He kept it simple, repeating that he was following up on a lead in a confidential investigation and had stumbled across the body. He'd never met Vadra Amhur, and didn't know if the victim was her or not. No, neither he nor his driver had touched anything or seen anyone else. Yes, he'd briefly looked through the rest of the apartment in case someone else needed help. No, he couldn't discuss the nature of the confidential investigation, but they could put in a request to La Plata's lawyers if they liked. He knew his rights and volunteered nothing.

At the scene, he'd refused to go back into the apartment again. Considering one of their rookies had nearly passed out, the detectives couldn't justify forcing a civilian to do it. If it hadn't been for Mairwen, he knew he'd still be lost in the sights and sounds from the talent-driven phantasms. As the interrogation had progressed, he was privately amused at seeing her turn taciturnity into an art form. He could tell the various interviewers had mutually concluded she was possibly hard of hearing and probably dumb as a rock.

She was many surprising things, thought Luka as he ate the last bite, but dumb wasn't one of them. Solitary, inscrutable, and impossibly lethal, if he believed what he thought he'd seen her do in front of the chems shop three days ago, but most definitely not dumb.

He was pleased to see she'd polished off the entire carton of fried rice with enjoyment. It was the first time he'd seen her show a preference for anything. A gust of wind rattled tree branches at his windows, and he shivered involuntarily.

She gave him a clinically assessing look, but there was concern behind it. "Are you all right?"

"Yes," he said reflexively, then remembered he'd promised her honesty. "No. I'm always cold after..." He hesitated, groping for the right words.

"A hard day?" A corner of her mouth quirked with gentle humor.

He couldn't help but smile back, but the moment didn't last. "After I lose control of the visions."

"The visions that enable you to reconstruct a crime scene without instruments?" There was no accusation in her question, just a clarification of fact.

"Yeah, those." He wasn't surprised she'd figured out that part, as observant as she was. "It's a talent. A unique minder talent if you accept what my telepath mother believed, or non-existent if you go by both rounds of Citizen Protection Service minder testing. Up until a year ago, it was there when I needed it and went away when I didn't. Then I pushed it hard for a case, harder than I ever had, and now it's strong. Stronger than I am where violence is involved."

"The 'Collector' case?"

He sighed. "Yes, the 'Collector' case. Has everyone in the galaxy seen that *helvítis* publication?" It had turned the case into a bloody, salacious melodrama, complete with ultra-color evidence holos and tri-D reenactments, and was still selling billions of copies across the galaxy. "Velasco's practically memorized it."

"No. I read the court transcript."

He was startled. "Why?"

"When I was assigned to you, I researched reconstruction. I found your journal articles, and the citations led me to your court appearances. It was your last case of record."

He didn't know why he was surprised. This was the woman who'd somehow made time to read the million-word Etonver traffic study because her job now included driving him places.

He felt restless, but he forced himself to stay seated. "Ever since then, my talent is always running. I can't shut it off. It's like constantly getting information from everything around you. I've learned to not think about the low-level data, like knowing Seshulla sneaks smokes on the executive balcony, or that you walk the perimeter of my townhouse building before your shift because you know the others don't."

He pushed away from the table and began pacing. "Maybe it's some sort of stress trauma tangled up with my talent because of... Now when there's violence, the possibilities I imagine are like *mórar*... you might call them malevolent ghosts, forcing me to live their pain or their anger or fear, and they swamp me. I see them, hear them, feel them, and they drag me under. Like at the warehouse. Like today."

"I provided external stimulus," she said. "It must have helped you focus."

He stopped pacing to look at her. He knew this side of his talent scared people, himself included. It was why he'd avoided using it in the last year, hoping it would cure itself, since self-medicating had been both destructive and useless. He was deeply relieved she was taking this all in stride. Better than he was, most days.

"When I got out of rehab after that pervert stabbed me, I tried to go back to work, but I was useless for any case with violence. My talent has always been attuned to it, to violence, but it got worse. I'd go into overload. All they could do was sedate me and haul me back to the mind shop."

He'd come to hate waking up in medical beds.

"I resigned my commission and was looking around for a new career, except my friend Leo convinced Zheer to hire me. I agreed on condition that I don't do violence cases." He sighed. "This hasn't been a good week for that."

"You said external stimulus didn't used to help. What changed?"

He froze in mid-step as a strong flash of intuition provided the answer. He turned to look at her.

"You."

He sensed she was shocked, though she hid it well.

He settled back into his chair, facing her. "Twice now, you disrupted the visions, helped me keep my talent iced. Believe me, the mind-shop therapists and my coworkers tried everything they could think of before, and nothing worked. *I* tried everything." Including focusing on a co-worker when his talent ran amuck. It had never worked before meeting Mairwen, with her preternatural calm. "If you hadn't been there to bring me back, I'd still be in that apartment, and catatonic by now."

"How am I different?" she asked. Was she alarmed? Skeptical? Her body and face were too still to read.

His intuition twitched. "Maybe it's because you have exceptional control."

A succession of emotions flitted across her face, too fast for him to sort out, before her expression went flat. "I can't be what you need."

He hadn't realized until she said that how much he'd been hoping for her to accept him and want to stay.

It was unrealistic to expect someone he'd only known for a week, admittedly an intense week, to... He didn't even know what he wanted, except she intrigued him. Teased him. Attracted him. Offered salvation.

Despair weighed on him, and his head felt too heavy to hold it up.

"Foxe," she said, compelling him to look up at her. She was leaning toward him, a soft, serious expression on her face. "You can't become dependent on me to control your talent. It's not safe." She touched her fingertips to his knee. "I won't always be with you."

She wasn't leaving. Relief flooded him, and suddenly he was touch-starved for her. He took wrapped her hand in both of his. It took all he had not to pull her closer, but he didn't know how long she'd let him live after that. He consoled himself by memorizing the shape and grace of her hand as he held it. Her fingers were slender with short, unadorned nails.

He wanted to keep her there, but knew he couldn't. "I didn't look at the schedule. Will I see you tomorrow?" He twitched a smile at her. "No more spaceport trips, I promise."

She frowned and gently pulled her hand free.

"There's something you should know." Her tone said she wasn't sure how he would react. "It's about your case."

She briefly rubbed her upper chest, as if it pained her.

"My case?" He was reeling, which happened a lot around her.

"In the spaceport, the lead mercenary who talked with Green. His orders concerned you, and he was expecting payment from Loyduk Pharma."

He searched her expression, but she was back to her usual sphynxlike self. "When did... oh. Your errand." What she said certainly fit with his theory that whole deal had been twisted, and confirmed that Loyduk was a linchpin. "I don't suppose you'd be willing to tell me where you got your information?"

She shook her head. It irritated him that she hadn't trusted him, but he couldn't fault her for keeping secrets. He had plenty of those, though one less after tonight.

He might have pressed her, but a wave of exhaustion rolled through him, and another shiver.

"I'm wrecked," he said ruefully. He rolled his shoulders to ease the soreness of his neck muscles. He felt like he'd been run over by a cross-town metro.

"It's after midnight. We can talk tomorrow," she told him. "Go to bed, Foxe."

He took her words to mean she was on shift.

"Call me Luka." At her raised eyebrow, he amended, "In private, at least."

She sighed. "Fine. Go to bed, Luka." Her demeanor reminded him of caregivers everywhere.

Luka nodded and forced himself to his feet, then remembered something. "Ah, *helvítis,* I have to check in with Zheer to let her know we're free. She's still got the lawyer on standby."

Mairwen was already neatly putting her chair back. "I did that in the vehicle, as soon as we left the station. She was still at the office." She gave him a real smile. It was small, but it was the first he'd ever seen from her. "What language do you keep swearing in? It's not Russian or Swedish."

"Icelandic. My mother's family. Sorry. I still think in it sometimes when I'm tired or stressed." He would have asked what other languages she knew, but a yawn overtook him.

"Go." She pointed toward his bedroom.

He smiled again, more grateful than he could say that she was there. He trudged toward the hallway as she retrieved her overcoat from the hook near the front door. Just as he got there, she said, "Thank you."

He turned and looked at her, confused. "For what?"

"Your trust." Her expression was soft as she finished buttoning her coat, dimmed the lights, and walked out the front door, pulling it quietly closed.

Her simple words threatened to break him. He warned himself that he knew precious little about her. He didn't know if she was in a relationship, or why she'd buried herself in a dead-end job on the night shift, or how many knives she wore to bed. She was far too comfortable with death, and probably had enough secrets to drag a ship down from orbit.

But if he was honest, he knew he wouldn't remember a single one of those objections if he got the chance to kiss her.

On that dreadfully cheerful note, he left his clothes in a heap and collapsed into bed.

CHAPTER 7

HILDREE FANNAR HAD to admit that, if she was going to be personally supervising jobs in the field, the penthouse of the best hotel in Rekoria's first city of Etonver made a comfortable base of operations. Rekoria was old enough to be a well-established and civilized world, but not so old it had become insular and hidebound like most of the First Thirty. Etonver was large and sprawling with a rich and varied culture.

She sipped an exquisitely brewed cup of real coffee as she looked out over the skyline that rose out of the morning fog like an impressionist painting. She was naked and knew she looked good that way. She was a regular customer of an exclusive bodyshop on Mabingion. The room service cart still had some delightful treats she could share with her sleepy bed partners, a talented male and female exciter pair she'd selected from the hotel's companionship menu. Their minder ability to stimulate her and each other with a mere touch was phenomenal.

The full-service penthouse and the companions were some of the bribes she had let Loyduk Pharma use to entice her back on the project, after Harado's spectacular incompetence had nearly blown everything sky high.

In her carefully worded termination notice, she'd reported Harado's interference and blunders in exact, high-res detail, making sure that he took ownership for every one of them. Even if he'd been the insatiable sex toy of the entire executive suite, her report ensured they couldn't have justified his continued involvement to their board and stockholders. Especially when his incompetence had come perilously close to connecting Loyduk Pharma to multiple murders.

While Hildree had been in transit to Rekoria, Harado had intercepted information from her source at La Plata, uncovering an address for what he was sure was the missing researcher. The frecking halfwit then sent the theft crew, not a professional wetwork crew, to end the woman. The same theft crew he'd used before, who knew the Loyduk Pharma name. The same crew that had made a mess of the kills in the warehouse and were already being hunted by the police. And if that wasn't bad enough, because Harado couldn't be bothered with details while fantasizing about his soon-to-be crowning success, the crew had killed the woman in such a sensationally grisly way that the details were still topping the news trendlines, and it was the *wrong frecking woman.* Frecking freaks and amateurs.

The miserly pharma company had come to heel nicely by offering her double her already high fee, sidelining Harado, and giving her a generous budget and free rein to take care of business quietly and professionally. Not that she wouldn't be earning her fee and benefits. Harado's actions had left a jumble of burned sources and dead ends. Her instincts told her that competitor pharma companies were sniffing around for unprotected Loyduk assets. She was still buying her way into police investigation records, and she was days behind in knowing what La Plata was doing. The Etonver police were as underfunded and overworked as everywhere else, so she wasn't worried about them, but La Plata continued to be a problem.

However, from problems arose opportunities. The only good thing about Harado's ineptitude was that it lulled La Plata into thinking they were in control of their investigation. La Plata was likely a lot closer to finding the missing researcher than she now was, so if she played her cards right, they'd lead her to the target. Since her La Plata conduit had dried up, she was arranging for a civilized, painless conversation with a key player as to their progress and plans.

A soft gasp and a sensuous moan told her that her bed companions were waking and re-engaging in pleasures from last night. Hildree had only a couple more pings to take care of before she could rejoin them.

CHAPTER 8

SHIZUKESA YOROKOBI, AN upscale Japanese-themed joyhouse, prided itself on multi-talented and versatile employees, satisfied customers, and fulfilling special requests and custom orders. For an extra fee, they promised anonymity within their walls and had an impressive track record in keeping that promise. It made for an ideal location to hold a discreet business meeting with a woman by the name of Dr. Tansa Onndrae, who until six standard weeks ago, had been a research chemist for Loyduk Pharma on Gasprélodid Prime.

The day before, Foxe—Mairwen couldn't let herself think of him as "Luka" while she was on duty—had made good use of her information about Loyduk and had combed through Balkovsky's hidden files to come up with what they needed to find the real informant. Although it had officially been Mairwen's day off, she'd gone to the office anyway to qualify with a standard-issue projectile handgun and a beamer on the company's weapons range, as required by the contract for her new position. She'd been careful to end up with unremarkable scores.

She hadn't been able to stop herself from slipping by the third floor to check on Foxe, then ghosting away before anyone saw her. Seeing that he was all right had relaxed a tension she hadn't known she'd been feeling. She ran twice the usual distance that afternoon to try to neutralize the almost magnetic pull he had on her. It had been instantly negated when he'd pinged her later that evening to tell her he'd initiated contact with Onndrae and wanted her to go with him to the meeting. All it had taken was the sound of his voice and the low-res holo for her memory to fill in the rest—his scent, his warmth, the feel of his face against her palm, his thumb stroking her hand.

He was thinking she could somehow help him control his talent, and she couldn't even control her need to touch him and want more. The universe apparently loved irony.

Mairwen stood now in the tastefully decorated joyhouse client room, playing the role of the recording equipment operator for the meeting. The resulting holo wouldn't be admissible in court, but it would point any criminal investigation in the right direction. Onndrae was a tiny, almost painfully thin woman with long, deep black hair and light hickory-toned skin. She could have passed for thirty or been mistaken for sixty, though the bio La Plata had put together pegged her at thirty-six. Her voice was thin and reedy, and she was jumpy.

According to Foxe, it had taken a lot of persuasion, precautions, and assurances to get her to meet in person. Mairwen couldn't blame her. Onndrae had known the woman who'd been tortured and killed in the apartment. Mairwen still wasn't clear why Onndrae hadn't already fled off-planet, but that was part of what Foxe planned to ask her.

Mairwen had positioned herself so that she was mostly out of Onndrae's sight, but easily visible by Foxe, in case his talent ran wild. She assumed that was the real reason he'd wanted her there. She was becoming accustomed to her constant low-level awareness of him, which she'd given up trying to suppress or pretend wasn't there. She settled into a neutral stance and expression, which she hoped would help Onndrae forget about her.

The joyhouse's soundproofing was good, though she could still hear well enough to keep from worrying. The scents were sharp and plentiful, and it took her a while to identify and categorize them. She'd been in joyhouses before, but only as a hunter after a target, never as a client. With no interest in sex, it would have been a waste of time.

Even now, her interest stirred only for one man. He was attractive and personable, so he doubtless had a lot more ordinary experiences in joyhouses. Would he want that level of skill in a bed partner? She had none to offer, and her sexual experiences during her tracker days had been less than pleasant. She had never regretted her lack of normality until now.

Pondering her personal inadequacies was not productive. She made herself pay attention as Foxe patiently drew Onndrae into talking.

"Vadra died… horribly because of me." Her voice was shaky. "I knew her in school. I dragged her into it." Her English was softened by a Spanish accent.

"You couldn't have known." Foxe's voice was quiet and warm. It was a marked contrast to how he'd sounded when he'd talked to the imposter informant in the spaceport.

"I should have." Onndrae was close to tears. "All Loyduk Pharma cares about is profit, and their vaccine is killing people. What's one more life to them?"

Foxe handed her a tissue, then asked her to explain how the vaccine was produced.

"We all thought NVP 70 was just another novel virus-phage that someone could create a quick vaccine for and it'd be over before it started."

Mairwen guessed Onndrae's "we" meant the pharma industry as a whole. Loyduk didn't have other vaccines in their catalog.

"No one anticipated the pathogen would be so easily transmitted, or have such a long incubation period that it was spreading before quarantines could contain it. We'd already agreed to produce and distribute the drug that Thang Panjutamai Research was working on, as usual. But once NVP 70 went pandemic, it had higher than usual casualties. Now we were racing against every pharma in the Concordance to be the first to market and skim the profits."

Foxe had been smart to get Onndrae to give them a recitation of the facts, because it seemed to help her settle into her personal story.

"I work… worked in the lab that produced the vaccine. Like they always do, the research company provided us early prototypes, and we did test runs to work out any issues that might be encountered with mass production. Higher than normal quantities would be needed in this case, since NVP 70 had already hit twenty or thirty systems hard, and projections said it was spreading fast. Management was anticipating windfall profits. We all thought we'd get bonuses."

She started to take a sip of coffee, but her cup was empty. Foxe poured more for her from the carafe.

"We were working killer overtime. Every day brought news that the pandemic had arrived somewhere new. One of my co-workers lost both her great-grandparents when it hit her home city. The latest prototype from Thang Panjutamai was stable, and the preliminary production run looked smooth as ice. They told us the final trials were only one month from completion and to get ready for a full production run. They made it sound like the trials were a mere formality."

"That was the usual practice, wasn't it?"

Onndrae nodded. "Then the pandemic hit Shinnowar. That's where my whole family lives. I'm the only one who ever left. Local girl makes good." Her last sentence was laced with sarcasm.

Foxe's expression sharpened and Mairwen recognized the signs that his intuition was sparking. "You helped Loyduk release the vaccine early."

Onndrae nodded, her voice barely a whisper. "I panicked."

"What did you do?" Foxe's tone was soft, inviting.

Her fingers tightened on her cup. "I had access because of my position, and I knew how everything worked. I changed the records to show the prototype had been approved as is, and to start the production run. It's an automated process, and Loyduk doesn't encourage employee initiative, so no one questioned the production orders. Everyone did their jobs, and the vaccine started shipping."

Foxe was looking distracted, and he glanced at Mairwen more often. She realized his talent was now flaring. If Onndrae had been more observant, she might have registered the changes, but she was too wrapped up in her own troubles.

"At first, I thought I'd done the right thing, because the vaccine was slowing and stopping the pandemic. I made sure it got to Shinnowar in the first shipments. Then we started hearing rumors of side effects. Bad ones. Fatal ones."

"What were they?" asked Foxe.

"I never found out. By then, Loyduk was in full-blown siege mentality. They were thinking it was a communication mixup with Thang Panjutamai, but I knew it was only a matter of time before they'd discover what I'd done. I used the pandemic as an excuse to take emergency time off. Once I got to Shinnowar, I kept expecting to see formal recall announcements, but all I saw were stories about vaccine thefts. I was sure Loyduk was behind them."

"Why do you say that?" Foxe's expression was encouraging.

Mairwen was impressed that he was able to maintain his empathetic interaction with Onndrae while his talent was operating, and seemed to have it under control. Of course, it probably helped that Onndrae wasn't dead and bleeding on the floor.

"I don't have any proof. I worked for them for fifteen years. I just know their mindset. Saving money was always more important to them than people's lives."

"So you read about the thefts. What did you do then?"

"If those bastards were willing let people die from taking a bad vaccine, I knew my life wouldn't mean much to them, either. I didn't want my family in danger, so I contacted Vadra. I hadn't talked to her in years. I figured it'd be hard to guess I'd go to Etonver to see her. I told her I was coming to town for a job interview, and asked if I could stay with her for a few days."

Her hands started to shake. She slid them into her lap quickly.

"The only reason I wasn't there when… that day was because I'd moved into a cashflow-only hostel the night before. Vadra wasn't like I remembered her, or maybe she was, and I never knew it, but she was chemmed out of her mind every night. I told her I was turned down for the job and was leaving Rekoria."

Foxe nodded, his expression compassionate. "You heard about Vadra's death. You reached out to friends for help, which is how we found you."

Onndrae took another sip of coffee. Her hand was steadier. "The newsfeed says illicit chem dealers killed her, but I thought Loyduk had done it, and they'd be watching the spaceports."

Mairwen hadn't heard the police's theory of the murder, and suppressed a derisive snort. Foxe had been optimistic when he'd predicted it would take them weeks to figure it out.

Foxe asked Onndrae to give him the names of anyone in Loyduk Pharma who might be involved, but she said as far as she was concerned, all the executives were complicit, one way or another.

"I'm tired and scared, and I'm tired of being scared. I just want to keep my family safe."

Foxe's eyes had quit drifting to Mairwen, so she assumed he was done using his talent.

"I can understand that. We'll do what we can to help you." He tilted his head toward the camera controller unit, which Mairwen took to mean he wanted to stop the recording. She complied.

"Agent Morganthur will escort you to one of our security teams. They'll be staying with you until we can get you someplace private and safe."

That was Mairwen's prearranged cue. If Foxe had judged Onndrae to be another imposter, he would have had Mairwen call the team in and let them deal with it.

As Mairwen led Onndrae through the joyhouse hallway, she surreptitiously studied her temporary charge. She thought Onndrae might once have been a person who smiled a lot, but was now weighed down with fear, anger, and loss. She had an uncharacteristic urge to reassure the fragile woman that she'd been right to trust Foxe.

Their walk was without incident, and she transferred Onndrae to the two La Plata staff who would become her bodyguards and protectors for the next phase of her life. Mairwen nodded in response to Onndrae's whispered thanks and left.

Back in the meeting room, Foxe had packed up the holo camera set and was waiting for her. He looked worn but pleased. He'd already put on his greatcoat, as if the room had become too cold for him, or he was anxious to leave.

"Much more interesting than blackmarketers selling bad clones," he said as he gave the room one last check. "Thanks for making Onndrae feel safe." He caught her gaze with a warm smile. "Me, too."

For five heartbeats, the pull of him was so strong she had to fight to keep herself still and her breathing steady. He looked away and the moment was gone. She belatedly realized she hadn't responded, and hoped he wasn't offended.

After she drove him back to the office, the rest of Foxe's day was taken up with meetings. He later holed up in his office in deep thinking mode, barely aware of his surroundings, pouring and forgetting multiple cups of coffee, neglecting to eat. Hours after everyone else had left the building, he finally emerged from his office. He was surprised to find her standing outside the door.

"Have you been out here the whole time?" He looked unhappy as he yawned and rubbed his jaw.

"No, just the last four hours."

She'd followed him to meetings and back, then parked herself in the hallway, with periodic forays to the stairways, lifts, and the fresher. It was nice to have a stationary security post that was indoors for once.

He shook his head. "Remind me to tell Zheer you deserve a bonus. Let's go home."

She was puzzled that he was bothered by her doing her job. Where else did he think she'd be? And more disturbing, how were Velasco and Alhamsi providing security during their shifts if they weren't near him?

He grabbed their coats and handed hers to her, then put his on as they walked the empty halls to the lift. The lights came on and off as they passed by.

His greatcoat smelled of wool and him, which curled into her nose as she drove him home. He'd taken to always sitting up front with her, and she'd taken to allowing it as a harmless chance to immerse her senses in him. Less harmless was the comfortable familiarity of walking into his townhouse with him, almost like it was where she should be. She was glad he'd gone to bed almost immediately, because it gave her time to stare out the curved window in his darkened living room and think.

For nineteen years, she'd dreamed of freedom, and she'd patiently, painstakingly prepared her escape. The Citizen Protection Service thought she was dead, but as masters of deception themselves, they wouldn't be entirely surprised if they discovered she wasn't.

The CPS remade people like her into "paracommando pathfinders," though everyone, even CPS top brass, called them trackers. They were not-quite-human weapons trained to be patient and relentless hunters—and cold executioners when ordered—but those same skills made them good at deceiving their masters. She wasn't the first tracker to escape and wouldn't be the last.

The CPS taught extreme self-reliance and crushed any perceived relationships, but active trackers still found ways to communicate with each other. The fact that a significant percentage of trackers disappeared wasn't a secret; nor was the fact that a few were recaptured, blank-slated, and returned to limited service as little more than automatons, as if they were capital crime convicts. However much trackers distrusted or disliked one another individually, their common enemy was the CPS, and their common dream was freedom.

She'd made that dream real, but four years into her hard-won new life, she didn't have any new dreams. She'd read books and watched trids to teach herself to blend into normal society, but she hadn't recognized in herself the softer emotions they'd described. She'd proven she could live like an ordinary person with an ordinary job, but that was as far as she'd gotten. She had no relationships because she didn't know where to start, or with whom she wanted to start one. She'd thought she might be damaged beyond repair.

But now, meeting Luka Foxe and being plunged into his investigation was changing her. He cared about doing what was right, about justice. It was what drove him, what fired his intuition and his love of solving mysteries. He dreamed of justice for his friends, for everyone, and sacrificed for it. He cared about others, too, even people he didn't know. He even cared about her, a little, even if it was just to help him manage the talent that scared him.

Working for Luka and seeing how he lived made her realize she'd been merely existing, content with having freedom but doing nothing with it. And doing nothing with herself or her extraordinary skills, which she'd thought had no place in a civilized world. She'd taken more initiative and risks in the last week than she had in the nearly four years since she'd hidden herself away on Rekoria, and it made her feel alive.

Luka made her feel alive. All her actions had been to support him, protect him, or please him. She wanted to make him laugh, to know what he was thinking, to learn what he tasted like, to feel the pressure of his breath in her ear. Her body and her emotions responded to him, regardless of the constant warning pings from her brain, and it both thrilled and alarmed her. There was a fine line between want and need. She was afraid she was becoming as dependent on him as he was on her, but for very different reasons.

She quietly let herself out Luka's front door, checking reflexively for scents or sounds that might mean trouble. Nothing had changed; he was safe, and his townhouse was secure.

Maybe it was enough that she was free to worry about such things, and free to stay if she chose to see what she and Luka could discover for themselves and together. She could still escape and hide herself away again if she had to, though the thought of it made her chest ache abominably.

CHAPTER 9

THE FOG OF the day was still lingering when Mairwen arrived at La Plata, earlier than usual because Velasco had requested time off for personal reasons. As usual, when Mairwen took over the shift from him, he lit out the second she appeared, leaving her to figure out where Foxe was and what his plans were for the afternoon. She finally found him occupying a fourth-floor office that, from the smells in it, used to belong to Leo Balkovsky.

The new office was much larger than Foxe's and more easily accommodated his habit of pacing, but it was still a closet compared to Zheer's presidential suite.

Foxe was in an audio conference. He was as dressed up as she'd seen him, with tailored pants and fitted dark wool halfcoat with a high-necked green shirt that complemented his hazel eyes. She hoped her grey pants and simple waist-nipped blouse and sweater were acceptable for whatever activities he was planning.

He waved her in and pointed to a chair and narrow desk in the corner. She walked quietly to it and draped her overcoat over the back of the chair.

"...*asking you for your opinion,*" said the man on the other end of the call. "*It's not every day we could get the benefit of the preeminent reconstruction expert in the galaxy.*"

Foxe rolled his eyes at the blatantly insincere flattery. "As I said, I have an exclusive contract with La Plata. You'll have to ask them."

"*I looked up your record. You used to be a good cop.*" The tone was accusatory.

"Yes," agreed Foxe blandly, unmoved.

"*Fine. I'll see if La Plata is interested in doing its civic duty,*" said the man, the barb thinly veiled. The call disconnected.

Foxe turned to her and shoved his hands in his pockets. "The Etonver police have finally discovered who I am. They want me to reconstruct the Amhur murder scene for them for free, conflict of interest notwithstanding. I respectfully declined."

She was glad he refused. He didn't need to go through that again. "Cheeky of them."

He smiled at her words, then swung his arms wide. "Welcome to my new office. I guess they got tired of me monopolizing the conference rooms."

"Perhaps it was the wear on the carpet," she said, giving his pacing feet a pointed look.

"Or that," he chuckled. The sound of it washed over her like a balm.

"Would you like some coffee?" he asked, pointing to a new, elegant-looking dispenser on the credenza. "I made extra, just in case."

She shook her head. "I'm allergic to caffeine." He looked disappointed, and she regretted making him feel that he'd somehow failed her.

She walked with him to the conference room for what he promised was his last meeting of the afternoon, then took her customary post near the door. When he realized she planned to wait for him, he shooed her away.

"The only danger here will be terminal boredom during the finance discussion. Go use the gym or relax in the lounge or something. It's going to be at least two hours. I'll ping you when I'm done."

She didn't know what to do with herself. She went back to his new office. She decided to think like a tracker planning an incursion, and examined the office more closely to determine its security strengths and weaknesses, then checked the locations of available exits. She noted the nameplates for all the offices so she could look them up and know who should or shouldn't be on the floor.

That only ate up seventeen minutes, so she grabbed her overcoat and walked downstairs to the lounge on the second floor.

There was some sort of celebration going on, so she avoided it and continued down the hall toward the back stairs. From behind her, she heard her name called, and recognizing the voice, turned to see Beva walking toward her, waving with one hand and carrying a covered plate with the other.

"Just the person I wanted to see!" Beva said with a smile as she caught up. She petted Mairwen's upper arm. Where once Mairwen would have flinched at being touched, she now found it wasn't objectionable, at least from Beva. Perhaps it was a side effect of liking Luka's touch.

Beva smiled even wider. "Nice sweater. I hate you. You make even off-the-rack clothes look *trés chic*. Get you to a good autotailor for something flattering, and you'd be plasma hot."

Beva, bubbling over with good humor, steered Mairwen into a tiny office that turned out to belong to Beva. "There's a mess of berry seedcake left in the lounge, so help yourself. My co-workers are so sweet. They brought it in for me because I got the promotion."

"Congratulations," said Mairwen. She was surprised to find she meant it, even though she hadn't interacted with Beva often.

"How do you like your new job?" asked Beva. "Got to be a nice change from working for Isak Malamig." She winked.

"So would working the night shift in a riot zone." Ordinarily, she wouldn't have said anything, but Luka responded positively when she expressed her odd sense of humor. Her brain grumbled that he was a bad influence.

Beva let out a huge laugh that shook her whole frame. "*Mais oui,* ain't it the truth!"

Mairwen saw Beva was about to drop the plate of cake she was carrying, so she caught it in time and put it safely on the desk.

"*Merci, cher.* Reason I ask about your new job is because my new job is to direct a new division for providing personal security services. I want you to come work for me when your assignment for Foxe is done."

Mairwen was nonplussed. "I'm not qualified. I'm not… good with people."

Beva laughed again and waved away the protest. "I've seen your record. You're plenty qualified. As to the other, you're quiet, is all. It's nice to have a friend who talks less than me, and clients are looking for competence, not conversation. Besides, Luka likes you, and I like you, so you can't be that bad."

Beva looked at the clock and gasped. "Oh my, gotta run—our youngest son is graduating tonight. All his aunts, uncles, and cousins are coming. We're taking up an entire row in the auditorium. You think about my offer, hear? We'll talk again." She hurriedly rolled her thincomp and thumbed the desk lock.

"Yes," agreed Mairwen, because it was simpler that way.

Beva grabbed her overcoat and the plate of cake and was out the door in a flash. Mairwen felt like she'd been caught in a whirlwind.

She wondered when Beva and Luka had talked about her and why. Or perhaps Beva had merely observed Luka's ease with her. She wasn't as bothered by the thought of being noticed as she was before, but it still made her uneasy.

She also wondered what it would be like to be a part of a family, even a small one. Mairwen remembered Beva saying she'd been happily married to the same woman for nearly thirty years. Mairwen couldn't begin to imagine what that kind of familiar, trusting relationship felt like, but it sounded surprisingly appealing.

She walked down to the first floor to find the gym, which she'd seen but never used, since night-shift guards had little need to visit the office. The gym was larger than she'd remembered, but perhaps its size was dictated by being directly over the basement weapons range. The exercise equipment was well maintained, and the human smells not overpowering, suggesting the room was cleaned daily. The company had posted instructional displays in several common languages on how to use each machine, and the employees had added the funny, mostly sex-referenced, illustrations to go with them.

Since she still had well over an hour to fill, she got her spare running clothes from the vehicle and used one of the booths to change out of her civilian clothes. She supposed she'd have to buy more of them if she took the job Beva was offering, or for that matter, stayed with Luka, if he wanted her. Perhaps Beva, who was evidently interested in such things, would help her select appropriate clothing, regardless. She was still baffled by the choices available when shopping, so she avoided it as much as possible.

She didn't want to try a new exercise machine without first seeing how normal people used it, so although she was alone in the room, she selected one of the force isolation machines, and kept the isolation net mass within a believable range for someone her size. In full-tracker mode, she could handle significantly more, though without eating well, she'd pay with sore muscles and joints later.

It felt good to build up heat and sweat with the steady repetitions of each pattern, to use her upper body's physical exertion to keep her thoughts grounded, and not on the entirely too good-looking man who was now her boss. She stopped in time to shower quickly, change back into her civilian clothes, and stash her exercise clothes in the car. Though it was humid and chilly in the underground parking area, she was still feeling warm, so she carried her overcoat instead of wearing it as she walked back.

She was just approaching the door into the building when it slammed open, propelled by Malamig as he barreled through. His jacket gaped open, and his unflattering orange shirt looked wrinkled. The angry look on his face had her instantly wary, and when he saw her, he veered toward her with stiff strides.

"What are you doing in here?" he demanded. The wind shifted, and she got a good whiff of fresh bourbon from his clothes and breath. "Oh, right, you've got a vehicle now that you're a satellite to the star, the heir to the fecking throne." His regional accent was thicker than usual.

Mairwen stayed neutral and silent. Drunk or chemmed people were irrational.

"You think you're set now, don't you? Movin' up in the world?" His lip curled in a sneer. "Well, don't count on it. This company does what it fecking well wants, and to hell with rules."

He leaned closer, and Mairwen zeroed her offended olfactory sense.

"*I* should have been made director." He shook his finger in her face. "*I* have the seniority, and *I* worked my ass off for it, and they gave it to that jumping Rienville slut because she has 'field experience.' That's fecking code for 'gives great tongue.'"

So Beva's promotion was the directorship Malamig had been convinced he'd get. Probably wiser not to mention that Beva had offered her a job. She kept her face blank.

Malamig eyed her up and down with contempt. "But you'd know all about that, wouldn't you? You're probably bobbing and spreading for Foxe every chance you get." He stared at her crotch, then gave her a sloppy leer. "You owe me some of that. I was nice to you for three and a half feckin' years."

It suddenly occurred to her that now that she worked for Foxe, she didn't have to stay and listen to Malamig. She started to step around him, but he countered to block her.

"You need a lesson in cooperation," he hissed, and reached out to grab her arm.

She evaded him easily and he staggered, off balance, but he recovered and spun on her faster than she'd thought possible. He was fumbling at something under his jacket, and she belatedly remembered he carried a handgun.

She dropped into full-tracker mode and time *slowed...*

Mairwen counted the security eyes and calculated their angles. If she could lead him two steps to her left, the eyes would only see the back of him and nothing of her. She slung her coat at him from the right, causing him to shift and trip over his own feet in the direction she wanted him to go. Taking a chance, she followed with a slow shove with her shoulder, causing them both to step out of eye view. She used her foot to sweep his legs out from under him, and as he fell, she cocked her left wrist to release the hilt of a flat stiletto into her waiting fingers.

She waited until he was mostly down, then lunged and pressed one knee on his rounded stomach and sternum and slid the knife to his throat. She allowed him a few thousand milliseconds to register where he was and the threat she posed. She eased time into half speed so she could form understandable words.

"Be still."

Even as she spoke, she saw the raw panic in him, causing his head and shoulders to buck in an effort to throw her off. She didn't move the knife away fast enough to avoid a shallow slice on his neck, and blood welled up.

She put more of her weight on him and, with her free hand, pushed his head back down to the plascrete with more force than was strictly needed. She leaned in closer to his face, ignored his putrid breath, and stared into his wide eyes. "Be. Still."

He froze. Finally. She fished under his jacket and found his gun still in its unsnapped holster. She lifted it out with two fingers, then rose up off his chest and stepped back. She breathed deeply and allowed time to come back to full reality.

She took another small step away, still out of camera view, and showed him his gun as she flicked the safety on. "This will be at the front desk."

He must have felt something wet at his neck, because he felt for the cut, then looked at the blood on his fingers.

"You horse-shagging, helio skag! You cut me!" Malamig was trying to sit up, holding his bloody hand out in front of him, staring in disbelief. "You feckin' *stabbed* me!" Adrenalin was making him shake.

She slid her stiletto back in its sheath. "Perhaps you should see a medic."

She folded her coat over her arm and walked back into the building, ignoring Malamig's increased bellowing. She took the gun to the front desk and said she'd found it in the parking area, then rode the lift to the fourth floor rather than chance meeting someone on the stairs. She likely had at least another fifteen minutes to wait, so she used the fresher down the hall from Luka's office to clean the few drops of Malamig's blood from the stiletto and its sheath.

She examined herself in the mirror, but she looked the same as ever. Her asymmetrical spiked hair, her only vanity, didn't even look out of place.

In retrospect, it was reckless to have visibly injured Malamig, but she'd underestimated his ability to function while impaired. She felt no remorse for hurting him, but knew it might well cost her the job with La Plata. That thought brought a strong wave of regret. She now had two friends where she'd had none, and in Luka, maybe more.

She sighed. When she'd first met Luka, she'd wanted nothing to do with him, and now here she was, wanting to do nothing without him.

Emotional pain was worse than physical pain, but she couldn't afford to wallow in it. She forced it into a mental hypercube and stored it away as something to deal with later, when she was alone. It was cold comfort knowing CPS training was good for at least that. She went back to Foxe's office to wait to take him home.

When they finally got to his townhouse an hour later, he asked if she was up for a run—he was desperate after two and a half hours without being able to pace.

"Let's run to the cul-de-sac and back," he said.

She met his smile with a small one of her own and agreed. That direction was the longest distance he could have chosen. After the day she'd had, she might have suggested it if he hadn't.

She changed into her running clothes and added a hooded waterproof jacket to ward off the chilly fog that had never lifted that day. She liked fog better than wind because it carried scents better. Maybe they'd even see the early first moonrise.

When La Plata terminated her contract, she was going to miss the quiet camaraderie of loping along just behind him on his favorite scenic running trail. Most of it was wide enough for four or five people to run abreast, but the fog made it seem like they were cut off from the rest of the world. She indulged herself in opening her senses to him, letting his fog-borne scent slide across her thoughts like the caress of a silk scarf.

"Help me think, Mairwen," he said. He slowed his pace to make conversation easier. He hadn't used her first name often, and she decided she liked the way he said it, as if it was a new word he'd found.

"About what?" She eased closer so they were running side by side.

"The lab results on the vaccine packets. The DNA tests were 'weird,' to quote Dr. Tewisham."

"Technical term, is that?"

Foxe laughed. "'Weird' as in completely unknown basal structure."

She edged forward a few paces in front of him when another runner came into view up ahead, although she'd been hearing the sound of feet and fast breathing for some time. She kept herself between the woman and Foxe until she was gone, then evened up with him again.

"Before you ask," he said with a smile, "it wasn't a testing error, it's not registered for research or license, it wasn't a corrupt clone, and five other labs, including Concordance Prime, all said the same thing. That's what took so long, because Tewisham got stubborn and called in favors." At their slower than usual pace, Foxe was running and talking easily. "I'm out of probable explanations, so now I'm looking for the improbable."

She was flattered he imagined she would have thought of asking any of those questions. "What does 'unknown basal structure' mean to a biochemist?"

"Something about epsilon aminos with isomers that aren't right or left, and I have no idea what that means. Tewisham thinks he'll get at least a top journal article and a galactic conference tour if he can figure it out."

They ran along in silence for long moments. Foxe was the puzzle solver, but she shared the underlying curiosity that drove him. Something twitched in her memory, from long ago, about the origin of the carrier phage that made the tracker alteration possible. It was one of the CPS's bigger secrets. "Perhaps it came from a hybrid planet."

Foxe's whoop of laughter startled her. "A hybrid planet? I'd have never taken you for a fan of science fiction spectaculars."

Mairwen shrugged and said nothing. Like most people, he probably thought hybrid planets, those deadly cauldrons of combined alien and terraform seeding, were impossible. The Concordance Ministry of Health may have convinced the known galaxy that failed terraforms were always poisoned to protect civilization from novel microorganisms to which the populace had no immunity, but she knew better. The CPS even hid a hybrid planet right under the nose of Concordance Command headquarters. She should know, because it had been the location of her barracks for nineteen years. She definitely wasn't going to tell him about that.

Foxe gave her two quick looks. "You're serious, aren't you? It's improbable, I'll give you that." He smiled as if to reassure her, though she didn't know of what. He returned his gaze forward. "Even if the poisoning didn't kill everything, the odds of finding viable..."

His words trailed off as his intuitive imagination began bubbling. She knew that look. She'd be getting no more conversation from him for a while.

She heard distant footfalls from behind them on the trail. The fog changed the acoustics, but she thought the two runners would overtake them in a couple of minutes. She shortened her stride so she could drop behind Foxe. He didn't notice. He was probably slipping into focused intuition mode, and the sure sign came when he started a mumbled dialog with himself.

As usual, when his mind started sparking, his speed picked up. Running seemed to be just a faster form of pacing for him. She dropped back a few strides farther and slid the hood off her head, focusing more of her attention on the runners coming up from behind. She was relieved to hear their pace was slowing to a walk. At that rate, they wouldn't catch up any time soon.

The fog made the trees and decorative grasses along the trail look dreamlike, and it also carried Foxe's scent to her, which gave her a warm feeling that she didn't care to examine too closely. Though he wore a mid-weight loose jacket, his pants were sleek and form-fitting. He had the most beautifully proportional legs and rear she'd ever seen. He could stop traffic if he ever wore tight shorts. Maybe he already had and would be a footnote in the next Etonver traffic study.

She wondered if he admired her body as much as she did his. It was outside her experience to want that. She'd been preoccupied with keeping her senses practically comatose so she could blend in and be normal. If anyone had been interested in her in the past, she'd never noticed, and her sex hormones had never been engaged. She'd been repulsed by physical contact. Now she had no idea how to tell if Foxe noticed her, or felt the same fascination she did for him.

Hope, regret, and frustration threatened to roil up and overtake her, so she centered on the steady effort of running to soothe her thoughts and order her senses, dropping farther back so his scent wouldn't keep distracting her. She could meditate on unknowable things on her own time. Besides, the two runners from far behind them were on the trail again, and it sounded like they were racing each other. Imprudent behavior, considering the poor visibility caused by the fog and approaching twilight.

Chapter 10

THE INCIPIENT BURN in Luka's legs and lungs told him he'd gotten carried away again while he savored the possibilities that arose from Mairwen's out-of-the-box suggestion of a hybrid planet. Suddenly, he was in the trail end's cul-de-sac, and he couldn't remember the last kilometer he'd run. He'd also lost Mairwen somewhere, probably outpaced her without meaning to.

He slowed to a walk and started around the circular perimeter to give her time to catch up, and to let his breathing ease. The cul-de-sac was big, maybe twelve meters across, and was ringed by curved benches at the edge and an informal hedge beyond that. The fog was dense enough to make it hard to even see the benches on the far side. On impulse, he used his percomp to send a short message to Zheer, suggesting she contract with a finder to look for a hybrid planet that could be the source of the "weird" DNA from the drug samples. More than likely she'd think he was being absurd, but maybe her forecaster talent would see some merit.

As he got to the farthest point of the circle, he was starting to wonder what was keeping Mairwen when he heard crashing of bushes from behind him, and suddenly a man was tackling him. The only thing that kept him from going down was an instinctive quick lunge to the left, but a second man joined the first, followed by someone's hand on his neck. And with that touch, his body was no longer his own.

A telepath, a woman he thought, though he couldn't turn his head to look, compelled him to start walking toward the hedge, pinned between the two men gripping his arms. He tried to push the telepath out of his mind, but he'd never been good at that, and she already had multiple hooks into him. The best he could do was obscure his surface thoughts and ruthlessly bury any worries of what might have happened to Mairwen.

Though the telepath forced his gaze forward and blocked his speech, she didn't bother controlling his hearing. Unfortunately, the men who were guiding him weren't talking. From his peripheral vision, he could see they both wore nondescript cheap civilian clothes, but they carried themselves like gunnin—ground-based military personnel—or mercs. The taller one on his left was dark skinned and bald, and the shorter one on his right was pale skinned and sported an ugly diagonal scar across his face like a badge of honor. He saw and felt one of them attach a tech suppressor to the front neckline of his shirt, good for blocking any incoming or outgoing transmissions from his percomp or any tracking devices he might have.

Luka gained grudging respect for the telepath controlling him as they made their way past the hedge and up a slope to the sidewalk. She kept his movements fluid and balanced instead of jerky like a puppet. Anyone seeing them from a distance would assume they were all friends having a good time, and the fog would cover up any incongruous details. He could still feel the damp chill on his face, and the feeling of movement, he just couldn't do anything about it.

He'd assumed they'd get him into a vehicle fast, but instead they kept him marching down the sidewalk for eight blocks into a crumbling neighborhood that had seen better days. Even kidnappers avoided Etonver traffic, it seemed.

He got a glimpse of the telepath when she was reflected in an eye-level window, but she'd compelled his head away too fast for him to make out any details beyond very short brown hair and brown skin. The people they passed hunched their shoulders and didn't make eye contact. It wasn't a part of town anyone wanted to be in after dark.

Their destination turned out to be a grungy, single room in a rundown cashflow-only hostel. Once there, the two mercs efficiently taped him to the room's only chair, anchoring his legs, arms, and torso. A closeup look at the mercs' clothing told him it was disposable, meaning they intended to leave no forensic evidence behind. It didn't bode well for his future.

They removed his jacket and percomp and put them on the bed, but left the tech suppressor clipped to his shirt. The telepath's fingers never lost contact with the back of his neck. She loosened control of his body except for his head, which she kept facing forward. The bald merc stood near the door watching Luka, and the scar-faced merc stood next to the window and looked out through the cheap blinds. Neither looked angry or sympathetic, just two people doing their jobs.

"I'm going to ask you some questions," said the woman behind him. Her voice was surprisingly high-pitched, almost girlish, and her English was accentless. "If you scream or act out before I can stop you, Mr. Brown or Mr. Blue will hurt you." He guessed the pseudonyms were based on the respective colors of their thin jackets. "If you cooperate, I'll send you to sleep, and we'll leave you here unharmed for your people to find. Do you understand?" She eased up on her control of his voice.

"Forgive me if I doubt your benign intentions." He could already feel her nibbling at his shields. They weren't strong enough to stand up to a focused probe by even a low-level telepath or empath, and she'd already proven she was better than that. Thanks to his mother's tutelage, he had developed another line of defense, and he steeled himself to use it.

"We're professionals, Mr. Foxe," she chided almost primly. "Violence isn't nearly as effective in ensuring we're getting the information we need. We'll start with the binary. Is your name Lukasz Foxe?"

Like most people, she mispronounced his first name. He delayed answering as long as he dared. "*Ja*," he finally said. He switched to thinking in Icelandic. English was the Concordance's official standard language, and most people could get by in Mandarin and few other common languages, but Icelandic was obscure, almost a relic. She'd have to use his mind's language center to translate, and it would slow her down. A trick he'd learned from another telepath. The longer he took, the better chance for someone to get him rescued. Someone he wasn't going to think or worry about.

"How many moons does Rekoria have?" she asked, punching at his weakening shields to compel him to give up the information.

He gritted his teeth. "*Tvö*," he said. "*Nakú-aben Ússí hefur einn tungl.*" Naku-aben Uzzi has one moon. And two deaths. He plunged into his filed reconstruction memory to call up each and every pool of blood from the boy who had been unwillingly sacrificed to the moon by his own mother, who'd later thrust the knife up into her own throat. The clearing in the woods smelled like an earthy slaughterhouse, and the filtered sunlight made a halo on the child's face. That's why the mother had placed him there, because the boy had always loved the sunshine, despite his heart belonging to the moon like the shape of his birthmark. She'd cut open the boy's chest and removed the heart first, then washed his face clean with the hem of her dress so...

An impact sent Luka's head snapping back and the pain of a hard slap brought him to the present. Luka opened his eyes to focus on the bald merc in brown standing in front of him, the likely source of the blow. The merc nodded once to the telepath behind him and returned to his post.

"That wasn't very cooperative, Mr. Foxe," the telepath said. "Don't do that again." Her voice sounded shakier than before. "Let's cut to the chase, shall we? Do you know where Dr. Tansa Onndrae is?" She accompanied the question with a hard thrust that shattered his shields and imposed a strong compulsion to answer.

Luka didn't even have to work at it to associate the name with Vadra Amhur and let the phantasms flood his mind with recent visceral memories of how a killer had used a wirekey to mark the flesh of the naked woman zip-tied to a chair, and how the killer had centered on the sexual organs for his own gratification. Someone else had stood watching as the torturer plunged into soft tissue as the woman screamed into the gag wrapped around...

Luka's head snapped back with the force of another slap. The bald merc was already moving away by the time Luka looked up. He felt blood trickle from his nose and the side of his mouth.

"I told you not to do that again," said the telepath. Her voice was definitely shaky.

"*Farðu í rassgat,*" he thought to her. *Go fuck yourself.* He switched to standard English to speak. "It was your question," he said, then spat out blood onto the stained carpet. "I can't help it if you didn't like the answer."

He tried to project confidence, but he knew he couldn't hold out indefinitely. Eating up their time was all he could hope for. He was risking losing control over the memories, and maybe sending himself into a fugue state, leaving the telepath free to slip in and browse through his mind at will.

Why do you remember murderers like that? She asked the question in his mind.

I don't, he thought back with vehemence. *I remember the victims.*

He felt a wave of revulsion in her mind and body, though she tried to hide it. Her fingers were turning to ice on the back of his neck. Then she shored up her shields and with that, her resolve.

"If you do that again, I'll have Mr. Brown break something," she said with a steely tone.

"Then pick another subject," said Luka. "You saw what they did to her." Ice was freezing his blood and bones.

She was silent a moment. "Very well. What do you know about Loyduk Pharma?"

"*Það framleiðir og dreifir lyfjum.*" The telepath made his mind translate to English. "They make and distribute pharmaceuticals." He was quoting from an article he'd read the day before. He visualized each sentence and focused on translating them into Icelandic. She used it as a hook into other related memories, including the lab's report on the squibs. He tried to avoid the memory of the warehouse, but he was losing control and the horror started to saturate his thoughts. The telepath thought he was doing it on purpose and it made her mad.

"I warned you," she said with tight anger. "Mr. Brown, if you please. Something painful." Luka felt her take control of his whole body again as the bald merc stepped close. He lifted Luka's left hand and casually forced all four of Luka's fingers back until they cracked. The pain was overwhelming, and the telepath didn't allow him the outlet of vocalizing or even gritting his teeth. His eyes watered involuntarily and his breathing came in shallow gasps.

"What was in the lab report?" she asked, and probed deep again. Control on his body eased, and he thought maybe she couldn't both physically compel and deep probe at the same time. Luka let the throbbing pain radiating from his left hand fill his mind. He couldn't stop her from rooting around, but he could make her pay for it.

"What did Leo Balkovsky find out about Loyduk?" He felt her trace the connection in his mind and triggered the nauseating memory of Leo's lifeless body curled around the forceblade that had killed him. His gut roiled as he tried to think of something else, anything else. But not of Mairwen who had anchored him, who might be hurt, or might have sent for the cavalry. He could feel the telepath tracing his mental thread, getting closer. He pressed his broken fingers to the chair arm and gasped as the overload of pain fluxed through him, obliterating all coherent thought.

As the pain subsided, the scar-faced merc in blue watching at the window spoke. "Problem outside." His right hand hovered near a thigh holster, but Luka couldn't see what was in it.

"Company?" asked Brown.

"Street fight." Something hit the thick security window with a loud thump. "They're throwing rocks. Fucking fog. Can't see shit."

It sounded to Luka like a riot might be brewing, one of the unfortunately more regular things Etonver was known for. And with Etonver's open-carry policies…

"Weapons will be next," said Brown, proving he was well aware of the pattern. His accent sounded Russian. He looked above Luka's head to where the telepath was presumably standing. "We must move. Are you done here?"

"Soon. I need five more minutes," said the telepath. She sounded angry and nervous.

Two quick, loud thuds hit the window. Luka would have twitched if his body hadn't been locked down.

"Too dangerous," said Brown. "We must take him somewhere else." He crossed to Luka and used his large combat knife to cut through the tape. The telepath's touch kept Luka immobile, then compelled him to stand. Brown stood nearby. "Left or right?" he asked, presumably asking which direction they'd be taking once they got outside.

"Right," said the scar-faced merc. He crossed to the door, checked that Brown and the telepath were ready, then opened it.

All hell broke loose.

The scar-faced merc staggered back as the door slammed into the wall and bounced into him, but he was already falling, his face a bloody mass as his nose sprayed blood like a burst water balloon. Someone streaked into the room and out of Luka's view, but Brown was slowed by having to drop his combat knife before reaching for the beamer in his holster. The overhead lights went out.

Luka felt the telepath's unshielded panic as she lost control of him. He dove to the floor, then almost passed out from the pain when he landed on his broken left hand. He rolled onto his back and was bombarded by a shadowy kaleidoscope of images and sounds. Brown's leg extending in a high kick and someone's grunt of pain. A brilliant flash of light and a roar from outside the door. Brown's body spinning as he pointed the beamer. A glimpse of pale blonde hair. A crash of security coilglass. A flash, and a woman's high-pitched scream abruptly cut off. A sickening thump, and Brown's body dropping like a sandbag on top of Luka, smashing his broken hand between them and sending him into deep twilight.

When the darkness receded, the roaring chaos had subsided and all he heard was heavy, unsteady breathing in the room and the rumble of the riot outside, moving away.

Someone called his name, and he recognized the voice.

"Mairwen?" he croaked. He couldn't imagine how she came to be there.

It took him a couple of tries to one-handedly shove Brown's unconscious but still breathing body off of him. The pain from his left hand was blindingly intense. He cradled it against his chest as he sat up. The supposedly unbreakable window was shattered. The scar-faced merc's body was lying in the doorway, covered in some of the coilglass shards.

Next to the overturned chair was the body of a beefy, dark-skinned woman, presumably the telepath. She was dead, her shoulder and neck fried, likely unintentionally, by the beamer that was still in Brown's hand. Luka was grateful that the excruciating pain of his hand kept his talent dark for the moment.

Mairwen, who had been looking out the window, moved to crouch next to him. Her strong features were softened by shadows.

"It's not safe here," she said. "Can you walk?"

It took him a moment to understand her English words. Her tone was remarkably even and calm for someone who had just taken out two professional mercs in a matter of seconds. She wasn't even breathing hard, so the harsh lung sounds must be coming from him.

He nodded and got to his feet awkwardly. She rose as he did, unclipped the tech suppressor from his shirt and pocketed it, grabbed his jacket and percomp from the bed, and glided to the doorway. She stepped over scar-faced merc's body to look outside. To Luka's relief, the merc was still alive.

"Let's go," she said, and watched him closely as he crossed to her. Apparently satisfied he wasn't going to collapse, she led him outside.

The central mass of the riot had moved on or broken apart, he couldn't tell which, leaving the street deserted except for the scattered debris, some of it burning. It was quite surreal in the fog and smoke.

He didn't remember much about walking away from the hostel or the taxi ride that took them to her apartment building, except the bitter, subzero cold in his veins. He knew he should be worried about shock, but he couldn't make his pain-soaked brain think of what to do about it. It was doubtless a sign of stress trauma that he felt safer with Mairwen than he would have with a phalanx of bodyguards, especially after she told him she'd neutralized two other mercs in the park before finding him.

She had him sit on a stool at the breakfast bar in her tiny, spartan, sixth-floor apartment. She gently wrapped a flexible freeze pack around his swollen and rapidly bruising left hand, apologizing for not having any painkillers. The fog in his head had begun to clear by the time she put a warm mug of herbal tea in front of him and wrapped his good hand around it. He was still miserably cold.

"Drink," she said. "You need to decide who to ping and where to get medical treatment."

He sipped gingerly and found it was too sweet but not too hot, so he took several swallows, paying no mind to its hay-like flavor of dried ryegrass. He knew sugar didn't work that fast, but he felt better almost immediately.

"Zheer first," he said. She nodded and put his percomp on the counter in front of him.

He lucked into connecting live and encrypted almost immediately, which meant Zheer was still at the office despite the late hour.

He set the percomp to speaker only and told Zheer what had happened. He glossed over parts he didn't want to discuss in detail, such as how he'd distracted the telepath, and how Mairwen had taken down three armed kidnappers in only seconds. They both had secrets to keep. He hoped Zheer would infer the riot had been the main reason he'd escaped.

"I think it's a bad idea for me to report this to the police, at least for now. Being involved in a second violent death case in as many days is liable to get me iced for a week."

There was a pause. "*Only the telepath is dead?*"

He looked at Mairwen, who nodded slightly. "As far as we know. The mercs were still alive when we left."

"*As you wish, then. Nothing in Etonver law says you have to report being assaulted, and I doubt the mercs will file charges.*"

Her dry tone drew a brief snort out of him.

"I'd like to visit the company's contract healer. I could go to the nearest urgent care center, but planetary law makes it too *helvítis* easy for the police and other interested parties to see the records."

"*Of course. I'm sending the authcodes now. Is Morganthur still with you?*"

"Yes, she can hear you." Luka pushed the percomp toward her. His broken hand was aching from the freeze pack, but he kept it on.

"*How did you get separated from Foxe on the trail?*" Zheer's tone was chillier than it had been.

Mairwen's expression was completely closed down. "Two other mercs attacked from behind us on the trail. They delayed me."

"*I see. Then how did you find Foxe so fast? Or at all, for that matter?*"

"The mercs walked him to the hostel room. I found witnesses."

"*Lucky for you both, then.*" A thread of skepticism in her voice suggested she thought there was more their story. "*Luka, any idea on motive?*"

"Not really. They went to the trouble and expense of separating me from Morganthur and interrogating me, instead of just disabling or killing one or both of us. Some of the questions were… unexpected, like a new player late to the game, catching up."

"*Interesting. I was inclined to disregard your rather fanciful idea of a hybrid planet, but after this evening's adventure, I'm rethinking that. In the meantime, can Morganthur stay with you and get you to the healer? Where are you, anyway? We'll need to get you to a safehouse.*"

Mairwen spoke up, which surprised him. "He can stay in my apartment tonight. It's subleased, and would be difficult to trace. I'll get him to the healer."

Zheer approved, promising expense reimbursement and to send secure transport for them both in the morning.

Mairwen used her own cumbersome percomp to call and persuade the healer to treat him that evening. He was content to sit and listen. He liked watching her. She had an indefinable presence and grace that always caught his attention, even when he was exhausted and hurting.

It finally came to him that she hadn't come away from the evening's excitement unscathed. Her gait was off, and she was avoiding using her right arm. He was ashamed he hadn't noticed sooner.

"You need the healer, too," he told her.

"I'm fine," she said as she placed a hot bowl of beef and rice soup and a spoon in front of him. It tasted good for being from a pouch, and it felt better in his stomach than the overly sweet tea had. She put her bowl on the counter and ate quickly and efficiently.

"Sure, if by 'fine' you mean a posterior dislocation of the right shoulder, a stiff left knee, and a boot-print bruise on your collarbone and neck. You got them in the line of duty, so the company will pay, if that's what you're worried about."

She didn't say anything, but she didn't refuse, either. She looked as tired as he'd ever seen her. Another thought occurred to him. "Were you responsible for the riot?"

"No," she said, then gave him a slight smile. "But I may have nudged it in your direction."

The taxi trips to and from the healer's office took twice as long as the treatments themselves. They could have taken the free metro transit and gotten there just as fast. The healer spent most of the time repairing Luka's broken fingers. He warned him the whole left hand would likely be weak for a few days, and gave him some pain patches.

Luka didn't see Mairwen's treatment, but she refused pain meds, saying she was allergic. He suspected it was because she considered herself still on duty, but he counted himself lucky that he'd gotten her to submit to healing at all, and didn't push it. However much he might instinctively want to look after her, she probably wouldn't let him.

Mairwen's apartment was barely furnished except for a monstrously large platform bed in the only bedroom, which she said had come with the place. Luka could see why. It could easily accommodate four or five adults, and removing it would require demolishing a wall or two.

With no windows, and only a closeable solar diffuser on the ceiling, the apartment was ideal for someone who worked the night shift. The space had nothing personal like artwork, holos, or any sense of décor. It could have been quarters in a hostel, except for an older-model, force-isolation exerciser in one corner, and one far wall covered in extra-thick, dark cork. The exerciser hadn't become a clothes rack or collected dust, so it was likely she actually used it.

He was again sitting at the breakfast bar, watching her clean up the nook that passed for a kitchen. She'd showered and changed out of the slightly bloody running clothes and into loose, wide-legged pants and a long-sleeved loose tank. The drapey, faded black fabric outlined her slim but muscled form as she moved. Thanks to the healer, the bruise on her neck was fading, though it would take time for it to vanish completely.

For once, she wasn't wearing her wrist knives. He flattened both his hands on the counter to keep them still, grateful for the distraction of the residual pain. He'd been alone with her often in the past ten days, so he didn't know why being in her apartment now felt intimate and charged. He wanted physical contact with her—a need that left him almost breathless.

"Luka, I owe you an apology." She stood next to him at the counter. He hadn't felt her approach, and her voice was quiet.

"What for?" How was it she took him by surprise so often?

"I should have anticipated they'd exploit your routine." There was vulnerability on her face that he'd never seen before, and she wasn't skittering away from him like she usually did. His intuition started to stir, and he let his talent guide his question.

"How did you really find me so fast?"

She looked at him consideringly, then seemed to come to a decision.

"I followed your scent. It carried in the fog all along the route they took you. I was afraid they'd kill you if I breached the door, so I had to lure them out." She gently covered his recently healed left hand with hers and lightly caressed his still swollen and bruised fingers with her thumb. "It gave them time to hurt you."

His intuition flared arc-white as he made the connections. Her extraordinary hearing and reflexes, her familiarity with death, hidden depths, legends and memes, improbable truths... "If hybrid planets can be real, then so can you. Are you a death tracker?"

* * * * *

He really was amazingly brilliant, Mairwen thought. The dawning wonder in his expression made her cautious brain scream at her to get away, but the rest of her wanted to get closer. She kept her hand on his.

"Yes."

"Invisible, unstoppable military assassins with amazing supernatural powers, the force of stellar energy at their fingertips?" His gentle teasing eased some of the tension in her. "So mysterious that even the military's covert ops division knows nothing about them?"

"The Citizen Protection Service knows everything about us," she said with a touch of acid. "They created us."

"Created? Like cyberneuro implants, skulljacks, enhancement drugs?" He named the commonly known modifications the CPS gave its Jumpers and minders.

"No." She wondered what to tell him so he'd understand.

"The CPS discovered a treatment and procedure that only works on a very few people. They can't tell in advance who it will or won't work on, so they secretly test as many people as they can get away with. Nothing happens if you fail, but if you're the one in a billion that passes, you become CPS property. They tell your family and friends you died, they mask your DNA, and a CPS telepath cleans you of as many of your childhood memories as they can and still leave you functional."

She touched her fingertips to his mistreated knuckles. "We're hunters, but we don't always kill." She gave him a brief, wry smile. "Sometimes we leave the killing to others."

He topped her hand with his right one, his fingertips cool on the back of her hand. "Are you an uncatalogued minder?" Like he probably was. Unfortunately, she was nothing so normal or benign.

"I'm an alter."

The shock on his face didn't surprise her. Ever since the discovery of the grisly horrors that resulted from the secret experiments during the First Wave era, altering humans was considered appallingly immoral and illegal. He deserved to know the whole truth. "The procedure, if you live through it, transforms subtrans-DNA to expand all the senses, inputs, nerves, synapses, to a lot higher than normal humans. The alteration changed my body chemistry and my brain."

Instead of pulling back from her as if she were contagious, as she'd feared, he pulled her to face him, close enough to feel the heat of his body.

"No wonder you're so amazing," he said with such a sweet smile that her heart stuttered. The smile faded. "The CPS wouldn't have willingly let you go."

"No. None of us makes it out of the program alive."

His face showed he recognized the implications of that. She liked that she didn't have to connect the nodes for him.

He turned her hand over, palm up, and stroked her thumb with his. "What's it like? The expanded senses part, not the being dead part."

She'd never tried to describe it before, never imagined wanting to. "Sort of like… turning up the volume on a music player so you can hear every note of every instrument all at once, except that it's everything. Smells, sounds, colors, images, tastes, touch."

"Did your extraordinary control come with the alteration, too?" His buttery scent curled up into her nose. The power of his regard when focused on her was dangerously, deliciously potent.

"No," she said. "Nineteen years of CPS training."

She tried to read his expression, to see how he was taking it, but all she could think about was the empty, icy feeling in her chest that was spreading to her barely healed shoulder and making it ache, too. The only heat in her came from where his hands held hers. Everything warm had been viciously beaten out of her long ago. "It's a dangerous process and a brutal program. Only a few of us survive it."

She fought to keep even uglier memories moldering in their graves where they belonged.

Before she knew what was happening, he was standing with his arms around her, and she felt the warmth of his shoulder against her face, with only his thin knit shirt between them.

"*Fyrirgefðu.* I'm sorry," he said softly. His voice rumbling through his chest and his warm breath's moisture against her skin sent a tremor through her.

She realized her eyes were filled with unshed tears, a peculiar sensation. It was easy to ignore because he felt so very good against her. She slid her arms up his well-muscled back. She drew in the scent of him and listened to the rhythm of his heart. The ice in her chest was melting in the flood caused by his heat.

He stroked her back gently. "How long has it been since you, uh, left school?" The timbre of his voice resonated deep.

"Four years."

Another tremor ran through her.

"Are you cold?" he asked, and slid a hand up to the nape of her neck. His thumb gently caressed her hairline, and sent tingles through her.

"I'm fine." She was almost intoxicated by the feel of him, and her breath was ragged as she struggled to clamp down tight controls on her body's feedback to keep the tremors at bay.

"I think you should look up the meaning of the word 'fine' sometime."

A laugh escaped her, and he tightened his hold on her. "That's the first time I've heard you laugh."

"I don't, usually. You're a bad influence."

He laughed, and it rippled through his body and into hers. She pulled back so she could see his smile. His amusement changed to a look of intent, and he kissed her. It was warm and cool and wonderful all at once.

She opened her mouth to his, inviting him to deepen the kiss, and an electric shock of pleasure coursed through her at the complex taste of him when their tongues touched. He pulled her in tight against him, and she felt like she was being imprinted by their heat signature. Nothing of what she'd read or seen matched the reality of this moment.

From deep within her arose a trembling that threatened to shake her apart, and she had to break off the kiss and bury her face against his collarbone to get control of it.

His breath was as shallow as hers. "What is it?"

"I didn't think I was capable of feeling this much for anyone," she said, then regretted revealing her impairment. The strength of her feelings terrified her. "I'll be–"

"You're not going to say 'fine,' are you?" He stroked her hair with gentle fingers, and his unhurt hand caressed the small of her back.

She sighed and tried to release her tension. "Sensory overload can cause... problems." She didn't want to think about them now. "I'm more susceptible when I'm tired."

She'd used a lot of energy in tracker mode earlier, but she suspected the strength of the tremors had more to do with the depth of her response to him. The CPS issued dire warnings on the life-threatening dangers of strong emotions, and tried to eradicate them permanently out of all trackers to improve obedience and efficiency. They'd evidently failed with her.

She reluctantly stepped back, and he let her go slowly. He brushed her cheek with the back of his hand. "You're so beautiful," he said, his eyes dark with intensity.

She knew she wasn't, but it pleased her that he thought so.

"So are you," she said softly. "You need rest. Time to heal."

"You do, too." His tone was light, but his expression was an odd mix of concern and invitation.

She shook her head. "I'm on duty. Use the bed."

She wanted more than anything to curl up next to him, preferably entwined with him for comfort, but it would inevitably lead to other, more interesting activities that she had little experience with and wasn't sure she could handle. She'd barely handled one potent kiss from him. More important, right now he needed a guard more than he needed a bed companion.

He gave her a long look and started to say something, but hesitated because of whatever he read in her expression. "All right."

He turned and stepped toward the bedroom. When he turned back, his expression was dark, intense. "Just so we're clear. I want you, Mairwen."

She forced her arms to stay at her sides instead of reaching for him. She met his gaze. "Yes," she said, both acknowledging his desire and expressing her own.

"Until tomorrow, then," he said, and went into her bedroom.

Tomorrow, she promised herself, as she ate a high-calorie protein bar that could have tasted like ash or ambrosia for all she noticed. Tomorrow, when she would spend as much time as possible with Luka Foxe and memorize every scent, every sound of him, right up until they terminated her for assaulting Malamig.

CHAPTER II

EARLY IN THE afternoon, Luka and Seshulla Zheer sat in her office at the priceless antique she called a worktable, waiting for the expensive realtime intergalactic trid connection to be made with an equally expensive finder on New Ares named Elellor Jalinok, whom La Plata had hired to research the possibility of a hybrid planet. The man had an excellent reputation for uncovering the unusual. If the idea hadn't panned out, he'd have just sent a report, so there must be something to it.

Zheer was sipping after-lunch coffee from a delicate porcelain cup that was almost translucent and reading the news in Mandarin as they waited. Luka cupped his hands around his larger coffee mug for warmth. Zheer kept her office chillier than he liked. For once, Luka felt no need to pace. As interesting as the case was, as much as he wanted justice for his friends, he was far more intrigued and unsettled by the last twenty-four hours with Mairwen.

That he'd slept at all last night while knowing she was awake in the next room was a miracle. He felt a growing emotional connection with her that fueled his desire. He'd had to consciously keep himself away from her since she'd reported for duty at noon, especially when they were alone in his office. She'd retreated to the passivity of a dispassionate security guard, but he saw the subtle signs that she was aware of him in the same way.

There was also sadness in her at odd moments, and he was afraid she was regretting admitting she had feelings for him. Whether she would—or could—ever let herself care for him was another matter. She had formidable self-discipline and a lot of secrets, but more than that, because of what had been done to her to transform her into a death tracker, he was sure she had no experience trusting anyone.

He distracted himself by rolling his shoulders and dropping his head to stretch his neck. The too-loose collar of his new off-the-rack shirt chafed. He splayed and cautiously tensed the fingers of his still slightly bruised and puffy left hand, welcoming the twinges of soreness because they could have been infinitely worse.

He caught Seshulla giving him speculative looks, but he didn't care. There was no way she could guess that the kidnapping and assault had affected him far less than kissing the woman who had rescued him.

A pleasant chime interrupted his contemplation, which he'd decided was a better word for what he'd been doing than "brooding." The trid blinked to life with the holographic image of an older, almost grandfatherly man seated behind a desk. After polite greetings were exchanged, the man pivoted straight to the point.

"There is an eighty-six percent chance that at least one living hybrid planet exists, and an almost sixty-percent chance it is being exploited by a pharma company."

Luka expected the news, but the high percentages surprised him.

"Interesting," said Zheer, "but you could have just pinged us with that data."

"Yes, but I need input from you to narrow down the best probable locations for it." He laced his fingers on the desk and looked straight at them. "Hybrid planets are a danger to us all. I want to make sure that when it is found, it will be dealt with properly."

In other words, if La Plata hoped to use his information to exploit the planet for themselves instead of reporting it to Concordance Command, Jalinok would report it for them, regardless of the non-disclosure clause in their contract.

Zheer nodded. "We're in complete agreement."

By the end of the conversation, Luka believed La Plata had gotten its money's worth from Jalinok. He'd identified six planets and assigned probabilities to each of them. They would all be detailed in his report, but two of them looked promising. Insche 255C was the best bet, with Noongar 18E a close second. Both were listed in Concordance's exploration records as failed terraforms from the First Wave, so physical information about both should be available in exploration archives. After answering a few final questions, Jalinok signed off.

Zheer leaned back in her chair and took a deep breath, then let it out slowly.

"We're headed for interesting times. We might have enough to keep Juno Vizla from having to pay Centaurus Transport's shipping losses, but not enough to keep them out of court, which is why they hired us. If Loyduk Pharma *is* hiding a hybrid planet, a few additional discreet murders are the least of their worries." She shook her head. "I still can't believe we're discussing a secret, viable hybrid planet as if it's real." She sighed again and looked at her cup. "I need more coffee. You?"

"No, thanks." He couldn't tolerate the super-caffeinated blend she favored. He'd be bouncing off the walls and hallucinating. That's why he'd brought his own full mug with him.

She crossed to her ornate service cart for a refill. The cart was modern, but styled to match the antiques in her office. As usual, no wrinkles had dared to mar her expensive resilk suit, even though she must have been sitting for hours. "Pharma companies like Loyduk have deep pockets, and La Plata can't take on a battalion of mercs."

Luka nodded. "Deep pockets can also buy a lot of convenient forgetfulness and historical record modifications. We can't just tell the government what we suspect. We'll need public proof that can't be explained away or lost in a bureaucratic warp."

"Meaning someone independent has to visit the planet and get enough biological samples to show correlation with the Loyduk Pharma vaccine," she said. "And fast. I dislike being last to the party."

"Which planet? Or both?" he asked. "If Juno Vizla is paying, we can hire exploration xenobiologists. Wouldn't even need permission, since the post-poisoning interdiction period for both planets ended something like four hundred years ago."

She frowned. "True, but hiring one or more expeditions is expensive. I don't know what I can talk Juno into. Insurance companies hire us so they can *avoid* spending money." She reflexively rotated her exquisite cup in its saucer. "In the interests of speed and confidentiality, I'm considering getting sampling kits and sending our own team."

"Risky. We'd need security. I doubt the planet is unprotected." He could tell where this was heading. He had a lot of sample collection experience, albeit at crime scenes instead of unknown planets. She'd want him as team lead. Leadership wasn't one of his life goals, but the investigation was too important to give to someone who didn't care about it.

"I'll go," he said, "if I can take Morganthur." He trusted no one else.

Zheer gave him an enigmatic smile. "I can't say I'm surprised, after yesterday." She crossed to her desk and sat. "I'm calling in a contract pilot. We need some expert answers about undeveloped systems. Go find out what kinds of kits and equipment would be our best option, and be back here at three." She paused. "No, make that ten minutes before, and bring

Morganthur."

He found Mairwen in his office where he'd left her. He couldn't stop himself from smiling at seeing her. She was in the far corner and seated, for once, instead of standing. He wondered if her knee was still bothering her. Not that she'd admit it to him if it was.

"I volunteered you for something." He closed the door behind him.

"Did you?" she asked, with an undercurrent of cautiousness.

"La Plata is sending me on a hybrid planet hunt, and I said I wanted you with me, even though I didn't ask you first."

He sat at his desk to keep himself at a professional distance, but he couldn't keep the impish grin off his face. "In my defense, it's because of your idea that we're going at all."

She gave him a small smile that acknowledged his teasing. "My idea, your hypothesis. The finder concurred, then?"

"Yes, with a high probability. Seshulla wants us in her office in a couple of hours." He tried to read her expression, but she was inscrutable. "That is, if you're going. It's your choice."

"I'll go," she said with no hesitation. The firmness in her tone suggested he'd have a hard time stopping her.

He gave her a wide smile. "Good. Want to read up on xenobiological sampling?" He laughed when she rolled her eyes and activated her percomp. He didn't know how she put up with its tiny, low-res viewing field.

Two hours later, they presented themselves to Zheer's assistant and were ushered in immediately. Nothing in Mairwen's face gave it away, but Luka thought she was feeling wary, and he wished he knew why. Zheer could be intimidating, but she treated her employees well.

As they settled into the chairs at the worktable, Zheer said, "A contract pilot named Eve Haberville will be here at three, but first we need to deal with an internal matter."

She called up a short file on a thin display and handed it to Mairwen to read.

"Your former supervisor, Isak Malamig, filed a formal complaint alleging you tried to murder him in the company parking garage yesterday afternoon. He asserts that you became uncontrollably angry when he told you your attitude needed improvement, and you tried to slit his throat."

A jumble of emotions flashed through Luka, mostly disbelief and protectiveness. He looked to Mairwen, who had gone very still and expressionless.

Zheer continued. "The security vid suggests events may not have transpired as Mr. Malamig described them."

She touched the display and the silent flat video played. Malamig approached Mairwen aggressively and spoke to her, an angry expression on his face. When she stepped aside, he lunged for her. Mairwen flung her coat at him, and they both stumbled out of frame. About fifteen seconds later, Mairwen came back in frame, carrying her coat in one hand and a gun in the other, and went into the building. A few seconds after that, Malamig staggered into view, holding a hand to the side of his neck and yelling at the door. The recording stopped.

Zheer looked at Mairwen. "What happened?"

Mairwen was absolutely still, her back ramrod straight. "Supervisor Malamig expressed unhappiness about being passed over for a promotion." Her tone was dry and flat. "I tried to leave. He tried to grab me. I evaded. We tripped. He tried to draw his weapon. I threatened him with a knife to dissuade him. I misjudged his reaction and cut the skin on his neck. I took his weapon away and gave it to the reception desk."

"Why didn't you report it?"

She shrugged one shoulder slightly. "I wasn't injured."

She had a subtle look of resignation on her face, and Luka knew she expected not to be believed. He spoke up. "If my experience with her counts for anything, in the time I've worked with her, she's always acted rationally and professionally."

Zheer took the display back.

"Mr. Malamig," she said as she calmly folded the display, "is an abusive ass." She blithely ignored Mairwen's startled look and Luka's raised eyebrow. "He came with the security division La Plata acquired, and he's becoming more trouble than he's worth. I actually wish you would file a counter complaint for assault so I could talk the Security Division director into terminating his contract, but I'm guessing you won't. Next time, if there is one, please find a way to handle him without leaving a mark."

She stood and put the display on her desk, then took her ever-present cup to the service cart. "Coffee or tea, anyone?"

"No, thank you," said Luka. Mairwen looked bewildered, though maybe only to his eyes. He suspected she'd been expecting to be fired on the spot, not treated like a trusted colleague. He wanted to give her some sign of reassurance, but couldn't while Zheer was watching.

They were saved from further conversation by the arrival of Eve

Haberville, the freelance pilot Luka knew La Plata had used occasionally in the past. La Plata only had one interstellar pilot left on staff, since Adina Schmidt had been murdered in the warehouse. He'd heard Haberville had a military and exploration background, and came highly recommended, including by the late Adina.

Haberville looked to be in her early thirties with beautiful features, expensively shaded black hair woven with metallic gold and blue, and a lush, hourglass figure right out of classical paintings. Her corporate suit was expertly tailored to show it off. Luka was appreciative of her beauty but curiously unaroused by the woman herself.

Zheer, Haberville, and he discussed the pros and cons of using the company's slower corporate ship versus a faster but pricier rental with wilderness-landing capability. They also discussed logistics, such as how much firepower to carry, and how big the team should be. Zheer ultimately decided they'd tackle the most likely candidate for a hybrid planet on their own, in the interest of keeping it off net. If it turned out to be nothing, and she could get the client to pay, she would contract an independent exploration spacer for the second candidate.

Mairwen listened to everything but said nothing. Luka noticed Haberville giving her a few speculative looks, clearly wondering why Mairwen was at the meeting, but she didn't ask, and he didn't offer. He'd let Zheer handle it if Haberville brought it up.

Zheer gave Luka and Haberville top priority assignments to get cost estimates for their areas of expertise so she could put together a proposal for the client, then sent them on their way. After a brief discussion with Haberville on who would handle what, Luka stopped by the Tech Division to get a thincomp. He handed it to Mairwen. "You need more than that prehistoric percomp from Security Division if you're going to get anything done."

When they returned to his office, he said, "You have more patience than I do for reading odd things. See what you can find on hybrid planets, especially related to safety."

She nodded and sat as he opened the large display on his desk to start on the estimates. Not his favorite thing to do, but better than Zheer's job of having to present the budget to the client and convince them to pay. He worked diligently on getting the numbers quickly because Zheer, forecaster that she was, thought there was a need to hurry. So did he. He had the feeling that Onndrae wouldn't be the last target if they didn't take the initiative.

Forty minutes later, he shot the estimate into Zheer's dataspace and breathed a sigh of relief. He saw Mairwen was still making notes, but she looked up to meet his gaze.

"Where is your safehouse tonight?" she asked.

"I have no idea." He'd completely forgotten Zheer had promised to arrange something for him, since his townhouse wasn't safe for now. He pinged Zheer's assistant, only to discover no one had told her to look.

"I'll do my best, but at this point, I'd be lucky to find you a prepaid sleep pod at the spaceport. Can you stay wherever you did last night?"

He looked to Mairwen. She nodded.

He told the assistant he could, then asked her to find him something for tomorrow night and disconnected.

Another thought struck him and he turned to Mairwen. "Did they at least remember to retrieve your company vehicle?"

"Yes," she said. "Do you want to go somewhere?"

Mairwen's apartment had several virtues, chief among them Mairwen herself, but her cupboards were practically bare. "Have you ever had East Indian food?"

"No."

"Good, it will be a new experience, what with your sheltered life and all." When she returned his grin with a small smile of her own, he wanted to kiss her.

"I'm hungry. Bring that comp with you. We can work remotely."

* * * * *

Mairwen finished the last swallow of water and put her glass in the drawer with the rest of the dishes. The ancient, built-in sanitizer would cycle after it detected no activity for a while. It was the first time in months she'd had enough dirty dishes to use it. She watched Luka read the display she'd handed him with a summary of the mostly speculative information she had found on hybrid planets. It had taken her a while to think of him by his first name because it felt too distractingly personal, but now it felt… right.

He was sitting at the breakfast bar again, with one elbow on the counter. His short-sleeved, red knit shirt hugged his chest nicely, as did the dark flexsilk pants that covered the rest of him. She was amused that even his casual clothing exhibited a sense of style. The masculine shape and power of his well-defined bare arms and feet stirred her hormones, and she wondered if that was normal or a tracker aberration.

The autumn day had turned bitter cold with the promise of a hard winter, and she'd turned the heat up to compensate because she knew Luka would like it. She wished she'd thought to do it the previous night. She wondered idly if he'd grown up in a warm climate zone and missed it. He'd look good in a native sarong. Or out of one.

She thought about changing into more comfortable clothes, but concluded she was still on duty, and there would be no running on public trails that evening. She made a mental note to offer him the use of the exercise machine. It was the only form of entertainment she had, other than the cork wall she used for daily knife practice. Her apartment had no other amenities, not even a built-in wallcomp or an outside window. It was boring, but secure.

He looked up to meet her gaze and smiled, like he was happy she was watching him. It made her breath catch.

"I want to cook a real meal for you," he said.

"Why?" The direction of his thoughts baffled her.

"Because I'd like to do something nice for you." Her confusion must have shown, because his smile widened. "I'm trying to impress you so you'll want to spend more time with me."

Did he mean he wanted her as his primary security assistant, or did he want to meet with her when neither of them was working? She shook her head and looked away, then back to him, unable to hide her bewilderment.

"I have no..."

Would cooking for her signify he had feelings for her beyond the physical and wanted to change their relationship? And if so, to what? She tried again.

"Will we..." She trailed off. She didn't even know what to ask.

She was out of her depth and didn't know how to explain how profoundly inexperienced she was in social interactions and emotions.

Finally, she said, "I'm not normal." Her chest felt hollow.

He snorted. "No such thing." He closed the distance between them in less than a heartbeat and drew her into his arms. "I haven't had many friends, and fewer lovers," he said. "My talent makes it difficult."

He kissed her lips as lightly and easily as if he'd done it hundreds of times. "I've been aching to do this all day." He kissed her lightly again, and she felt heat rise in her.

She luxuriated in his scent and the feel of his lean body against her softer counterparts. "I think I have, too," she said, realizing the icy feeling in her chest always vanished when he touched her, like an addiction being eased.

He put his hand on the side of her face and tilted her chin up to meet his kiss. She opened to him immediately, reveling in the taste of him, the silky feel of his tongue against hers. His soft moan ignited a fire that made her instinctively arch into him. She repressed a tremor, but he felt it and broke off the kiss to look at her.

"Tell me more about sensory overload," he said, his voice ragged.

She took a deep, calming breath. "The first few years after we undergo the procedure, we can get overwhelmed by sensations before the brain finishes altering to handle them all. It's easy to become… lost in sounds or scents or tastes. The CPS trains with pain and discipline to prevent it." Her voice sounded husky to her ears.

"What about the shaking?" She felt his hand stroke her back in a gentle caress.

"A warning that the input center is about to be overwhelmed. In some, it causes seizures or coma."

He stilled. "What about in you?"

She tightened her grip on him. "I don't know." Not even in the first months after the alteration procedure had she ever felt like she did with Luka. It was frightening, but the stubborn part of her wanted to meet the challenge head on. "You are the first thing—the only thing—that's ever made me lose control."

"Flattering, but not reassuring," he said, gently stroking her cheek with his thumb. "It would kill me if I hurt you."

"If we go slow, I can stop if I need to," she said, hoping it was true.

He trailed nibbling kisses to her ear and along her neck. "I can do slow."

Air suddenly seemed in short supply. "So I see," she whispered, not trusting her voice. Her powerful sense of duty warred with her strong desire. Both had grown exponentially, but her desire was winning. *Bad, bad idea,* hissed her cautious brain, but was overridden by another, less-familiar part of her mind saying this was *good, perfect…*

Somehow her hands had burrowed under his shirt, splayed on the warm expanse of his skin. She loved the way his back expanded when he drew breath. His arm felt deliciously firm angled across her back.

* * * * *

Luka moaned as the sensations from her hands and mouth made his hair stand on end with desire. He was on the edge of abandoning "slow," and desperately tried to find something distracting to think about, like how many knives she had on her person and how sharp they were.

"Why didn't you tell me about what happened with Malamig?"

She gave him a hazy look that took a moment to clear. "Wasn't your problem."

"You don't have to do everything alone, you know." He couldn't help it, but he felt fiercely protective of her.

He slid his hand around to the silky smooth nape of her neck. Her skin was velvety soft and warm and... lumpy.

"What's this between your shoulder blades?"

"Knife."

"Of course it is," he said, amused. He kissed her again and nibbled at her bottom lip, then groaned in protest when she slowly stepped back and smoothed his shirt down where her wandering hands had rumpled it. He was sorry he'd reminded her about the real world, where people were trying to kill him.

"I'm your personal security detail." She clasped his left hand in hers and lightly stroked the fading bruises. "I can't do my job if I'm distracted."

"I know." He sighed and smiled. "I'm glad you find me distracting. I'd hate to be alone in that." He caressed her upper arm, unwilling to stop touching her yet. "I suppose sleeping together in that insanely large bed of yours tonight is out of the question?"

"It's not safe," she said, and he understood she was talking about much more than security duty. There wouldn't be much sleeping if they shared a bed, even if they had good intentions. They were too combustible. Chaos, but he wanted her. Wanted to find out how hot they could burn.

"No, not for us," he agreed, not hiding his regret and reluctance to move away even as he did so. He returned to the barstool and picked up the display to keep his hands busy.

She stepped into the kitchen, and as she did, visibly reasserted her redoubtable control. It was hot and sexy as hell. He'd take strong, sleek Mairwen any day over all the Habervilles of the galaxy.

He made himself look at the information on the display, though he wasn't able to actually comprehend it for several more minutes until his body cooled and blood circulation returned to his brain.

The protocols for xenobiological sampling, while useful for their intended mission, were mind-numbingly boring, so he was glad when she interrupted.

"Is Zheer your friend?"

"Not really. More of a respected colleague. And my boss, of course." He gave her a questioning look.

"Why didn't she terminate my contract?"

He considered it for a moment. "My guess is, you told the truth and took responsibility for your actions. Malamig did neither."

Privately, he wondered if Zheer's forecaster talent told her that Mairwen's continued employment would benefit the case or the company. It was also possible Zheer suspected he and Mairwen had something beyond a professional relationship, though he couldn't have defined what that something was. He only knew he'd fight for her to stay.

Leo would have laughed at him and told him all women were mysterious. Luka missed him. They'd probably never catch the specific crew assholes who had killed Leo and Adina, but at least they could find the person who'd given the orders.

Mairwen had moved to near the door, standing in what he thought of as her sentinel stance.

"Do you have any friends, Mairwen?"

"No," she said, then seemed to think better of it. "Perhaps. Beva Rienville said we're friends. I don't know how to tell. She said she wanted to hire me for her new division after my assignment with you is done."

"What did you say?" he asked, feeling a stab of possessiveness. He didn't care if Beva wanted to be best friends for eternity with Mairwen, but he'd be damned if he'd give her up as his assistant, or anything else, so easily.

"Nothing. She was running late."

He laughed, relieved. "She's always running late for something."

He wanted to ask Mairwen if she wanted to stay with him, be with him, be his lover, but he didn't have the courage to hear the answers just then.

A few hours later, as he was again in her bed alone and dreaming she was with him, Mairwen nudged him awake to take a live ping from Zheer. He wondered groggily if either woman ever slept. La Plata was sending a vehicle in four hours to take them to the spaceport, where they'd board the *Berjalan*, an interstellar ship bound for Insche 255C, the best-guess candidate for a hybrid planet.

CHAPTER 12

MAIRWEN LOOKED AROUND her small but private stateroom for a place to store the low-res beamer and holster she'd been issued, but no luck. She placed them in her duffel bag with the upscale flexin armor she'd been issued and her spare knives and sheaths. While on the ship, she saw no reason to carry the beamer, since she already wore her usual knives. Besides, incautious use of a beamer was a quick way to breach the hull. She'd stowed her overcoat and expedition gear in the shallow closet, above where she'd put her boots and running shoes.

At least she could wear comfortable clothing for the next few days. Good thing, because she had little else. She slipped on pants that hung loose from her hips and a sleeveless tank top. Her breasts were too small to make it worth the trouble to wear a bra. The stateroom's unexpectedly plush carpeting felt good on her bare feet as she wiggled her toes.

Luka's stateroom was next to and the mirror image of hers, with a shared fresher between them. Across the short hall were similar staterooms for DeBayaud and Adams, the two security specialists Zheer had assigned. Both men appeared competent and pleasant. They moved like they had military training, and were probably ex-gunnin. DeBayaud was tall and athletic, and Adams was compact and well muscled, and they both appeared to be in their late twenties or early thirties. She gathered they were both La Plata employees, not subcontractors, and that they'd worked together before.

On the other side of the mid-sized ship were two larger staterooms plus two tiny cabins. Haberville and the La Plata pilot, Ta'foulou, had taken the staterooms, which were probably meant for a pilot and a captain. Having two pilots on their team would allow them to travel nonstop, and provided backup in case of trouble.

Ta'foulou was in his fifties and had no hair, and his hands, neck, and bald head had surface tattoos on practically every square centimeter except his face, almost like a permanent hooded jacket. He preferred speaking in Arabic and didn't seem comfortable talking to people. Mairwen sympathized.

The common areas included a kitchen, a well-equipped exercise room, an open, convertible dining and lounging area with various seating and entertainment options, and a desk and bookshelf area along one bulkhead meant to serve as a work area. All told, it was about six hundred square meters of flat-level living space, plus the engine and navigation pods, which doubled as escape pods. Comfortable enough for six people for a few days, but she planned to keep her extraordinary senses dampened to subnormal levels while in such close quarters with others. Even so, she could still hear the phantom sonics that meant they were in transit.

She was more concerned about Luka at the moment. Zheer had put the pressure on for a quick liftoff window that suited her sense of urgency. Between arranging for delivery of more clothes for himself, weapons and armor, camping gear, and a portable medical kit, he'd only gotten an hour's nap. From the moment he'd seen the *Berjalan*, his tension had increased. She caught hints of his old, bad memories look flitting across his face when he thought no one was watching. He'd declined Haberville's safety tour, saying he already knew this ship model well.

Something finally clicked in Mairwen's mind as she slipped on a long cardigan to cover her knives and walked through the fresher to the open door of Luka's stateroom.

He was seated on the low, padded platform couch that doubled as a bed, wearing only a loose pair of knit pants. Earlier, he'd mumbled something about sleeping, but he hadn't closed the door or darkened the room, and she doubted he could rest in his current state.

"I'm not good company," he said, closing his eyes as if his head throbbed. "And little pilots sometimes have big ears."

It was unfortunately true that some pilots abused their access to the emergency occupant-monitoring system and used it as their personal entertainment channel. Mairwen thought they were lucky the ship didn't have the upgraded system that included visuals.

She sealed the entry door and stepped closer so they could speak quietly. "I know why. Is it exactly the same make and model of ship?"

"Different stateroom configuration, but close enough." He ran his fingers through his hair. "My talent feels hot right now, like it did when I reconstructed the 'playroom' those sick fucks made." His low voice dropped to a whisper, and he shivered as if his talent was consuming his body heat. "I can see everything. Hear everything. Like it was yesterday."

She didn't know what to say. She felt hopelessly out of her depth, but she couldn't leave him like this. Maybe whatever it was about her that cooled his talent could help him now. She pulled up the room's only chair to face him, close enough to thread her knees between his. She took his hands in hers.

"Look at me."

He shook his head. "No, you don't know what you're asking." He looked down and refused to meet her gaze.

"Yes, I do." She leaned closer so she could pitch her voice just to him. "It's what you did at the spaceport with the woman who called herself Green and with Dr. Onndrae. It's how you found the collector when he hid among the joyhouse kitchen staff." The thought of his focused, talent-enhanced intuition directed at her made her nervous, but he already knew a measure of her secrets. He was afraid of his talent, fighting it, and that couldn't be good for him. Her unease was mostly old habit, not present danger.

"Luka, look at me."

She thought he'd refuse again, but after a moment, he looked up and into her eyes, and his pupils slowly dilated. She stilled her sensory inputs until there was nothing in her universe but the sound of his breathing, the exotic scent of him, the warmth of his hands in hers. She admired the lines of his sensual mouth, the stunning colors in his eyes, the well-defined, sculpted shape of his broad chest and taut abdomen, the two old scars on his ribs, the thin line of dark body hair that trailed down from his navel, the heady maleness of him. It was almost like relaxing into full-tracker mode meditation.

"Mairwen," he said, after what could have been short seconds or long minutes. He made her lose track of time. His voice was thick with emotion, and his expression had gone from haunted to something she couldn't name, but it made her heart skip a beat.

"You are..." He trailed off, as if searching for the right words. She couldn't describe what she was feeling, either, just that it was powerful and melted inside her like hot wax.

She gave into a rising, aching need and rose from her chair to kneel on the platform, facing him and straddling his thighs. His hands tightened on her waist as she sank into his lap. She grasped his wonderfully naked shoulders and kissed him fiercely. He responded almost immediately, then took over the kiss with sensual strength.

She loved the feel of his skin under her hands and wanted more. They broke for air, gasping, and he slid his hands up to gently push the sweater back and slide it off her arms onto the floor, then glided back up her arms to her shoulders, where his hands hesitated.

"What are these?" His passion-hazed expression darkened as he circled the furrowed, irregular scars with his thumbs. "Souvenirs from vocational school?"

She quirked a smile. "No. When I... graduated, I had to leave their tracers behind."

He kissed the scar on each shoulder, then returned hungrily to her mouth, and she couldn't suppress a deep tremor. He dragged his lips away from hers to drop his forehead onto her shoulder and stroked her sides, generating heat and goose bumps at the same time. "Someday soon, let's do this when neither of us is exhausted or hurting."

"Or about to be interrupted," she whispered, hearing the approach of booted feet on the carpet outside Luka's door. She slid back and off his marvelously strong thighs and scooped up her sweater, resigned to it being a pitiful substitute for the heat of his chest on hers. She pulled the sweater on as the entrance chime sounded.

She moved the chair back, then unsealed the door to reveal DeBayaud, who glanced at her with mild curiosity, then apologized for interrupting. He asked Luka what schedule he wanted to set for the three subjective ship days it would take to get to their first destination, a flux and supplies stop called Horvax Station.

"Ask the pilots to sync us to the local day length on Insche 255C, if the exploration records have that data. One of us besides the pilot should be awake at all times, but that can't be me right now. I'm flatlined." He looked at the display clock on the wall. "Let's meet at fifteen thirty ship time to set shifts and talk about plans."

DeBayaud nodded and headed toward the navigation pod. Someone, probably Adams, was puttering about in the kitchen area. She turned back to Luka. He no longer looked distressed, just tired.

"You need rest, Luka."

She resolutely ignored her body's crying need for his and turned to go. She needed a few hours of sleep herself.

"Mairwen," he said, and she stopped and looked back. "Could you help me find... control?"

She hesitated, then said, "We can try."

It was the glimmer of hope in his eyes that made her agree. Even though she had no clue where to start, and her own controls eroded the moment she was anywhere near him.

At the meeting six hours later, Luka summarized the case thus far, saying that they suspected Balkovsky and Schmidt had been killed to cover up the fact that the source of the bad vaccine was a hybrid planet, and that their trip was to see if they could prove it. The team's pre-flight briefing hadn't included the part about the deaths, and Adams, who had worked with Balkovsky, was visibly angered by the circumstances. Mairwen thought the others were calmer, or at least hid it better.

Luka opened the portable display. "We'll be stopping at Horvax Station for a resupply and to pick up the xenobiological sampling kit that hadn't been ready when we left Rekoria."

"Will we load flux, too?" asked Ta'foulou. It took Luka a moment to understand the question through Ta'foulou's thick Arabic accent.

"Yes," said Luka. "We may need the extra fuel. No telling what we'll need when we hit the Insche 255 system."

He gave them the briefing Mairwen had prepared on the few facts and many conjectures about failed terraforms and hybrid planets, and emphasized the extra safety precautions they'd need to take. He asked Haberville to report what she'd found in the navcomp datacube.

"The exploration data is sparse. Gold G-type star, of course. It was a First Wave terraform candidate, so 255C has a similar day length and orbit period to old Earth. Records say it was poisoned five hundred and three years ago. Six continents, a few tectonic plates. One small moon. Nothing else worth mentioning. The solar system has an asteroid belt in fourth position. The in-system transit point is between that and 255E, a gas giant."

Haberville and Ta'foulou set up alternating six-hour shifts to pilot the ship, and DeBayaud and Adams set up their schedules to correlate. Luka had already introduced Mairwen as his assistant, which exempted her from a security shift.

Adams, it turned out, was an excellent cook who cheerfully volunteered to make all their meals, which she and the others promptly agreed to. She didn't used to care about food until she met Luka. Her grumbling, cautious brain insisted that he continued to be a bad influence.

After the meeting, Luka went back to his room, and DeBayaud, an avid redball fan, hooked into a trid of one of the dozen prerecorded games he'd brought with him. He leaned his whole body into each play he watched, but kept any vocalizations to himself. Mairwen thought it made him look like a demented mime.

She went to see Haberville in the navigation pod for her turn for the personalized safety briefing. While everyone else on the ship was dressed in old, comfortable clothes, Haberville looked like she was going to a party, though to be fair, perhaps wearing tight, shiny outfits counted as comfortable to her.

Most safety briefings were prerecorded holos, so Mairwen was impressed that Haberville took their security so seriously. However, she turned out to have a disconcerting habit of crowding personal space and touching often, most of which Mairwen managed to subtly evade. When she would have made her escape, Haberville asked her to stay and chat a minute.

"How long have you been with Foxe?"

She was still standing and was wirejacked into the navcomp from her unobtrusive skulljack, so she was multi-tasking the realspace conversation with whatever the nav and engine comps were telling her.

"Two weeks," said Mairwen. It seemed a lot longer, like she'd known him for years, but they'd been an eventful set of days.

"Throbbing as a pulsar, if you like your partners lean and wiry." Haberville said with a wink and a lascivious smirk. "From what I've seen, half the women and some of the men at La Plata would hot-connect with him if he flashed the 'go' light." She made some adjustments to a holo readout of the light drive's flux. "Have you had him yet? Is he as good as he looks?"

Mairwen affected selective deafness to Haberville's personal questions, the same way she'd done with Malamig's similarly inappropriate inquiries over the years. It was oddly unpleasant to think of others wanting Luka as a lover. Or more accurately, to think of Luka wanting them. Logically, it shouldn't matter if he engaged in sex with multiple other partners, but logic wasn't very comforting.

Haberville apparently took Mairwen's expressionless silence to mean she was offended.

"Don't mind me, I'm just naturally nosy. Gets me in all sorts of trouble." There was little contrition in her tone. "So, how'd a good-looking woman like you end up here?" she asked, and managed to briefly touch Mairwen's upper arm. Mairwen twisted out of range quickly. The only person she wanted touching her was Luka.

Mairwen drew breath to answer, but Haberville held up a hand and closed her eyes a moment, signaling she was communing with the navcomp.

Mairwen was glad of the interruption, finding the thread hard to follow and not sure what Haberville was asking. She already knew about the investigation, and probably wasn't looking for a recitation of Mairwen's history. The personal flattery was meaningless, so she ignored it.

When Haberville opened her eyes again, Mairwen said, "I'm usually a night-shift guard. I'm temporarily assigned as Foxe's assistant for this investigation."

"Lucky you. You're better with Foxe than Velasco is." The way she said Velasco's name suggested she didn't like him. Mairwen wondered when Haberville had met him. Knowing Velasco, he'd drooled when memorizing Haberville's generous breasts.

"I have no basis for comparison," said Mairwen, relieved she'd answered the earlier question without engendering further probing.

Haberville laughed. "You definitely belong in the Investigation Division. You fit right in."

Haberville was distracted by the navcomp again, and Mairwen took the opportunity to escape. She was perplexed by the whole conversation. Haberville the pilot was sharp and competent, but Haberville the person was uncomfortable to deal with. Mairwen felt a momentary pang for her old days on the night shift, where the only interaction required was with comps and equally anti-social co-workers.

She drifted through the common area, where Luka was discussing cooking techniques with Adams. They were of similar height and coloring and, from a distance, might have been mistaken for cousins, but Adams' dark hair was short and well behaved compared to Luka's riotous spikes, and Adams had the noticeably more muscular build of a dedicated weightlifter. She decided she liked Luka's long-distance runner's build better.

She went to her room and changed into running shoes and a long-sleeved, thin pink T-shirt and navy knit pants that covered her knives, then went through to the exercise room. Luka smiled briefly at her as she passed by, and she nodded. He looked better after having slept, and smiled a lot during his light conversation with Adams, but there was still a brittleness to the edges of him. Had they been alone, she might have touched him in reassurance, though whether it would be for Luka or herself, she wasn't sure.

She engaged the treadmill unit, then disabled its monitoring functions. She'd rather not leave a record of anything that might be different from normal human behavior. The unit was high quality, but still didn't feel the same as running on stable ground, regardless of the manufacturer's claims.

She remembered something Luka had said about preferring to run on a planet surface, and she had to agree. Planets smelled of a million living things, while exercise rooms smelled mostly of stale sweat and machinery, even with her senses dulled to practically dead.

Luka's request to teach him control had her dredging up memories of her first months after surviving the final alteration procedure. She tried to analyze them objectively.

CPS trainers introduced the candidate trackers to pain and brutality on day one and never let up. The first few weeks, when the candidates didn't know how to ignore sensations, all it had taken was loud sounds, powerful smells, or a simple bruising pinch. The better the candidates got at handling the painful input, the more creatively savage the trainers got, all to make sure the CPS owned them, mind and body. Some trainers loved their jobs. Those that loved their jobs too much sometimes suffered fatal accidents once their trainees acquired useful skills.

Pain wouldn't work for Luka, even if she could bring herself to suggest it. Physical pain would just feed the emotional trauma his talent and imagination were already creating. Pleasure required time and relaxation, usually in short supply in situations when his reconstruction talent was needed. All she had to go on was that he regained some control over the talent and the talent-reinforced memories when she touched him, or at least when she was close. She couldn't very well be at every violent scene he saw. He needed a way to stop the cascade before it started, whether or not she was there, but she couldn't think how. She wished she was as clever as Luka.

She heard footsteps approaching the exercise room and identified them as Luka's. She looked at the clock and realized she'd been running for over an hour. Thinking he'd probably like some time on the ship's only treadmill, she slowed to a stop just as he entered the room. He was wearing running clothes and a towel draped around his neck, so she'd guessed correctly. And universe help her, he was wearing shorts that displayed his perfect hips, thighs, and calves.

She pulled at the front of her tank top where it was plastered to her chest from sweat. As always, his smile fluttered something in her heart. The first hint of his woody scent reached her and curled up into her thoughts like a caress. Images and ideas blossomed in her mind as he strode toward her. She dismissed the ones that started with licking him and stepped closer so she could speak quietly.

"You use pacing and running to help you think. Perhaps it could help you with... what we talked about earlier." Despite her flattened senses, the welcome full scent of him gave her a floaty feeling. She could almost feel the hormones flooding her system when her body was near his. It was hard to make herself remember that she needed to keep her mind on his security.

"I'm game." His eyes were looking down at their almost-touching chests, and his breath was shorter. "Tell me what to do."

Mindful of audio that might feed to the pilot's console, she kept her voice low and her phrasing oblique. "The... possibilities seem to overwhelm you with everything at once, like overload flux in a light drive. Start running, slow, and draw out a single piece of one of your memories at a time. Maybe isolate only the sounds, or only the strongest image. When you feel the overload coming, focus on the feeling of running—the flexing of your feet, the pumping of your lungs, the impact on your hips, the burn in your legs." She briefly touched his chest, his hip, and his thigh as she spoke. "Once you're back in your body, try the same isolation again."

He looked dubious but nodded. He handed her his towel, stepped onto the treadmill, and adjusted the settings for his stride. He started running, and she had to force herself to look away to keep from staring at how stunningly graceful he was. She hung his towel on the nearby rack, then crossed to the weight bench closer to the door, needing the distraction.

"Please stay," he said, not looking at her.

"Yes," she said. Even if she'd been planning to leave, the subtle desperation in his tone would have kept her there.

She set the weight machine for light repetitions, snapped her arms in, and began smooth, controlled anterior lifts. She was relieved that the shoulder she'd dislocated was performing as it should, with only minor residual pain. The healer had wanted to do more, but Mairwen couldn't risk discovery of her alteration abnormalities. The CPS drummed into all trackers the absolute imperative to only use designated CPS minder healers, meaning there were noticeable differences to be found.

She wished she could see Luka's face, to know if he was in trouble, but her selfish desire to keep him from harm wouldn't help him develop the internal controls he needed. She switched to diagonal dorsal pushes and poured her unnamable emotions into the physical effort, letting them energize in and flow out with each repetition.

The first time Luka stumbled, she froze, only relaxing when he picked up the rhythm again. The second time, she was up and in front of him in a flash. He focused on her. He didn't smile, and he looked uneasy, but he didn't look like he was in over his head yet. She caught his eye. "Just run."

He nodded and she relaxed. She was tempted to simply stand guard and wait for him, but she suspected he'd feel guilty about it and cut his run short if she did.

"I'll be in my room," she told him. With one last glimpse of his glorious backside and thighs, she went straight to the fresher.

After her shower, she finger-combed and smoothed her hair back away from her face and looked at herself in the full-length mirror. She was muscular, lean, and not curvy, though she'd become more rounded in the last four years, since she hadn't been using tracker mode and constantly taxing her body's resources. Active trackers often looked like famine victims. Her skin and coloring were night-shift pale. She doubted the rest of her scars, from where she'd removed the other tracers with her own knife, plus more recent scrapes and bruises, added to her appeal. Luka was the first person who'd ever caused her to worry about it. She wondered if he preferred his lovers to look less battered.

She found Luka attractive because of all of who he was, not just his seductively masculine form and unique scent and taste. She could only hope he was similarly inclined.

* * * * *

Luka finished his run, which was shorter than usual because he disliked treadmills and, if he was honest, because he wanted to be with Mairwen. After stopping by the kitchen, he showered and put on a T-shirt and sweatpants. He went around through the hallway to Mairwen's door, which she'd left partly open. He knocked very lightly for the sake of politeness, knowing she already heard him coming. It made him smile as he poked his head in.

"Adams says dinner will be served in an hour," he said. "Got a few minutes?"

"Yes," she said, waving him in. She was sitting on the far corner of the cushioned platform, currently configured as a couch, while she fiddled with the small in-room clothes sanitizer. He sealed the door behind him and sat.

She was wearing form-fitting dark knit pants and a thin, sleeveless, white tank that barely counted as covering. Her skin was even paler than the light tan wrist sheaths she wore, and he wondered what it would look like when flushed with the heat of desire. He clasped his fingers together in his lap and focused on them instead of her, or there wouldn't be any talking.

"I think it worked, somewhat," he said, circumspectly referring to his experience in the exercise room. "But I started easy, and I still needed y... an anchor." He had tried an older memory, less ferocious than most, and nothing similar to recent events. Even so, he'd nearly face-planted the first time the memory started saturating his thoughts, and the second time, he'd needed to force his talent to focus on Mairwen to cool it off.

"It'll take practice." She followed his lead in speaking quietly.

He knew he had to learn not to depend on her, because if he didn't, he was afraid she'd pull away from him for his own good, and that was the last thing he wanted.

"I can't run at a..." He stopped, frustrated at the lack of privacy. Another reason he didn't like traveling on ships with strangers. Fortunately, she got the drift.

"Memories of a physical experience can help with... overloads." She started the sanitizer, and a quiet humming filled the room. She drew one foot up to the couch and rested her elbow on her raised knee. "At least they do for me."

The neckline of her tank gaped open, exposing the top swell and tip of one high, firm breast. Coherent thought was leaching out of him as he felt arousal start to rise. He looked away and down, and found his hand gripping the sweater next to him. His desire for her was surging high, and he thought she wanted him, too, but anything other than slow and easy could hurt her. Besides, he wanted their first time to be more than a frenzied coupling in a rented ship's stateroom.

He made himself let go of her sweater and stand up. "I'd like to try again after dinner, if we can."

"Yes." She looked up at him, and he saw subtle hunger in her expression. Her ice-blue eyes were hypnotic.

"Ah, hell," he said under his breath, and pulled her up tight against his chest for a heated, open-mouth kiss.

He wrenched himself away and left quickly before he lost control altogether.

To Luka's delight, Adams's culinary skills lived up to his claims. He served excellent fish with a light sauce and several side dishes. Ta'foulou took his plate to the nav pod, relieving the more sociable Haberville so she could join them for the meal. She chatted easily and wittily, making the meal almost feel like a party. Adams and DeBayaud enjoyed her open flirting, DeBayaud especially.

Luka, disliking her habit of constant touching, strategically placed himself well away from her when they sat at the table, with Mairwen as a buffer. It was cowardly of him, but he rationalized that, as his personal security detail, she should be protecting him from all dangers, including grabby women.

He almost felt sorry for Haberville when she tried to engage Mairwen in several personal topics, but found it heavy going with Mairwen's mostly monosyllabic responses. Mairwen was also skilled at seemingly accidentally avoiding being touched. Haberville became increasingly ruffled by Mairwen's bland indifference. It was petty of him, but he thought it served Haberville right.

Luka noticed that Mairwen tried tastes of everything first, then ate everything except the spicy parsnips. When she'd told him she'd led a sheltered life, she wasn't exaggerating, at least food-wise. He made a mental note to discuss some options with Adams to give her more opportunities to try new things.

He couldn't begin to imagine her life as a death tracker, or why someone so amazingly competent and skilled would keep herself so locked down, even after escaping the clutches of the brutal program. It satisfied his masculine pride that he'd been the one to tempt her out of the shadows, and he wanted to keep giving her reasons to stay in the daylight. To stay with him.

He wanted to be alone with her, to ask her what she was thinking. The nature of the talent he'd focused on her in his stateroom might be a variant of telepathy, but he'd never had conscious insight into anyone's thoughts, just their overall emotional outlook and essence, and it always felt uncomfortably like prying. Except with Mairwen, when it had felt stimulating and soothing at the same time. His talent had never before been soothing.

After helping Adams clean up after dinner, Luka went to the exercise room to try the control technique again. Mairwen came in a few moments later and sat, reading a portable display. Instead of running, he set the treadmill to a brisk walking pace, but it didn't go well. Maybe he was trying too much too fast. Or maybe he was spending half his time wanting to pluck the display reader out of Mairwen's hands and take her right there on the weight bench.

It was just as well that he was interrupted when Adams came in to use the free weights, or Luka might have completely exhausted himself. Mairwen left the room, and he found himself wanting to follow her like a puppy, which would be pathetic.

He lasted ten minutes more, doing cool-down stretches to relieve the tightness and chatting briefly with Adams, then went to his stateroom. Mairwen was already in hers. It was bittersweet comfort knowing she was so close, even if he couldn't have her in his arms or bed.

He was cold, even though he jacked up his stateroom's temperature several degrees. He despaired of ever getting control of his talent. And if he couldn't, what good was he to anyone?

CHAPTER 13

THE NEXT SHIP day at breakfast, DeBayaud and Adams were in rambunctious good humor. Luka moved to the other end of the table out of self-preservation.

Haberville arrived just in time to see DeBayaud narrowly evade a snap of a dishtowel from Adams. She inserted herself between them, hands on each of their chests, and smiled widely at both of them. "Now, boys, let's use our inside manners." The men laughed.

DeBayaud held a chair for Haberville to sit close to him, then handed her a napkin and poured a cup of coffee for her.

Luka, seated near Mairwen, wondered if she'd like that sort of solicitous behavior. He eyed her briefly, and decided against it. He'd probably have to explain it to her.

Toward the end of the meal, Haberville asked, "Would anyone mind if I used the floor of the common area for thirty minutes to exercise to a cardio dance holo?"

"Okay with me," said Adams.

"We'll help move the couch pieces out of the way," said DeBayaud, pointing to himself and Adams.

"Foxe?" she asked.

He shrugged. "Sure." He was amused to note she didn't ask Mairwen.

Haberville left to change clothes, leaving her dirty dishes on the table as usual. By tacit agreement, Luka and Mairwen cleaned up after the meal while Adams and DeBayaud cleared a space in front of the trid entertainment unit.

Mairwen left for the exercise room. While Luka was still wiping down the counters, Haberville returned, wearing scraps of fabric that strategically covered her considerable assets. Adams smiled appreciatively, and DeBayaud watched her every move with predatory interest.

Haberville turned out to be fit and flexible, at least from what Luka could tell, and she clearly enjoyed the attention she was getting. While the others were distracted, he took the opportunity to grab his running shoes and slip into the exercise room.

Mairwen was setting up the force isolation machine for more arm work. She was wearing a loose, long-sleeved T-shirt, but it didn't stop him from remembering the previous evening when her sweat had made the thin tank she wore effectively transparent. It had made him heat up and pant well before he stepped foot on the treadmill. Haberville's near nakedness and blatant sexuality left him unmoved, but tantalizing glimpses of Mairwen's body woke up everything in his.

"Trying again?" she asked.

"Yes, since the others are busy." He slipped behind her and slid his arms around her waist to pull her against him. He dropped his head to inhale the clean smell of her.

"Unlike Haberville," he whispered, "the only admiring audience I want is you."

She turned in his arms and kissed his neck under his ear, sending electricity along his nerves. "Then don't let them see you in shorts," she murmured.

So she'd noticed. "Glad you like them."

He kissed her because he could, then stepped away because he had to, or he'd be dragging her back to his stateroom no matter who saw them.

Running had always helped clear his head, even when he was young. He woke his legs up with a few slow lunges, then started on the treadmill at an easy pace, enjoying the impact of his feet and the bellows of his lungs.

Once he settled into a steady rhythm, he warily called up the reconstructed scene of an older woman who had been savagely beaten, stabbed with a screwdriver, and left to die. She'd left a trail of blood as she crawled from the back office to the front, where the lobby security guard found her. The splatters and casts, plus the wound patterns, told a tale of an assailant who was short, weak, and uncontrollably angry.

He called up the image of the victim's body, but it was too much, too strong, so he dragged his mind away to focus on the pumping of his arms, the filling of his lungs. He tried again, this time remembering just the defensive wounds on the woman's hands and arms, then moved to other aspects. In fifteen minutes, according to the clock, he had reviewed the whole crime scene and seen the phantasms of the possible, and only lost control of the rhythm of his run a couple of times. He was cautiously encouraged.

He lowered the speed but kept on running until he felt the runner's groove, the cadence automatic. He had to know if he could handle a more horrific memory.

He called up the one he'd used to distract the telepath in the hostel room, about the boy in a forest clearing whose mother had cut out his heart, then killed herself. He balanced his visions with the physical sensations from running, speeding up the treadmill to cope with the memory as it swelled and threatened to overload him. It was hard and unnerving, and left him covered in icy sweat. He stumbled several times, but gritted his teeth and kept going while he still could. In the end, he had to focus on Mairwen, or he'd have gone under, but he'd lasted longer than he had in previous attempts. He managed to shove the memory back into its dark closet and slow the treadmill again.

He looked at the clock and was astonished to see it had taken close to fifty minutes. He counted that as progress, because it had seemed like hours. He felt like hell. He was nauseated, and his legs and sides burned like he'd been running wind sprints. His core felt as cold as when his talent ran wild. Still, it was better than waking up in another unfamiliar medical bed.

He slowed to a walk, breathing heavily as he stepped off. He grabbed a towel from a nearby rack and wiped the sweat off his face, then draped it around his neck for warmth.

He turned to Mairwen, who was doing force isolations with her lower torso, and caught an expression of concern on her face before it smoothed away. She released herself from the machine and stood to look at him.

"I'll be okay, once I catch my breath." His throat was parched.

He stepped closer, stopping only when their bodies were not quite touching. He put his hand on her shoulder, and he couldn't help but smile. "I'm glad my personal security detail is worried about me."

She twitched an eyebrow. "I'm more worried about my towel," she said with an almost straight face.

He laughed when he remembered he hadn't come in with one. "I'll bring you another."

She cocked her ear slightly toward the entrance. "No, I'm done for now."

She turned and headed for the door, getting there just in time to cross paths with DeBayaud. Luka shook his head in wonder. Her acute hearing was astonishing.

He headed for the kitchen for something to drink before hitting the shower. The couches had been returned to their original positions. Adams was probably in his quarters, and he didn't care where Haberville was.

The odd shift schedule they'd set up reminded him of his early days with the military police investigation division. The crime units had been chronically understaffed and overworked, and the commander was liable to send them to a crime scene halfway across the galaxy at any time. He'd been glad when he'd moved up in rank and could focus on the specialty cases. Not that they were any more conveniently timed or located, but there were fewer of them.

He had since become quite happily accustomed to having something that resembled a predictable schedule, with regular meals. He made a mental note to ask Mairwen how she was handling the schedule changes that had been thrust upon her since she'd begun working with him. He had a tendency to think of her as superhuman, and that wasn't a fair expectation.

Luka tried again in the exercise room after lunch, with no better or worse results. He'd chosen what he'd thought was a less difficult memory, and still had to use Mairwen as a lifeline. Irritably deciding he needed to think about something else, he holed up in his stateroom to read a couple of technical journals and take a short nap. He'd run more treadmill miles in the past two days than he usually did in a week on the trails at home.

The evening meal was a mix of more good food courtesy of Adams, a spice-rubbed duck and grilled squash and onion, and more sparkling conversation, courtesy of Haberville. The dinner party atmosphere was nice for Adams and DeBayaud. Luka might have appreciated it more if he hadn't been frustrated by his lack of progress with his talent, and if it hadn't reduced Mairwen to monosyllables. It didn't help that the conversation often wandered into personal matters. Still, as nominal leader, he made an effort to interact with his team.

"…her parents made her wait until she was sixteen to get her birth control implant," DeBayaud was saying. Luka gathered he was talking about a former lover.

"Heavenly Sovereign, why?" asked Haberville, with indignation.

"I know, right? Some notion that it would stop her from having sex." DeBayaud shook his head.

"That's insane," said Adams. "I got mine at twelve, when I started puberty."

"I was eleven," said Haberville. "What did her parents have against sex?"

Luka swallowed the bite he'd been chewing. "Maybe they didn't dislike sex so much as the thought of their child growing up."

DeBayaud nodded his agreement. "Wouldn't surprise me. They were kind of creepy, the one time I met them." He smiled mischievously. "I bet her career as one of the top sex feelie artists in the industry really pisses them off."

Haberville laughed. "Karma's a bitch." DeBayaud and Adams laughed with her, and Luka smiled.

She speared another bite with her fork, then waved it in Luka's direction. "I've been meaning to ask you, what's with all the running?"

Luka counted himself lucky that he had another mouthful of food, giving him time to come up with even a vague answer. "I'm training." He should have thought of an excuse before this.

"For a race?" asked DeBayaud. "The Etonver Invitational isn't for another six months."

Luka shook his head. "I'm not that good." He was coming up blank on the names of any other races.

Unexpectedly, Mairwen came to his rescue. "For a track run for a charity. He asked me to coach him."

That he was able to hide his surprise was only due to years of experience testifying in high court against the galaxy's best adversarial lawyers. He wondered if she'd just made it up, or already had foreseen the possible question and prepared a plausible story. He'd bet on the latter.

"Really? Have you raced?" asked Haberville, latching onto the first bit of personal information Luka had heard Mairwen offer since the trip began.

"Yes," said Mairwen.

Haberville gamely tried again. "I love watching runners, especially when the men wear those little thongs or better yet, go full native. Any races I would have seen you in?"

Mairwen shook her head and went back to eating.

Luka looked down to hide his amusement. Haberville was no better at getting anything out of Mairwen than the Etonver police interrogators had been.

Haberville might have pressed, but she was distracted by DeBayaud.

"Did you see the Prime City Classic three years ago? I came in seventeenth. My best time ever."

"Only because he was being chased by his cohab partner at the time," teased Adams.

DeBayaud groaned. "Don't remind me. I was lucky to get out of that contract with my bank account intact. That woman went through cash like it was past its expiry date, and kept expecting me to bail her out."

The conversation turned to memorable vacation trips, of which Luka had none worth mentioning. His career choice had never lent itself to predictable leisure time. If he didn't get a handle on his talent, he might have unintended leisure in his near future.

He caught Mairwen's eye, then subtly tilted his head toward the exercise room. She nodded slightly and continued eating. He made a mental note that she seemed to enjoy the duck and squash, but only ate one bite of the cinnamon apple compote before abandoning it.

Since Adams cooked, Luka had suggested the rest of them should take on cleanup duty. Haberville once again managed to duck it, this time by taking Mairwen's unfinished apple compote to Ta'foulou in the nav pod and not coming back. Once Haberville was asleep, he'd have to check the nav pod for any other dishes she'd left around.

After changing into running shoes, he headed for the exercise room with Mairwen. He was doubly glad for her cover story, because it meant they no longer had to pretend to meet in the exercise room by chance.

She stationed herself near the wall, facing the treadmill. He followed and hung his towel on the nearby rack. Knowing they were alone, he leaned in for a quick kiss, then whispered, "Thank you. Which charity?"

"Rashad Tarana Survivors. It's a half marathon in eight weeks."

It was an event he might actually have chosen had he known about it. No one deserved what had been done to the people of Rashad Tarana. "When did you look it up?"

She brushed calloused fingertips along his neck and jawline. "This morning, when I saw how… focused you were going to be."

He smiled. "That's a nicer word than 'stubborn.'"

"I know." She kissed him, then stepped back.

He set the treadmill for an easier pace, since his legs were already sore. He chose one of the mildest violence scenes he could think of and managed not to trip or lose control even once. It wasn't a hard test, but it was a start.

After a quick shower, he fell into bed, and for once didn't think about anything else but sleep.

At breakfast the next morning, Luka's legs felt like overstretched elastic, though he was pretty sure only Mairwen noticed. Haberville and DeBayaud were asleep, so it was just a quiet meal with Adams.

He'd awakened with a renewed determination to wrestle his talent into submission. He had to. He couldn't think of anything else he'd rather do than use it to bring justice for the dead, which now included his friends.

He decided to use weightlifting as his physical distraction, and Mairwen thought it was worth trying. It wasn't his preferred form of exercise, but he needed to give his legs a rest, and it was good to keep his upper body strength balanced. The position of the weight bench gave him a clear view of Mairwen on the treadmill, if need be. He no longer needed to see her for his talent to find her if she was close enough, but he liked watching her run. She made it look so effortless that he could almost believe counteracting gravity was one of her extraordinary skills.

His new method worked better than he'd hoped, especially considering yesterday's disappointing results. He successfully called up two blood-drenched crime scenes and put them away again, and only lost rhythm a few times as he struggled to keep control. He didn't have to focus his talent on Mairwen even once. Maybe he'd just needed the time away from it. He was cold as always, but a quick, hot shower made him feel better.

After a stop in the kitchen to consult with Adams on upcoming menus and food supplies, he retreated to his stateroom and spent some time working on the case. He'd been too wrapped up in wrestling with his talent, and not focusing on the real reason he was on the ship in the first place. The planetary exploration data was as sparse as Haberville had said, and the fact that it was five hundred years out of date didn't instill confidence. If the planet was dead, as it was supposed to be, they wouldn't even have to land, and they would have made the trip for nothing.

On the other hand, if the planet truly was a hybrid, there'd be no telling what they'd find. The pre-terraform native fauna and climate had been reported as jungle-like, but that vague description allowed for a lot of variation. If the hybrid mix of native and terraform life was viable, he almost hoped it *was* being exploited by a pharma company, because that would mean it wasn't inimical to human life, and improved the odds his team could survive it long enough to get in and out with samples.

He was reviewing the contents of the specialized med kit when he was interrupted by a quiet knock on his door. It was DeBayaud.

"Morganthur says you should eat soon, before all the lunch stuff Adams made is gone."

"Did she really?" It didn't sound like her. Too many words.

"Well, not exactly. She just said you hadn't eaten yet, and wouldn't let me put the stuff away until you did."

Luka looked at the time and saw it was mid-afternoon. Now that he thought about it, his stomach had been complaining for a while. He'd intended to work on his talent control again after lunch, but maybe it would be better to wait until after dinner for what he wanted to try.

He followed DeBayaud into the kitchen and made himself a quick sandwich, then helped DeBayaud store the rest of the food. He found Mairwen in her room, sitting in the far back corner of the platform, reading.

"Thanks for looking out for me," he said, waving what was left of his sandwich at her. He sealed the stateroom door behind him.

"You're welcome." She closed her display. "How are your legs?"

He smiled ruefully. "Stiff. I'll be better tomorrow." He stayed near the doorway, mindful of not dropping crumbs on the carpet or her bed, and finished the last bite. "After dinner, I want to try…" He broke off, remembering they couldn't speak openly. "*Svei því.*" Damn it.

With fluid movements, she stood and crossed to him, her body almost touching his, angled so he could speak quietly in her ear. He rested his hand on her lower back. The weave of her sweater was silky soft, and she was pleasantly warm.

"I want to try using a less violent reconstruction, and use only the memory of running instead of actually doing it." He took a deep breath and released it. "I have to know if I can do it."

She looked at him, then nodded. "This morning must have gone well. Your stateroom?"

He was relieved. He'd been afraid she'd think he wasn't ready. "Yes, and yes."

He had the answer to his question, but now he found himself reluctant to leave. "What are you reading?"

"The xenobiological sampling safety protocol. Even though we have a decon chamber, I'd prefer not to infect the ship."

The *Berjalan* had been retrofitted with the decontamination chamber in front of the portal, but it wasn't perfect. Careless procedure might mean both the personnel and the ship would have to be quarantined, which would be expensive and time-consuming. And in a worst-case scenario, fatal.

He smiled. "You're admirably patient with reading the most boring things. I needed two cups of coffee to get through it."

She shrugged. "I don't sleep much."

He slid his hand up her back to the nape of her neck, skirting around the knife she wore to stroke the edge of her soft blonde hair. "Vocational training?" he asked softly.

She shook her head minutely.

"Rewiring?" He kept his voice so low he barely heard it himself.

She nodded uneasily, her eyes on his.

Did she think he was bothered by what she was? He smiled and brushed her cheekbone with his thumb. "You're amazing." She relaxed and gave him a small smile back.

A little louder, he said, "Let's talk after dinner." He pulled away and left before his brain and his hormones could invent another excuse to keep him in her stateroom.

For the evening main course, he'd collaborated with Adams to serve lamb meatballs and mushrooms in a fragrantly spiced sour cream sauce over spinach-flavored pasta. As usual, Ta'foulou took his plate away with him to the nav pod. Haberville once again appointed herself social director, as if they were on an interstellar pleasure cruise.

"I love traveling, so it's always interesting to hear where people grew up," Haberville said as she unfolded her napkin. "I was raised on Helonne, in a melting-pot neighborhood. Opposite side of the planet from the famous glassworks. Where do you hail from, DeBayaud?"

He was sitting to her right, with Adams to her left. Luka was across from Mairwen, with one empty chair between them and the others.

"Lumentye Bashkonen. Third Wave. Kind of a backwater. Mostly known for having a lot of rivers. Big French and Belgian population."

"I think I was there once," she said. "Prime city is Moshra or something like that?"

"Moesia," supplied DeBayaud with a smile, perhaps pleased to have something in common with her. He seemed very taken with her.

She turned to Adams. "What about you?"

"Lots of places, but ended up on Vaylamoinen. University Town." He took a bite of green pasta.

Haberville nodded. "I had a conference there once, I think. Why a city of fourteen million is still called a town, I have no idea. I never saw so many bicycles in all my life.

"That's the place," agreed Adams.

"Foxe?" She smiled at him.

"Kaldur Fjall on Lumi Silta. Coldest city on the coldest planet in the Concordance. Lots of snow."

Haberville gave a mock shiver. "I'll bet you're glad to live in Etonver, then."

He nodded his agreement. He'd been happy to leave, and happier to never go back. Too cold, and too many bad memories.

"Morganthur? Where are you from?"

Luka was surprised when Mairwen answered. Usually she ignored Haberville's prying. "Duau, on Waimaakole."

"Never heard of it," said Haberville. Her tone encouraged Mairwen to share more.

Mairwen shrugged, clearly not caring. A look of annoyance crossed Haberville's face before she turned to ask DeBayaud for more water.

Mairwen's answer had Luka wondering how she'd created her identity after escaping from the CPS. He remembered she'd said that memories of her childhood had been wiped clean. He couldn't imagine how that would feel. He wouldn't wish his childhood on anyone, but at least he could remember having one.

Luka cleared his throat. "As soon as we leave Horvax Station tomorrow, I'd like to go over our plans for what we'll be doing once we transit into the Insche system. We can meet in the nav pod so everyone can be there."

Adams and DeBayaud nodded, and so did Haberville, but she waggled a finger at him. "No more business talk over dinner. We should be enjoying ourselves while we have the chance."

Luka didn't mind, since he'd gotten agreement on his request, but her assumption of authority rankled him a bit. He might have to assert leadership more forcefully for the things he cared about.

Adams made it a point to thank Luka for coming up with the excellent dinner idea, and Haberville and DeBayaud expressed their appreciation. He was glad the others liked it, but he only really cared that Mairwen did. She would abandon it if she didn't, but he didn't know how to tell if she was enjoying it.

"A glass of wine, and it'd be perfect," said Haberville.

Adams shook his head. "Transit-stable wines are expensive. Besides, I'm glad to have the salary bonus for being on duty for the entire mission, even if that means no alcohol or chems on board."

"I'm with you," said DeBayaud. "I'm going flitter-drop skiing on Artesonraju next year, and the equipment alone is costing a fortune."

"Are you going with him?" asked Haberville.

Adams snorted. "Oh hell, no."

DeBayaud laughed, then looked to toward Mairwen and Luka. "What sports do you like? Besides running, I mean."

"Just running," said Luka. He wouldn't have admitted to skiing even if he liked it, though he'd done a lot of it growing up. He had a feeling DeBayaud was entirely too competitive to be a relaxing companion.

Haberville touched DeBayaud's bare arm with her fingertips and gave him a seductive smile. "I much prefer indoor sports." DeBayaud's answering smile was wide and only for Haberville.

From there, the conversation turned to love versus lust, with Haberville arguing they were entirely separate, or there wouldn't be a joyhouse on every street corner of every civilized planet. That led to a discussion of the best joyhouses in Etonver and their specialties, which Luka had no experience with. Most people enjoyed an occasional joyhouse visit alone or with a partner, but after the initial hot rush of puberty, he'd discovered he needed an emotional connection to make sex enjoyable, probably because of his talent. Another reason his lovers had been few and far between.

It was dismaying to realize he had so little in common with the rest of the team, and felt more comfortable with quiet, self-contained Mairwen. He was never going to be the hopelessly gregarious, natural leader that Leo Balkovsky had been. The best he could hope was to make the best decisions he could when needed. He took his dishes to the kitchen and made his escape.

He left his stateroom door open so he could see when Mairwen passed by, which was only a few minutes later. Haberville went back on duty and Ta'foulou returned to his quarters, leaving Adams and DeBayaud in the kitchen. Just to be safe, he waited ten minutes more, then sealed his door and used the shared fresher door to invite Mairwen into his room. She started for the chair, but he intercepted her and pulled her into his lap, needing the contact with her. He loved the feel of her, the weight of her on him.

"What did you think of dinner?" He was learning not to make it easy for her to give one-word answers.

"Good."

Well, he was still a novice. "It's an Icelandic recipe of my mother's." He let her warmth soak into him and pulled her in closer. "Do you have any memories at all of your family?" He kept his voice low and quiet.

"No," she said. "I used to think I remembered warm feelings, but it might have been something I made up because I needed it at the time. I was younger than most candidates."

"How old were you when you… started school?"

"Fourteen."

It hurt to think of her so young and so alone, but he knew the weight of his pity wouldn't be welcome. He tried for a breezy tone. "Ah, makes me feel ancient at forty-one to your thirty-seven tender years." She smiled, and he continued. "Someday, I'd like to hear more about Mairwen Morganthur. If you're willing." He nibbled on her earlobe and was gratified when her flesh pebbled and her breathing became ragged. Her responsiveness sent his blood racing.

"I'm willing," she said, turning to give him a kiss. "But not when we're on duty." She kissed him again quickly and slid off his lap to sit in the chair facing him.

Knowing he'd put it off long enough, he took a deep, slow, centering breath and closed his eyes. He constructed a detailed image of running in his mind, especially remembering how it felt in his body, then called up a milder crime scene memory, returning as often as he needed to the remembered sensation of running. It worked. It was hard work, juggling them, and he felt as cold and tired as if he'd been running a marathon in winter, but it worked. For the first time since he'd nearly lost everything, he had hope that he could get his life back, maybe find a new normal.

His back complained, and his head throbbed. The clock said he'd been working for nearly half an hour, so no wonder he was wrecked. Mairwen had been there the whole time. "I don't know how you have the patience for this, but I am eternally grateful that you do."

She gave him a slight smile and a shrug. "Better than midnight guard rounds in an ice storm."

The image sent a shiver through him. He wished he was doing this on a secluded tropical beach.

"You're cold."

He nodded. "Always. It's a side effect of…" He was too tired to think of a cagey way to explain that it was an aftermath of using his talent. The coldness, like his talent, had gotten a lot less controllable after the "collector" case. He was tired of having to dance around words and subjects because someone might be listening.

He was really tired of not being able to spend private, off-duty time with Mairwen. He'd be glad when they could get back to Etonver and their normal lives, whatever that might bring. He stood and held out his arms to her, and she stood and melted into his parting embrace and kiss.

Maybe he would have eventually regained control of his talent if he'd never met her, but he doubted it. He didn't believe in fate or destiny, but he did believe he was a very lucky man.

CHAPTER 14

HORVAX STATION WAS a mid-size orbiting platform above an unprepossessing planet of the same name. The station had enough portlocks for thirty or forty smaller ships and a dozen large commercial liners or military transports. From what they could see upon arrival, it looked about half full.

In the interest of efficiency and keeping a low profile, Luka sent DeBayaud and Adams to pick up the xenobiologic sampling kit that he'd arranged to be sent from the manufacturer, and authorized Adams to purchase some fresh groceries. It was always good to keep the chef happy. He asked Haberville and Ta'foulou to both stay with the ship to handle the supplies and flux reload. Meanwhile, he and Mairwen would visit the station's communications center and retrieve any incoming packets externally, rather than connecting the ship to the station directly. He also wanted to look at some extras for the med kit. No one seemed to think he was being overly cautious, or if they did, they didn't say anything.

The comm center was in the middle of the station, near the restaurants, stores, joyhouses, and chem shops that were always open. The commons area was decorated to look like an old Earth-style town square, but it couldn't hide the station's industrial origins. There were plenty of people, from station employees to corporates to passengers, but it wasn't crowded.

The retail pharmacy didn't have much in the way of medical supplies that their expedition kit didn't already have, but he did buy some extra broad-spectrum antivirals, just in case.

Mairwen was as quiet as she usually was in public. He'd come to recognize the very subtle signs that she was taking in sounds, smells, and sights like a bloodhound, though he thought of her as more cat-like, all predatory power and lethal grace. He allowed himself a short daydream of taking her to one of the restaurants, then window-shopping, as if they were an ordinary couple with time to kill, but he tripped up when he tried to imagine her thinking of shopping as a recreational activity.

"What do you do for amusement?" he asked, as they passed a store selling trids, holos, feelies, and other publications. The store claimed to cater to all known languages, and he had a momentary impulse to ask them for something in Icelandic, just to see what happened.

She gave him the tolerant look she usually did when she thought his topic was random. "I read."

"Yes, I know, and you run. I mean, what do you indulge yourself with when you get the chance? See live theatre? Swim the Xochoptl Straits? Volunteer at a pet-trade shelter?"

She eyed him as if he might be teasing her, then gave him a fleeting smile before blandly saying, "I follow brilliant men around spaceports."

He covered an irrational stab of jealousy with a teasing smile. "Men? There are others?"

"No, it's a recent interest."

"Lucky for me." He wanted to kiss her, but settled for briefly stroking her hand. It reminded him of the first time she'd touched him, her fingers interlacing his on the crowded crosswalk in Etonver, when he'd so desperately needed that contact and gentle comfort. He realized he'd started falling for her even then.

The comm center was large, with evidence of a recent expansion, and though not particularly crowded, was unusually noisy. The changed configuration had probably impaired the original acoustics. He chose a corner console and entered his biometric and access codes to retrieve several routine system and personal info packets for the *Berjalan*, which he dumped to a longwire.

A separate private message from Zheer had several interesting pieces of news. Juno Vizla, La Plata's insurance company client, had agreed to pay for the whole trip, which made Zheer suspect they had knowledge they weren't sharing. There had been two recent breaches in La Plata information security that related to the case, and Zheer urged extra vigilance from the team. Velasco, his erstwhile assistant, had resigned. Luka was pleased because it saved him from having to release him in favor of Mairwen when they got back to Etonver, which had moved to the top of his to-do list after she'd rescued him from the kidnappers.

The most interesting, if least actionable, item was that a pharma company by the name of Korisni Genetika kept coming up in the data analysts' deep diving of Leo's files and on the net, and there were indications they'd had a long-standing relationship with the dead telepath who'd tried to interrogate him. He cleared the terminal and pocketed the longwire. He was frustrated that Zheer's message hadn't described the nature of the security breaches so he'd know what he was supposed to be vigilant about.

When he told Mairwen about the message, she insisted they take a different route back to the ship. Mairwen again walked companionably by his side, rather than the usual three-steps-back position she took when she was in simple guard mode, though he didn't doubt she considered herself still on duty. It was only as they got back to the *Berjalan*'s entry lock that Luka realized he hadn't once felt the stir of talent that used to make him almost queasy in crowds. He was congratulating himself when Mairwen put her hand on his arm to stop him.

"We need Adams and DeBayaud." Her tone was neutral, but she was taking shallow breaths and her eyes were dilated. He'd seen that behavior when she was scenting something of interest. She stepped to within bare centimeters of him and spoke quietly. "A stranger has been here in the last ten minutes. The fluxing should have been automated."

"Maybe there was a problem? Or someone got lost?"

"Maybe," she conceded.

There was nothing visible to make his talent bubble, but Mairwen's caution was contagious. "I'll go find Adams and DeBayaud. Go check on Haberville and Ta'foulou."

"No. I'm going with you." There was a determined intensity behind her words and in her unwavering gaze. He got the feeling she'd disobey any order he gave her if she thought he was in danger, maybe because she still blamed herself for the kidnapping and interrogation. He knew he'd survived it only because of her.

He gave her a small smile and brushed the side of her face with the backs of his fingers. "Lucky for me."

* * * * *

Mairwen was unhappy. The incident had disturbed her, and she'd instigated a full security sweep as soon as they got back to the ship, but found nothing. Her nose and Luka's talent told them whoever had been at the portal hadn't been on the ship. Haberville and Ta'foulou insisted the resupply process had gone like clockwork, and the portal logs agreed. All she could do was tell Luka her misgivings, but it was ultimately his decision to continue the mission. It had been his friends who were murdered, not hers.

The *Berjalan* entered transit without incident. The phantom sonics of the light drive sounded ordinary, but she didn't know the ship well enough to detect subtle variances. Luka held his planned meeting to talk about the types of samples they'd need from the planet, and the safety precautions they should all take. If it was a viable planet, the owners would likely have ways to protect it. He mentioned Korisni Genetika, the new pharma company player, but everyone said they'd never heard of it.

Adams was in the kitchen chopping fresh vegetables for omelets, and DeBayaud and Haberville were napping while they had the chance. Mairwen had followed Luka into the exercise room, where he was pacing, his mind a thousand light-years away. She didn't envy Luka his leadership position, and hated putting pressure on him because of her strong, quite possibly pathological, sense of caution. Trackers who didn't assume the universe was malevolent didn't live very long, but she wasn't a tracker any more. Didn't want to be one any more.

She now stood indecisively in the doorway, torn between wanting to stay close to see that he was safe, and recognizing that it was a kind of arrogance on her part to think he couldn't take care of himself. She was afraid she'd lost her sense of objectivity when it came to his well-being.

Besides, the proximity enforced by the ship would evaporate once they returned to their normal routine on Rekoria. She knew it would be harder if she didn't start separating herself now. Alone in her stateroom, perhaps she could find her elusive equilibrium and start thinking like a hardened tracker instead of a soft human. She had just about convinced herself to go when they were interrupted by Adams.

"Something's wrong with Ta'foulou," he said. "I went to ask him what he wanted in his omelet, and I found him out cold, still jacked in. Haberville's with him now."

"Get DeBayaud," Luka ordered, but Adams was already on his way. "*Helvítis,*" he swore, and headed toward the nav pod. He put his hand on her shoulder as he passed, as if he needed the brief contact. She let herself find her own comfort in his touch.

In the nav pod, she narrowed her focus to the sight and scents of Ta'foulou unconscious and slumped in the pilot chair. Blood trickled down his tattooed neck from his skulljack. It was stark, wet red against the pale grey of a tattooed eagle's wing.

Haberville held up a bloody wire. "Mal virus payload. If he blacked out in time, he might still have a few brain cells left."

Mairwen allowed herself a moment to be grateful that tracker brains didn't work with implants. Modern skulljacks were designed to stop all input when the host was unconscious, but malicious viruses had been known to override safety features.

"What can we do for him?" asked Luka. Adams brought their medical kit in and set it next to the main console.

"Damned little," said Haberville, "unless you've got a healer or a telepath hidden in that kit. Give him an auto-hydroline for dehydration, I guess. He'll have to sleep it off on his own for now."

Adams pulled out a fluids bag and pressure line and slapped its adhesive patch on the back of Ta'foulou's hand, where the unit would find a suitable vein and insert itself. DeBayaud shouldered Ta'foulou's bony frame easily and headed out of the nav pod and toward the pilot staterooms.

Meanwhile, Haberville tossed the bloody wire into the recycler, and pulled hers out of her skulljack and tossed it, too. Mairwen approved of her caution.

Haberville called up a holographic interface and began manipulating it with rapid-fire gestures. "So far, everything else in the navcomp looks okay. We should check the other comps, in case there's something we missed."

"On it," said Adams and headed out of the nav pod.

Mairwen decided to do her own investigation, as well. She'd start with the engine comp, then access the shipcomp from there as well. Not that she had reason to distrust Adams, but she didn't know his skill level.

By tacit agreement, they all ended up in the nav pod again forty-six minutes later, and the news wasn't good.

Haberville reported first. "Ta'foulou was, to use an old-fashioned word, a pervert. He liked to covertly watch or listen to people having sex. I caught him spying early on and warned him about it, and I thought that was enough. It's probably been a dull trip for his tastes. After this afternoon's meeting, the log says he accessed the emergency monitoring system to listen to my room and DeBayaud's. Maybe he was hoping we'd be making a hot-connect instead of sleeping in our separate rooms." She shrugged. "That system was where the payload was, and it launched as soon as the idiot accessed it. I don't know if someone targeted him specifically, or maybe they thought all pilots do that sort of thing." She frowned at them all. "We don't, in case you're wondering."

Haberville sounded more irritated that Ta'foulou made pilots look bad than she was worried about his health. Unfortunately, that was just the start of their troubles.

"Morganthur and I found two more virus payloads," said Adams. "The obvious one is in the navcomp, targeting the pilot during transit exit. It's like the one that got Ta'foulou. We can't flush the navcomp while we're in transit, but as long as Haberville isn't jacked in, she should be fine." Adams gave her a brief nod. "The other one's really subtle, in the shipcomp. If we hadn't isolated it, in about eighty minutes, the habisphere would change the air and pressure mix to give us all nitrogen narcosis. The logs look clean, but the recovery array says none of the viruses were there before we docked at Horvax."

Mairwen had also checked Adams's work and snuck further queries into the navcomp modules when Haberville wasn't using them. Neither Haberville nor Adams had given her reason to think they were behind the attacks, but the only person on the ship she fully trusted was Luka.

She thought Luka was feeling the need to pace, but there wasn't enough room. She didn't think the others recognized the signs that his intuition was firing.

"Someone," he said, "wants us to have a lot of chances to die, and in ways that would look like an accident."

Haberville looked shocked, and Adams and DeBayaud looked grim.

Luka didn't look happy, either, as he ran his fingers through his hair. "We need to get to Insche before the timed virus would have started making us dopey and delusional. It's too easy to have sabotaged the ship's hull on Horvax." He looked at Haberville. "What's our ETA for realspace?"

She brought up a holo countdown clock and pinned it to the permanent display. "Two hours, three minutes."

"Is there any way we can get there in eighty or ninety minutes?"

"Impossible," said Haberville.

Mairwen knew that wasn't true, but pointing it out would reveal knowledge that a night-guard-turned-security-assistant shouldn't have. On the other hand, keeping her secrets was likely to leave them adrift in uncharted realspace. She cleared her throat. "We could decouple the light-drive safeties and overload flux to the light drive, which will bounce the ship rather than let it skim. If we start now, it would cut transit time by forty objective minutes or more."

Haberville's jaw dropped. "Holy Mother of…" She stared at Mairwen a long moment. "That's suicide!"

Luka looked at Mairwen, and she met his questioning gaze with tacit assurance. He nodded, then turned to Haberville.

"It's a good bet the virus is timed to go off with something else. We can't check the hull for an exterior problem while in transit, right?"

"No," she said. "We'd have to be in realspace. We could drop at the next packet beacon and check." She brought up another countdown clock. "The next beacon is only ten minutes away if we angle and do an emergency drop."

"Which puts us where?" asked Luka.

Haberville shrugged. "The middle of nowhere." She glowered at Luka and Mairwen both. "But we'd be *alive* in the middle of nowhere."

Luka shook his head. "Not if the hull is breached. Is Morganthur's solution invariably fatal?"

Mairwen wondered uneasily if Luka was thinking of making her the pilot. He clearly trusted she had skills, but she'd have to talk to him privately about her limitations. For now, he was focused on Haberville, his expression hard.

"No, it's doable," she grudgingly conceded. "But you're depending on the engine being well maintained, and the navcomp to keep up with the new data and manage the overload, and hoping like hell the bounces don't hit an anomaly. And it goes through flux like an exploration spacer goes through lube at a joy palace."

"As opposed to hoping the people who breached the comps, and targeted our pilots, don't know how to sabotage a ship's hull?" Luka was as unyielding as Mairwen had ever seen him.

Haberville stared at Luka, her eyes narrowing.

Mairwen spoke up, anticipating Haberville's next likely objection. "We'd still have enough flux to get back to Horvax."

Haberville looked to Adams and DeBayaud for support, both of who raised their hands in the universal "don't look at me" gesture.

"Do it," said Luka. His air of command was unwavering.

After a long moment, Haberville caved. "Shit," she said. "Shit!" She glared back and forth at Mairwen and Luka. "Fine, but I'm not covering up a goddamn thing if we live through this. Morganthur's solution is a jack trick."

She released the webbing on her chair and launched herself toward the door, then stopped and turned.

"I looked up that planet she said she's from. Its colonies failed twenty years ago, so there are conveniently no records. If she was just some mouth-breather night-shift guard before this, then I'm the fucking First Flight Queen of Albion Prime!"

Haberville stalked out, headed toward the engine pod. Mairwen silently followed her to help, and to ensure Haberville complied with Luka's order.

* * * * *

Luka's appetite was nonexistent, but he forced himself to eat every last bite of the excellent omelet Adams made. It would go to waste, otherwise, and no telling when they'd get the chance to eat well again. Thankfully, Haberville was eating hers in the nav pod, where her continued hostility toward Mairwen was out of view. Luka wanted to defend Mairwen, but the real reason for her astonishing skills was a lot less believable than a suspected stint on a jack crew. DeBayaud and Adams didn't seem to be fazed by Mairwen's knowledge, though if other evidence appeared, he knew they'd remember Haberville's accusations.

Adams and Mairwen agreed that the two virus signatures that targeted the pilots were very different from the one hidden in the shipcomp. Luka was playing with the theory that the virus attack on the pilots was meant to divert attention from the more subtle ship sabotage, but he wasn't comfortable with it. Ultimately, it didn't matter, because the end result was the same. The ship and everyone on it were in trouble, and he was responsible.

With less than fifteen minutes before the rushed exit into Insche realspace, Luka ordered everyone to armor up, put on the exosuits, and gather up any weapons they had. He asked Mairwen to move the xeno sampling kit from his stateroom to the kitchen area, while DeBayaud and Adams brought the medical kit and camping gear up from the lower hold.

Luka was sure he was forgetting a thousand things they could be doing to prepare for unknown trouble, but his jumble of emotions swamped his rational thoughts. He should have trusted his own intuition and Mairwen's suspicions more and never let them leave Horvax Station. Now, everyone was in danger because of him, and if he'd guessed right about the exterior hull sabotage, they'd be lucky to live long enough to get rescued. He wanted to apologize to them all, but he knew he couldn't until they were safe again. He wasn't inclined toward command, but he knew enough not to wear self-doubts and regrets on his sleeve.

Regardless of what anyone might think, Luka led Mairwen into the exercise room and wrapped her in a long embrace, even though he couldn't feel the warmth of her through the suits. He didn't know what to say, so he just held her tight, needing the pressure of her arms holding him. They only disengaged when Haberville announced the two-minute warning for exiting transit.

The drop to realspace was textbook smooth. For all that Haberville was a pain in the ass, she was a damned good pilot. As planned, she immediately sent a repeating distress packet to the local comm relay, and an automated exobot to examine the hull. She used the system drive to arc over the rocky asteroid belt and approach the solar system's third planet, Insche 255C. She also began passive scanning for tech signatures, in case there was something to find. She sent Mairwen into the engine pod to return the flux field to normal and re-engage the safeties. DeBayaud and Adams were in the kitchen area organizing the gear they'd brought up from the hold.

According to the ship's clock, they should have just started feeling the effects of the nitrogen narcosis, had they not isolated the shipcomp virus. Luka, having secured the xeno kit, headed to the nav pod to ask Haberville if the hull scan found anything, when he felt the ship shudder.

He took another step and the ship shuddered again. Gravity fluctuated, then stabilized. Luka yelled for DeBayaud and Adams while launching into a run. His forward momentum slammed him into the door jamb. He tumbled inside the nav pod and landed on his knees next to the med kit, behind the co-pilot chair. Haberville was snarling curses at the nav interface as she worked it, fingers flying.

A sharp, horrendous sound of metal groaning assaulted his ears, and lighting and gravity failed as the floor shuddered and tilted under him. The pressure in the pod suddenly popped his ears, and he realized the pod was self-sealing to maintain atmosphere. He fumbled with the neck controls on his exosuit to get the containment working. His hands were now sealed, too, at the cost of some dexterity. Worry and fear for Mairwen flooded him, even though he knew the engine pod was also self-sealing, and she wasn't inclined toward panic. He hoped Adams and DeBayaud made it in with her, because he didn't want to imagine what was going on with the rest of the ship, where poor Ta'foulou was.

Emergency lighting came on. With great clumsiness, he secured the med kit to a hold-down, then maneuvered himself into the co-pilot chair and strapped in. He could see Haberville's lips moving, but he couldn't hear anything. He finally remembered to switch on the exosuit's heads-up display. The audio came through loud and clear, but no projected images. He didn't know if his suit had that, or if it just wasn't working.

"...at a time. Adams, sit rep and injury status." Haberville had the calm, no-nonsense tone of the Space Div pilot she'd been before contracting with La Plata.

"The exercise room and pilot staterooms are gone. I can see black space. Zero atmosphere, zero gravity. I'm in the kitchen, and I have some lights." Adams' voice sounded breathy, but not panicked. *"I'm concussed but functional."*

"Adams, find a hold-fast and tie in. How's your exosuit?"

"I'm already anchored. Display says nine hours of air at average exertion rate, sixteen hours of heat, twenty hours of fluids."

Luka pictured the layout of the ship in his head. "Adams, if the autodoc survived, it should have at least five hours breathing mix, and maybe self-contained heat packs."

"Okay."

"Good," said Haberville. "DeBayaud?"

There was no answer.

After a long pause, Adams said, *"Last I saw, he was headed toward the staterooms to get Ta'foulou. That part of the ship is gone."* There was a forlorn quality to his voice.

"Understood," said Haberville. "Morganthur, report."

Luka hadn't realized he'd been holding his breath until he heard Mairwen's slightly raspy voice. *"Engine pod sealed, engines undamaged. Full atmosphere, full heat, full charge capacity, zero gravity. I am functional."* He would have felt better if he could see for himself what she meant by "functional," considering her loose definition of the word "fine." She didn't seem to worry about herself as much as he did.

"Haberville," he said, "can we can get Adams into one of the sealed pods?"

"Not without losing all atmosphere," she said. "We're going to have to try to land this clusterbucket and pray to the Baby Jesus it will hold together."

* * * * *

Mairwen unsealed her exosuit to save its breathing mix for later, then strapped herself to the bench facing the display. The engine pod was mostly dark, even to her extended visual range. She'd been lucky to escape with only bruises, though some of them were likely to be lingering. According to the engine comp, the pod had thirty days of breathing mix and longer than that for heat. Haberville had said she expected to have them down on the planet within the next five hours.

Trackers were trained in zero-G, but Mairwen had never had any assignments that required her to function in it. The lack of gravity was playing havoc with her stomach, making her nauseated, as if she'd ingested caffeine. She was glad her high metabolism meant she didn't have much left in her stomach to throw up if it came to that.

There was little else to do besides wait and think. She selfishly wished Luka were in the engine pod with her, where she could see he was safe, but knew it was better that he was in the nav pod where he could direct Haberville as needed.

The sabotage, she decided, had been effective but generic. She was uncertain as to whether their ship, specifically, had been expected to approach the Insche 255 system, or if they'd simply been caught by a signature-based security protocol protecting approaches to the system.

If Insche 255C was indeed a hybrid planet, there would definitely be an in-system perimeter, but it would have to be well camouflaged to hide it from casual observers. If she were designing it, she'd have passive telltales that automatically reported any visitors via packet, the way the *Berjalan's* distress call had gone out. All surveyed systems in the Concordance, habitable or not, had a comm relay, which couldn't be destroyed without bringing a military crew to investigate and replace it. But comm relays could be subverted...

Mairwen brought up the specs for the engine and the spare parts inventory for the engine pod, then asked Haberville if she could provide directions for building an exploration-style comm relay.

"*Why?*" Haberville sounded impatient.

"To improve the chances our distress message will get to its intended destination," Mairwen said.

"*The system's comm relay is working fine. There's no need.*" The tone was snappish.

Mairwen considered how to explain it, but Luka jumped in first. "*If I were hiding a hybrid planet, I'd find a way to read or delay any outgoing packets that didn't come from my people.*"

"*You mean like jack crews do?*" Accusation colored Haberville's tone.

Mairwen sighed. She'd never been part of a jack crew, but the CPS had been happy to incorporate their techniques into the official paracommando pathfinder curriculum. It wasn't ideal that Haberville now thought she was hiding a criminal past, but it might save some explanations later.

Luka's voice had a sharp command edge. "*Can you help Morganthur or not?*" Mairwen guessed he was feeling protective of her, since she often felt that way about him. It was unexpectedly comforting.

Haberville's "*Yes, sir*" had more than a hint of disrespect in it, but the instructions appeared on the engine pod console.

Mairwen spent the next two and a half hours fashioning the rudimentary comm relay. It would have gone a lot faster if she'd been in full gravity, and she wouldn't have lost so many bolts and fasteners that would undoubtedly get in her way later. The trickiest part was launching it away from their damaged ship, the planet, its single moon, and anything else it could run into. Fortunately, Haberville was cooperative and they got it deployed and the repeating distress call transmitted.

Luka periodically asked Adams to do trivial things and report back, which Mairwen thought was odd, until she realized he was trying to keep Adams from worrying or drifting off to sleep. Mairwen liked hearing the sound of Luka's voice, and regretted she'd never told him so.

She stayed as still as possible, resting as best she could in zero-G, knowing she'd be grateful for it later. Haberville's voice woke her from a semi-doze.

"*If it's any consolation, ladies and gentlemen, Insche 255C is definitely not a dead, poisoned planet like Concordance records say it is. Morganthur, check your console. Adams, I sent the scans to the shipcomp, if you've got a working display.*"

Mairwen found the feed and opened it. Temperature and gas composition values suggested a hot, steamy, high-oxygen but breathable atmosphere, and a wide swathe of green that expanded far above and below the equatorial zone. There were no oceans in the section they'd scanned, but many big lakes. Haberville pointed out several energy concentrations that she said meant tech was in use, and said she planned to try to land near one of them.

"*I'd like to be more precise than that, but I won't know how bad off the ship is until I try to land it. We'll hit exosphere margin in ten minutes. Seal up your suits.*"

Adams reported that he'd crammed himself, exosuit and all, into the autodoc unit that was installed in the ship wall next to the engine pod. It was the best of a bad lot of options for surviving the descent.

"If I don't make it, and any of you do, would you please tell my daughter I love her? I didn't record a last-chance packet for her this trip like I usually do."

"Goddamn it, Adams, don't talk like that..." began Haberville angrily.

"Yes, we'll tell her," said Luka, overriding whatever else Haberville was going to say. *"What's her name?"* Mairwen knew Luka's voice well enough to hear the compassion and guilt behind his words.

"Peregrine, but I call her Pico," said Adams. *"She lives with her mother on Vaylamoinen. La Plata has the coordinates."*

Mairwen didn't know the words for what she felt, but it hurt to think Adams might not see his daughter again. Somehow, over little more than a few shared meals, Adams had become a friend. If they lived through the landing, Mairwen was determined to protect Adams, too, if only so Luka wouldn't take on the added burden of Adams's death.

Before she'd met Luka, she wouldn't have had friends to worry about, but no one would have cared whether she lived or died, either. Like everything else worth having, being a normal human had a price.

CHAPTER 15

THE LANDING, WHEN it came, was beyond the worst Mairwen had imagined. Noise and lights assaulted her senses. Each bone-jarring impact did more damage to the engine pod's skin, and the ship tumbled and felt like it was shaking apart plate by plate. She'd have been bounced and broken if she hadn't been strapped in. The fasteners she'd lost while making the comm relay became tiny missiles that threatened to pierce her exosuit.

It felt like hours, but her time sense told her it was only eighteen minutes from the first turbulence to gliding through the troposphere, if a ripped-apart mass of incalloy could be said to glide, and another seven minutes until her pod came to a jolting, lurching stop.

Total darkness enveloped pod, the display having died in the last big shuddering flip once it hit the stratosphere. She hung suspended from the pilot bench, which was sticking out perpendicular to what was now down.

Luckily, her exosuit's interior display still workws. She had a few new bruises, but no significant damage. The flexin armor she wore inside the suit had done its job distributing the kinetic energy of the impacts.

"Adams? Foxe? Haberville?" she called as she released the straps and cautiously stretched her feet to the wall that had become her floor.

No answer.

She pushed her worry and dread into a tight cube in her mind and sealed it.

She flipped on the hand light zip-tied to the wrist of her exosuit. The pod looked surprisingly intact, but the water creeping under her feet told her it was no longer sealed. When she directed her light to the entry door, she could see muddy water flowing in where the frame had warped. She sloshed over to the other side of the pod, where the built-in tool bin lay submerged under her feet. She wrestled it open and fished out the manual crank and the meter-length bent alloy bar. She tried vocal pings again and got no answers.

Her exosuit would protect her from the inevitable flood of water, but would also impair her mobility and leverage. She concentrated on the task of prying open the door, and not thinking about the dark and heavy water above her that might soon swallow her whole.

Her fear of large bodies of water was instinctive, possibly from some childhood trauma she had no memory of, thanks to the CPS. She pushed her fear aside and focused on escape.

She dropped into half-tracker mode to power her muscles, knowing she had to get out to stay alive, and hoped that the ship landed close enough to a shore for them to swim. Slowly, reluctantly, the door slid up into its pocket, and water poured in, but equalized when the water level was just above her knees. After one last push using her leg and back muscles, the opening was wide enough for her to slip through underwater in her exosuit.

She stood up in the hall and shined her hand light around. The hall's intact walls angled up to the right to where the nav pod should be, and there was a glimmer of emergency lighting in that direction. To her left, against the outer wall of the engine pod, the battered autodoc unit was miraculously intact, powered, and still sealed.

She climbed up on its rounded end and pointed her light in the transparent view window. All she could see were exosuit boots, so Adams's head would unfortunately be below water when she got the autodoc's clamshell lid open. She stuck her head underwater and turned the light on what should be Adams's head, but the light died almost instantly. From the glimpse she got, she didn't know if he was conscious or not, but at least water wasn't leaking in. The unit's external controls were submerged and nonfunctional.

Next, she waded around the wall of the angled nav pod until she got to the pod's door, which unlike hers, was at least two meters up from the waterline and looked deformed in the middle. Water wouldn't be a problem at that height, but the deformed door would be a lot harder to get open. She stretched up and grabbed the doorframe with one hand, then pulled herself up high enough to bang three times on the door as hard as she could with the pry bar. She hung on and waited, cursing the sound impedance caused by the exosuit. After thirty of the longest seconds of her life, she heard three muffled answering thuds. It didn't mean that Luka was alive or uninjured, but it was a start. She dropped back to the flooded floor.

She needed a way to create leverage if she was going to get the door open. She made herself go back underwater through the engine pod door and retrieve the repositionable panel lift handles, then used some plastic sheeting to wrap them up, hopefully keeping them dry enough to stick to the wall surface. She found some flexline and wrapped it around her torso and shoulders to create a temporary sling for the pry bar.

Back at the nav pod doorway, she pulled herself up far enough to slap two lift handles onto the wall. They proved sturdy enough to handle her weight, and she hoped they could handle more. Using them, she raised her feet, wedged them into the doorframe, and pulled her body up. The door and frame definitely bowed in toward the pod. She slid the edge of the pry bar around the inside edges of the frame, hoping she'd find a place where she could jam the bar in and start working the door open. Just when she was afraid she'd have to try something else, the bar caught. The angle was awkward, but by moving the lift handles, she was able to use her leverage to rock the bar in, bit by bit, until at last she saw a puff of dust move and knew she'd broken the seal.

She badly wanted to call out for Luka, but she couldn't risk opening her exosuit for that unless there was enough oxygen in the trapped atmosphere to breathe. She used more half-tracker mode strength to make lurching but steady progress on getting the door open. When she had it open about a quarter of the way, she rested, and noticed the pod interior still had emergency lighting. Encouraged, she kept prying until she had it open half way and her muscles were screaming for relief. She turned off her awareness of the pain, not caring that she'd be paying for it later. She slid the pry bar into the makeshift sling on her back and poked her head into the pod.

About two meters below, she saw an inert-looking Haberville still strapped into her chair but hanging sideways, and next to her was Luka, standing, looking up at Mairwen. His smile was visible through the faceplate. All the fear for him that she'd been suppressing suddenly dissipated, making her shudder in relief, and she barely managed to hang onto the lift handles. When she could finally drag her eyes away from him, she saw he'd tied electrical conduit around Haberville's torso and legs in the form of a harness, from which Mairwen inferred that Haberville was still alive but incapacitated.

Thinking a moment, she signaled to Luka that she'd be back. She dropped back into the ruined corridor and returned to the engine pod, where she cobbled together a five-meter line made of short lengths of braided wire, fiber cable, and miscellaneous equipment straps, then secured metal pipe elbows to each end to act as weights. She counted seconds in her head to stave off her flaring emotions, none of which would be useful to her now. On the way back to the nav pod door, she checked on Adams again, but couldn't tell if anything had changed.

At the top of the nav pod, she wedged a length of heavy pipe as a cross brace, then draped the line over it and dropped both ends down to Luka. Clever man that he was, he figured out what she intended and was soon pulling on one end to lift Haberville up with the other. The makeshift line was holding, but she didn't trust it. As soon as Haberville was in range, Mairwen hauled her up and rested her on the door ledge. Close up, Mairwen could see Haberville was groggy and marginally responsive. At least her exosuit looked to be intact. As gently as she could, Mairwen lowered Haberville down into the water. She was mostly submerged but didn't quite sink to the bottom. Mairwen jumped down herself and untied the line so she could send it back down to Luka. He insisted on sending up the medical kit first before using the line to haul himself free of the nav pod. Mairwen pulled Haberville into a half sitting position in the water as he climbed down and joined them in the hall.

When he finally stood next to her, knee-deep in water, he pulled her to him and wrapped his arms around her. The exosuit prevented any body contact, and the transit vibration dampeners prevented contact communication, but she clung anyway and let the comfort it provided wash over her for an uncounted number of seconds.

She stepped back and pulled him toward the autodoc unit. In clumsy sign language, and hindered by the poor lighting, she tried to indicate that Adams was upside down in the unit and she needed Luka's help getting him out.

As she'd hoped, Luka's knowledge of the ship gave them a better way to open the unit than assaulting it with the pry bar, and they soon had Adams out and floating in the water. He was unconscious but alive.

Completely unexpectedly, Adams had shared the autodoc with a high-end sniper's railgun, and had jammed a case of ammunition and the xenobiological sampling kit into the end near his head. Had either gotten loose, it could have injured or killed him. He'd been stupid to take the chance, but she admired his dedication to duty.

By her estimation, Adams only had about thirty minutes of breathing mix left. They were running out of time.

The intermittent emergency lighting was enough for Mairwen to function, but left Luka mostly blind. They couldn't communicate except by gesture and lip reading, which neither she nor Luka was good at. She went looking for a safe path.

Getting out of the ruined ship was alternately frustrating, harrowing, and tedious. The worst part came when she had to dive completely underwater and search through jagged metal for a route that would accommodate pulling unconscious bodies through without risking the exosuits that were keeping them dry and breathing. The suits were designed to resist tears and punctures, but it paid to be cautious.

The only thing that terrified her more than being in open water was being in enclosed water, like a flooded ship. She focused on her strong desire to get Luka and the others to safety, telling herself she could fall apart later. She finally found a route that would take them to a spot beyond the hull, where they could float to the surface. Then they could tackle the next hurdle of finding dry land.

She swam back to Luka and found him propping up a shaky but now awake Adams. Adams grinned weakly when he saw her, which surprised her because no one but Luka ever did that, until she realized Adams hadn't known until then that she'd survived the crash.

It was easier to keep Haberville's form moving with Adams helping, though he insisted on taking his railgun and the xeno kit with them instead of coming back for them, and Luka did the same with the medical kit. It seemed to take forever to escape the wreck, and they nearly lost the xeno kit more than once because Adams was still impaired.

Once in open water, they used the buoyancy of the waterproof kits to lead them to the surface. It was either dawn or dusk, she couldn't tell which. All she could see as she treaded water were oily patches and floating debris. The exosuit made movement awkward, and a part of her mind was still gibbering in the corner about being in the water. She looked for a bigger piece of flotsam that could help support Haberville so Luka didn't have to keep holding up her weight.

Luka had other ideas. He began swimming with purpose, towing Haberville's exosuit by the conduit harness he'd rigged. Mairwen let Adams go next, and followed in case he needed assistance. She narrowed her focus to just following, just swimming, so she wouldn't have to think about the surrounding water that might stretch for endless kilometers.

It came as a surprise when her foot hit something sloped, and she looked up to realize they'd reached a sandy, rock-strewn shore. The increased light told her they'd landed at dawn. Adams was struggling with the kit, and ahead, she saw Luka dragging Haberville and the medical kit in the silty mud. She helped Adams first, then Luka.

They ended up sitting on dry ground among some scraggly shrubs, about six meters from the water's edge. Behind them was what looked like the edge of a forest, but it was still too dark to see details. Luka got her and Adams's attention, then unsealed his own exosuit and took a deep breath of air. They both unsealed their suits, and Adams took several deep breaths. They helped steadily improving Haberville with hers.

"The planet's oxygen levels are a little high, but probably not enough to hurt us," said Luka, reading from his exosuit's display.

"I never want to get that close to flatlining my air supply again," said Adams feelingly. "And no more ship crashes, either. My head *hurts*."

Luka laughed sympathetically, and the sound soothed Mairwen, though she couldn't have said why, since he was obviously alive and unhurt. Perhaps because she wasn't in the water anymore and could hear him.

"I've never blacked out like that before," said Haberville. "Maybe my blood pressure bottomed out or something. I'm still dizzy."

"Maybe syncope," said Luka. When both Adams and Haberville gave him a blank look, he added, "Sudden loss of blood to the brain. That final bounce was intense."

Luka and Adams helped Haberville stand so she could try walking, but she couldn't reliably stay upright when they let go. She kept tilting over to her left, like her sense of balance didn't know which way was up.

Trusting they'd ask for her help if needed, Mairwen stepped away and turned up her senses, trying to get a feel of the sounds and smells of their new environment. The lapping water had a rhythm to it, like ocean tides, but shallower, and it smelled slightly salty. She hadn't seen or heard any insect or bird sounds, but that presumed the hybrid planet's fauna was terra-like. The air was warm, even though it was dawn and near water. From what Haberville's scan data had indicated, heat could become a problem.

The smells were all new and complex. All Mairwen could do was start tagging them in her memory for later association with sources.

The light breeze shifted and brought a whiff of lubricant and fluids from the ship, which in the increasing light, appeared to be about a hundred meters from the shore. From its silhouette, it looked like it was stuck in the lakebed at an angle, with the nav and engine pods at the waterline. She imagined the ship's manufacturers hadn't envisioned a crash landing on a lakeshore when they advertised the ship as being "wilderness ready."

She went back to where Luka and Adams were. Haberville still sat, looking pale and nauseated. The scents of Luka and the others were comfortingly familiar.

"Luka, where did we land?" she asked. Since he'd unerringly taken them to shore, she assumed he'd seen visuals after they'd hit the atmosphere.

He gave her a quick smile, perhaps because she'd unthinkingly called him by his first name in public, if Adams and Haberville counted as public.

"On a peninsula. Haberville aimed the ship for it, but we hit some trees and tumbled in just short. I saw the shore as we went in. The lake is big, probably a hundred and sixty kilometers across and five hundred kilometers long. We're about sixteen kilometers from what looked like a large building and a landing field with an interstellar ship. The base was well lit." He pointed vaguely toward the trees. "We have the coordinates, so we should be able to find it with the xeno kit's readers. This part of the continent has low-energy geoposition transmitters about every six hundred kilometers or so, in a grid pattern."

He made eye contact with Adams and Haberville. "The installation may not be the safest place to go, but the alternatives are worse."

Adams and Haberville nodded their agreement. Mairwen nodded, too, for their benefit. Luka already knew she'd go wherever he was going.

She didn't see any way to avoid going back into the ship to look for salvageable supplies they'd need to stay alive, and that meant going back into the inky brown water. Despite the temperature control in her exosuit, she shivered. She decided she could at least wait until there was more sunlight.

"Adams, Haberville," asked Luka, "did your gunnin training include wilderness survival skills?"

Adams snorted. "Just the basics, like don't drink unpurified water and stay away from predators." His sweeping wave indicated the crashed ship in the lake and the trees. "It sure as hell didn't cover anything like this."

Haberville just shook her head, then winced and put her fingers to her temples to rub.

Mairwen sighed. She'd have preferred not to admit any knowledge at all, but they needed her expertise to survive. "I have training. I participated in planet-fall expedition challenges."

It was the best excuse she'd been able to come up with to explain her skills. She'd actually been on one once, but only because it gave her access to a target.

At this rate, she should just issue a press release to the top newsfeeds that she was a legendary death tracker and get it over with.

CHAPTER 16

LUKA COULDN'T HELP but smile at Mairwen's cover story as Adams expressed amazement and interest.

Actually, Luka kept wanting to smile ever since he'd seen Mairwen's face above him through the nav pod door she'd pried open. It had taken the heart-freezing fear of losing her to realize he was deeply and madly in love with the woman. She was ferociously competent with the extraordinary, and quirkily awkward with the simplest of things, especially human interactions. He had no idea how to make it happen yet, but he wanted her to be a part of his life and wanted to be a part of hers. But first, they had to get off this planet alive.

"I have to go back to the ship," she was saying. "We need water containers and edible food, and if we're lucky, weapons and camp gear." Something in her tone made him look at her more closely, and he thought he detected uneasiness. Knowing how reserved she was, he probably wouldn't get a straight answer out of her if he asked directly.

"Adams," he said, "how much breathing mix has your suit regenerated?"

"About ninety minutes' worth," Adams said, peering at the display. "Call me Jerzi, by the way. I figure fellow crash survivors should use first names."

Luka nodded his acknowledgment. "Call me Luka."

"I'm Eve," said Haberville, then gave Adams a coy look. "We could have been Adams and Eve." Adams looked puzzled, clearly not understanding the reference. Eve gave an exasperated sigh.

Luka waited for Mairwen to give them her first name, but she didn't. Maybe she didn't care. He smiled at her. "Breathing mix?"

"Seven hours, forty-one minutes."

He nodded. "Mine says six hours plus a little." He turned back to Jerzi. "If we swap rebreather units, are you up for another swim? Since Morganthur is our survival expert, you and I should become her security detail."

He heard her soft snort and gave her an amused smile in reply. He ignored Eve's peeved frown, which had become her current default expression. She probably had a killer headache.

"Fine with me," said Jerzi, and started peeling out of the suit so the rebreather could be removed and replaced. "Too bad we don't have dive gear. That'd be more fun."

Once out of the suit, Jerzi took off down the shore to go relieve himself, claiming he hated the way it felt in the exosuit.

Luka took the opportunity to ask Mairwen if there was any reason they should wear exosuits on their upcoming trek.

She looked toward the trees, then back to him and Eve. "No," she said. "It'll make you clumsy, and if the temperature controls fail, you'll overheat too fast. But keep your armor on. Don't roll up your sleeves, and keep your cuffs and collar tight if you can." She looked at the forest again. "I want a closer look at the trees."

"I'll come with you," said Luka. He wasn't willing to let her out of his sight again so soon.

He looked at Eve. "Jerzi can help you get your suit off when he comes back."

"Good," she said, massaging her neck and wincing as she eyed the lake. "It's not safe out here. We need to get to that base."

He and Mairwen walked in companionable silence over the hardened sand to the tree line. She was looking intently her surroundings, as if all her extraordinary senses were fully engaged. He imagined no one but other trackers had ever seen her like that. He glanced back to see Jerzi just returning to Haberville's position on the shore, about fifty meters from where they stood.

"Why are you nervous about going back to the ship?" he asked quietly.

She looked away, then down. "I dislike deep water," she said. Her mild words belied the brief glimpse of fear he saw in her eyes. It was the first time he'd ever seen her afraid, or at least the first time she'd ever let him see it.

"Then I'll go..." he started to say, but she cut him off.

"I'm better suited for it." She had the quietly stubborn look he'd come to know well.

He sighed, knowing she wouldn't let him put himself in danger. She didn't seem to understand he felt the same way about her, especially since she'd admitted the lake scared her.

With another quick look to make sure Jerzi and Eve were distracted, Luka closed the distance to Mairwen and cupped her face in his hands. "You are a wonder," he said softly, then kissed her thoroughly, letting her needy response nourish his soul. He stepped back, though not as far away as he had been. The slightly dazed look and small smile she gave him made him almost light-headed.

Ultimately, it took three trips back and forth, but Mairwen and Jerzi managed to salvage a fair amount of useful gear and additional weapons, mostly personal hand weapons and one rifle. Each time she was gone, Luka worried, and each time she came back, he found a way to touch her, and once even steal a brief kiss while Jerzi and Eve weren't looking.

An hour after sunrise, the temperature had already ramped up to sweaty hot, so they rigged a temporary sled and dragged the gear into the shade of the trees. There, they spread everything out to take inventory and figure out how to make packs of it. Jerzi and Mairwen removed and packed their exosuits, but kept the grey flexin armor, the same as Luka and Eve already had. Although the suits made their packs heavier, they were their only protection from possible future inhospitable conditions. Under her armor, Mairwen wore a black shirt and pants. The color combination reminded Luka of the first time he'd met her, and he was startled to realize it had been only two weeks ago. It seemed like he'd known her for months or longer. How had he fallen in love with her in such a short amount of time?

If they were going to make it to the installation, their first need was potable water beyond what they'd gleaned from the ship. The lake water was too salty to drink, so Mairwen told them to look for puddles, cupped leaves, and the like. She also had Jerzi find broad-spectrum antibiotics in the medical kit and made them each take a dose.

"None of us has immunity to anything on this planet," she explained. "Try not to swallow or inhale anything, or get stung or bitten."

Jerzi was amused. "No drinking, no breathing. Got it."

Luka grinned when he saw that it took Mairwen a moment to realize she was being teased, and laughed aloud when she raised an eyebrow at him in mild exasperation.

The xeno kit had three geoposition readers, and Luka used one of them to calibrate the kit's two compasses, one of which he gave to Mairwen. They'd been able to salvage a few hand lights, but not enough to allow them to walk safely in the dark. They were close enough to the planet's equator that they should have about twelve or thirteen hours each of light and dark, since the axial tilt was close to Earth standard.

By tacit agreement, they took turns swapping out the heaviest pack, except for Eve, who still had balance problems. Jerzi refused to let anyone carry his railgun, but he grudgingly let Luka take the ammo case for part of the journey. Away from the lake, the terrain grew rockier and less flat, making the travel hard going in some spots. The trees blocked the worst of the heat, but the high humidity made for hot, thirsty travel. They'd stopped for a rest after a particularly difficult section in early afternoon, and Eve asked for a meal pack. She'd been gamely keeping up and apologized that she wasn't in as good physical shape as the rest of them.

While Jerzi and Haberville dug for meal packs, Mairwen drew Luka aside near a tree a few meters away.

"I want to scout ahead for the easiest path," she said quietly. "Give me thirty minutes."

"Okay." He helped her unload her pack so she carried only what she considered essential. When she shouldered the pack and started to leave, he stopped her and turned her to face him.

"Be careful," he said, emphasizing each word. He clasped both her hands and brought them together between their bodies. He gave her fingers a gentle squeeze. "I worry about you."

"I know." She gave him a small smile. "It's nice." She raised their joined hands up and kissed his knuckles before letting go and vanishing into the trees.

Her tender gesture was such a little thing, but coming from her, it meant a lot.

He turned back to Jerzi and Eve, glad that only Jerzi had noticed Mairwen's affection. He didn't want a renewal of Eve's hostility, which he suspected was owed somewhat to her suspicion that his impartiality was compromised.

* * * * *

Mairwen dropped into half-tracker mode and ghosted through the trees, looking for a tall one to climb. The canopy overhead was high and rainforest-like, but it was eerily silent at ground level. She saw mosses, and the leaves of the low-growing ferns and shrubs looked simple, though her botany training had only focused on identifying useful poisonous plants. She also heard the low buzz of insects, though she had yet to see any, and the distant sounds of tumbling water suggested a stream or river to the northeast. The humidity level suggested they should prepare for rain.

She selected a likely tree at the top of an incline. She attached the climbing spurs they'd salvaged to her boots and wrists, adjusted her pack, and started up the tree. The wood where she'd gouged it started leaking a sticky, pungently acidic sap, and soon clouds of tiny flies hovered around the drips and the residue on her spurs. Fortunately, the flies weren't interested in her sweat or eye moisture, but their numbers made them a nuisance. They also weren't the right frequency for the buzz she'd been hearing, so she was deliberately cautious about moving leaves and vine tendrils as she climbed, not wanting to disturb a hidden insect nest.

When she'd gone as high as she could without chancing broken limbs, either the tree's or hers, she let time come to normal speed and surveyed the terrain. The wind at that height was hot, humid, and gusty. The canopy went on for kilometers in every direction except back toward the lake. About three hundred meters to the east, she saw a winged creature with a long tail zoom up and back down, too fast and too far away for her to make out any details. It was the first non-insect animal life she'd seen.

There was a distinct lack of diversity at the canopy level, where she would have expected the greatest variety. It was like an unfinished interactive exhibit meant to look like a rainforest.

To the northwest, toward the installation, she saw several hillocks of trees, but nothing that suggested an insurmountable obstacle. They'd have to deal with any rivers as they came to them. The greyish clouds to the north looked billowy and dense, and considering the surprisingly strong wind was southward, the clouds were probably bringing rain. She thought Luka would have liked the view, then realized she didn't know if he liked heights. There was still a lot she didn't know about him.

Enough sight-seeing, she told herself, and climbed back down the tree. She used some damp moss to wipe the sap off the climbing spurs before putting them in her pack. She was grateful that the canopy protected the ground level from the wind, although she would have liked more sunlight. Her muscles were sore from exertion and her bruises hurt, and she felt itchy under the clothes and armor, light as they were.

She made herself drink several swallows of water, then slipped back into half-tracker mode and ran northwest as far as she figured they'd be able to get that day and looked for places to rest for the night. She'd only had to backtrack a couple of times to find the easiest routes. Sleeping off the ground was best, if they could rig the tarps into hammocks and none of them were restless sleepers. She used her wrist knife to test a tree with rougher bark and discovered it didn't leak sap when pierced, which was good to know.

On her way back, following her own scent to retrace her route, she made a point to note the locations of high ground, in case the rains were sufficiently intense to flood the swales.

About twenty trees before she got to the clearing where she'd left Luka and the others, she shifted herself into realtime. She could feel the burn from her metabolism and knew she'd have to eat soon and sleep that evening, or risk collapse later. She made shuffling noises with her feet so they'd know she was coming, and hopefully not shoot her.

Luka appeared almost immediately to meet her halfway and hand her a protein drink, which she gratefully accepted. His smile at seeing her made her heart skip. She was still feeling profound relief that he'd survived. She busied her hands with the drink pouch to keep herself from reaching for him. If she started, she'd never stop.

"Did you have a nice walk in the park?" he asked with a teasing smile. His hands were balled in his pockets as he walked, as if he had to fight the same temptation she did.

"Yes." She smiled because he was there and smelled so nice, so familiar. "We can make good progress until dark, if Haberville remains mobile."

"She will. She wants to get to the base as much as any of us." He companionably nudged her shoulder with his as they walked. "Jerzi plans to ask you all about exploration marathons."

She gave him an exasperated look. Luka laughed and put a companionable arm around her shoulders for a quick squeeze. "Just tell him you were young and frisky, and you didn't compete."

"Frisky?" Her dubious tone made him laugh even louder.

There was a disconcerting sameness to the terrain, reinforcing the impression it was like traveling through an unfinished exhibit. They made good progress, stopping when it looked like Haberville was in need of a rest. Each time, Jerzi determinedly collected samples of the plants using the xeno kit's equipment, and enlisted the others to help. Haberville cooperated grudgingly, complaining it was a waste of time.

"Could be," said Jerzi, as he sealed a packet filled with a sample of reddish moss and stored it in the kit. "But if we make it out of here, I want something to show for it besides a 'lived to tell the tale' story for my great grandchildren. Whoever killed our ship, whoever thought letting a freaking hybrid planet live was a good idea, needs to pay."

Mairwen hadn't given much thought to the politics or ethics of human galactic expansion. As she walked, she considered Jerzi's underlying premise that safety could only be found on Earth-like worlds, even if it required finding viable alien worlds and either remaking them in Earth's image or killing them. She wasn't so sure it was right. It felt too much like what the CPS had done to her.

The threatened rains finally came late in the afternoon, but they weren't heavy enough to require stopping and waiting them out. The tree canopy filtered the rain into fine mist, making it like walking in a wet sauna. Their clothes were sopping with sweat and steam.

When they at last got to the hill Mairwen had found earlier, she called a halt and explained her notion of rigging the tarps they carried to the trees so they and their supplies would be high enough off the ground to avoid floods and any possible predators. None of them had seen recognizable signs of any large mammals or reptiles, but that didn't mean there weren't any.

She let Jerzi and Luka plan where tarps and ropes would go, and she and Jerzi did the climbing to secure them. Even though she tried to be slower than Jerzi and made a few deliberate mistakes, Jerzi was enthusiastic in his praise of her skill, and even Haberville looked grudgingly impressed. Mairwen would have much preferred to be ignored, although she admitted to herself that she enjoyed seeing the admiration on Luka's face.

Her joints were starting to ache, meaning she needed food and rest soon, or she'd be no use to anyone. She was increasingly stiff and sore from her earlier exertions with the pod doors and getting out of the ruined ship. She must have let it show, because Luka made her sit on a high tree root and eat a self-heating meal pack while he and Jerzi finished the setup. Jerzi handed out meal packs to himself, Luka, and Haberville, and Mairwen accepted a second one.

Too soon, the comfortable, companionable silence was interrupted.

"This reminds me of my first cohab, Moswin," said Haberville. "He loved to hike, the farther from the comforts of civilization, the better. Which was still better than my second cohab, who never saw a mountain he didn't want to climb. A few years after we terminated our agreement, he got himself killed on one."

"Sorry to hear that," murmured Jerzi.

"Don't be. He was mostly a jerk." She smiled wistfully. "But nova-hot in bed."

She smoothed a stray lock of hair off her face. Her perfect fire-opal fingernails and the woven strands of bright blue and shiny gold in her hair looked incongruous with the dirt and grime on the rest of her.

"Now Heike, my third, was a city boy, through and through. Intergalactic banker, liked the finer things, and spoke about twenty languages. I'd still be with him, except he wanted me home all the time. It's kind of hard to pilot a ship from your living room." She rolled her eyes. "Plus, he wanted to get married."

Jerzi sighed. "I'd like to be married, but it's… complicated."

"Marriages are always complicated. It's an outdated concept. Cohab agreements are much easier to get in and out of."

He shrugged. "I prefer marriage, but my kid's mother's family hates me. The feeling is mutual. Dhorya and I are saving all we can so she and Pico can move to Rekoria. If we married now, the family would throw them out immediately."

"Family can bleed the life out of you, that's for sure," Haberville said sympathetically. "What do you say, Luka? Marriage or cohab?"

For once, Mairwen wanted to hear the answer to Haberville's overly personal inquiries. Luka's past was his own, but Mairwen couldn't help being curious.

"I've never been in either." He used his fork to scrape up the last of the green goo that the package claimed was creamed spinach.

Haberville was amused. "What, no near-misses? No prospects?"

"Nope." His tone was bland, but Mairwen sensed the irritation in his voice.

"You know what they say," Haberville said, waving a dismissive hand. "There are plenty of fish in the sea if the local minnows aren't biting."

She turned to Mairwen and smiled. "Your turn, Morganthur. Marriage? Cohab? String of broken hearts?"

Mairwen affected deafness and ignored the question. She would tell Luka if he wanted to know, but it was no one else's business.

"Come on, Morganthur. You know about all of us." Haberville's wheedling tone had an edge to it.

Mairwen was too tired to listen any more. She folded her empty food container and sealed it, then slid it into the bottom of her pack. No sense attracting hungry local critters unnecessarily.

In an unlooked-for bonus, Haberville's evident irritation caused her not to speak for a full seven minutes. If Mairwen had known that was all it took to silence the social interrogation, she'd have tried the tactic days ago.

There were only three tarps and nets big enough for sleeping humans, meaning two of them would have to share. Mairwen rigged slings for watchers above each tarp. At least there was enough clear plastic sheeting to protect each of them if it rained again.

Haberville was not a climber, and needed both Luka and Jerzi to help her into her tarp. She was lucky they were along, because Mairwen had no patience with intentional helplessness and would have left her to fend for herself. Particularly since she had continued her habit of leaving the cleanup for others. Mairwen flattened the empty meal pack container Haberville had left on the ground and put it in the bottom of her own pack.

Mairwen estimated they had one more day of travel until they got to the installation, and wished they could go faster. When the *Berjalan*'s saboteurs eventually came looking to confirm their kill and didn't find orbiting wreckage, the first place to look would be the planet. Their only slim hope was to find safety in the more defensible building on the base.

She climbed the tree, then flipped up and over into the rope sling she had rigged just above Luka's tarp. She'd slept in worse conditions, but not since she'd left her former life. Civilization had made her soft, her brain said sourly. She ignored it. Being civilized, being human, was a price worth paying if it kept her with Luka.

He was stretched out below, hands behind his head. Even in shadow, he was dangerously handsome, and her memory filled in what her eyes couldn't see in the rapidly failing light. The scent of him made her feel warmer than the noonday sun.

"Come be with me," he murmured quietly, and reached out a hand to her.

His smile and rumbling voice were so enticing that she melted inside, and her chest and arms ached with a hollowness that only his touch could relieve. They'd been amazingly lucky thus far, surviving a crash on a hybrid planet that hadn't killed them yet. Suddenly, she didn't want to spend another second apart from him.

She piked and kept her knees bent, then slid down and straightened so she was only supported by her flexed feet in the sling. She reached down to the connector line that supported the tarp and released her feet. She balanced on her hands long enough to drop her legs one at a time onto the tarp, then lifted the net and slid her body down along Luka's, into the circle of his arms.

"Show off," he said, so quietly he was almost whispering.

It had been showing off, because he openly delighted in her abilities. "You're a bad influence," she breathed. "You make me want to."

She snuggled closer to him and let more of her body drape over his because he felt so wonderfully good, and it soothed her sore muscles. She didn't mind the heat of the night, and thought Luka must be happy to be warm. He had to have been miserable on the cold planet where he grew up.

She wanted to talk to him about arranging watch shifts, but a yawn surprised her.

"Hey, Jerzi," Luka said loudly. "Could you take first watch? Four hours, then wake me?"

"You bet, sir," came the good-natured response. "I'll set a timer."

He turned his head toward Haberville's tarp. "Eve, we'll give you a pass for tonight. Mairwen will take third watch."

Haberville coughed and mumbled something that sounded like assent.

Mairwen nestled her head on Luka's chest just under his shoulder. She felt his fingers stroking her hair, and she couldn't resist sliding her thigh over his and splaying her hand on his chest, feeling the power and sound of his breathing, like a soothing metronome. It felt right, and comforting. Her hormones stirred at the feel of him, but fatigue won. She sighed and settled into the bliss of his buttery, pearwood-scented warmth.

"Relax, *sæta*," he whispered, the air from his breath ruffling her hair. "Let me watch over you for just this once. You can be our dedicated sentinel again in the morning."

She drifted into a deep sleep punctuated with dreams of running with Luka by her side.

CHAPTER 17

BECAUSE LUKA HAD taken second watch, she'd gotten a full eight hours of sleep, which she'd needed to compensate for her use of tracker mode. That she'd only stirred when Luka had gently awakened her for her turn at third watch was a testament to how much she'd come to trust him.

As soon as it was light enough, she downed a bland protein bar, then went scouting while the others ate, broke camp, and repacked their supplies. Her foray confirmed her worry that today would be a rougher trip. Already, they'd begun seeing denser vegetation as they'd traveled farther away from the lake. Today it got worse as she went on. They'd have to detour around large, dense thickets, adding unwelcome distance between them and the installation.

The intermittent low humming she'd been hearing was more noticeable, though she still couldn't determine its source. An increasing sense of urgency drove her to stay in half-tracker mode all the way back to camp, even though it meant she'd need more food and water immediately and more rest later.

When she arrived back at the hill, sweat pouring down her face and neck, Luka and the others were ready to go. Without asking, he handed Mairwen a hot meal pack. Fortunately, they had more than enough to get them to the installation. After that, it was anyone's guess as to what they'd find.

It was hard and hot travel, but at least Haberville seemed to have more stamina after a good night's rest, although she'd developed a cough. She complained more, too, but Jerzi was well able to handle her, and his attentive care kept her mollified. During a break later in the day, when Luka and Jerzi had gone off to relieve themselves, Mairwen's sensitive hearing picked up part of a conversation between them.

"...piloting skills saved our asses, so I'm willing to cut her some slack." said Jerzi. "She reminds me of my mother."

"I advise you," replied Luka with mock seriousness, "to never, ever tell her that."

"Don't worry," Jerzi said with a snort. "I only *look* that stupid."

In the afternoon, they lucked into a freshwater stream and filled all their containers, though it added to the weight they had to carry. Fortunately, their medical kit had plenty of chemelec water filters, more than was usual. Luka's forethought, she imagined.

The inland thickets were home to a new kind of fly, larger and slower than the sap-loving version that congregated under low-lying leaves. When a passing boot or knee disturbed them, they puffed up in swarming clouds before settling down again a few minutes later. Jerzi caught a few of them in stasis vials and stored them with the other samples.

At sundown, they were still a good two kilometers from the installation. The waning moonlight wouldn't make it past the tree canopy. Moving in the unrelenting darkness wasn't an option. It made Mairwen edgy to be so close to the installation and potential danger.

As they finished eating, Luka proved to have been harboring the same concerns as Mairwen.

"Considering that ship and how well lit the base was when we came in, we have to assume it's staffed and protected on some level. If whoever tried to kill us at Horvax finds our ship in the lake, they'll likely be using the base to organize their search operations. We didn't try to hide our trail."

Mairwen frowned. It was something she should have considered. Another mistake she hoped wouldn't cost them.

Luka continued. "This forest is amazingly quiet, which means we'll hear anyone on foot a lot sooner than usual, but they can hear us, too. We'll need to travel clean and quiet from here on out." He scooped up a discarded wrapper that Haberville had left on a high tree root. "Eve, how good are you with projectiles or beamers?"

She made an equivocal gesture with her hand. "I can hit stationary targets with either, but firefights aren't my ace, and I don't think I can run here. The air feels heavy when I breathe. I'm usually at the flight controls." She pointed at Jerzi and smiled indulgently. "There's your marksman, or so he says."

Jerzi confirmed it with a nod that wasn't cocky, just confident. "That's why I saved my railgun." He pointed to the shoulder bag that hadn't left his side. "It's part of why La Plata hired me."

"Good." Luka turned back to Haberville. "We'll give you the projectile rifle and its magazines. Mairwen and I will pick from what's left."

After helping Jerzi settle Haberville on her sleeping tarp, Luka led Mairwen to the pitifully small pile of other weapons they'd salvaged from the ship. Not counting the few knives and one machete, or the projectile rifle already reserved for Haberville, the selection included two tiny low-res beamers, two handled beamers and various powerpacks, a solar-charged cutting laser, and one wide-array plasma gun, which would have stopped a rampaging rhinoceros, but for which they had no extra chargers.

"Pick your poison, milady." He gave her a courtly bow.

She shook her head. "You should choose a weapon you're comfortable with."

"I'm a decent shot with any of them. I've learned to shoot practically every personal weapon on the market in the last twenty years. Fringe benefit of my job." He gave her an impish grin. "Keeps me entertained."

She was amused that his career suited his personality and talent so perfectly. A job without new experiences or mysteries would have bored him to distraction.

She selected a small low-res beamer and a handful of its power beads as the stealthiest option and slipped them into her pack. At her suggestion, she and Luka tried pulling out a couple of the exosuit comms to see if they could serve as a makeshift comm net for the team. Unfortunately, they required the suit's power to work, and wearing clumsy exosuits would make them easy targets.

Jerzi volunteered to take first watch again that night. Haberville declared that she'd be useless for a watch shift and exempted herself. Mairwen was glad Luka didn't fight it. Haberville was still coughing, and Mairwen wouldn't put it past her to be deliberately incompetent just to prove her point.

Mairwen didn't bother creating a sling for herself; she simply went straight to Luka's tarp. She needed the rest, and she wanted it to be with Luka. If Haberville wanted to comment on the sleeping arrangements, Mairwen would deal with her later.

She crawled into the tarp and arranged the netting, then rolled aside to make room for Luka as he slid in. She put her head on his chest and draped her arm and leg across him.

He wrapped his arms around her and kissed the top of her head. His breathing was rhythmic and his heartbeat was strong and steady, and she felt sublimely content in those few dozen seconds.

Despite her exhaustion, Mairwen the tracker wanted to ghost into the night and check the installation, but Mairwen the woman wanted to stay with Luka and memorize every contour of his body with hers, and steep herself in his warmth while she had the chance. The feel of him next to her was addictive. It would be hard to give up. Even assuming they made it back to civilization, she didn't know what the future would hold once their normal routine was restored.

Resolving to quit worrying and just live for the moment, she allowed herself to be lulled to sleep by the quiet syncopation of his heart and breath.

She came awake to a new sound in the deep dark of the night. She was alone, but she knew Luka couldn't have gone far. She sat upright and turned up her senses to nearly full-tracker mode.

She heard and scented Luka on the corner of the tarp where it attached to the anchoring line around the tree. It was pitch black, except for the faint indicator light on a powerpack for the beamer he'd selected. The slow-motion time of tracker mode made it surreal.

"Mairwen?" he said very quietly, though to her, it seemed like he was shouting. He'd probably felt the tarp move and heard her movements. She turned down her senses to a more manageable level.

She kept her voice barely above a whisper so as not to wake the others. "Flitter, probably a high-low. Coming this way from the northeast. About ten or fifteen minutes out." She looked up at the tree canopy, where only a few slivers of weak moonlight leaked through. She slid carefully across the tarp toward him. "Spectrum and bioscans won't see us at night, but if they deep-scan for tech, they might find us if they get close enough. If we're lucky, they'll think it's bleedover from the base's security perimeter. I think that's the low buzz I've been hearing."

"It's at least five hours until dawn," he said. "Nothing we can do right now without killing ourselves." He eased off his perch and down into the tarp. She slid back to the center, and he followed. Still sitting, he wrapped his arms around her and kissed her lightly, then whispered in her ear. "Can you see in the dark?"

The banked fire of her desire started to flare, and she nuzzled his neck to fill her nose with his complex, exotic scent. Her softer chest, with a life of its own, arched into the hard wall of his. It took effort to remember what he'd asked. "No, but I don't need as much light. I'll scout about thirty minutes before sunrise."

She felt him nod. He kissed her lightly, then with more heat. She responded, and her heart rate increased along with his. She strained to prevent herself from moaning in pleasure. He broke off the kiss with a ragged sigh.

"I'm on duty," he whispered. He blew out a long breath. "I wouldn't notice a battalion of mech-suited Jumpers if we keep doing this."

She caressed his beard-roughened jawline. "Neither would I."

"Are you…" He hesitated, then began again. "This is probably indelicate of me to ask, but do you have a birth control and cycle implant?"

"Yes," she said quietly. "Menses and reproduction would have impaired my effectiveness. But just to be sure, they harvested all my ova before the full alteration procedure."

"Harvested, not destroyed?"

"Yes. Rumor said it was for a reproduction program, trying to make more of us."

Luka was silent for a long moment. "Does it bother you?"

"No, it's done." The past was past. "Does it bother you?"

"That you can't reproduce? No. That they treated you like an exotic pet to be bred? *Fökk*, yes."

There was nothing more to say. She settled for nestling into him while they waited and listened. She could easily hear Jerzi and Haberville breathing, and even Luka could hear Eve's occasional coughs.

Eleven minutes later, the preternatural quiet of the forest allowed him to finally hear the flitter engine, too. To her ears, it got closer, changed pitch and echo, then went silent.

"I think it landed on the airfield," she whispered.

She felt him shift. "Will you go back to sleep until then?" He slid his hand up and around to her face and neck and stroked her jaw with his thumb. "You've been running yourself ragged for us. You need the rest." His tenderness flushed some of the tension out of her, and she turned herself more fully into him and wrapped her arms around his waist.

"If it pleases you," she said softly, smiling even though she knew he couldn't see it.

"It does, *hjarta mitt*." He gently laid her back down and adjusted his legs so her head rested on his thigh as he sat cross-legged. He stroked her hair. "You do."

She drifted into sleep, only waking when he nudged her for her turn for third watch. He stretched out next to her where she sat and was soon asleep. She was glad that somewhere in his career, despite his civilian occupation, he'd learned the skill of sleeping at will. She admired him for the variety of things he'd learned and could put to practical use. She resisted the temptation to stroke his hair, not wanting to wake him, and not trusting herself to stop there.

She used her time in the dark as a tracker should, monitoring their environment and evaluating various scenarios with the flitter at the installation and how to use them to achieve her goal of keeping them safe until they could be rescued.

In the best-case scenario, they could neutralize any installation defenses, avoid getting killed by whoever was in the flitter or the ship, and dig in until help arrived. She had to assume at least one of their distress calls had gotten through to La Plata, and that they'd be bringing firepower. In a discussion earlier that day, Luka and Haberville had thought it likely that Zheer would call in Concordance Command as the best option for countering a pharma company with big secrets and deep pockets for multiple squads of mercs. The question was how quickly Zheer could get Space Div to respond.

Non-tracker thoughts kept intruding every time Luka stirred in his sleep or she became aware of the sound of his breathing or his scent.

It was going to be difficult to go back to Etonver, seeing him only when he needed a personal security detail. Assuming she'd be allowed to continue in that capacity once they heard Haberville's accusations of a jack crew background. While the last two weeks may have been unusual for Luka, he'd be able to pick up where he left off as a top investigator for La Plata, and would do even better since he was doggedly regaining control of his talent.

But her life had changed forever. There would be no more anonymity of the night shift, no more camouflage of the dull and ordinary, no more safe solitude. It terrified her, but the thought of never seeing Luka again terrified her even more, even though she knew the CPS would destroy him if they ever discovered her.

She was used to planning everything, and the unknowns made her uneasy. Her carefully mapped, invisible life had become a puzzle to which she had only some of the pieces, and only the vaguest notion of what the whole might look like.

CHAPTER 18

DAWN FINALLY APPROACHED. Mairwen shouldered the lightened pack she'd prepared the night before, drank the nasty-tasting but nutritional protein drink, then tugged on Luka's booted foot to awaken him. He stretched and groaned softly, then lifted the netting and sat up. His thick hair looked even more wavy and disarrayed than usual, and they all desperately needed basic hygiene and clean clothes. She'd do anything for a clean pair of socks.

She touched his shoulder and spoke softly. "When it's light enough, eat and break camp. If you think I've been gone too long, don't come after me unless you take at least Jerzi as your security detail."

"How long is 'too long'?"

She shrugged, then remembered it was still too dark for him to see. "I don't know. Two hours at least."

"Okay." He found her hand and kissed the back of it. "Try not to get killed."

She slid her hand to his face and cupped his jaw, enjoying the unexpected texture of the soft stubble of his beard. "Stay safe."

She swung down to the forest floor and started a fast walk toward the installation. The closer she got to the security perimeter, the more annoying the low humming became, until she finally had to shut down her awareness of it, at the cost of some sensitivity to sounds beyond it.

The field fence would have been a lot quieter if one of its ground points, about ninety meters to the west, hadn't been downed by a recently fallen tree. The leaking acidic sap made a feedback loop with every power pulse. It only took a careful walk along the tree trunk to breach the fence.

About two hundred meters beyond, she found the landing field and nearby large, flat building, which someone had helpfully lit up like a holiday display. The interstellar ship Luka had seen before the *Berjalan* had crashed was still parked on the landing field.

Although nearby trees had been clear-cut when the installation was built, it looked like no one had bothered since then to keep the undergrowth from encroaching. Mairwen dropped into half-tracker mode as she circled the irregularly shaped one-story building. She had plenty of time to hide behind a thicket when a uniformed man carrying a beam rifle rounded the corner. He might have discovered her if he'd been wearing his night-vision lenses in front of his eyes instead of on top of his head, but his attitude said he believed guard duty was a waste of good sack time.

She spent another forty-two minutes oozing her way through the rapidly fading shadows, listening, scenting, and gathering intelligence. The unnatural quietness of the area made it easy to hear conversations among the mercs, and their inattentiveness made it easy to avoid them as she scouted the building, ships, and perimeter. Just outside the building's oversized cargo bay doors, she lucked into an unattended stack of supplies, which she raided for useful items, the grand prize being a full case of variable frequency communication earwires and a booster. Now their small team would be able to communicate, and the mercs would have to rely on voice if they had no other earwires.

She slipped away into the forest and across the fence via the fallen tree. She took a quick reading with the compass, then made a beeline back to where she'd left the others. Luka smiled when he saw her. She wondered if she'd ever get used to the relief she felt when she saw he was alive and well.

They'd organized the gear into four packs and readied the weapons. Haberville and Jerzi sat on the forest floor, tying knots of mono line around leaves. It took her a moment to realize they were making a sniper's camouflage cloak. She handed out the liberated earwires, then told them what she'd found as Luka dug out and triggered a self-heating meal for her.

"The landing field has a light-drive ship, twice as big and three or four levels taller than the *Berjalan,* and a heavy high-low flitter that seats twelve and is outfitted with beamers. No identifying marks. The building is one level with living quarters, lab, and storage. It hasn't been occupied for a while except the last few days."

"Prophet Ayeleh's tears," muttered Haberville. "So much for taking the base quietly."

Mairwen used a stick to draw a rough map of the installation, pointing out doors and windows, and describing what little she'd gleaned about the interior. She paused to eat several quick bites of what purported to be meat.

"There are fifteen mercs wearing blue uniforms with a starburst and lightning logo. They speak a mix of English and Spanish. From what I overheard, some of them spent yesterday afternoon transferring cases of samples from the base's cold storage onto the ship. They're preparing to destroy the installation, but are waiting for a laboratory specialist to identify things worth saving. They expect her and another squad tomorrow with more samples to transfer to the ship. They have four more bases to empty and destroy on this continent, and will move the flitter and the ship to each. There are other ships on the planet of unknown type and quantity."

"Shit," said Jerzi. "They're sparking out."

"For now," said Luka. "I'd lay odds that Loyduk Pharma, or whoever, won't kill the planet. They'll just vacate it and hope they can come back in a few years after everyone has forgotten about it."

Haberville nodded. "Besides, killing a planet is expensive. If the government wants the planet poisoned, let *them* pay for it." She snorted, but it turned into a cough. "Your taxes at work."

Haberville stood and brushed the dirt off the back of her pants, a largely wasted effort considering how filthy they all were. Even their flexin armor was stained and streaked.

"That light-drive ship... Is there any way we can take it from a whole squad of company mercs?"

Luka ran his fingers through his hair, but his expression was determined. "Mairwen, any recommendations?"

Mairwen hated the pressure of sharp scrutiny from Haberville, but she knew Luka didn't really have better options than to use her expertise. Haberville already thought she was a jacker, so Mairwen wouldn't be exposing much that Haberville didn't already suspect. Haberville had little gunnin ground force experience; Jerzi was a specialist, not a tactician; and Luka had already told her his combat experience was limited to abbreviated military basic training for civilians from fourteen years ago. She'd been trained to act alone and in stealth, but at least she had plenty of experience in planning infiltrations and assaults.

"Our options are narrowing by the hour. They're planning to send five mercs in the flitter to investigate the *Berjalan* later today. They weren't expecting it." She organized her thoughts as she drank half a cup of chemically filtered water, an improvement over the taste of the meat sauce. Before Luka's continued bad influence, she hadn't paid attention to her preferences in the tastes of foods.

"The installation has two dormant shipkillers, and two mercs are working to get them and the surface-to-orbit scanners back online. If we want to neutralize them, the best time is now while they're still bottled up and distracted. They believe nothing could have survived the crash and won't expect us."

"What kind of shipkillers?" asked Luka.

When Mairwen described them in more detail, he nodded. "Üler Mark Twenties, I think. They'll be cabled with compulsator power. Ammo is loose but racked for autofeed. The targeting gimbal is comp controlled." Mairwen gave him a brief smile to tell him how much she liked that he knew things like that.

"If Lord Buddha loves us, we can take the light-drive ship, which gives us a whole lot of other options," said Haberville. "Did you see any gunports on the ship?"

"No," said Mairwen. "It looks like a transport. The flitter's two beamers are amped large-array. The mercs have rifles, sidearms, and military-grade wilderness gear. More weapons may be stored in the ship or in the building. They plan to use thermobarics to destroy the facility."

She finished the last of her meal and folded the container for packing as she talked. "We should neutralize their pilots and the shipkillers first. We can't stop them from calling for help, but based on conversations I overheard, I think it would be several hours in coming. Maybe we can get away in the flitter or the light-drive ship long enough to buy us time to be rescued."

Luka looked directly at her, then at them all. "That's what we'll do, then." Jerzi and Haberville nodded. They all looked at Mairwen expectantly.

"Our team is too small to give Jerzi a spotter. He'll have to find his own vantage points. He'll be needed to protect the rest of us and to take out the two merc pilots, if he can."

"Agreed," said Luka.

Mairwen described to Jerzi the two men she'd seen during her reconnaissance.

"Copy," Jerzi said, as he strapped an extra railgun ammo pack around his waist. Mairwen noticed his normally amiable expression had been replaced by the detached look she'd seen in people who had experience delivering death. It probably looked a lot like hers.

Mairwen fingered the low-res beamer in her pocket. "I'll run point and take down targets or identify them for you. Luka, you and Haberville will be the followup attack force, taking out as many as you can."

Luka looked grim but resolute as he handed the projectile rifle and its ammunition to Haberville. She checked the magazine and safety, then slung its strap across her right shoulder and stuffed the magazines in her pockets. Jerzi distributed the unclaimed energy weapons among the packs.

Mairwen would have liked to ask them all to disable instead of kill, because Luka didn't need to feel responsible for any more deaths, but with such an asymmetric assault force, they couldn't afford the luxury of mercy.

Haberville surprised Mairwen by pulling her aside. "You're jack crew or worse, and I don't trust you. You only care about Luka, but it's kept the rest of us alive. Get me that ship, and I'll get your lover boy and the rest of us off this Godforsaken mudball."

Mairwen nodded. She respected Haberville's piloting skills. The woman's personal opinions didn't matter as long as she did her job.

They each attached the stolen earwires to their mandibles, hooking the thin wire in the ear, then tested them while pocketing the spares. Mairwen gave Jerzi the range booster, figuring he'd be better able to protect it. She hoped they wouldn't need it, but it would be a nice fallback for when, not if, things went twisty.

It only took them twenty minutes to get to the downed tree. She crossed first, just to make sure the mercs hadn't decided to add a guard. They hadn't, so she gave the all-clear sign.

Once beyond the fence, they could hear shouting from the direction of the installation. When they got close enough, they saw two mercs fighting. Several others were cheering them on instead of separating the combatants.

Jerzi took the opportunity to slip away toward the east to find a nest for himself. Mairwen led Luka and Haberville to one of the larger dense thickets southwest of the landing field. They shucked their packs and hid them under the foliage, along with the medical and xeno sample kits.

Mairwen subvocalized into the earwires. "Give me ten minutes to check status. Luka and Haberville, take out any singles who come your way, if you can do it quietly. Jerzi, protect us as long as you can." Luka's expression was focused and determined. Haberville was, thankfully, in professional pilot mode, and had no comment, though her cough was back.

She hoped to hell Luka would be all right, because there was nothing she could do about it if he wasn't. She'd never been on a mission with a team, let alone with people she cared about.

She used the vigorous undergrowth for camouflage as she eased around the airfield toward the building. She listened closely as she circled the light-drive ship that took up about half the field, but heard nothing, not even near the ship's portal. She'd need to get inside to take control of it, but that would have to be done later.

Once clear of the ship, she got a better look at the mercs watching the skirmish. The fighters, a small man and tall woman, were still going strong, and the spectators now numbered eight. She had no idea why the squad's commander allowed the fight to continue, but she wasn't going to let the opportunity go to waste.

She slipped into half-tracker mode and ghosted closer to the corner of the building, where she discovered the mercs had rolled one of the shipkillers onto the landing field and locked its anchors. She eyed it quickly, looking for the features Luka had described, but had to duck away fast when two mercs pushed the second shipkiller, with its trailing cable, out of the big equipment storage area. It was slow going because the field's plascrete pad had cracked and buckled where vigorous rainforest plants had pushed up through it. The two mercs complained to each other about not getting any help.

It was hard to pass up the chance to disable the mercs and slag the guns with her beamer, but the likelihood of being discovered was too high, and she still needed to find the other mercs. She also decided against infiltrating the building for now, since she'd lost the cover of darkness. She subvocalized to the team what she'd seen so far. Someone snorted—Jerzi, she suspected— when she described the continuing fight and its growing audience.

She eased around the northeast side of the building, peering into the small, high windows of the sleeping areas she'd discovered during her pre-dawn reconnaissance. The rooms were empty, but the beds had been slept on. She slowed as she approached the southwest corner of the building, listening to the fight. She dropped into full-tracker mode and time *slowed...*

The smells of the vegetation were more varied, and she detected hints of charring and harsh chemicals mixed with it. She dropped into a low crouch, then stretched into a lunge that let her peek around the corner at the area where the flitter was resting.

It may once have been intended as a shaded area, but the hard canopy had fallen apart and left pieces on the ground. The burned vegetation smell came from a blackened spot on the far side of the flitter, and the chemicals were unburned accelerant, meaning somewhere there was flame-throwing equipment. More likely in the building than on the light-drive ship or the flitter, she judged. Considering the squad's lack of discipline, it wouldn't surprise her to learn they'd found a flamethrower in the building and had been playing with it.

The flitter was half-angled in between the canopy's support posts. It was unattended with its side doors wide open, but they faced toward the fighters, who were only about six meters away. Mairwen studied the mercs for a few hundred milliseconds to confirm they weren't looking her way at all, then leaped and rolled to the far side of the flitter, out of their view. She contemplated whether or not to take the unexpected opportunity to disable the flitter, knowing it to be a gamble either way.

Finally, she decided on the simple expedient of using her wrist blade to cut the control cables to the front and back airflows. It could be fixed, but it would take the mercs time to track down the problem. She chanced a peek around the back end of the flitter to see what was happening with the fight. One of the fighters had misjudged a kick and hit one of the spectators, and the group dynamics were changing.

She allowed time to speed up to half-tracker mode as she faded back to the partially charred thicket behind her and used it for cover. She told the team what she'd done as she made her way quickly to Luka and Haberville's position.

She crouched next to Luka and subvocalized the plan she'd come up with. She hoped it would survive first contact with the enemy.

CHAPTER 19

ANOTHER SHOT WHINED by, and the projectile thudded into the dirt. Luka was pinned down behind the long side of the flitter, with shooters targeting him from both ends. Thus far, the mercs had taken care not to damage the flitter, but they might be willing to sacrifice it if they got desperate. His emotions made a roiling mass in the pit of his stomach. It was completely insane to be taking on an enemy squad of fifteen, except the alternatives were even worse.

They'd started with good luck. When the fight ended, the mercs had dispersed and gone their separate ways, and he, Eve, and Mairwen had neutralized five mercs before anyone even noticed they were missing. He'd chosen the hand-held beamer with the best cohesion range, and it did the job.

Their luck continued until someone's shout drew two people out of the light-drive ship to see what was happening, and Jerzi took them both down. The remaining mercs came alive after that and the battle was on.

The mercs were using the cover of the building to shoot from, but it had several blind spots. His small team had managed to keep any of the mercs from getting to the ship, but so far hadn't been able to pry them out of the building. Luka felt the pressure of time, knowing the mercs would have called for reinforcements by now.

His and Eve's task had been to keep the mercs distracted so Mairwen could disable the shipkillers. He thought she'd already gotten one. From what he'd overheard, the mercs thought there were six or seven attackers, probably because Jerzi moved between takedowns, Luka was good at anticipating movements, Eve only took guaranteed shots, and Mairwen was devastatingly fast and deadly. It kept the remaining mercs cautious and behind the building's walls instead of boiling out to kill him, but he was still pinned.

Without the tree canopy for protection, the base was hot and getting hotter as the sun rose higher in the sky. He was sweating rivers. His beamer wasn't recharging itself anymore. He hadn't heard or seen Mairwen in the last ten minutes, and he couldn't keep the worry from intruding, no matter how much he tried to subdue it.

He almost had coronary arrest when someone slid down beside him in the dirt.

"It's me," said Jerzi, only just avoiding Luka's elbow to the face.

"Have you seen Mairwen?" Luka asked.

Just as Jerzi was shaking his head, he heard Mairwen's voice through the earwire. *"I lost my first wire. I'm fine."*

"How bad?" he subvocalized. Jerzi's puzzled look said he wasn't aware of Mairwen's overly broad definition of the word "fine."

There was a moment of silence. *"A scrape or two,"* came the answer. *"You?"*

"Functional," he replied, ignoring the blood oozing from a large, long scrape on his right thigh. It had soaked his pant leg and seeped through the armor. He looked at Jerzi, who looked uninjured but was covered in dust and dirt. "Jerzi, why are you here?"

"For you," Jerzi said, giving him a hand-beamer. He subvocalized so the team could hear. "I'm extracting Luka. Eve will keep them busy while we fall back to the shrubs where they can't see."

Mairwen gave more precise orders. *"Skirt around toward the ship. Adams, set up to take anyone coming out of the building or going to the ship. Haberville, get as close to the ship as you can so we can get in fast. Luka, on my mark, slag the second shipkiller, the one closer to the flitter."*

"Will a beamer to the compulsator be good enough?" he asked.

"Yes."

Under the cover of a flurry of weapons fire, Luka followed Jerzi as he slithered backward, aiming the hand-beamer at the window where a merc could have line of site. The window was empty.

He and Jerzi slid into the undergrowth. Somewhere along the way, Jerzi had abandoned his homemade sniper's cloak. Luka felt vulnerable as they moved, knowing the mercs had more than enough firepower to kill them. They stopped long enough for Jerzi to retrieve his railgun and ammo bag, then worked their way toward the ship.

As they traveled, Luka made it a point to confiscate several unsafetied weapons from fallen mercs. He didn't want to be caught without a working weapon again. He thought he saw Eve moving on the other side of the ship, but he couldn't be sure. Jerzi found a spot he liked and waved Luka on.

Luka crept carefully toward the end of the building where the big shipkillers were. When he had a good view of the guns, the closest one looking distinctly charred, he focused on the high bay doorway and the storeroom beyond. He thought he saw at least one merc in blue behind some stacked crates, and he knew there had to be more. He was a fast runner, but not faster than weapons could shoot. Even if his armor prevented major damage, the impact of a projectile would still knock him sideways.

Jerzi's voice came quietly in his ear. *"I've got a clear vector on one target, north corner, second window in. Should I take the shot?"*

"Not yet," Mairwen's voice said. *"You'd have to move too soon."*

"Copy," said Jerzi. He sounded marvelously calm.

Luka wished he could say the same. Waiting was almost more difficult than running for his life while dodging beams and bullets. His adrenalin pumped in fits and starts, and his stomach was in knots. He was heartily glad that he'd stayed in the civilian side of law enforcement and the military, because he'd have hated to do this for a living.

After what felt like hours but was probably only minutes, Mairwen's voice came over the wire.

"Explosion coming in five seconds. Jerzi, take your shot if available. Luka, wait until I say 'go.' Haberville, get in the ship if you can, but don't get hurt. We need you."

"Copy," said Jerzi and Eve, at the same time Luka said "Okay."

A second later, Luka heard the high-pitched whine of a projectile and shattering glass. He doubted the unlucky merc's body even had a chance to fall before a huge fireball of an ear-ringing boom shattered the silence. The northeast end of the building erupted in flames.

Inside the storage area, he saw a flash of movement as someone in blue ran toward the explosion. A high-pitched whine and a collapsing body said Jerzi had seen the runner, too. Another merc hulked out of the shadows holding a larger weapon, aiming toward the area where Luka had last seen Jerzi.

"Jerzi, move. Heatseeker pointed at you," he said.

"Already gone," said Jerzi.

Luka remembered that heatseekers were more useful in urban settings. Hot, humid climates threw off their targeting, but it would only take one hit to ruin Jerzi's whole day. Luka was tempted to shoot the merc aiming the heatseeker, but if he missed because of the bad angle, he'd give away his own position. The merc, watching the display, started swinging the muzzle in wider sweeps, trying to lock onto a target. Luka flattened himself on the ground even more and angled his body away to make himself less detectible. He hid his beamer underneath him, to mask its heat signature. He hoped Eve was doing the same.

The merc stepped toward the open doorway and froze. "You're mine, *chingado*," he said loud enough that Luka could hear. The merc took another step, but instead of firing, he sank to his knees, dropping the weapon, then collapsed. Luka thought he caught a glimpse of blood at the man's throat.

Silence prevailed.

Luka had lost count of the remaining mercs. He didn't see any in the storage area, but maybe smarter ones were hiding in the shadows.

In his ear, Mairwen said, "*Luka, go.*"

He rose to his feet and half-ran to the shipkiller, willfully ignoring how incredibly vulnerable he felt to anyone who might be in the open bay of the storage area. He pulled out one of the large hand beamers he'd acquired. He tried to visualize the specs in his head to locate the power unit so he could fry it.

Suddenly he heard the rapidly rising whine of a flitter in emergency lift mode. The flitter only got about a meter off the ground before it started listing badly to the far side. A wide-array plasma beam from the flitter cut through the awning support pillar and scored a path through the undergrowth and onto the airfield pad, then up toward the sky before cutting off. The flitter's front end swung around, and he got a glimpse of a snarling woman in merc uniform in the pilot bay. Luka knew she'd seen him. The wide-array beam stabbed out, but suddenly the flitter bucked out of control, and its beam went wide and seared the armored hull of the light-drive ship.

Luka couldn't let the flitter destroy their only hope for getting off the planet. Dropping the beamer, he unlocked the shipkiller's gimbal and free-aimed the barrel toward the flitter, then pushed the firepin. Nothing happened. The whine of tortured flitter airfoils assaulted his ears. Luka frantically looked for the problem and found a safety release. He aimed and pushed the firepin. The kickback knocked him on his ass, but the shipkiller round shot straight through the flitter, leaving a gaping hole.

Unfortunately, the flitter was still airborne, though sagging toward the back. The wide-array beam sheared off the tops of some trees.

Luka scrambled frantically for the manual feed mechanism to load another round, then re-aimed for the cockpit and fired again, bracing himself this time so he stayed upright. The round pierced the front and spun the flitter around like a wobbling top. The wide-array beam sliced up into the sky and then down into the building as the flitter broke apart and the pieces tumbled into the clearing and nearby undergrowth.

Luka bent to pick up the dropped hand-beamer. Suddenly he saw a flash, followed by an earsplitting *whump*, and the shockwave of a massive explosion slammed into him, knocking him off his feet and onto his left shoulder. Dust and burning debris stung his exposed skin as he curled into a protective ball.

He'd have liked to stay there until everything quieted down, but Mairwen was counting on him to slag the shipkiller. Telling the eye-watering pain in his shoulder to get in line behind the screaming pain in his thigh, he crawled back to the big gun, found the hand-beamer, and used it to thoroughly destroy the target controls. Even if he hadn't gotten its power, the shipkiller would now be useless.

As the dust cleared, Luka saw that the whole north end of the building was obliterated, with only rubble remaining at the base. Whatever they'd stored in that part of the building had gone off like a supernova.

The only sound came from the ringing in his ears. He knew he needed to crawl to safety, but he didn't know where that would be.

From far away, he heard someone calling his name. He looked around, then realized the voice was coming from the earwire still attached to his jaw. He tried to speak, but inhaled a cloud of dust and had to cough it out first. Finally he was able to croak, "This is Luka. I'm okay, but I can't hear *sjitt*."

Jerzi's voice was loud enough to hear this time. "*Same here. Eve's in the ship, I think. Have you seen Mairwen?*"

"No," said Luka, as a new surge of adrenalin spiked through him. He needed to find her. He pulled himself to his feet and limped to what was left of the storage bay, hand-beamer at the ready. Inside, he found the body of the merc who'd had the heatseeker, with a knife impaled in his throat. The knife was one of Mairwen's, so Luka pulled it out. He used the merc's uniform to wipe the blood off, then slid the blade in the back of his belt.

He stumbled through the rubble and found more bodies and another of Mairwen's knives, but not her. The walls had collapsed, so to go further, he had to leave the building and approach it from the outside. He found what was left of two other bloody bodies, but they were wearing merc uniforms.

He was blackly amused that his wild reconstruction talent was meekly silent in a war zone, and planned to tell Mairwen about it. If she was still alive.

CHAPTER 20

MAIRWEN AWOKE IN hot, humid, pitch-black darkness. Pain seeped into her awareness, but it meant she was alive, so she took it as a good sign. She was able to ignore most of the pain except for her head, which ached abominably. She was lying on her side, knees bent, and felt pressure above her shoulder and hip.

She cautiously opened her senses. Her hearing was impaired by multi-threaded high-pitched tones that signified temporary damage. At least she hoped it was temporary. As much as she'd once resented the senses that made her irreversibly different, she'd grown to embrace them if it meant keeping herself and Luka alive. She'd like to continue doing that in the future, assuming they had a future.

She smelled dirt, a mix of plants, plascrete dust, various unknown chemicals, metal, and her own scent, ripe with sweat and blood, some of which wasn't her own. She tried moving her shoulder and hip and found she could without shifting whatever was on top of her, which smelled metallic. She had no idea how long she'd been there. She struggled to regain her sense of time.

Last she remembered, the flitter's beamer was arcing down toward the building. She'd calculated she had only a few thousand milliseconds before it sliced into the corner where the negligent merc squad had stored their thermobarics, and a few more thousand milliseconds before the beam's energy ignited the whole stack. She'd taken a running leap off the building's roof into the shrubs and rolled when she hit the ground to channel her momentum. She'd just come up running when the shockwave threw her forward, out of control, and... nothing.

She concluded she'd been hit in the head, and that it was likely she was buried under debris. She'd been lucky, and hoped Luka, madman that he was to manually shoot down a flitter with a shipkiller, had shared her luck. Jerzi and Haberville had been farther away, so perhaps they escaped relatively unscathed, at least enough so that they could see to Luka and find her.

With some painful maneuvering, she got her left arm free enough so she could touch her face and neck, trying to see if the earwire had survived the impact. She couldn't reach it and had no room to turn her head, so she excavated the dirt under her face, which stirred up enough dust to make her sneeze, causing sharp pain in her cracked ribs and pounding in her head. After all that, all she found was abraded and bloody skin along her jaw where the wire used to be.

She rested, breathing as shallowly as she could until the dust settled. Even with that bit of exertion, the heat was oppressive. She was in a poor position to get any leverage to move whatever was on top of her. With some painful twisting and maneuvering, she managed to get her last remaining knife out of her right ankle sheath. They'd been good knives. She'd miss them.

Just as she was considering where to dig and where to put the dirt she'd have to move, she thought she heard voices. It was hard to tell with the constant ringing, but she cut off her awareness of it and tried to listen in the between tones.

She thought she heard her name called, and it alarmed her that she couldn't tell if it was Luka's voice calling. Reversing the knife in her hand, she tried pounding the pommel into the metal above her three times, then waiting five seconds and repeating. She could hardly hear it, but the painful vibration in her hand convinced her she was making all the noise she could.

Time was still slippery, and she'd lost track of the number of repetitions she'd pounded by the time the metal was lifted off her. The sunlight blinded her. She felt her eyes start to water when she heard Luka's voice asking where she was hurt, then calling for Jerzi. She felt rather than saw him kneel beside her.

"Head hurts... hearing loss," she managed to croak. When the involuntary tears subsided and she could finally see again, she was relieved that Luka looked more or less intact, and Jerzi the same, though he sported an incipient black eye and his chest was thickly coated in wet grime. She smelled Luka's unique scent and something more.

"You're bleeding," she said, her voice sounding like gravel.

"So are you," he said with a small, worried smile, gently smoothing her hair back from her face. "Can you sit up?"

When she nodded, he took the knife from her hand and helped her up, then because she insisted, helped her get to her feet.

As near as she could tell, she'd been covered by a piece of the flitter, which had protected her from the thermobaric fireball. Although the side of her head and neck felt wet, she didn't feel too bad until she turned her head too fast. Then dizziness caused her to tip sideways and almost take Luka down with her.

"*Taktu það rólega...* easy," said Luka, holding the side of her hip and pulling her close to him for support.

For once, she was content to stand with him awhile, letting his solid strength soothe the worries and panic she'd been trying not to think about. Somehow they were both still alive. Again.

"The mercs?" she asked Jerzi, who was hovering anxiously in front of her. The muck on his armor and clothes looked like a mixture of mud and soot. His railgun was strapped across his back, and his pocket had at least one ammo pack sticking out.

"Dead, or as good as. The building fell down while we were looking for you." His voice sounded nasal, and his nose looked crooked, like it might have been broken. "The light-drive ship took one beamer shot and was hit by some debris. Eve's in there now. She'll have to tell us if it'll fly."

She looked up to Luka, moving slowly this time. "She needs personal security."

Luka nodded, but didn't take his eyes off her. "Jerzi, go find Eve. The high oxygen hasn't been easy on her. I'll help Mairwen." He tightened his arm around her hips.

Jerzi took off at a half run. Mairwen was glad he was young and resilient, and wished to hell she didn't feel like she was a hundred and fifty years old. The sun position looked unchanged, so she'd likely been unconscious for only a minute or two, and she guessed it had taken them ten minutes to find and unearth her from her resting place. She didn't feel very rested.

As they walked, she saw Jerzi hadn't exaggerated about the building. Only the southern wall was left standing, and it looked none too steady. Luka, muttering to himself in what she presumed was Icelandic, remained determinedly at her side as they made their way toward the ship as fast as they could through the debris, body parts, and burned plascrete.

Twice he made her slow down to purposefully hyperventilate, telling her it was to keep oxygen flowing to her brain, which he was worried had been injured. He was favoring his right leg, which was matted with blood, dirt, and soot, and he winced every time he moved his left shoulder. At least the beamer wounds on her left arm and ribs had been instantly cauterized, although they hurt almost as much as her head and neck now that she was moving. She'd hate to think how much worse they'd be if the flexin armor hadn't taken some of the damage before failing. The flechette projectile hole through her lower left calf was hardly worth noticing by comparison, though the blood from it made her sock and boot sticky.

The ship looked none the worse for wear, despite the shiny mark where the beamer had raked its hull. She and Luka had just made it up the long ramp and past the wide airlock into the cargo area when the shipcomm sparked to life with a synth voice announcement in standard English: "*Attention. Incoming communication. Attention. Incoming communication.*"

"*Andskotinn,*" said Luka vehemently. She was getting quite an education in Icelandic cursing.

Haberville's voice boomed through the shipcomm. "*I set the navcomp to autoreply, but it won't fool anyone once they get a visual on what's left of the base. Jerzi, strap in. Luka, get the ramp retracted and seal the door so we can launch.*"

Luka left Mairwen's side go to look for the control panel. He found it, then swore at the agonizingly slow wakeup sequence.

If the ramp moved that slowly, they'd never make it. She looked for the emergency release and finally found it on the floor. She dropped to her knees, knowing dizziness would overwhelm her if she tried bending over. She fumbled with the safeties on the handle, then pulled it up hard. The ramp dropped suddenly, and she let the handle fall back into place. The airlock closed so slowly, she thought she'd unthinkingly dropped into tracker mode, but the heave of Luka's chest and her own heart rate told her she was still in realtime. She let out the breath she'd been holding when the airlock indicators finally showed a complete seal.

Haberville's calm but acerbic voice came over the shipcomm. "*Incoming seven minutes out, launch in one. Strap in if you can, because a high-speed lift will make this gods-cursed bus handle like a pregnant cow.*"

Mairwen tried to stand, but her dizziness made it almost impossible. She dropped into half-tracker mode and got to her feet. Pain messages exploded from her head, side, ribs, and leg, but she'd expected it and paid no attention. They couldn't stay on the cargo level because any unsecured supplies or equipment could crush them like bugs.

"We need jump seats." She grabbed Luka's arm and pulled him toward the upward ramp.

She squinted at the curving ramp floor to narrow her visual focus and ran up it, nearly overshooting when she arrived at the landing. He caught her and pulled her toward the interior of what looked like a common area. She looked around frantically and finally pointed.

"There!"

She and Luka hobbled together toward the row of jump seats against the wall. He pulled down two seats and practically slung her into one, then waited to see that she was strapping herself into the webbing before sitting and doing the same for himself. The ship vibrated deeply under her feet and thighs. She leaned back and let time come up to normal speed.

The chair's headrest wasn't particularly comfortable, but it would keep her immobile and save her from whiplash or spinal injury, neither of which would improve her condition. The vibrations were just shy of earsplitting, so she cut off her awareness of all sounds, even the ringing, and turned her head slightly so she could look at Luka. He was pale and exhausted, and he was covered in grime and caked blood, especially his right thigh. At least he didn't smell like fresh blood any more.

He smiled a little when he caught her eye and said something she couldn't hear. Probably telling her she looked like hell, which, considering how she felt, was shameless flattery. She gave him a small smile in return, then faced forward and flattened herself into the jump seat.

The ride was bone jarring. Even with the gravity compensators, it felt like Haberville was evading airborne weapons fire, and possibly ground-based, too, if one of the other installations on the continent had managed to get shipkillers online. Or maybe it was just because their ship was fat-assed and wobbled like a drunken sailor. She hoped Haberville's skills would continue to keep them safe and that the other merc squads were as inept as the one they'd already encountered.

Finally the vibrations began to diminish. The jolting settled down to the intensity of a mild thrill-ride, then tapered to nothing and normal ship gravity.

"*Clear thermopause,*" announced Haberville over the shipcomm. "*Engaging system drive. I'm looking for a hidey hole. Otherwise, our tech and propulsion signature will light us up like a beacon to any asshole who's looking.*" There was a brief pause. "*It's safe to unstrap. Welcome to the good ship* Beehive. *Come on up to the nav pod, top level, and bring the med kit. I left it in cargo by the lifts.*"

Mairwen was surprised to find her hands were shaky as she released the webbing. The ship's vibrations had masked the telltale signs that she was perilously close to flatlining. She stood up cautiously. The room stayed steady, so some of her dizziness had subsided, or maybe she was just getting used to it. She looked around to find the lifts, then took a couple of trudging steps toward them, promising herself she'd eat as soon as they were done meeting with Haberville.

Luka stepped in front of her, and she almost ran into him. He grabbed her shoulders gently and steered her to a chair at a long dining table. "You need to rest and eat. Now." She took a breath to argue, but he put a finger over her lips to prevent her from speaking. "You are the most stubborn person I've ever met. Stay here, and stay sitting up."

She sighed, knowing he was right. She wouldn't be good for anything if she was passed out in a corner.

He started rummaging in the nearby open kitchen and quickly found some slices of cheese in an oversized cold box. He pulled those out, but continued pawing through the rest of the contents.

"*Gull verðlaun!*" he said, and pulled out a container of liquid labeled "Electrum Gold" in bright shiny letters. He opened it and handed it to her. "Drink all of this. It's an electrolyte balancer, and you need it."

He only relaxed when he saw she was complying with his order. It came to her that he'd been field treating her for possible traumatic brain injury. She took a moment to be grateful for the practical nature of his vast store of knowledge.

He put the cheese and some apple slices on a plate. "Appetizer," he told her, handing it to her, then went back to foraging.

She ate and let herself be amused by his running commentary about the mercs' poor organizational skills and nutritional habits. He was entertaining her so she would stay awake, like head injury patients were supposed to. Similar to what he'd done with Jerzi in the hell ride down to the planet surface. Luka was good with people that way. He was good with her.

He handed her another plate, this one with a ham sandwich with unidentifiable vegetables. "Main course," he told her, as he handed her a napkin and a glass of water.

"Does this count as cooking a meal for me?" She took a bite.

He gave a short laugh as he examined the contents of various cartons and pouches in the cold box. "No. When I cook for you, you'll know it."

Her stomach was starting to cramp, which meant her already high metabolism was still operating in top gear, trying to compensate for all the tracker mode she'd used that day. She drank half the glass of water to try to soothe her stomach before swallowing more bites of sandwich.

They were interrupted by Haberville's voice over the shipcomm, heavy with peevishness. *"Any time now with the med kit would be good."*

Luka set a glass of orange juice in front of her. "Drink this. I'll be right back. Stay awake." He started to go, then turned back to her. From his back waistband, he pulled not one but three of her knives and set them in her lap. She felt tears well up at how much that meant to her. He put his hand to the side of her face, then limped over to the lifts and was gone. She wished she was better with words so she could tell him how happy it made her that he was still alive and caring about her.

She also wished the ringing cacophony in her ears would go away. Unfortunately, the tracker alteration had only sped up her ability to heal a little, by dint of her higher metabolism, so it would take hours, or even days, to see any improvement. She also knew Luka and Jerzi had it worse than she did, so she told herself to quit whining. She needed to get her battered brain thinking about the next steps, not wallowing in her woes. She wanted to follow Luka to the nav pod, but knew it'd be better if she finished eating and drinking so her body would have enough fuel to keep going a while longer.

He was back in ten minutes. He put a pill in her hand. "It's a vasodilator from the med kit. Good for possible brain injury. Can you take it?"

"Yes, but it won't last long. I have a fast metabolism." That was an understatement. Still, she swallowed the pill with the last bit of orange juice.

"More?" he asked, indicating her empty plate.

"No," she said, then pointed upward. "Trouble in nav?" She was pleased that her voice was sounding less throaty than it had before.

"Not really. Jerzi neglected to mention he'd been shot in the shoulder with a projectile, and he passed out. We revived him and got him into the autodoc for a quick diagnostic." He snorted and shook his head. "I am surrounded by stubborn people. Eve not only retrieved the medical kit, she saved the sample kit and all our packs, too. She says the previous pilots left the navcomp wide open, or else we might not have gotten off the planet so fast."

He stepped behind her and began massaging her shoulder muscles in gentle circles. It felt surprisingly good. "How's the head?"

"Fi... better," she said. "Your thigh?"

"Needs patching. Eve says there's something wrong with the navcomp, and she doesn't trust it for faster-than-light until she resets it. Something about stuttering the system drive to jump scatter our tech signature, whatever that means. All I know is we're stuck in-system, and we're looking for a suitable rock in the asteroid belt to give us cover."

"Any ship weapons?" Luka's touch was making it hard to think. She'd trade a dozen physical therapists for Luka's hands on her any day.

"Lean forward a little. Your back is really tight. No, it's just a small troop ship. We might luck out and find some personal weapons in the hold, but they won't help if some *skíthæll* wants to smash us to atoms from a distance."

She knew an unorthodox method or two for defense, but mentioning them would only add to Haberville's already long list of suspicions. Still, better that than being dead.

"If the ship has debris lasers and some extra fibret cable, we could modify the lasers to extend their range. They burn out faster, and it takes more flux, but it's an unexpected weapon if we can lure a target close enough."

Luka laughed, and she felt it through his hands on her shoulders. "You're amazing. Eve's going to think you're pirate clan by the end of this."

She gave into long-suppressed need and stood to turn and lean against him, resting her aching head on his undamaged right shoulder, and breathing in his sound and scent. His arm enfolded her gently and he sighed. "Let's get those lasers modified, then find the nearest showers. We stink, even to me."

In the end, it took an hour and both Luka's and Jerzi's help to add an overload flux line in the engine pod, then reconfigure the ship's four lasers and get them back online. Haberville was busy plotting asteroid paths and finding the optimal location for avoiding possible firing solution vectors. Mairwen had no doubt she'd complain about the "jack trick" later. Once the lasers were ready, Luka, who didn't want Haberville to be without help, sent Jerzi to scout for freshers first while he remained in the nav pod with Haberville.

Mairwen stayed out of the way in the engine pod. She sat on a padded bench, keeping upright as Luka wanted her to, and allowed her thoughts to drift, with the ringing in her ears as an accompaniment.

She hoped the inactivity would convince her metabolism to gear down a notch or two, so she tried to sit still and just think. She wondered why Haberville was so professional one minute and galling the next. She wondered how incompetent mercenaries stayed in business, and worried that the competent ones, like whoever had sabotaged the *Berjalan* and attacked their pilots, might be coming out to play soon. She thought about what Zheer could tell Space Div that would get them to come to their rescue but not arrest them. She longed for another sandwich, but the trip to the kitchen seemed like kilometers.

Twenty-one minutes later, Luka, carrying the med kit, came and got her. He led her down to the sleeping quarters level and into the large fresher with its eight community showerheads that Jerzi had discovered. Each showerhead array had its own settings, plus dispensers for soap, shampoo, depilator, and lotion. She helped Luka out of his armor and boots, and he did the same for her. They spread their armor and clothes under one shower head and set it to a pounding wide spray. Her upper armor was irreparably compromised on the side where the beamer had burned through.

Luka opted for the simple expediency of starting his shower with the rest of his clothes on, then peeling them off once the worst of the muck had rinsed off and the dried blood had softened. Mairwen had to help him with his T-shirt, giving her a closeup look at the massive, swollen bruise that covered his right shoulder. Without a minder healer or treatment, it would take weeks to heal. Other scrapes and cuts materialized as the dirt washed off, and she winced at the awful extent of the laceration on his muscular thigh. She hated to think how much worse off he'd have been if he hadn't been wearing flexin.

She'd rather hoped the first time they got to see each other naked would have been under different circumstances.

She felt unexpectedly shy once she'd removed her own clothes and knife sheaths. She'd never been modest before, but she'd never been naked with someone she wanted to want her. *Stop being ridiculous*, she told herself. She stepped into the deliciously warm, soft spray.

The water at her feet swirled oily brown with grime and pink with blood as it poured into the drain. She hoped the ship had a good filter and recovery system. The warmth felt good on the bruise over her cracked ribs, and she got used to the sharp sting from the water on her abrasions and burns. She rejected the cloyingly floral shampoo in favor of the unscented liquid soap. She couldn't help but hiss in pain as she massaged it over the bump on her head, discovering a gash hidden by her filthy, matted hair. She worked the snarls, trying to untangle them.

"Let me help." Luka's voice startled her because he was suddenly close, and she hadn't heard or smelled him.

He gently pushed her hands away, then turned her so the back of her hip and shoulder angled into his side. He gently cupped water over her head wound and used delicate touches to cleanse her hair and the laceration.

She wouldn't have thought that the feel and slide of his bare skin against hers would be more powerful than the pain, but it was. Pleasure fluxed haphazardly through her, like a river finding a new path through storm debris.

Driven to make more contact, she leaned closer, causing her hand to encounter his mangled right thigh. It was his turn to hiss in pain.

"Sorry." She clasped her hands in front of her and made them stay still.

"I'm okay, *ástin mín*," he breathed.

He added more soap to his fingers and delicately swirled them through the rest of her hair. It was a strange mixture of pain and relief when he finished and guided her under the soft spray for a final rinse.

His left hand slid down her neck and onto her shoulder, and his right slid around to her waist, where he pulled her gently against him and his arousal. Even though it felt good, she couldn't help but gasp in pain as her broken ribs grated under his touch.

"Sorry." He glided his hand over her shoulder and sighed. "We have the worst timing."

"We do," she agreed, though she was on a knife's edge of not caring. It was killing her not to turn and rub herself up him like a cat, melding her body with his.

"You really took a beating." The pressure of his breath in her ear sent tingling warmth through her that had nothing to do with hot water. She only barely suppressed an overload tremor. "Could I persuade you into the autodoc?"

She shook her head. "It's not safe." She couldn't afford to leave personal biological samples in a strange unit, and she didn't trust it not to administer unknown drugs with unknown side effects on her altered body.

"I'll keep watch if you'll use it for you," she said, half turning to look at him.

His expression shadowed. "I don't like medical beds." He stepped away. "Let's patch each other up with the med kit."

She felt suddenly cold, despite the warm water still misting over her. And along with everything else, her lower left calf was starting to remind her that it had been pierced by a flechette.

She dropped to one knee to pick up her sopping wet underclothes. She turned off her showerhead, then limped to the one on the other side of the room, where she'd left her outer clothes and flexin armor. She turned everything over to get the last of the gunk off, picked up her three remaining knives and five sheaths, then turned off the showerhead and left the clothes to drain.

She looked around for the solardries and was surprised not to find any, especially since this was a community shower. Quick-dry blowers were the easiest way to get people out faster. Even her no-frills apartment had one. She headed for the towel cabinet.

Luka rinsed off the last of the depilator, leaving his handsome face smooth once again. She idly wondered why he hadn't had his beard stopped more permanently, like Jerzi obviously had. He turned off his showerhead and met her at the towel cabinet, limping only slightly. His thigh still looked like ground meat.

He handed her a towel and took one himself. The room was chilly now that she wasn't being sluiced by hot water, so she dried quickly and wrapped the towel around herself, knotting it above her breasts to give her some semblance of warmth. The scrape on Luka's thigh smelled obscenely fresh, but it was no longer dripping blood. He took another towel from the cabinet and helped her dry her hair, gently blotting the area around the head wound. She would never get tired of his touch.

"Jerzi said he found clothes in one of the staterooms. Let's see if we can find some, too," he said, dropping the bloody towel on the floor near her wet clothes. Nudity didn't bother him, for which she was privately very glad.

On their way out, she saw her boots, and wondered what to do about them, since the inside of one was sticky with congealed blood. Luka's boots looked no better.

A search of the fifteen identical double-occupancy rooms yielded a hodge-podge of wearable items that would do until the industrial-sized clothes sanitizer they'd found finished cleaning and drying their own clothes. She could make do with the large, long-sleeved faded blue T-shirt. A large pair of men's red boxers would serve as half pants, though she had to knot the elastic waistband to keep them up around her smaller body. She reattached the sheaths to her upper back and forearms and slid the knives in place. She left the empty ankle sheaths with her boots and damp armor.

Luka wore mismatched socks, loose knit boxers, and a tattered bog-green long sweater, all of which made him look like he'd dressed out of the lost-and-found box. He'd mock-growled at her when he'd caught her smiling at his attire.

He made her sit in a stateroom on the lower drop-leaf bed. He gave her an infraheat pack to hold on her ribs while he sprayed dermaknit on her various burns and abrasions. He used a wound pack on the through-and-through hole in her lower calf before spraying it, too. On her head wound, he applied dermaknit paste, which hurt more than the burns because he had to press it in. She gritted her teeth against the pain and resisted flinching, using the delicious clean scent of him to distract herself. She could shut pain off when she had to, but it was better to heed her body's warnings when she could.

When it was his turn, he sat patiently still but swore under his breath while she applied dermaknit and liquid skin sealant to his thigh. She was beginning to recognize the individual Icelandic curse words.

He carefully pulled on the pair of stained, loose cargo pants. She was glad he'd found them, since the ship felt cold even to her.

He dug in the med kit for painkillers and found both jets and orals. She shook her head when he offered them to her.

"Are you really allergic to pain meds?" he asked. He dry-swallowed a pill.

"No, they're just pointless. My high metabolism and body chemistry burn them out in minutes. The vasodilator you gave me earlier probably lasted ten minutes at the most. If I'm really hurt, a healer can help, but…"

"…it's not safe," he finished when she trailed off, tenderly stroking the side of her face, avoiding the scrape along her jawline.

He slid back in the bed until his back was against the wall, then pulled her gently into his arms, her back to his chest. His arms and legs cocooned hers. She leaned her head back on his good shoulder and closed her eyes. His head dropped back to the wall. Despite her stinging pains and bone-deep aches, it was the most comforted she'd ever been in her life. A peaceful lassitude stole over her, and she drifted into a blissful, hazy doze.

And because the universe hated her, they were interrupted only four minutes later.

"*We've got company,*" announced Haberville over the shipcomm, "*and someone needs to get her skinny ass up here and be ready to handle the jacked laser.*"

Luka's deep groan expressed Mairwen's feelings exactly. She reluctantly slid off the bunk.

He stood and leaned in for a quick kiss. "If we live through this, I swear I'm going to pop that woman."

Mairwen caressed the side of his entirely handsome face. His rebellious hair was already starting to go its own way, in spite of having been determinedly slicked back. "Ignoring her works better," she said.

"I'm not as good at that as you are." He pushed a stray lock of her hair away from her eyes.

"You're a nice human being. I'm not."

He kissed her forehead. "Just because you were created by monsters doesn't make you one. Need anything?"

"Socks and a jacket, or a blanket." She put a hand on his broad chest, feeling his warmth through the ragged sweater. "I'm cold without you."

The smile he gave her took her breath away. "And here I thought I was the only one," he said, his voice low and intimate. He rubbed her arms up and down twice, then let her go.

Chapter 21

IN THE NAV pod, situated in the top center of the ship, Haberville had several holo displays going at once. She wasn't jacked in to the navcomp, probably because she didn't trust it. Considering what had happened on the *Berjalan*, Mairwen didn't blame her. Haberville hadn't had a chance to shower, so she was more than a bit rank. Mairwen cut off her awareness of the smell.

"Krishna's flute, what did you do, volunteer for target practice?" She was staring at Mairwen's various bandages.

Mairwen shrugged, not bothering to comment. None of them would win the company good health bonus for a while.

Haberville gave Mairwen a shipcomm earwire from a drawer full of them, then had her sit in the co-pilot chair and gave her a brief explanation of how she'd modified the co-pilot interface to direct the lasers.

"I don't have space combat experience," said Mairwen.

"Really?" asked Haberville, her disbelief evident. Mairwen gave her a bland look. Haberville rolled her eyes. "Fine. Let the navcomp find the targeting solution. Use your brain for strategy and tactics."

"Understood," Mairwen said. She began decluttering and reorganizing the interface to be more manageable.

Haberville scowled at her. "No test firing. So far, our two little friends don't know we're here."

Mairwen let Haberville's unnecessary admonition slide. "What are they?"

"One's a glorified bus like ours, but the other is a surplus military corvette, probably with aftermarket armament." She gave Mairwen a wolfish grin. "They think they're on a wild goose chase, so they're active-scanning all over the place. Even their comms are in the clear. Not the sharpest knives in the drawer."

Mairwen gave Haberville a small smile in return. Whoever hired this merc company had obviously selected based on price instead of performance. Perhaps even deep-pocket pharma companies had budget pressures.

Haberville manipulated her interface to enlarge one of the holos. "Here's us, in green, hiding among this big cluster of rocks, tucked into the shadow of an icy chunk with an iron core." Two more moving icons appeared, each with labels. "And here are our little friends. The transport like ours is designated Blue One, the corvette is Blue Two."

Mairwen may not have known much about space combat, but she had a lot of experience analyzing and evading search patterns. After a few moments of reviewing the recent movements, she said, "The transport won't go in the asteroid belt. The corvette believes asteroids aren't a threat."

"Noticed that, did you?" said Haberville. "I bet he's up-armored with a shield generator, making him feel invincible. If I had even a single mass driver, I'd send that corvette our icy chunk with its heavy iron core. That would take him down a peg or two."

"Would thermolytics do? There may be some in cargo." She remembered them from a merc conversation she'd overheard during her scouting reconnaissance of the base.

"Nah, too uncontrolled, but they might make a nice diversion." Haberville keyed the shipcomm. "Hey, boys, when you get a minute, check the cargo area for anything fun our merc jerks might have left for us to play with, like things that can go boom in space."

After a long moment, Luka's voice came through the console speaker. *"Jerzi's gone to look. I'm coming up with soup in about five minutes."*

"Oh thank the billion gods of the multiverse," said Haberville. "My stomach thinks my throat's been cut." She released the shipcomm key and began muttering unintelligibly to herself.

Mairwen ignored her and considered non-suicidal strategies for luring the corvette into laser range. There weren't many.

Luka was a welcome diversion, and the soup was hot and satisfying. He also brought a scrounged scarf and overcoat and insisted on helping her into them, careful of her cracked ribs. The overcoat was entirely too wide for her and smelled like a smokehouse, but it was long and warm. She gave him a soft, amused smile as he pulled the overcoat's collar closed over the scarf and buttoned it, like he was bundling a child up for a walk in the dead of Etonver's winter.

Haberville gave a loud, obnoxious sigh. Mairwen ignored her and focused on Luka, willing him to do the same. He tried, but the tension in his shoulders gave him away. He gave her a brief, rueful smile and turned to go, but stepped back to her side again when Jerzi arrived carrying a tray with four steaming mugs.

"Coffee for us, homemade Nuevalle hot chocolate for Mairwen. No caffeine." He handed out the mugs.

Mairwen nodded her thanks, then took a tiny trial sip. Sweet, smoky, creamy chocolate flavors danced across her tongue. She was sorry she hadn't tried it before. She savored more sips as Jerzi reported what he'd found in cargo.

"About twenty thermobaric shape charges and sixty self-contained thermolytics, all det-value five Gs, a hundred packaged KemX cubes, and enough timed detonators for the bicentennial fireworks show. Even better, we've got at least four wrapped pallets of lab supplies and a huge cold unit with what looks like thousands of samples from the planet. If we can save them, there's no way Loyduk can explain them away. Oh, and I also moved our packs and stuff to the big sealable hold closest to the lifts. They got scattered during takeoff."

"Is the cold unit tied down?" asked Haberville.

"Built in. It's not going anywhere."

Mairwen noticed Luka watching her as she drank, so she concluded he was responsible for the hot chocolate.

"Good?" he asked quietly. He was looking pleased with himself.

"Yes." She flashed him a quick smile to let him know she was charmed by his quest to expand her gastronomic horizons.

Haberville whistled to get their attention. "The engine pod's available if you two want to be alone for a quick hot-connect."

Luka sighed and started to respond. Jerzi beat him to it.

"What are you, five years old? Quit being an asshole." His normally genial face showed deep irritation.

Haberville's look of smartass challenge faded under his uncompromising stare. She turned and concentrated on the nav interface.

"Fine. Go make as many twenty-G thermo packages as you can," she said, not looking at anyone. Jerzi and Luka exchanged a silent look, then left together.

Mairwen shifted her attention to monitoring the two merc ships as they bumbled their way along a search pattern. Wargaming children could have done a better job.

Underneath, she wondered how much longer it would take for La Plata to realize something had gone wrong and call Concordance Command.

Even if none of the distress messages had made it out, Zheer should have taken action when Luka didn't report in on schedule. Regardless of Haberville's considerable skill and the merc company's considerable incompetence, the longer they were forced to stay in-system, the more their odds of staying safe deteriorated. They needed to leave.

"What's wrong with the navcomp?"

Haberville snorted. "Whoever piloted this piece of shit was a tweaker." She said the last word with the loathing usually reserved for discussing rotting fish.

Mairwen shook her head, not familiar with the term.

"Tweakers reprogram the navcomp because they think they can do transits better than hundreds of years of experience, all so they can make faster jumps or exit closer in-system. There are no old tweakers." She gave Mairwen a pointed look. "Not even among jack crews."

Mairwen gave her an expressionless look. Haberville frowned in irritation, then scratched under her shirt and winced.

"Lord Buddha, I think even my bruises have bruises. At least I'm not coughing any more." She stretched in her chair. "What I wouldn't give for a long, hot bath. Preferably with several hard-bodied attendants to help me relax." Haberville winked, then rolled her eyes when Mairwen didn't respond.

Mairwen checked the location of the two merc ships, which were distant and moving slowly on a vector that took them away from the icy chunk below. "I can pilot long enough for you to take a shower."

Haberville gave her a startled look, then narrowed her eyes suspiciously. "Where'd you get your training?"

Mairwen kept her face bland. "I can keep us near the asteroid. I'll ping if something changes."

Haberville was patently torn between displeasure at Mairwen's non-answer and the strong desire to get clean. She gave Mairwen a long, assessing look, then agreed. She spent the next few minutes providing instructions on the ship's systems, the telltales she'd set up, and how to recognize changes in the passive scan results. Then she left, and the nav pod fell pleasantly quiet.

Mairwen spent a few moments closing drawers and cabinets in the nav pod that Haberville had left open and in disarray. The smelly borrowed overcoat felt awkward and heavy, reminding her to increase the ambient temperature in the living areas to a more comfortable level. Fortunately, the ringing in her ears had finally started to fade. She rather liked using her extraordinary hearing instead of suppressing it as she had for so long.

She heard Luka's footsteps as he approached the nav pod a few minutes later. As always, he smiled when he saw her, and as always, it made her heart skip. She was relieved to see he wasn't limping. The anesthetic in the dermaknit and the painkiller he took must be working.

He leaned against the doorway. "I don't know how long it will take for help to arrive, so we need to talk about pilot shifts. Eve says her limit is twelve hours before she needs rest or stims, assuming the med kit has the right kind. What about you?"

"My 'jack crew' experience doesn't include big ships. I can keep us out of trouble, but we need Haberville if trouble comes looking for us."

"How about I tell Eve to sleep for a couple of hours now? Assuming our pursuit hasn't changed."

"It hasn't changed. You can give her four hours if you bring me socks." She'd been sitting cross-legged in the chair to keep her feet warm.

He smiled more broadly that time. "I can do better than that. Our clothes are done."

* * * * *

Luka looked at a wall display to see it had been three hours since he'd delivered Mairwen's clothes and armor. It felt longer, maybe because his body clock said it was close to midnight and he was running out of energy, despite the nap he'd managed to squeeze in earlier. He thought he would have slept better if Mairwen had been with him, remembering their two nights together on a suspended tarp. Sleeping with her just felt right.

Having finished staging the thermolytic packages in the launch bays, he and Jerzi were investigating the biological samples in the cold unit. Jerzi was wearing nothing but a T-shirt and pants as he crouched on the threshold of the cold unit's door, examining trays of tiny boxes.

"Assuming the first two numbers indicate the base of origin, then we've got the samples from five of them," said Jerzi.

Luka stood to the side, reading from a portable display that showed the inventory he'd found in the shipcomp. He tried not to shiver. "Should be six. Maybe the last set was still in the building when it blew."

"I'll count the boxes from the zero-five group and see if that matches." Jerzi may as well have been part polar bear for all the cold bothered him.

"Okay, I'll see if I can find better records." Luka moved to get away from the blasts of frigid air. It was warmer in the rest of the ship, finally. His flexin armor wasn't designed to be warm, the flexitape holding his shredded pant leg together felt cold, and his feet felt clammy. He and Jerzi had found a way to clean out the worst of the blood and dirt in their boots as well as Mairwen's, so at least they weren't gory, but they were unpleasantly damp.

He heard a lift door open and was surprised but pleased when Mairwen appeared. He went to meet her. Under her burned and beat-up armor, she was wearing her black pants and long-sleeved knit shirt, both of which she'd patched with blue fibret tape. She probably thought it slightly odd that he was always smiling at her, but he couldn't help it. He was in love with her, and she was gorgeous. Even though she still looked like she'd recently been in a war. They all did.

She handed him an earwire and took one to Jerzi. "Now we'll all hear alerts from the nav and shipcomps. In case something happens to Haberville. She relieved me early."

Jerzi accepted his and absently pressed it into place along his jawline, still engrossed in counting.

Luka put his on, but gave Mairwen a speculative look. His intuition and his talent, which had been dormant while he'd been fighting for his life, flared.

"I'm going with Mairwen to the kitchen," he told Jerzi, then headed for the lifts, and Mairwen obligingly followed. Instead of stepping into one, however, he walked farther to a shallow alcove just beyond. He drew her into the corner and brushed his lips over hers, for the benefit of any nosy pilots with access to monitoring cameras.

"Why don't you trust Eve?" he asked quietly.

He reveled in the feel of her arms sliding around his neck. He needed her touch like he needed oxygen.

"The merc pilot wasn't a tweaker." She explained the term, then said she'd found no evidence of it in the navcomp. "I think Haberville wants to stay in-system."

"Why?" He skimmed his hands down her back and lower to her hips, subtly pulling her toward him. The feel of her chest and pelvis against his was derailing his thought processes, overwhelming them with memories of her beautifully sleek, wet, and naked body in the shower, her velvety moon-pale skin a sensuous contrast to his own light brown.

"No idea. I follow brilliant men, I don't lead them." Her breathing was irregular, and her raspy voice was like a caress.

"You'll have to introduce me to those other men you keep mentioning. I'd like to know who my competition is." He kissed her again, this time with open, raw passion, to let her know how badly he wanted her. She arched into him with a low moan.

"Luka, we can't..." she entreated, her breath shallow.

She was right, of course. He gave himself a mental shake to throw off the drugging effects of her and took a deep breath. "Which alerts will we hear?" His voice sounded as husky as hers.

"Launches, significant movements, ship system changes, outgoing comms, anything I could think of."

"Can't she just delete them?"

"Yes, if she can find them. I learned from whoever hid the air-mix virus in the *Berjalan's* shipcomp." She stroked the side of his face where he'd attached the earwire. "I customized these. If you subvocalize, only I will hear it. I can make Jerzi's do same, if you trust him enough to tell him."

"You don't?"

"I trust your talent. I trust you."

Given her life experience and what had been done to her, he considered it a gift from the universe that she did.

Over the earwires, they both heard a synth voice alert.

"*Attention. Infrared signature on Insche 255C planet surface.*"

A moment later, Eve's voice came over the shipcomm. "*In case you care, fems and gents, the mercs on the planet just blew another installation.*"

He cupped Mairwen's face in his hands and kissed her one final time. "I'm a very lucky man," he whispered, then reluctantly pulled away.

He captured her hand in his and led her toward the lifts. If they ever made it back to Etonver, he was never going to let her go again. He wanted to tell her he loved her, but he was afraid it would throw her into turmoil worrying about how to respond, and he couldn't do that to her while they were still in danger. Her CPS handlers had drummed into her that she wasn't capable of normal human emotions.

He knew better, but he didn't think she did.

They'd no sooner arrived in the kitchen when another alert, and then Eve, told them a new ship had launched from the planet surface to join in the hunt.

"*Another corvette is coming... and damn, it looks like the adults have come to see what the commotion is.*" A tone sounded, and suddenly they could all hear playback of the new ship's commander yelling at the others about open communication and ordering immediate encryption. The signal flatlined.

"Sorry to say, but the new guest at the party is organizing a better search pattern. It's going to be less likely we'll stay hidden behind our iron-core asteroid. Morganthur, I need you in the nav pod for the lasers. Jerzi, Luka, get to the launch bays. Be ready to set the timers on the thermolytic packs you made."

Luka helped Mairwen find a protein bar and fruit cube to take with her, then reluctantly left her and went to meet Jerzi at the launch bay crossover to coordinate their efforts.

Jerzi took the initiative to locate and distribute exosuits for everyone and to take their xeno sampling kit up to the engine pod, which was well protected because it doubled as one of the ship's escape pods. Eve used the shipcomm to publicly express her irritation that Jerzi wasn't following her orders. Jerzi used the shipcomm himself and said he'd be damned if he'd be caught in hard vacuum again. Luka found the shipcomm in his launch bay and announced his support of Jerzi's actions. He felt like he was supervising preteens.

As he waited in the bay, he decided he disliked being in an exosuit, but would dislike being dead even more. He made a point of sealing it a couple of times to get the hang of the various controls, remembering how he'd fumbled with them on the *Berjalan*. At least this was a new, clean suit from the *Beehive*, instead of the filthy, malodorous one he'd hauled through the hybrid rainforest. He found that even while wearing an exosuit, he could still pace and think, and he took advantage of it.

He kept coming back to Korisni Genetika's involvement. If, as Zheer suspected, they'd hired the dead telepath to interrogate him, it implied they already knew the eight-hundred-kilo secret, the existence of a viable hybrid planet. Maybe their real goal had been to hijack it out from under the company exploiting it now, whether that was Loyduk or one of their partners. Based on what Dr. Tewisham had said, it wouldn't surprise him if Korisni Genetika found out about it because they had a spy in the research operation. Was it too Machiavellian to think that Korisni Genetika dangled a cheap merc company in Loyduk's path, meaning they'd be easy to beat? Or maybe they'd simply suborned the merc company.

He wished he had Mairwen around so he could bounce ideas off her and get her unconventional take on things. He thought better when she was nearby. Or maybe he was just rationalizing his selfish desire to be with her.

CHAPTER 22

"SHOOT," SAID HABERVILLE. "I was hoping they'd take the idiots' word for it that they'd searched our little corner of the system." She seemed much calmer now that she'd showered and rested. Unfortunately, she'd used the floral shampoo and lotion, making the whole nav pod smell like a cheap perfumery.

Mairwen had already analyzed the new and improved search pattern and estimated they had at least another thirty minutes before their pursuers would come anywhere close. One of her private alerts told her there was an incoming transit. The alert was followed directly by one Haberville had set.

"Oh, hello there," said Haberville, checking out the newly arrived ship. She looked at Mairwen. "Have they come to help or hurt, do you suppose?" Mairwen shrugged.

Haberville keyed the shipcomm. "We have another new player, just in from transit. Look sharp."

Through Mairwen's earwire, Luka asked her if it was possible to give him ship commander's rights. She turned away from Haberville briefly to subvocalize a "yes," then updated the command module under the guise of checking flux and laser status. Mairwen kicked herself for not having thought of it earlier when she'd had all the ship's systems to herself for three hours.

The merc ship Haberville had designated as Blue Three sent a broadbeam but encrypted ping at the newcomer. The *Beehive* only detected it from the fringes because the beam wave passed nearby. The newcomer didn't respond, at least via broadbeam. After several minutes, the original Blue Two corvette sent a long and wide active-scan, which strongly suggested the new ship wasn't expected.

Haberville slapped her thigh. "Thank you, Great Spirit, for sending idiots to do me favors." She manipulated the nav interface with rapid fingers and called up comparative signatures. "Bounceback says the new ship is an exploration-class deep spacer. Bigger than us, smaller than the corvettes.

Spacer is tagged as Purple One."

On Mairwen's holo display, the newcomer's purple icon appeared and started to move in-system. She rotated the perspective to make it easier to see the relationships. The transit exit point was outside the asteroid belt, and to get to Insche 255C, most ships would angle over the elliptic to avoid the cosmic debris, just as the *Berjalan* had done. So far, the spacer was behaving predictably for that destination. Mairwen remembered that Zheer had been planning to contract a freelance exploration spacer for an expedition to the second hybrid planet candidate. She wondered if La Plata had diverted it to Insche 255 instead.

"Shit," said Haberville. "Ship number four just cleared from the surface. Looks like another corvette. Fuck. Tagged as Blue Four."

Instead of joining the search pattern, Blue Four appeared to be on an intercept course for the spacer. At present velocities, Mairwen estimated fifteen minutes to firing solution, and twenty minutes to intercept. The spacer seemed oblivious.

Haberville announced to Jerzi and Luka what was happening.

Mairwen tried to put herself in the mind of the exploration spacer's commander for various scenarios. None of them had the spacer expecting to be up against three armed merc corvettes. Unless the spacer had vastly superior weapons and heavy armor, it was in trouble.

Haberville proved to be thinking along the same lines. "That spacer will be dead meat if the mercs shoot first and ask questions later."

"Can we get the mercs to show themselves, or warn the spacer?" asked Mairwen. Any other approach would light up the *Beehive* and get it slagged in short order.

"Maybe." Haberville looked thoughtful, then smiled and snapped her fingers. "Emergency comm relay. Change the message, delay the broadcast, boost the output. It'll fry quicker, but who cares? We'll launch it toward an area the idiots already cleared."

Her fingers flew in the interface. "Shipcomp says the relay is in cargo six, near the airlock. Go get it. I'll do the message and plot the vector while you're doing that."

Mairwen was already halfway through the doorway by the time Haberville had finished speaking. In the lift, she heard Haberville using the shipcomm to tell Luka and Jerzi.

So far, Haberville had done everything aboveboard, and Mairwen was having doubts about her suspicions, as well as doubts about her own ability to detect the tweaker's adjustments.

She quickly located the relay unit in the cargo hold, but it was too heavy for her to handle. She found a grav cart and wrestled the unit onto it. She followed Haberville's announced direction to take it to the number two launch bay. Jerzi helped prepare the payload and get it into the launch claws.

They stepped back to the safety zone for Haberville's five-second countdown. Despite his stint in the autodoc, Jerzi's eye and nose were still swollen, making him look like a competition fighter. She made a brief search for hearing protectors and handed the rigid cups to him before putting on a set for herself. The launcher's noise was hard on her, despite blocking her senses, and Jerzi winced in pain.

She could have used the earwire to tell Luka he'd need them, too, but she chose to visit his launch bay in person and give him her hearing protectors, since she wouldn't need them in the nav pod. She didn't pretend the reason for her visit was anything but her own need. Despite knowing it was irrational, she worried about his well-being when she couldn't see him.

"I… evaluated Jerzi. He knows about these," he said, pointing to his earwire.

She grinned, knowing it meant he'd once again successfully used and controlled his talent. For once, she initiated the kissing senseless activity, leaving them both breathless.

"I'll fix it so you and he can talk." She gave him one final kiss, then returned to the nav pod.

Her body stayed heated from the encounter for quite a few minutes afterward, despite her exosuit's environmental controls. When Haberville was momentarily distracted, Mairwen surreptitiously adjusted the comm system to connect Luka and Jerzi.

The combination of the launch energy and the comm relay's own tiny engine propelled the relay surprisingly close to the merc transport ship before it began broadcasting. Whatever Haberville's repeating warning message was, it definitely got the spacer to change trajectory. It also stirred up a hornet's nest of active-scans and movement from the hunters, and demonstrated that two of the four corvette commanders knew what they were doing.

The Blue Four corvette anticipated the spacer's actions and started serious pursuit, while Blue Three followed back along the relay's path. Although Haberville had craftily bent the relay's angle with the launch spin, Blue Three was looking for the origin a lot closer to the *Beehive* than they had been.

Blue Two's commander demonstrated continued stupidity by destroying the relay with a missile, which also set off the thermolytic package that Mairwen and Jerzi had thoughtfully included with it. The Blue One transport responded to the detonation as if it was under attack and retreated to put Insche 255C between it and any combat.

Mairwen used the shipcomm to briefly describe the action to Luka and Jerzi. Haberville gave her an annoyed look, then announced, "Everything but critical systems going low tech."

The air handlers went silent and the nav pod's ambient lighting went out. The primary light came from the displays, which lit up with the passive intercepts of bouncebacks from the numerous active-scans by the mercs and the spacer.

The Purple One spacer proved to be a worthy adversary and evaded the pursuing Blue Four corvette, finally luring it into a weapons firing solution for a strike. The corvette would have been crippled if it hadn't dodged at the last second, but it didn't get away entirely unscathed. The Blue Four icon moved noticeably more slowly on the holo display.

The alerts were startling. Somehow they seemed louder in the dark.

"*Warning. One minute to long-range firing solution from enemy Blue Three.*"

"*Warning. One minute to long-range firing solution from enemy Blue Two.*"

Haberville swore as her fingers flew in the interface. Mairwen keyed the shipcomm and told Luka and Jerzi to seal their exosuits. The launch bays weren't independently sealable the way the nav and engine pods were. If Haberville was unhappy about the announcement, she could complain later.

"Pray to Allah they still don't know where we are." Haberville used docking thrusters to nudge the *Beehive*'s position ever so slightly to keep them hidden from two corvettes. "Move along, you godless infidels. Nothing here but a little cluster of rocks."

Haberville fired the thrusters again and kept nudging their ship around the asteroid.

"*Warning. Long-range firing solution from enemy Blue Two achievable.*"

For a moment it looked like the Blue Two corvette might be oblivious to the *Beehive*'s presence, but an active-scan from it said otherwise. Instead of firing, however, the Blue Two changed vector to a new course straight for them. Before Mairwen could think about that, a syncopated flurry of announcements bombarded them.

"*Warning. One minute to long-range firing solution from enemy Purple One.*"

"*Warning. One minute to long-range firing solution from enemy Blue Four.*"

"*Warning. Long-range firing solution from enemy Blue Three achievable.*"

"*Warning. Long-range firing solution from enemy Purple One achievable.*"

Mairwen nearly flatlined her hearing to block out the distraction of the synth voice announcements. She dropped into half-tracker mode to give herself more time to think.

All of the three merc corvettes were now in range to kill the *Beehive*, but that didn't tell the whole story. The unknown spacer had turned aggressor and was firing on the crippled Blue Four corvette. The other two corvettes abandoned pursuit of the *Beehive* and went after the spacer.

Blue Two's incompetent commander proved true to form and waded into the orbiting rocks instead of arcing over them. The path would take Blue Two within ten kilometers of the *Beehive*'s hiding place in two minutes, and within range of their enhanced lasers. Alternatively, they could launch a timed thermolytics package and let Blue Two overtake it. Mairwen plotted the firing solutions for both and showed them to Haberville.

When Mairwen eased into realtime, she felt light-headed. She had nearly burned herself out during combat, and her body was fighting injuries. She couldn't afford much more time in tracker mode, even half-tracker, until she got food and rest.

"Let's save the lasers as a surprise," said Haberville. She keyed the shipcomm. "Luka, load all five of your packages in the tube, tied together if you can, and set the timers for..." She plotted vectors rapidly on the display. "...six minutes. I'll control the launch."

Her fingers moved in the display, and the lights in the nav pod brightened. "Powering normal systems," she announced. "No point fumbling around in the dark now that they know we're here."

After forty-nine seconds, Luka reported that the payload was set and ready to launch.

Haberville set the firing solution in the navcomp, then announced over the still-open shipcomm, "Launch from number one bay in ten seconds from... mark."

"*Warning. One minute to long-range firing solution from enemy Blue*

Two."

"*Confirm launch from bay one.*"

Mairwen closely watched Blue Two's progress on the display. It was active-scanning almost continuously, but the homemade thermo package was too small to detect that way, even if they'd been looking for it.

"*Warning. Long-range firing solution from enemy Blue Two achievable.*"

"*Warning. One minute to long-range firing solution from enemy Blue Three.*"

"Yeah, yeah, we know," growled Haberville at the navcomp, eyes never leaving the Blue Two icon. "Go open your present, *pendejo.*"

It was a tense few minutes as Blue Two kept its straight-on course for the wounded Blue Three corvette.

The result was worth the wait. Blue Two hit a rock just as the thermolytic package detonated. The scans and the panicked comms made it clear the corvette's shield generator was offline. The hull was compromised catastrophically when the ship careened out of control into another larger asteroid. Blue Two broke apart, shedding debris and several life pods. It was an unexpected piece of good luck.

"One down, one and a half to go," announced Haberville via the shipcomm.

The Blue Three corvette commander, despite having a clear shot at the *Beehive*, didn't take it, and chose to take on the spacer instead.

That was twice the mercs had opted to let the *Beehive* live. While Haberville was distracted with trying to find a new place to hide, Mairwen turned away and subvocalized her observations to Luka. He said it confirmed his belief that their cargo, specifically the samples, was valuable. It also meant they personally were expendable, especially after they'd cost the mercs a squad, a flitter, and two ships.

The battle between the spacer and the corvettes continued, but it was soon obvious the corvettes were outclassed by whoever was commanding and piloting the spacer. Crippled Blue Four was the first casualty, and was set adrift, broadcasting distress calls. Blue Three got in a few good shots, but within fifteen minutes, it was sent damaged and spinning out of control toward Insche 255C. Without a pilot of Haberville's caliber, they'd be lucky to survive the descent, much less the landing.

The merc transport that had been hiding behind the planet took advantage of the melee to make its escape. It arced under the asteroid belt and successfully went transit just as Blue Three took the last hit from the spacer.

The displays went quiet. With no more active-scans blanketing the area, the *Beehive* would have to do scans of its own to find out what the spacer was doing.

Haberville's fingernails drummed on the armrest. "The spacer knows we're here and will find us quick." She gave Mairwen a pointed look. "Question is, Queen Jack, what do we do about it?"

Mairwen gave Haberville a steady look back. "Luka is the commander."

Haberville rolled her eyes and keyed the shipcomm and started to speak. She was forestalled by a synthvoice alert.

"*Incoming communication, broadbeam, open.*"

Haberville played it via the shipcomm.

"*This is deep exploration ship* Seraika Shamsa, *on behalf of La Plata Security. Do you need assistance?*" The voice was in standard, unaccented English and could have been male or female.

To Mairwen's disapproval, Haberville responded immediately without asking Luka.

"This is transport *Beehive*. Yes, we need assistance. We expect reinforcements from the merc company that attacked us both. We'd like to be out of this tin can before that happens." Because the shipcomm was still keyed, her answer was broadcast throughout the *Beehive*.

"*Do you have external transports?*"

"No, we'll have to join airlocks, and we'll need your ramp. We have some cargo, too." Haberville manipulated the nav interface, then sent size and shape specifications data. "Our system drive is operational. We can meet you above the asteroid elliptic."

"*Acknowledged. Sending target coordinates.*"

Haberville checked the incoming data stream. "Got it. Our ETA is about eight minutes."

She plotted a safe course out of the asteroid belt and engaged the system drive.

"*Acknowledged. Will you need medical assistance?*"

Haberville eyed Mairwen's bandaged head and lower calf, where the wound pack was visible through her torn pant leg. "Yeah, we're a little banged up. Nothing critical."

She was about to turn off the shipcomm when Luka's voice came over it. "*Eve, ask them where they'll be taking us.*"

Haberville complied, and was told simply "home." She relayed the answer, then told Luka and Jerzi they'd need to be near the airlock when it came time to join with the spacer. She also unnecessarily reminded them it was standard procedure to seal exosuits and tie in. Everyone who'd ever traveled interstellar knew airlock joins were riskier than external transports when it came to transferring cargo or people.

The spacer's response had been an inadequate answer to Luka's question, but perhaps Haberville thought it impolitic to question their rescuers. Haberville's actions had committed them to close interaction with the unknown spacer crew. Doubtless she wouldn't care that Mairwen didn't like it.

Via her earwire, she heard Luka tell Jerzi to put the weapons on top when they packed their equipment. She assumed he'd subvocalized it for her benefit, so she'd know he didn't like the situation, either. He was becoming more untrusting since she'd known him. Perhaps she was a bad influence on him, too.

As much as she wanted to be where Luka was, she decided she needed to stay in nav as long as possible, where she could be more useful if trouble arose. Even though the spacer had been hired by La Plata, her tracker instincts demanded more caution than Haberville was displaying.

From the visuals, the exploration ship was easily three times the size of the *Beehive*. Like most, it had enough defensive and offensive capability to fend off an alien invasion, even though humans had never encountered other intelligent life in a thousand years of galactic exploration. The spacer could slag the *Beehive* without breaking a sweat. On the other hand, they hadn't so far, despite multiple opportunities.

To soothe her prickly sense of unease, Mairwen set up and hid a small instruction set in the shipcomp that silently added herself, Haberville, and Luka to the commander's access group. It would reinitialize even if someone else specifically tried to remove them.

The airlock join between the ships was connected and sealed quickly and expertly. Haberville told Luka and Jerzi they could unseal their exosuits and open the *Beehive*'s airlock door whenever they were ready.

Haberville turned to Mairwen. "Why don't you go meet the spacer crew? I'll negotiate telemetry with their pilot." She waved toward the door. "I'm sure Jerzi will want every last sample from that cold unit transferred to the spacer's cargo hold for evidence."

Mairwen nodded, then folded the interface closed. She wished she could be both at the airlock and in the nav pod, but her series of hidden alerts would have to do. Haberville hadn't remembered Mairwen's earwire, and she had no intention of mentioning it. Nor of mentioning the spare in her pocket.

Instead of going straight down to the cargo area, she stopped off in the kitchen to chug a protein drink and slap together a sandwich and wolf it down. It would tide her over for a short while.

In the lift, she determinedly settled under the mental and physical camouflage of a simple night guard with dull senses. After days of freedom, it was harder to achieve than she would have imagined. She couldn't remember if it had been as hard right after she'd escaped the CPS and was trying to blend in. She'd been in considerable pain at the time, and it colored all her memories. She wondered if she needed to explain to Luka what she was doing, but it was too late because the doors opened, and she was immediately among strangers.

The spacer's crew had no uniforms, but there was a similarity to their clothing, body art, and jewelry that marked them as a unit. As Haberville predicted, Jerzi was supervising the offloading of the Insche 255C biological samples, tracking the crates against the inventory. She found Luka in the sealable hold with three of the spacer crew, loading their motley gear onto a long, narrow grav cart. Curiously, none of their weapons were on the cart.

She took a couple of steps inside, then assumed an at-ease stance and gave Luka as impassive a look as she could manage.

"Haberville said to report to you." She added a tiny bit of boredom to her tone. The spacers gave her a glance, then dismissed her, as she'd hoped they would.

An astute observer might have noticed that Luka's eyes widened in momentary surprise, but he covered it smoothly. "Good. Get the med kit from the third level and anything else we left."

She nodded and went back to the third level where the showers were. She checked them briefly for any equipment they may have left behind, then went through the staterooms.

She found the medical kit in the hall outside the stateroom closest to the clothes sanitizer. It felt heavier than she remembered. She checked and discovered it was now home to some of their stash of captured hand weapons, concealed under the top layer of medical supplies. She pocketed one of the small hand-beamers, just in case. She was definitely a bad influence on Luka. She smiled briefly as she rearranged the contents to hide the weapons again and closed the case.

She was about to head back down when she remembered that Jerzi had stashed the xenobiological sampling kit in the engine pod. Since he'd been so diligent in collecting the samples it now carried, it would be a shame to leave the kit behind. She walked up the circular ramp to the engine pod door and stepped inside.

The kit wasn't in plain view, but the evidence of the jury-rigged overload flux connection they'd added to power the rigged laser was. She didn't know what would happen to the *Beehive* after they abandoned it, but if military investigators went poking about, she'd rather not be questioned about the modifications they'd made, and she knew Haberville would give her up in a heartbeat. She put the med kit down and sat on the bench to open the engine console so she could adjust the flux controls before decoupling the connection.

Mairwen shook her head. Haberville seemed constitutionally incapable of putting things away. She'd left the emergency communications relay module running, including the recorder. There were two messages queued, and Mairwen assumed one was a copy, until she noticed one was encrypted and considerably larger. The encryptor was still open with the last key used, so she was able to decrypt the longer message.

Just as she was about to listen to it, she heard two sets of boots clomping on the circular ramp one level below, coming up toward her. She didn't recognize the footsteps, so it must be more of the spacer crew. She clamped down on her senses, becoming the dumb guard again, and had the engine comp convert the message for display. While waiting, she opened the cabinet beneath the console to see if Jerzi had secured the xeno kit there.

Far too late, she realized she'd made several mistakes. The words on the screen shocked her, and the sudden sound and floral scent of Haberville behind her caused her to jump, but not fast enough to avoid the slap patch applied to her vulnerable neck. She threw herself to the side to avoid any weapon Haberville might have, but the anesthetic patch did its job, and submerged her into numb, despairing twilight with alarming speed, and then unfeeling blackness.

CHAPTER 23

EVE HARBERVILLE WAS so royally pissed she was ready to shoot the next person who spoke. She'd been so fucking close to winning the high-risk, high-reward gamble that she could pull off this mission, and now everything was in jeopardy.

It had gone as planned to begin with. It was child's play to lure perverted Ta'foulou into using the emergency monitoring system where she'd hidden the mal virus. She'd promised he'd be hearing memorable sex between her and the lusciously hard-bodied, but now sadly departed, DeBayaud.

Then everything had gone chaotic, starting with the sabotage and damage to the *Berjalan,* which wasn't her doing. If she ever got her hands on whoever did, she'd give them a one-way trip off the wheel of life.

She'd rolled with the punches, though. Even after surviving a crash landing and living through a firefight with a merc squad, she'd gotten the gods-cursed samples off that lung-rotting, stinking boghole of a planet and into the contract exploration spacer's hold. She'd even, amazingly, gotten the drop on Morganthur, but now that hellspawn freak of nature had vanished.

Eve *knew* the anesthetic slap patch had made full contact because she'd checked it before stripping off Morganthur's earwire. She should have found a weapon and shot Morganthur then and there instead of taking the time to wipe the nav history and bottle up Foxe and Adams. It was partly her own fault for indulging her soft spot for Jerzi, wanting to protect him from whatever her generous but exacting employer might do to him.

Eve had been planning to quit the piece-of-shit *Beehive* with good riddance when she remembered Adams's precious xenobiological sample kit. Maybe her thoroughness in getting the samples would make up for the fact that one of the merc transports got away, possibly with another cold unit full of samples, although that hadn't been her fault, either.

Besides, it was too dangerous to leave Morganthur alive. Even if she wasn't a jacker anymore, she likely had friends who were, and Eve didn't want to be at the top of some jack crew's payback hit parade. The impatient spacer crew had given her a beamer and five minutes to take care of loose ends.

Now the mutant bitch was gone, and Eve had no idea how or where. She'd even taken the med and xeno kits with her. Christ only knew what the bitch was thinking, but Eve did know Morganthur's weakness, which was why she was standing outside the cargo hold where Adams and Foxe were trapped. She keyed the hold's door comm.

"Jerzi? Luka? You in there?" she shouted, as if she'd only just discovered where they might be.

Adams's muffled baritone came back after a short moment. "*Eve, are we glad to hear you! We're locked in.*"

"Oh God, I'm so sorry." She smiled at how sincerely apologetic she sounded. "The spacer crew said you were already aboard their ship, so I sealed the holds out of habit. I'll get you out right now."

She entered the proper code sequence, and the door opened. She hugged Adams when he came out, taking care to make skin contact with him so he'd feel a little wave of pleasure. Her exciter talent was so low-level that it barely registered in CPS testing, but she'd learned to use it very effectively. She'd tried the same trick with Foxe, but unfortunately, there were always a few who were immune or averse. At least he felt normal. The few times she'd tried with Morganthur, it was like trying to excite a reptile.

Eve angled away so her back was against the wall, then pointed her high-res beamer at them. "Park. I have a deal to make."

Adams's mouth gaped in disbelief. Her tone and the look on her face must have told them not to fuck with her, because they froze in place, their full attention on the business end of her weapon.

She subvocalized a command into her earwire, then spoke. Her voice boomed over the shipcomm.

"Morganthur, I have something you want. You have something I want. Bring me the xeno kit and don't fuck with me, and I'll give you Foxe and Adams. Find a wall comm and respond, or I'll start frying delicate parts of your loverboy."

Foxe's face was admirably stoic, but Adams was looking sadly shocked. If she let him live, maybe it'd be a lesson to him.

Long seconds went by. The ship was silent.

Eve stamped her foot in frustration and swore. The spacer crew didn't seem like the indulgent type. "On a schedule here, Morganthur. Two minutes and I cut my losses."

After a long moment, Morganthur's voice sounded from the shipcomm and echoed in the cargo area. She sounded calm, as if discussing whether or not to have tea.

"*Leave alone now and live. Stay and die.*"

"I'm holding a high-res beamer on Foxe, you subhuman freak!" Eve bit out angrily, and it boomed throughout the ship. "I don't know how you're awake, but get your goddamn ass down here with that kit! Ninety seconds."

There was no response, and no sound from the lifts. Eve swore again, steeling herself to shoot Foxe's torso. She didn't like close-up wetwork, but she'd do it if she had to. At this distance, his exosuit and flexin armor wouldn't hold and she couldn't miss.

CHAPTER 24

IT HAD TAKEN Luka an embarrassingly long time to figure out that he and Jerzi hadn't been locked in the hold accidentally.

After the door automatically sealed but didn't respond to his commander's access, and no one answered their calls on the shipcomm, he assumed it was because Eve was temporarily busy. When Mairwen didn't respond right away via the earwire, he'd thought she was waiting until she could do so without being noticed.

He'd already explained to Jerzi that she preferred to let strangers think she was an inconsequential security guard with barely two brain cells to rub together. Jerzi was skeptical that anyone who spent more than ten minutes with her would believe that, but had been willing to play along if Luka wanted.

Worse than being sealed in was not knowing what was going on outside the hold. When Eve had finally shown up at the hold's door fifteen minutes later, he was just happy to be rescued, after torturing himself with visions of them having been left to die, and anguishing about what could have happened to Mairwen.

Eve's beamer pointed at him had been a shock, but less so than he would have imagined. Mairwen had been right after all. He wanted to tell Eve that the person not to fuck with was Mairwen, but of course she'd never believe that.

Too late, his intuition began filling in the gaps and drawing conclusions. Eve had been on someone else's payroll from the beginning, and her objective was to retrieve the biological samples from the hybrid planet. The exploration spacer's presence was just too damned convenient, and the fact that they weren't accompanied by Space Division should have set off alerts in his mind a lot sooner.

He'd bet a month's pay that Eve worked for Korisni Genetika, Loyduk Pharma's rival, looking to take advantage of Loyduk's emergency withdrawal from the hybrid planet. Other players were possible, though, such as a blackmarketer, or even the Citizen Protection Service, which had turned up in the investigation too many times for coincidence.

He didn't know if Eve had planned the attack on Ta'foulou, but he thought she definitely hadn't expected the *Berjalan* to be sabotaged. Looking back, he conceded that Eve had done an excellent job of keeping everyone off balance the whole trip. He resolutely fired up his talent and focused on her, like he should have done a lot sooner. They needed any advantage they could get.

"...your ass down here with that kit! Ninety seconds." Eve was practically vibrating with rage. The look on her face reminded him of the berserking ramper in Etonver. The beamer's barrel centered on his chest, and he knew she wouldn't miss.

His talent said Eve was corrupt, narcissistic, and amoral, but not an ice-cold killer. His intuition said to distract her.

"Do you believe in any of those deities you swear by?" he asked conversationally.

It visibly derailed her train of thought and relaxed her trigger finger. "Not really." She shrugged. "Hedging my bets."

Luka nodded, projecting calm. "Protagoran logic, then." He felt a draft and suppressed a cold shiver, the price of using his talent.

Eve looked startled, then annoyed. "What?"

Through his earwire, he heard his beloved angel of death. "*Luka, Jerzi, down.*"

Luka dropped like a stone, gratified when Jerzi did the same. Faster than he imagined, even though he'd seen her in action, Mairwen blurred into view and closed her hand over Eve's. By the time Eve started to react, the beamer was already up under her chin and triggered. In his mind, Eve's essence faded to nothing.

Her face still wore its annoyed expression as her body slid down the wall and slumped forward. The back half of her head was missing.

A whiff of burned hair stung his nose. Mairwen was already halfway to the airlock controls.

Luka shook off his daze and spoke urgently to Jerzi. "Get our package. When we decouple the airlock, we need to give our spacer friends something else to think about."

Luka ran to the airlock and took the beamer from Mairwen to cover the airlock door, in case someone from the spacer came looking for Eve. The *Beehive*'s painfully slow airlock sequence was still engaging when Jerzi joined him, holding the cube they'd made to blow the hold's door. Luka was glad neither the spacer's crew nor Eve had noticed they'd been sealed in the hold with four flat cases of KemX explosives.

"Set it for thirty seconds and throw it down the ramp as far as you can," ordered Luka.

Jerzi complied and achieved admirable distance. The package landed in the corner of the ramp, right outside the spacer's hull.

"Nav pod, now!" ordered Mairwen. She started toward the ramp.

The *Beehive*'s airlock was still closing with agonizing slowness as he and Jerzi ran up the ship's circular ramp as fast as they could. Mairwen outdistanced them like they were running in place.

"Seal your suit!" Luka shouted as he ran, fumbling at his exosuit's controls. If the KemX explosion pierced the *Beehive*'s hull, they'd lose air mix violently fast.

The circular ramps were dizzying, and Luka had time to decide that whoever designed them should be launched into the nearest black hole.

They had just cleared the third level when the whole ship shook, and the grav compensators stuttered. Jerzi stumbled, and Luka dragged him up. Luka could have run faster, but he didn't want to chance leaving Jerzi behind. Not again.

The ship shuddered again, throwing off his gait and triggering sharp *deja vu* from when he'd been aboard the *Berjalan*. He grabbed Jerzi's arm and dragged him into the nav pod. Mairwen was already at the nav console, fingers moving so fast they were a blur. The nav pod door sealed and locked quickly behind them.

"Our hull is intact," she said. "It's okay to unseal for now." Luka gladly opened the exosuit so he could hear and breathe better. Jerzi did the same.

She pointed to the co-pilot seat. "Jerzi, lasers." The interface popped into view.

Jerzi adjusted the angle on the holo. "What am I looking at?" he asked. "Oh, I get it. Like an oversized 3-D scope."

"I highlighted targets on the spacer. Their torp tubes are priority. Be ready to fire on my mark."

"Copy," he replied. He adjusted the holo viewing angle again. His expression settled into his detached sniper's look.

Luka moved out of the way to a corner, only to discover it was already occupied by the medical and xeno kits. He couldn't imagine when she'd had time to drag them in. He leaned against the wall instead, trying to stay focused. Mostly all he could do was stare in wonder at Mairwen, who'd saved their lives so many times he was losing count.

"Jerzi, tube is coming around. Five-second burn. Track target movement manually."

"Ready," said Jerzi. They both sounded so calm.

"Now," said Mairwen.

Jerzi powered the laser, counted the burn time out loud, then shut it off.

Mairwen watched her display intently, then smiled slightly. "Dead bang."

Jerzi smiled in response but didn't take his eyes off his targeting display.

"Luka, I need your help." Her voice was suddenly thready.

Luka was deeply alarmed. She *never* asked for help. He was beside her in a heartbeat. She was ash pale. "What do you need?"

She pointed to icons on the navigation interface with shaking fingers. "This is us, this is the spacer. Their airlock is gone. They're spinning out, but they'll get control soon. They're guessing we used regular debris lasers on their torp tube, so they're trying to get away. We have to be within a hundred K for our lasers to slag the other torp tube before they can use it on us, but we can't be closer than fifty K, or their lasers can cut us open." She closed her eyes a moment, then opened them and met his gaze. She looked deathly tired.

"I'm having trouble reading. I can control the system drive, but I need you to read out the distance and angle to me every ten seconds, or sooner if something changes fast." She pointed at two numbers on the interface.

"I can do that." He knelt in front of her and read off the first set of numbers.

She made a minute adjustment to a control on the interface, then closed her eyes and went inert, like a power switch had been turned off. Although he was scared out of his wits for her, he waited the full ten seconds before reading off the numbers again. Some of his terror eased when she opened her eyes. How would she get any rest in ten-second intervals?

"I'm fine," she said, so softly he almost didn't hear it. She met his gaze with the hint of a smile, and he realized with astonishment that she was teasing him. He smiled back at her with all the cockiness he could muster, but he was sure his anxiety was still glaringly obvious.

A shipcomm alert startled them all.

"*Attention. Four transit displacement signatures detected.*"

If Luka had been a religious man, he would have been praying right about then, because the arrival of four new ships meant they were either saved or damned.

He read off the numbers again.

CHAPTER 25

LUKA'S DEEP, STEADY voice soothed her like velvet. As long as he was safe, all was right with the universe.

"Active-scan detected from unknown ship A."

From the readings, it looked like the spacer they'd targeted was firing its trim jets all at once, apparently in an attempt to startle her into moving the *Beehive* away. She couldn't think why the spacer hadn't just engaged its system drive and taken off, since it had gotten what it came for.

Actually, she was having a hard time thinking at all. Despite her bravado for Luka, because he'd looked so vulnerably scared for her, she wasn't fine.

As soon as she'd woken from Haberville's slap patch and staggered out of the engine pod, she'd downed two abandoned cups of cold coffee in the nav pod to help counteract the residual effects of the anesthetic, knowing the caffeine would be a double-edged sword. It had helped her to recover enough to use full-tracker mode to find Luka and Jerzi, and then to kill Haberville, but she was now perilously close to flatlining. Her stomach felt like she'd swallowed lye. When she wasn't losing focus, she kept seeing spots, and the lights made her head throb. She was afraid if she tried even a single second of half-tracker mode, she'd pass out cold.

"Incoming broadbeam message from unknown ship B."

It took her two tries to hit the shipcomm key to play the message out loud.

"This is the Concordance Command dreadnought Khong Met Moi. *Stand down and identify your ship."*

The message was in Mandarin and English, and accompanied by the Space Div identification signature that was almost impossible to counterfeit. Mairwen aimed a tightbeam comm at the dreadnought and spoke as clearly as she could. "This is transport *Beehive*. Luka Foxe from La Plata Security in temporary command. We're under attack by exploration spacer. We need help now."

She never realized how much energy talking took. Her vision grayed out, and her hands became too heavy to hold up to the interface.

From far away, she heard Luka's voice. "This is Foxe. Our only pilot is badly hurt. If you don't help us now, we're dead."

She regretted that she hadn't told Luka how much she loved his voice. The world faded, and she fell into black, and silence, and oblivion.

"...*ljósið mitt*, you have to wake up."

She felt more than heard the murmur of Luka's vocal vibrations through her body. She awoke enough to realize she was being cradled in his lap, her head against his chest. His scent curled up into her nose and soothed her.

Her left hand had an IV unit that was delivering fluids or nutrients, she couldn't tell which. Her right hand, too. She was still in an exosuit, and they were still in the *Beehive*'s nav pod, so not much time could have passed. She tilted her head up to meet Luka's gaze.

"Hi there," he said, with a soft smile.

"Are we safe?" Her voice sounded weak to her ears.

"The dreadnought's pilot talked Jerzi through getting us stabilized. They're setting up an airlock join, and Jerzi's down there now. The spacer is disabled, and its crew is under lockdown. When we blew their airlock, it damaged their system drive guidance. I'm guessing the KemX set off the thermobarics they took from the *Beehive*."

"How long?"

"You passed out twenty minutes ago. You need to listen. Jerzi and I took apart the overload flux line and cleaned the laser guidance system, but if anyone looks at the lasers themselves, they'll see the modifications. None of us knows anything about it. If there are healers on the *Khong Met Moi*, I won't let them near you, and I won't let the medics put you in an autodoc."

"Thank you," she said. Her hands felt cold.

"There's more. Eve Haberville saved us with superb pilot skills, led us safely through the forest, and led the assault on the base. She was trying to rescue all of us from the hold when she was tragically killed by the thieving, murdering spacers. We escaped and blew the airlock with the KemX. Jerzi and I didn't like Eve, but we concede she was a hero."

It was simple, believable, and hard to disprove without a telepathic scan. She tried to smile at him, but was feeling numb, so she wasn't sure she was successful.

"Okay," she said.

He gently pushed a lock of her hair out of her face. "So, what made you suspect her?"

"Engine comp. Left it open. Saw the message she sent to the spacer. Too late." She knew she was sounding like a newsfeed burst, and made an effort to string words together better. "She gave them our names... told them to say they were from La Plata. Wanted all the hybrid samples. She surprised me with an anesthetic slap patch."

"Which she expected to keep you down for hours." He stroked her hair softly. "You moved the kits, then tracked her." The corner of his mouth twitched. "I'll clean the engine comp before we leave. Wouldn't want messy details to get in the way of a good story."

She was flooded by emotion she could finally put a name to.

"I love brilliant men," she whispered.

He tenderly kissed her forehead. "I love you more than any of those other men do."

She discovered tears could come with happiness. "There's only you."

His smile widened and his eyes were bright. "Then I'm a very, very lucky man."

He kissed her lips softly and rocked her in his arms for long moments. Her world shrank to only him, only the exotic, buttery pearwood scent of him.

Jerzi's voice came over the shipcomm. "*The lock is open and we've got company. I asked for a stretcher for Morganthur. They're on their way.*"

"Mairwen, promise me something." The look on Luka's face was suddenly serious. "I want you in my life, and to be in yours, but I know that may not be possible because of your former employer. All I ask is that if you feel you have to leave, tell me. Otherwise, it'll become my life's obsession to find you again."

She lifted her fingers to caress his face, the attached IV unit on her hand making her clumsy. "I promise." He was so perfectly handsome, so perfectly human. Maybe he could teach her to be, too.

CHAPTER 26

LUKA LEANED BACK in the military briefing room chair and arranged his face and limbs in the attitude of relaxed boredom, in case anyone on the *Khong Met Moi* cared to look in. Jerzi was trying to do the same, but the younger man couldn't quite stop fidgeting in small ways. Mairwen, of course, surpassed them both with her ability to remain completely, impassively still. Her only concession to her recent injuries was to sit instead of stand.

They'd been asked to wait while La Plata's lawyer and Seshulla Zheer herself tried to pry them loose from Space Div's care. The room had no door, and they weren't being detained, exactly, but Lieutenant Commander Omharu, the *Khong Met Moi*'s security officer, didn't want to let them go without more "fact finding." Little clues had sparked Luka's intuition, and he'd ruthlessly used his talent on the woman. He wasn't going to make the same mistake of avoiding using his talent and putting them all at risk. What he'd sensed made him believe Omharu was a CPS telepath, whereupon he'd instantly ceased cooperating and demanded the team's formal arrest or immediate release.

Commodore Morris-Seeley had been indifferently unresponsive, but the second in command, Captain Okeanos, had surprisingly taken their side and used a fine knowledge of military code and procedure to keep Omharu at bay. Luka ordinarily disliked being a pawn in someone else's conflict, but in this case, he wasn't going to complain.

Luka's talent said Okeanos was a good man—idealistic, loyal, and surprisingly lonely, probably from having to work with people like Morris-Seeley and Omharu. It was Okeanos who'd finally communicated with the La Plata ship that had accompanied the Space Div contingent to let them know there was a problem. So now they were stuck in jurisdictional limbo.

In truth, Luka was almost completely out of patience with everyone and everything. He'd been glad to get Mairwen onto a large, well-armed ship where she could recover her strength. He hadn't left her side the entire time she was being examined and treated, and both he and Jerzi enforced her wishes with the medics when needed. She'd refused drugs and full-body imagers, but allowed them to use a portable bone knitter on her ribs, and to reapply dermaknit to her burns, lacerations, and leg wound. He would have liked a diagnostic scan on her brain, in case it was swollen from the concussion, but conceded that discovery of her secrets would kill her a lot more quickly than a possible mild brain injury.

When she'd finally been released from treatment, he returned the knives she'd entrusted to his safekeeping, then allowed the medics to treat his own injuries. Luckily, his thigh was knitting nicely and his shoulder bone had only been bruised, not fractured, as he'd feared. Multiple microjets of meds flushed the blood out of his tissue, leaving only hints of bruising. Jerzi's broken nose and black eye were almost erased, and he said his bullet wound felt a lot better.

For the thirty-six hours after that, he, Jerzi, and Mairwen all agreed not to be separated from one another. They asked for shared quarters, ostensibly out of politeness to the personnel who might temporarily be displaced to accommodate them. They slept in shifts, so at least two of them were always awake, acting as personal security for each other. They went everywhere together and were only apart when being interrogated about the events of the prior week.

The *Khong Met Moi* and the two accompanying Space Div frigates were still in the Insche 255 system. Luka hadn't heard what had happened to the exploration spacer or its crew, or if the hybrid planet was being investigated. At this point, he really didn't care. All he wanted to do was go home and spend a month curled up with Mairwen.

It was a new kind of hell being so close and not being able to talk to or even look at her freely, much less touch or hold her, and he was aching for her. He sensed she was feeling it, too.

She was, thankfully, looking much healthier after sleep and food. She still favored her left leg, where the projectile had pierced it, and the sealed laceration on her head made a visible furrow through her asymmetrical haircut, but her eyes were bright and her color was normal.

At every meal in the dining hall, he'd made it a point to load extra selections he thought she might like onto his tray, then surreptitiously transfer them to hers. She raised her eyebrow at him a couple of times and said nothing, but she ate everything he gave her. He was secretly amused by the taciturnity she'd steadfastly maintained since they arrived, mostly because it pissed off Omharu.

After ninety additional minutes of enforced leisure in the briefing room, Luka used the shipcomm to politely request that the operator ask Captain Okeanos to authorize food and drink for them, since they'd missed the second-shift dining hours. When someone finally came, it wasn't with a meal, it was Captain Okeanos himself with two others. Luka recognized the older man who wore civilian clothes. The younger, uniformed man's collar insignia indicated he was an ensign, but his size and demeanor were those of an enforcement guard.

The older man stepped into the briefing room.

"Razumovsky," Luka said. He sat up a little straighter but didn't stand. He was tired of games.

"Foxe," the man acknowledged, then turned to Okeanos. "I'd like to talk to my clients alone for a few minutes."

"Regrettably, privacy is hard to find these days, even on Space Div capital ships," said Okeanos. His voice was a deep, rumbling bass. "This public briefing room will have to do." His eyes darted briefly to two of the light panels in the room.

Razumovsky nodded. Okeanos and the other man stepped out into the hall and politely turned their backs to the open doorway.

"I see you're all looking tolerably well, considering," Razumovsky said, eying the blue taped patches on the side and sleeve of Mairwen's shirt and the round hole in the shoulder of Jerzi's. "Zheer is wrapping up details with the commodore. You'll have to be available for an official recorded statement for Space Div investigators once we get back to Rekoria, but I expect you'll be released from here in the next thirty minutes." His gaze rested on Mairwen. "I understand some of you refused medical treatment?"

"Oh, please," said Luka, mindful of the monitors Okeanos had subtly warned them about. "Morganthur doesn't like hospitals or medics. They tried to make it out like she wasn't competent to decide for herself. We convinced them otherwise."

Razumovsky nodded his understanding. "Do you need anything from your bunks before we leave?"

"No," said Luka, and Jerzi echoed it. Mairwen shook her head.

"Sit tight. I'll be back soon."

He left with Okeanos, but the ensign stayed put outside the door. Luka exchanged a look with Jerzi and saw he also thought it unusual for the ensign to stay.

Luka knew Mairwen would hear someone coming a lot sooner than he could, so he casually angled himself so he could see her instead of staring at the corridor. Besides, he liked watching the beautiful woman he was in love with. The woman who miraculously loved him back.

They didn't have long to wait before Mairwen subtly flicked her eyes toward the door. About ten seconds later, Omharu tried to stride through the doorway, only to be blocked by the ensign.

"Sorry, sir, no one in or out. Captain's orders," The ensign didn't sound the least bit sorry.

"Countermanded," snapped Omharu. She tried to step forward, but the ensign blocked her again.

"Sorry, sir, you'll have to take it up with the captain." There was a perverse enjoyment in the ensign's tone. Maybe Omharu had made more enemies than just Okeanos.

Omharu was obviously used to overriding the chain of command. "Ensign Águila, if you want to keep your rank, you'll let me in *right slagging now*." Her voice was controlled, but her face was flushed with anger.

"Funny, that's the same thing the captain told me about keeping people out." Águila shrugged. The man's body language said he was feeling confident. "Maybe we should ping the captain together and ask."

Luka carefully schooled his face to keep his enjoyment from showing. Jerzi hid his smile by bending down to adjust his boot fastening.

"Ensign, you just bought yourself a whole galaxy of trouble." She gave one last sweeping glare at Águila and everyone in the room, then stalked off.

"Asshole," said Luka, just loud enough to be heard. Águila snorted, then turned it into a cough.

Razumovsky's time estimate turned out to be optimistic, but an hour later, all the La Plata employees were finally transferred via pinnace to La Plata's commercial ship, the *Padrashan Librero*.

Zheer met them in the small landing bay and graciously thanked the pinnace's pilot in flawless Mandarin, then ushered them all into the formal dining room that doubled as a conference room. Luka liked the *Padrashan* better than most ships, but he was more than ready for solid, planetside ground under his feet.

He was happy to hear the *Padrashan* would be going transit within ten minutes, with an ETA at Rekoria in three ship days. He'd had enough of the Insche 255 system to last a lifetime, and the farther away he was from the zealous security officer, the better.

A buffet had been set up so they could help themselves. He tried not to watch Mairwen, because he knew he couldn't hide his feelings for her, and keen-eyed Zheer was bound to notice.

A lot of questions were coming, and Zheer and Razumovsky needed information now, but he wasn't willing to spend all night at it. Or was it day? He really had no idea. He wished he'd had even five minutes alone with Jerzi and Mairwen to discuss what he was about to say, but it couldn't be helped.

He started by telling Zheer and Razumovsky the story they'd been telling Space Div, with Eve Haberville as the martyred hero. Then he told them what really happened, more or less, with the emphasis on *less* when it came to anything that hinted at Mairwen's abilities and skills, and the emphasis on *more* when it came to assigning certain extraordinary events to luck or to Haberville. Such as how they'd avoided being killed by the *Berjalan*'s sabotage, or how the four of them overcame a merc squad of fifteen, stole a light-drive transport, and defeated a military-style corvette with a rigged laser.

Jerzi, to Luka's deep gratitude, supported Luka's mostly true but slanted version of events, and the one outright lie, wherein Luka blamed the spacer crew for Haberville's death. Mairwen only contributed when asked a direct question, and otherwise maintained her usual reticence. Luka had to continually fight his impulse to look at her to see how she was taking it.

Zheer rotated her coffee cup in its saucer, a familiar habit of hers when she was thinking. "Why did you tell Space Div that Haberville was the hero?"

Luka had an answer ready. "Because once they start stomping around, all the cockroaches will head for the dark corners, and we won't have a chance to confirm who she worked for, or find out who sabotaged the *Berjalan*, or even who hired the mercs, here or in Etonver. You can't hide a hybrid planet without help, or at least willful ignorance, from the Concordance government or the military. And I sure as hell didn't want a CPS telepath mucking about in our minds, or one of their cleaners removing inconvenient memories that might contradict whatever official explanation they concoct."

Most of the Space Div investigators he'd ever worked with tended to be linear thinkers, so he'd told them a story that suited their view of the universe. He personally didn't care if they ever solved the *fökking* case or not, as long as Mairwen was as safe as he could make her. That included misleading his employer and lying shamelessly to Concordance Command. Even if it meant no justice for the murders of Leo Balkovsky and Adina Schmidt.

"Haberville never said who she worked for?" asked Razumovsky.

"No," said Luka, "but I'd lay odds on Korisni Genetika. Like Tewisham said, the pharma industry is full of spying, dirty tricks, and double agents."

He took a sip of water, glad it didn't taste of purification chemicals.

"My working theory is that Korisni found out Loyduk Pharma, or its partner, was having to abandon Insche 255C for a while, and saw a golden opportunity to hijack their samples and research. Or maybe they'd already had someone on site, siphoning off the best discoveries, and decided to steal everything once Loyduk terminated the operation." He splayed the fingers of his left hand. It was fully healed, but he hadn't forgotten the pain. "I think Korisni arranged my kidnapping and interrogation in Etonver. They asked what I knew about Loyduk, which was a stupid question if Loyduk had hired them."

"You believe Haberville was responsible for the virus that attacked Ta'foulou?"

"Yes," said Luka, keeping his tone nonchalant. "She knew he entertained himself by monitoring the emergency comm system, and didn't want him listening in on anything she did." While possibly true, it was more likely that she'd disabled him so she'd be the only pilot, and had been unpleasantly surprised by Mairwen's expertise. "I imagine she listened to all of us from time to time, too, in case we made decisions that threatened her agenda."

Zheer's icy look would have stopped a star in mid-solar flare. "Had I known of Ta'foulou's weakness, I would have terminated him immediately. I don't tolerate such abuse on any ship I operate."

Luka wasn't sure Zheer's policy was enforceable, but at least her words put the *Padrashan*'s pilots on notice that they'd better not get caught.

Jerzi spoke up. "When we hit Horvax Station, Foxe got a message saying there'd been two infosec breaches. What were they?"

Zheer's expression went sour. "Someone cloned our entire info hypercube when we did a network upgrade a couple of weeks ago. It was auctioned to at least two bidders we know of. If Luka's suppositions are right, one was Korisni, which caused them to hire Haberville, and the other was Loyduk, through a fixer named Hildree Fannar. Needless to say, we've improved our procedures in that area. We believe one of the bidders found the Amhur address and hired a crew to go there, looking for Onndrae. The Etonver police think members of a theft crew they recently detained might have been involved."

Luka nodded, pleased that another loose thread was being addressed.

"Connected to Loyduk, I'd say. Their corporate culture is stupidly tightfisted. I bet they thought they could save money by using their cheaper theft crew instead of hiring wetwork pros."

"And the other breach?" prompted Jerzi.

Zheer and Razumovsky exchanged a look, and Razumovsky answered. "On the day the *Berjalan* left Rekoria, Foxe's assistant Velasco went missing. La Plata assumed he had taken an unannounced vacation, which he'd been warned against several times before. Therefore, we terminated him, as Foxe knows from the message. However, he turned up three days later claiming to have been kept prisoner at a joyhouse and mentally interrogated by his sex partners. We later confirmed his explanation."

Luka was amused by the lawyer's careful answer, which implied a lot of damage control. Reading between the lines, they'd assumed Velasco to be an irresponsible oaf, which he mostly was, and had fired him, then discovered evidence that he'd been the victim he'd been claiming all along. La Plata probably had to offer Velasco his job back, or a monetary settlement, or both.

"Taking La Plata to court, is he?" asked Luka. Zheer's acid glare confirmed his guess.

Razumovsky gave him a calculating look. "Since he's your assistant…"

Luka interrupted. "I was already planning to request a new assistant as soon as we got back." He knew the company lawyer, of all people, would know Luka's contract made it his choice. Luka didn't care what La Plata did with Velasco, as long as they assigned him elsewhere.

A wave of mental exhaustion washed over him.

"Look, we'll be happy to answer more questions and make all the reports you want, but Morganthur, Adams, and I have had one hell of a week. Could we take this up again after we've had about twenty-four hours of downtime?"

After only a moment's hesitation, Zheer said, "Of course." Razumovsky nodded his agreement.

Zheer looked at each of them, her eyes darting to the various patches and holes in their clothes. "Captain Okeanos was kind enough to inform us that you arrived on the *Khong Met Moi* with little more than the shirts on your backs, so we made some purchases from their supplymaster. I'll have Ravan show you to your quarters." She stood, which was the cue for everyone else to do the same.

More than clothes, sleep, or a hot shower, Luka wanted time alone with

Mairwen, but he couldn't think of a way to make that happen, not without making them both the center of attention, which she'd hate. *Helvítis*, but it was going to be a lonely few days.

CHAPTER 27

FOR THE ENTIRE debriefing, Mairwen had listened attentively to Luka's careful weaving of truth and misdirection, confirming details when asked but volunteering nothing. It would take someone with Luka's brilliance to unravel it, and no one else in the room came close.

All the while, she'd wrestled with herself over what to do about Luka personally. Actually, the wrestling had started when he hovered over her like a guard dog on the *Khong Met Moi*, ready to defend her with the nearest bone laser to prevent the medic from taking even a blood sample without her permission.

The cautious part of her brain, the part she'd diligently cultivated after escaping the CPS, urged her to fade into the background and wait to see what happened once they got back to Etonver. The fact that she finally figured out that she loved him with shocking intensity didn't mean a relationship would work. Even if it did, it would at least be prudent to keep it secret.

They were all excuses. She'd known days ago there would be no going back into the shadows, not if she wanted to stay with Luka. She wanted that more than anything. She was deathly tired of merely existing, avoiding risk, not using her skills, never enjoying the freedom she'd fought so hard for.

That was all very well, but she didn't know what to do about it. Was there some sort of social protocol for telling friendly co-workers like Jerzi, or powerful company officers like Zheer, that she planned to stay with Luka? She hadn't even told *him*. It suddenly occurred to her that even that wouldn't be possible if she was still considered to be on duty.

"... I'll have Ravan show you to your quarters," Zheer was saying. It was suddenly the end of the meeting and everyone was standing up.

Before she lost her courage, Mairwen spoke up.

"What about the security detail for Foxe?"

Zheer stopped mid-step, nonplussed. "I wasn't aware he still needed protection. We're in transit, with trusted employees and contractors... Oh, I see your point." She gave Mairwen a considering look. "Your dedication is... unanticipated. I imagine it's part of why you're all still alive. Are you volunteering?"

Mairwen felt Luka step up behind her, so close she could feel the heat of his body on hers. She just barely stopped herself from melting against him.

She needn't have bothered, because he put his hands on her shoulders and pulled her back to him possessively. Her heart skipped erratically.

"No, she's not," Luka said firmly. "She needs rest as much as I do. All three of us will need protection until we can record our official statements. I'm sure you brought enough staff depth to cover it." She felt his breath against her ear, and she had to slam down her senses to stop her body from responding.

Mairwen mentally held her breath, waiting for Zheer's reaction.

Outside of a momentary eyebrow lift, Zheer's only response was to say she'd take care of it, then to blandly lead them to a corridor and point. "Your names are on the doors. Breakfast will be at seven. We'll talk tomorrow evening."

Their rooms were clustered together. Jerzi found his and said he'd see them all later, then sealed the door behind him.

The singleton rooms assigned to her and to Luka weren't much bigger than utility closets, but the pull-down beds were wider and better padded than those on the *Khong Met Moi*, and the control panels had individual lighting and temperature controls. Each room had bags of military-issue work clothes and toiletries. Luka took charge and brought her bags into his room and put them all on the chair.

He sealed the door, then pulled her tightly into his arms and hard up against him. Any doubts she might have had about whether or not he wanted to stay with her faded away. She clung to him as if he was a life raft in a turbulent sea.

He reached out one hand and fumbled for the control panel, turning up the heat and setting the lights at half-glow. He stroked her back and gently kissed her face around the wounded areas.

"I'm never playing games of chance again. I used up all my luck when I met you." His smile was teasing, but there was a tinge of desire to it.

Happiness bubbled in her, and she laughed at his hyperbole. "Probability doesn't accrue."

"I know, but I love the poetry of it."

He reverently took her face in his hands and kissed her expertly and thoroughly.

"I love your laugh." He kissed her again. "*Ég elska þig.* I love you."

"I love you," she whispered, then kissed him with no expertise, but with everything she was feeling, everything she had to give him. The taste and the scent of him drenched her senses.

The aching that had plagued her chest and arms turned to liquid fire. She pulled out his shirttail so she could burrow her hands under and splay them on his warm skin and firm muscles. A moan vibrated through her and she couldn't tell if it was his or hers.

"You're not still in pain, are you?" he asked. The moan must have been hers, then.

He started on the buttons of her shirt. She tried to help, but the tremors had already started, and she couldn't hold her fingers steady.

"Not much. You?" Her command of words was slipping fast.

"No." He kissed her neck behind her ear, making her gasp. "Right now, I wouldn't care if I was."

He undid the last button and pushed her shirt off her shoulders. She let it drop behind her on the floor. She released her wrist and ankle sheaths and put them on the shelf above the desk. He practically ripped his shirt off.

His muscled chest and bare skin were entrancing, and she had to touch. She traced the remnants of the bruised discoloration on his right shoulder with delicate fingers. It troubled her that he'd been injured.

He grabbed her fingers and brought them to his lips for a kiss.

"Don't you dare apologize for me getting hurt." He pulled her close and lowered his voice to a whisper in her ear that sent a tingling wave through her. "We'd be dead three times over if it wasn't for you. If anything, I owe you an apology. I should have... evaluated Haberville a lot sooner."

She appreciated that even when deeply distracted, he remembered that little pilots might still have big ears, and they each had secrets to keep.

He traced the bottom edge of the narrow-strapped, tape-patched tank top she wore. "Have I told you how plasma hot you are in these?"

His questing hand swirled under and up to the pebbled peak of her breast, and she arched into his caress. She tried to speak, but a tremor rippled through her like overload flux in a light drive. She gasped involuntarily and struggled to regain control of her sensory inputs and her body's response.

To her regret, he moved his hand away from her breast, but his other arm tightened around her and brought her flat against him. "We'll go as slow as you need, *elskan,*" he said.

She wanted this so badly, but she was afraid she was too impaired. She wished she knew what to do, other than try not to have seizures.

He slowly caressed her back under her tank. "I know it's rude to ask, but have you had other lovers?"

She remembered he'd said he'd had a few, and she was glad at least one of them had.

"Not… lovers."

She didn't want to distress him, but he deserved to know that she didn't have the right kind of experience in what they were about to do. Or at least, in what she hoped they were about to do.

"In the first few months of, uh, school, trainers used sex on all of us for discipline. That stopped once we learned… skills."

"Defensive skills," he said.

She could hear the anger in his voice, and she wanted to soothe it away, but didn't know how. She couldn't change her past, only her future.

"Some students found relief with each other, but I had no interest, even after I left. I thought I was permanently broken." She nuzzled her face into his neck and inhaled his exotic scent, letting it curl up into her nose. "Until I met you."

"I'll try to make it good for you, *ástin mín*. My love." The rumble of his voice and the pressure of his breath against her ear made her tremble. She licked his neck with little touches of her tongue, savoring him, then kissed and licked along his collarbone. The taste of him was irrevocably associated in her memory with love and desire.

She moved back from him long enough to pull her bedraggled tank off over her head and drop it on the floor. She pressed her chest to his, drawing little soft moans from them both.

His breath was ragged. "Chaos, but I've wanted this. And for once, no one's trying to kill us."

She smiled. "So far."

"Hush, woman, you'll jinx us." He kissed her as if to keep her from saying more, but the kiss grew more sensual when she took his hands and brought them back up to her breasts. This time, she managed to hold off the tremor until his mouth found their pebbled tips. The sensations shredded her control and drowned coherent thought.

He kissed her mouth again, then pulled away. "I have too many clothes on, and so do you."

He pulled her to the bed and sat her on the edge, then kneeled before her and started undoing the fasteners on her boots. She awakened from the haze of desire enough to get the idea and did it for herself, while he removed his boots and everything else. He was gloriously, rampantly male. She wanted to taste every centimeter of him.

She stood and fumbled at the hook for her pants. He sat on the bed in front of her and gently pushed her hands away. He undid her pants and helped her slide them and her underwear down so she could step out of them.

"*Falleg*," he breathed. "Beautiful." He skimmed his hands up the sides of her hips, thumbs skimming over the matching scars, and onto her abdominal muscles. He stood and wrapped her in his arms, molding his body to hers.

"We fit together perfectly." He kissed her long and deep.

She slid her hands down his back to skim and cup his beautifully muscled rear, pulling his pelvis into hers because it felt right.

She felt a deep shiver flow through his core. Worry washed through her. He'd turned up the heat, so he shouldn't be cold. Was his talent working?

"What's wrong?"

"Nothing," he whispered, "I just want you." He tightened his hands on her hips and ground his hard arousal against her. "A lot."

She was thunderstruck. "Trembling is normal?"

"It is when you desire…" he trailed off. He took a deep, uneven breath and looked at her with dawning revelation. "When we kissed in your apartment, you were afraid it was because you're…"

"…no longer human," she whispered.

He smiled at her with such loving compassion she thought she'd melt. He pressed butterfly kisses to her face. "It's because you *are* human."

Her eyes were filling with tears again, and she added profound relief and hope to the list of things that made her cry. The list was getting disconcertingly long.

He pulled her onto the platform bed, entangling his limbs with hers and kissing her wherever he could land his mouth. "Delectably… delightfully…"

She found the most sensitive part of him with her greedy tongue, and he bucked.

"I won't last two minutes if you do that… *human*."

CHAPTER 28

SHE HAD NO words to describe making love with Luka. Becoming lovers. Becoming one.

Her body still simmered and her emotions still swamped her rational brain. Slow had turned into fast, and into slow again, and pleasurable release was only part of what they'd shared with each other.

She lay at his side, half draped over him, their heart rates only quite recently slowing to something like normal. He was caressing her with smooth, lazy strokes. Every breath she took was laced with the perfect scent of him. She didn't know how she could feel both energized and drained at the same time. The floor of the stateroom looked like an explosion of clothes.

His wonderfully sculpted stomach growled, and it made her smile.

"How long until breakfast, do you suppose?" His voice was deep and quiet as it rumbled in his chest and vibrated against her ear. "I need a flux resupply."

She calculated from when they'd stepped into the stateroom together. "Three hours, seventeen minutes, if they serve on schedule."

"You're really accurate with time."

"Yes," she agreed. Honesty made her add, "Except I lose track of it when I'm engaged with you."

"Do you have a chrono implant?" His voice was so quiet that only she could hear it. As was often the case, the direction of his thoughts was mysterious to her.

"No, just training. Time slows when I'm in full... action. I need an anchor to the real world."

"Action, like what you did with Haberville, or the ramper in Etonver, or the mercs?" He smiled at her, his eyes sparkling with intuition. She delighted in his mercurial, brilliant mind.

"Yes," she said, responding to his smile with one of her own. She'd known he'd eventually figure out the right questions to ask. He was the one person in the universe she would ever trust with the answers.

He kissed her forehead. "I've been meaning to tell you, by the way. I noticed you didn't kill those two mercs who jacked me in Etonver."

She guessed he was wondering why she'd let them live. She shrugged a shoulder and looked toward his face. "It would have been easier, but I thought you'd seen enough death already that week."

He laughed and kissed her lightly. She loved that he laughed so easily. "That's the nicest thing anyone's ever done for me."

She slid her hand lazily down his chest. She couldn't get enough of the feel of him. She lingered on two jagged scars between his ribs.

"Why do you still have these?" She knew they were from a year ago, when he'd nearly been killed by the collector pedophile he'd cornered. Any half-decent body shop could easily erase them for a reasonable fee.

"A memento, I guess. Some people have skin art; I have scars."

She'd found another, longer scar when memorizing every surface of him with her hands and mouth. She slid her hand to his hipbone and touched the much older, faded mark, but still pale against his exquisite light brown skin. "And this?"

"The reason I went into forensic investigation."

"An old, bad memory?" She didn't want to make him think of painful things. His extraordinary talent made him remember more than enough as it was. She started to slide her hand away, but he caught it and held it fast.

"Bittersweet. I was thirteen, and a friend of mine was beaten and killed. I found his body and the crime scene. The man who did it was my friend's uncle. He was a respected business owner and charity director, but he also liked anal intercourse with adolescent boys. My friend resisted, and the man panicked. My mother had died only a month before, and the detectives thought I was delusional when I said I could see some of the things that happened. But the forensic investigator not only listened to me, he believed me, and it led them to the uncle. He tried to kill me because he thought I had to be a witness."

She wove her fingers through his, then pressed a kiss to the back of his hand. It reminded her of the first time she'd touched him, barely knowing how to offer comfort. She would never willingly go back to being the person she was then.

"Have I told you I love the sound of your voice?" She'd meant to tell him several times, but couldn't remember if she'd actually said it. She wanted to be better about words with him.

"I thought you loved my scent. And my taste." He began to caress her with less-than-lazy strokes, and her arousal began to surge along with the pace of his heart.

"I do," she agreed, as she released his hand so she could rise and slide herself sensuously up and over him, to where their hips fitted together perfectly. "Let me show you what else."

Chapter 29

LUKA FINISHED HIS official report for La Plata and sent it to Zheer's workspace in the shipcomp. He'd volunteered to compile it with input from Mairwen and Jerzi, rather than making them create separate reports. The *Padrashan*'s ship days were synced to Etonver time, but his body clock was still confused. The ship's food was passable, but not as good as Jerzi's, and it was about time for the evening meal, but his stomach thought it was mid-morning at best. They'd be arriving in Rekoria space in about thirty hours. He could have used something from the med kit to reset his sleep pattern, but since Mairwen couldn't take it, he'd rather stay synced to hers.

Jerzi was young and resilient, and his bullet wound was almost healed, but he'd grown increasingly quiet as they got closer to home. Now that Luka had filed the report, he sought Jerzi out and found him sitting in his room, feet up on the narrow desk. The brand-new, military-issue pants and pocket-covered tunic were a marked contrast to his battered gunnin boots.

"Everything okay?" asked Luka.

"Yeah, sort of. It's just little things, now that I have time to think about them." He waved, inviting Luka to sit.

"Dom DeBayaud was a friend, and I'll miss him. I feel like an idiot that Haberville manipulated me. I know the pharma companies involved in all this won't get what's coming to them because money can buy a lot of immunity." He sighed. "I don't know that I want to go back to being just another ex-gunnin on a security team, but I don't know else I can do."

Luka knew the feeling, from when he'd left the military, before Leo had brought him into La Plata. "What do you *want* to do?"

Jerzi shrugged. "Whatever I can so I can get my kid and her mother away from where they are. We needed her family to support them while I was still in the service, but that family is nasty crazy. Now it's just a question of money. I miss them a lot. I'm going to use some of the extra downtime Zheer authorized to go see them."

"Before you do, talk to Beva Rienville when we get back to Etonver, and tell her I sent you. She's heading up a new division for personal security. I can personally attest that you're damned handy in a firefight."

Jerzi looked a little surprised. "Thanks. I will," he said after a moment, then gave Luka a knowing look. "I'm a piker compared to Mairwen."

"Aren't we all," said Luka, with a small smile for the shared secret.

After that, he went looking for Mairwen and found her in one corner of the large exercise room. He didn't recognize the other man in the room using the free weights, but then again, he didn't even know how many people were on the ship. He hadn't spent much time outside of the room he shared with Mairwen.

She was working gingerly on the force isolation machine to strengthen her lower left leg where the projectile had pierced it. The wound pack had done its job promoting rapid healing, but the bruising and scarring were still evident. All her injuries were getting better, but he knew she was still in moderate pain. He wished his minder talents included healing so he could help her.

He watched her do five more repetitions, then turn the machine off. She grabbed her towel and crossed to where he was standing. She'd been working hard and sweating. The dark military-style sleeveless tank she wore was plastered to her chest, outlining her firm, high breasts with their delightfully sensitive tips. He drew a deeper breath, suddenly in need of more oxygen.

"Want to read our report?" He tried to achieve a business-like tone.

"I don't know. Is it odd?" She gave him a small smile.

He grinned at the unexpected teasing. "Yes, and boring, too. It'll be ready after your shower."

He was waiting for her when she came back to their room. He openly admired her as she dressed, glad she wasn't shy about her body. She wore the new tunic over her own patched pants because the ones purchased from the *Khong Met Moi* were hugely too big for her slender hips. She sat at the small desk to read his report on the display. Tempting as it was to make love with her again, they needed to talk. His discussion with Jerzi had him thinking about the future.

"Mairwen, what do you want to do when we get back to Etonver?"

She froze, her face suddenly neutral. He remembered seeing that look when she'd thought she was going to be fired. That wasn't what he'd intended at all. He pulled her up and into his arms, and felt her stiffness.

"I'll tell you what I want, my love. I want you in my life, any way I can have you. I'll visit you and stay the night as often as you'll let me. Better yet, come live with me. Be my partner, work cases with me, help me think." He took a deep breath to steady himself. "I don't want to stampede you or pressure you, because I'm afraid it'll make you pull away or leave me, so I'm asking, what do you want?"

She'd relaxed slowly as he spoke. She took a long time answering.

"I feel things with you. I didn't used to care one way or the other about people, or different foods, or having preferences, because they weren't real to me until I met you. I don't know if our relationship will survive a normal, daily routine that doesn't involve murder, combat, and running for our lives. I don't know if La Plata will let me stay, because Zheer knows my records are incomplete. I don't trust other people to keep you safe, except perhaps Jerzi because he admires you, but I'm not even sure I can keep you safe, because you distract me to where all I think about is having sex with you in inappropriate places."

It was the longest personal speech he'd ever heard from her. He held her strong, beautiful face in his hands and kissed her with thankful reverence. He sat in the small padded armchair and pulled her into his lap, cradling her in his arms.

"Three things. First of all, I've been dreaming of a normal, daily routine with you, preferably one that has us going to sleep together every night, like we did in the hybrid forest, though I prefer actual beds to tarps. If you hate my townhouse, I'll sell it and we'll find something together, when you're ready. Second, La Plata damned well *better* let you stay and be my partner, or I'll find somewhere else to work. Zheer may suspect you're much more than what your records say, but you already passed a mid-level background check, and I'm betting there's nothing to find. More importantly, I don't think she'll care. Something she said yesterday makes me think she sees value in a surprisingly skilled employee with such an innocuous background."

"I can't be your partner. I don't know how to investigate. You're creative and brilliant and good with words and people. I'm just a…"

"…a night-shift guard?" he finished. "To quote the late and entirely unlamented Haberville, then I'm the First Flight Queen of Albion Prime."

Mairwen, his beloved warrior, had invaluable unconventional knowledge in the ways people could be traced or killed. She was controlled, well-prepared, and crafty, not to mention as tenacious as he was, and together they made a formidable team. And that wasn't even taking into account her extraordinary senses and tracker skills. He'd tell her all those reasons and more when he was sure they were truly alone.

She snorted, half in exasperation, half in amusement. "What's the third thing?"

He'd forgotten his third point. The feel and smell of her were sending warmth into his core, and his brain was getting short shrift as his blood flow went south. He kissed her neck and nibbled her earlobe with teeth and tongue, which made her tremble in response.

"Third, *engillinn minn*, my angel, tell me about these inappropriate places you have in mind..."

CHAPTER 30

FOUR MONTHS LATER on Rekoria, winter winds blew with full force, rattling the dark windows of the small but luxurious apartment. Mairwen saw Luka suppress a shiver, despite the thick dark green sweater he wore. The storm was only one reason he was cold. The other was because he was using his talent to reconstruct the crime scene of an unknown blond male lying on the floor in a pool of congealing blood. From what the preliminary police investigation said, and Luka was confirming, not all the blood spilled and splattered on the walls belonged to the dead man.

Mairwen looked at Nouri, the police officer who'd been ordered to stay with them, to see if he'd noticed Luka's reaction. So far, the older, thick-bodied man had paid them scant attention. It was late enough that he probably didn't care what Luka did, as long as it was expeditious and didn't involve tampering with the evidence. Fortunately, Nouri wasn't the chatty type, and didn't seem to be disturbed by the violent crime scene.

To reinforce her role as Luka's uninteresting assistant, Mairwen parked herself in a security-guard stance near the large forensic kit. Luka had done most of the talking, though she had pointed out that the apartment's upscale security recording system had been turned off.

Someone who knew Luka would have said he was looking distracted and stressed, but not unduly so. Seshulla Zheer hadn't expected him to agree to do the rush crime scene reconstruction job, but it didn't surprise Mairwen. Since they'd returned to Etonver, he'd worked diligently with his brutal memories to gain control of his reconstruction talent. A fresh, violent crime scene would be the acid test.

He rose from where he'd been crouching and crossed to the kit. He pulled out a small instrument and handed it to her.

"Do a preliminary check of the other rooms for blood splatter."

He caught her eye and rubbed his nose briefly. He was suggesting she use her extraordinary sense of smell. The hemolytic vapor spectrum analyzer, known as a blood sniffer for short, would be a cover for her actions. He'd been using forensic reconstruction instruments as a cover for his own talent for years. She nodded her understanding and headed down the tiny hall.

Although it had been simpler in this case to let the police assume she was Luka's minimally skilled assistant, she'd actually been promoted to investigator and Luka's partner two months ago. He professed innocence, but she was still convinced he'd pressured Zheer into it. The new position made her far more visible than she'd ever imagined being able to tolerate. But then again, she'd never imagined having friends or falling in love with Luka. She would have taken almost any job that let her keep that.

Her examination found nothing to contradict their client's story of having been alone before the dead man broke in, raped and tortured him, and nearly killed him. The bedroom, closet, and fresher only had one person's scent, and it wasn't that of the dead man. The client's rich parents had hired La Plata when the focus of the police questions implied they thought it was a lovers' disagreement turned tragic, meaning they might be arraigning the young man for homicide.

She returned to the living area, where Luka pointed out other specific areas of interest where she should use the sniffer. For tiny samples such as blood drops, the device was better than her nose at differentiating between sources. She thought she might be able to taste the difference since the crime was only hours ago, but she thought Officer Nouri might object if she licked blood splatter from the wall.

The dead man had died from being gutted with a carving knife. If the client's story was true, the painful death was deserved. The client was in the emergency trauma ward with multiple contusions, lacerations, and burn wounds, and would likely need post-traumatic experience treatment with a good minder sifter and a therapy telepath.

Luka was still taking images and measurements around the body, especially the outstretched right hand. He frowned.

"Officer Nouri, did the investigators remove anything from this hand?"

The man nodded. "Illegal weapon."

"Really? What's illegal in Etonver?" asked Luka, with a tinge of cynicism in his tone.

The officer snorted. "Amped wirekey. It was still sparked."

Luka raised an eyebrow. "That's a theft crew tool."

Adding power to a wirekey made it better for forcing cheap locks, which is what made it illegal. Etonver law placed a high value on the sanctity of possessions.

Nouri grunted, but didn't say anything. Mairwen suspected he knew the lead homicide detective was on the wrong track with the "lovers' spat" theory, but wasn't going to admit it to civilians. Nouri looked restive, and it wasn't long before he asked when they'd be done.

Luka looked around, then at the clock. "In about thirty minutes."

Nouri frowned. "I need to use a fresher. Protocol says I should seal you out while I go find one that isn't part of the crime scene." He looked at the front door, which was barely staying upright on a single warped hinge, and sighed. "Oh, to hell with it. I'd rather have you in here than some sticky-fingered neighbor. I'll be back in a few."

Nouri walked faster than she'd seen him move all evening as he left the apartment. She turned up her hearing to listen as his footsteps led him down the hall and down the stairs.

Luka drifted her way, watching her. When Nouri was out of her hearing range, she nodded, and he glided to within inches of her.

"What does your nose say?" he asked quietly. The buttery pearwood scent of him was a welcome change from all the blood in the room.

"Outside of police personnel, only two humans have been in the apartment in the last few days—the person who sleeps in the bed and him." She tilted her head toward the dead man. "He didn't get further than the couch. It smells of blood and burned flesh. He smells like coconut oil, chems and smoke, like from a pub, and sex fluids. I think I've run across his scent before, but I can't remember where." Scents she'd imprinted, like Luka's, were unforgettable, but the hundreds of others she ran across daily she tended to forget after a while.

"Our client has wirekey wounds on his genitals, like the torture marks on Vadra Amhur. Could that be the smell you remember?"

Mairwen shook her head. "I never got close enough to Amhur's body." Luka had been her main concern at the time. She gave him a searching look now and lightly brushed her fingertips across the back of his hand. "How are you?"

He caught her hand and squeezed it gently before letting it go. His fingers were cold.

"I'm okay. Thank you."

She knew he was thanking her for more than just inquiring about his status. She gave him a small smile.

He took a deep breath, then stepped back. "Let's get the camera cloud running while Nouri is out of the way."

She'd assisted him at other more mundane crime scenes, and she'd read the complete instructions for most of the tools in his reconstruction kit, so they had the little flying cameras working quickly. She and Luka stepped into the hallway so the cameras could do their job. He was using the gridded composite viewer to control them when she heard footsteps on the stairs.

She pitched her voice just loud enough for Luka to hear. "Nouri's coming. Someone's with him."

Luka nodded. "We're good." He led her into the apartment to stand just to the left of the doorway.

Nouri's companion turned out to be one of the detectives who'd been leaving just as she and Luka arrived three hours and forty minutes earlier.

Both Nouri and the detective, a short Chinese woman with even shorter hair, were intrigued by the cameras that were now swarming the bloodstained kitchen.

"I'll wager those glossy toys cost a month's salary," Nouri said.

Luka grinned at him. "Four month's, but they're stellar, aren't they?"

Mairwen, once again standing at the open forensic kit near the door, suppressed a smile. She was glad when Luka ran across other technology fans. She wasn't a good partner for him in that regard. She trusted her own senses more, especially since she'd allowed herself to use them more often. It helped that Luka still marveled at them and encouraged her.

The detective turned to Luka.

"I'm Investigator Hsu Wei. I'm the new primary on this case. Anything you can tell me now that will help?" Her English was impeccable, but Mairwen thought Mandarin was her primary language.

Luka raised an eyebrow. "I thought Harless was leading."

Hsu Wei exchanged a glance with Nouri, then looked back at Luka. "Harless was reassigned." She kept a straight face, but Nouri snorted.

Mairwen guessed it involved internal politics. She was getting better at recognizing them since she'd started attending meetings with Luka and interacting with co-workers and clients. It made her occasionally wistful for the night shift.

"Depends on your theory of the case," said Luka. Mairwen heard the thread of resolve in his voice. If the detective proved as arrogantly opinionated as Harless, she'd get nothing out of Luka.

"I don't have one," Hsu Wei said. "That's why I'm asking what the evidence says. Just an overview."

Luka gave her an assessing look, then nodded.

"The dead man forced the lock with the wirekey your techs collected earlier and assaulted the man in the apartment. Zip-tied his hands, dragged him to the couch, had rough sex with him there. Used the wirekey to burn him. The zip-tie was cut." He pointed to the floor near the couch, where the zip-tie with burned edges lay. "They fought. They hit the door hard enough to pop the hinges. They ended up in the kitchen area, where the knives were knocked on the floor. The apartment man stabbed the dead man in the gut and crawled to the wall comp and pinged for help. He dropped the knife there and stayed. The dead man moved a little but bled out where he is now."

"Did they know each other?"

Luka shook his head. "Evidence doesn't say."

"Yeah, that's what I thought. Thanks." She looked around at the mess and sighed. "Nouri, I'll be in the cruiser. Ping me when they're done."

"Yes, sir," he said.

The detective left, and Luka sent the swarm of cameras into the bedroom.

Twenty-two minutes later, Mairwen and Luka packed up and went out the door.

* * * * *

Even though he'd turned up the heat in his townhouse, Luka was still cold. He put the finishing touches on his report, then encrypted it and sent it to La Plata with a flag for Zheer. The samples he'd secured in his closet safe could wait until tomorrow. Zheer would forward the report to both the client and the police, as they'd agreed. He never wanted his work used to hide the truth, although it looked like it wouldn't be a problem in this case.

He stretched in his chair, from his fingers down to his bare toes, then looked at the clock. No wonder he was nearly flatlined. It was almost one in the morning, meaning he'd been up for more than twenty hours. He needed sleep, but first he needed to get warm. He went in search of Mairwen.

He found her in the kitchen, where she handed him a mug of hot chocolate. Her own mug was already half empty. She had no interest in cooking, but she had learned to make excellent hot chocolate. He was glad he'd introduced it to her before they'd left the ill-fated *Beehive*. He'd heard that both the *Beehive* and the exploration spacer had been deemed irreparably contaminated by exposure to the hybrid planet samples, and had been given one-way trips into the Insche 255 star. Expensive losses for the owners.

"How was your night?" she asked.

He knew she meant with his talent. "Good, but I was careful. I imagined I was running anytime there was even a hint of trouble. It made me slower than usual. I'll get better."

"Then you plan to take more violent crime cases." There was a note of concern in her statement. She was still fiercely protective of him. It warmed him in a way no external heat source ever could.

"Maybe. They're always hard, but I'm good at them. The dead and the living deserve the truth." He took a sip of hot chocolate. It was just the right temperature to have several swallows more.

She sipped from her mug. "Is the client telling the truth?"

"Unofficially? Yeah, I think he is. What do you think?"

She gave him a slight smile and an eyebrow twitch. "That you're a brilliant man."

He laughed. "Thank you. Nice dodge."

He knew she thought she didn't deserve to be an investigator, and that Zheer had promoted her as a favor to him. As if Zheer did anything she didn't want to do. He had suggested it, but hadn't expected Zheer to jump on it so fast. She'd been right, though. Mairwen was already proving her value to the company.

He sidled closer to her. "Will you stay tonight?"

They'd spent more nights together than apart since the pharma case, and she was already half undressed, wearing only a winter undershirt and leggings, but he didn't want to take her for granted.

"Yes." She set her empty mug in the sink. "If the storm keeps up, we could send the samples to the lab by courier and work from here tomorrow."

Which meant she'd stay all day. He used to be annoyed by the storms that kept him cooped up with only the net and his treadmill for company. Now he looked forward to them, as long as she was there.

"Good. I got groceries yesterday, so we won't starve." He finished the last of his hot chocolate, then put his mug in the sink next to hers. "That reminds me, Jerzi wants to borrow the kitchen next week. He wants to make meals in advance for when his fiancée and daughter arrive."

"Has he found a larger place to live yet?"

"Not yet. He's barely managing to do everything for the wedding." Luka smiled, remembering Jerzi's blind panic when he realized he had less than a month to plan a wedding and reception. The hazard pay from La Plata for their hybrid planet adventure made it possible for his family to afford to be together at last, and they were arriving in ten days. Fortunately, Beva Rienville and her large, boisterous, and generous family had stepped in to help and had things well in hand, meaning Jerzi could relax and start thinking about details.

She nodded. He knew she didn't see what the flurry was about. Her equanimity was one of her many charms.

"Should I tell him 'yes'?" he pressed.

She gave him a puzzled look. "It's your kitchen."

He put his hands on her shoulders and met her gaze. "I'd like you to think of it as yours, too."

He watched her as she thought about what he'd said.

"Are you asking me to move in with you?" Her voice was soft.

"Yes, *ljósið mitt*, I am." He'd called her his light, because she was. He gave her a warm smile and tried not to wear his heart on his sleeve. It had to be her choice.

They were interrupted by the distinctive ping tone that meant a live call from Zheer.

Djöfull, thought Luka darkly, as he walked to the desk to answer. Did that woman live at the office?

He activated the comp, and the holo of Zheer, seated, sprang to life. It was the middle of the night, and yet she was impeccably dressed. Maybe she really did live at the office. Or maybe she considered corporate suits as casual clothes, and she wore ballgowns the rest of the time. He mentally shook his head. Lack of sleep was making him whimsical.

"Excellent report, as usual," she said. She wouldn't have had time to do more than skim the conclusions section. Not that she'd ever read the whole thing. Only Mairwen did that.

"The client's parents will be pleased that they were right in pressuring the police to remove Detective Harless from the case."

"I wondered," said Luka. "The new primary, Hsu Wei, will likely do a better job, from what I saw."

He'd been distracted by testing his control over his still dangerous reconstruction talent, or he'd have used his other talent to confirm his opinion. He'd gotten over his reluctance to pry. He never wanted to be surprised by another Haberville again.

"Luka," Zheer began, then hesitated. "I've been refusing cases like this one for you. Has that changed?"

"Let me get back to you on that," Luka hedged. He wanted to select his own cases and set some boundaries, and needed time to get them straight in his own mind.

"Fair enough. Is Morganthur still there?"

Luka looked at Mairwen as she stepped into camera view.

"Good," said Zheer. "You have a new industrial security assessment case. It's down in Boetîa déș Luan, and it's a rush job, as usual. It's a large complex, so you'll need help. Take Luka."

"Should we plan on using charter, commercial, or suborbital?" asked Mairwen. A valid question, since the site was in Grand Sur, the continent south and east of Norutara, where Etonver was.

"Suborbital. They're in a hurry. I sent the details to your percomps. I'm told we had two more assessment inquiries today. At this rate, La Plata is going to need to hire an assistant for you." She gave them an enigmatic smile. "Oh, and since I have you both, I thought you might be interested to know that Juno Vizla Casualty is offering La Plata a special bonus for the successful completion of the pharma theft case. In exchange, they want us to not sue them over the fact that they knew about the high number of 'accidents' befalling ships that left Horvax Station, a fact they neglected to tell us when they saw and approved your itinerary. With the poisoning of Insche 255C scheduled for galactic-wide broadcast in three weeks, they'd like to keep their name out of the coverage."

Luka raised an eyebrow. "Will we sue?"

"If we must. I prefer to win the war instead." With that cryptic statement, she wished them a pleasant night and signed off.

He closed down the comp and looked at Mairwen. "That was interesting."

"Why?"

"Forecasters like Seshulla Zheer don't chat. They play *n*-dimensional chess." He planned to contemplate what she'd said in the morning, after a full night's sleep.

Mairwen gave him a small smile. "I don't chat, either."

He reached for her hand and pulled her into an embrace. She felt perfect in his arms. "You do so, *ástin mín*. You're just picky who you do it with."

He leaned his head against hers, thinking it was probably too late to pick up their interrupted conversation. He schooled himself to have patience. He'd rather win a whole life with Mairwen, not just a part of it now. He sighed.

"*Ég munu flytja inn með þér,*" she said.

Delight bloomed in him. "You will? I'll call the movers tomorrow. Later today. Whatever." He tightened his arms around her. Then it hit him. "Wait… that was Icelandic." He pulled back to look at her face. "You said you'd move in with me *in Icelandic.*"

She nodded and smiled.

"*Þakka þér, engillinn minn.*" He kissed her soundly. "It's the most thoughtful gift I've ever received."

"You're welcome, but I'm not an angel." She cupped the side of his face with her hand and stroked with her thumb. "There is strategic value in us both knowing a language only spoken on one underpopulated planet."

He smiled and kissed her again, then let her go, but kept her hand to lead her toward the bedroom. "I would expect no less from a woman who wears five knives." He waved the lights off as they left the living area. "That was how I knew you were something special, that first night in the warehouse."

She usually demurred when he told her things like that, but instead, she looked unexpectedly thoughtful.

"Yes?" he prompted.

"The dead man tonight."

Not the direction of thought he was hoping for.

She stopped walking. "He was in the warehouse. His scent was all over the forceblade that killed Balkovsky. I didn't connect it until you reminded me."

"How sure are you? Enough for me to make an unofficial suggestion to Hsu Wei that she look at him for Leo and Adina?"

"That, maybe, but nothing more. I didn't imprint the scent, I just remember it."

She took off her top and leggings and put them on the chair, then put her percomp in the drawer he'd cleared for her. It was still mostly empty, despite the fact that most of her things had migrated slowly into his townhouse. She had the least amount of possessions of anyone he'd ever met, male or female. The movers would have an easy job, except for her small but heavy force exerciser.

He used the fresher, then pulled his sweater off over his head and removed his pants quickly. "If he killed Leo, it's a fair guess that he killed Amhur, too. It was the same theft crew." He got into the heated bed where it was warm. "If it's the same man, the mode of his death tonight was deserved." He raised his voice a little so it carried to her in the fresher, even though he knew she could hear him even if he whispered.

She returned and gave him a sardonic smile as she released the knives and sheaths from her legs, arms, and back. "That's very frontier justice of you. I'm a bad influence." Naked, she was still lethally beautiful, not to mention blue-star hot.

"Not at all. I'm just more pragmatic these days." Having survived a stabbing, being kidnapped, a combat firefight, and a space battle, he'd gained some perspective. He'd been afraid of losing his compassion, but Mairwen, with a far more horrific past and a likely body count of untold numbers, was still very much human.

She slid under the covers and along his side. She rested her head on his shoulder, and her legs twined with his. He loved the smell of her, the glide of her skin on his. She'd get up before he did, as always, but he was glad she liked sharing the bed with him for a while. He couldn't help but use a thread of his talent when she was near because he loved the feel of her essence in his mind.

He reached up and waved the lights to almost nothing.

Despite being tired, he was still keyed up from the evening. He'd proved he could control his talent, and he'd achieved the first step in his grand plan for building a life with the woman he was deeply and desperately in love with. Who was moving in with him.

"You once said you'd tell me about Mairwen Morganthur..."

He focused carefully on her breathing and the feel of her body. He didn't want to bring up bad memories for her, but he had to know if he needed to worry about who the real Mairwen Morganthur had been. She passed civilian background checks with flying colors, but someone might look more thoroughly someday.

Her hand flattened on his chest. "It's not pretty."

He knew she was worried about how it would affect him, especially after the evening's experience. "I figured, *ljósið mitt*. I'll be all right." He tightened his arm around her waist with gentle, reassuring pressure.

She took a deep breath. "Most tracker targets are political or covert, but sometimes they're criminal. Two years after I... graduated, I was sent to a frontier planet to take down slave traders. When I found the camp in the middle of a monsoon jungle, the slaves had revolted and the traders had killed most of them. I followed my orders and killed the slavers and guards, then against orders, I looked for surviving slaves. I found four: a woman, about my age, and three children. The woman had protected the children, but at the cost of her own life. She was mortally wounded, and I could do nothing except stay with her while she died. I promised to get the children to safety."

He felt her shake her head, perhaps at some memory that made her regretful. He stroked her back slowly.

"The woman was an orphan, the last of her maternal and paternal lines, from a failed colony on a different frontier planet."

"Waimaakole," he said. The planet she'd said she was from.

"Yes. The foster house illegally sold her as an indenturee to care for the slaver's younger 'merchandise.' She was unafraid to die if the children were safe. I was... sad she wouldn't be missed or remembered."

His intuition twitched. "So you took her name, in her honor, when you got out."

He was continually amazed that the CPS imagined they had obliterated the humanity from Mairwen. Her feelings ran deep and strong, no matter how well she controlled the surface.

"Honor, yes, but expedience, too. All trackers dream of freedom. It's the only thing we ever agreed on when we weren't trying to kill one another."

"Kill? Why?"

"The CPS makes sure there are no tracker alliances. We're hard enough to control as individuals. There were rumors of a rebellion early in the program, long before my time. It took battalions of Jumpers and telekinetic minders to crush it."

He smiled in the dark. "Considering your extraordinary skills, I'm not surprised." He caressed her shoulder with his free hand. "So there was a woman your age, now dead, with an off-the-net past."

She nodded. "I was already planning to escape. Since my own identity was irretrievably lost, I knew I'd need a new one. Hers was ideal. When I took biometric samples of the slavers as proof of death, I took her samples, too, and hid them. I used them to build a life for her. I taught myself some Welsh, the language of her mother, plus computer twists, under the guise of improving my tracker skills. Each time I was on a mission and unobserved, I hunted for the few real records of her and altered or destroyed them. I kept her alive in new records and created accounts to funnel any untraceable funds I could find. She moved often. She was on Rekoria when I 'died' on my last mission. She moved to Etonver and accepted a night-shift guard job at La Plata."

"How did you handle the biometrics? Your former employer must have virtual tripwires throughout the galaxy just waiting for a stray biometric from the 'lost' to show up somewhere."

"Blackmarket chimera implant to match the samples I'd saved."

He tightened his arms around her as he realized the implications. Without a healer or the ability to use pain medications, she'd have been very sick and in excruciating pain for weeks, maybe months, and very vulnerable. The CPS had already meddled with her DNA, and the implant could easily have killed her.

It was such an unlikely convergence of chance that had brought them together that first night in the spaceport warehouse. He shivered in spite of himself. No wonder people were tempted to believe in fate or destiny.

"I am," he said, tilting his head down to kiss her, "a very lucky man."

"We're both lucky. Who else would teach me how to be human?"

He took several long, deliberate breaths and stroked her skin slowly, letting the simple actions and her warmth help clear his mind of the sadness and anger he felt for the too-young woman who'd had to steal another's identity because the CPS had erased hers. And had treated her and her fellow trackers worse than slaves, making them disbelieve their own humanity. The ironically named Citizen Protection Service had gotten away with far too much for far too long.

"Your former employer deserves to be taken down, piece by nasty little piece," he said, with more vehemence than he'd intended.

"Yes," she agreed, "but not by us." He heard determination in her tone, and worry.

She must think he wanted to single-handedly take on the whole government covert operations organization. He didn't. He wanted to enjoy a long life with his socially artless, impossibly skilled woman. Putting her in the CPS's sights would cut that decidedly short.

He laughed. "No, my heart, the men you follow are brilliant, not insane."

She laughed and touched his face with gentle fingers. "There's only you." Her voice was soft and warm. "*Ég elska þig.*"

"I love you, too, more than I can say." He found her mouth for a long, sense-drenching kiss. "Like I said, I'm a very lucky man."

EPILOGUE

SESHULLA ZHEER SMOOTHED the front of her gold gossamer caftan, enjoying the color and the freedom from the restricting suits she usually lived in. The view from her fifth-floor executive office overlooked a park that had floating fairy lights all night long. The early summer weather made Etonver more bearable than usual.

From an ornate and velvet-lined box, she gently removed the hand-blown bottle of two-hundred-year-old, flamed, five-barrel cognac, then put it carefully on the serving cart.

It was the first day of the Galactic Standard new year, but still a few minutes before midnight on Rekoria. It was a minor event, hardly celebrated at all compared to the local summer solstice, which was still a couple of weeks away. Still, it meant something to her. She'd been born on a galactic new year, far longer ago than she'd ever admit.

As her guests seated themselves at her worktable, she served them the beverages she'd arranged with them each in mind. For Jerzi Adams, in casual clothes that showed off his muscular physique, a perfectly chilled dark lager from Rekoria's best brewery, served in a stein decorated with ancient rifles. For Luka Foxe, stylish in a grey resilk shirt and black vest, white champagne in an antique ice flute, the closest she could come to acknowledging his maternal Icelandic heritage. She knew he didn't care for hard alcohol. For Beva Rienville, comfortable in a brightly floral sundress, a classic black Nero d'Avola in a handmade Bordeaux stem, because she knew Beva's tastes. And for Mairwen Morganthur, in non-descript dark red knit, with long sleeves as always to hide the plethora of knives she was never without, an artistically minimalist glass of iced herbal Schisandra tea steeped slowly in triple-filtered water.

Lastly, she poured herself another snifter of outrageously rare cognac, then sat in the only empty chair at her worktable. She knew they were genteelly shocked at her casual appearance, and the fact that she was undeniably tipsy.

She smiled at them all. "I know the rumor is I don't sleep. I actually do, but not for long." She centered her snifter on the coaster protecting the worktable's hand-polished finish. "You all know I was a forecaster for the CPS, and Beva knows I retired on disability. The 'enhancement' drug they used on me gave me permanent hypnolepsy."

She'd been lucky. Most of the others in the secret "study group" who'd received the same experimental version of the drug had died within a year. She ran a finger along the rim of her snifter.

"I can take a regimen of daily drugs and be normal, or I can be an effective forecaster, but not both. Since I choose the latter, I have to sleep in two-hour intervals, day and night."

It wasn't news to Beva, but it was to the others. Jerzi looked surprised, and Luka looked intrigued. Morganthur looked… quiet. It was what made people underestimate her at first, the way Seshulla had.

She knew she should gently lead them up to the reason she'd called such an inconveniently late meeting, but she was suddenly chafing at the rituals of politeness.

"I know you all have secrets and may know some of them about each other. Now you know one of mine." She took a deep breath. "Here's another. There's an upheaval coming, and it'll affect the whole Concordance. Not tomorrow, or even next year, but in six years or eight years at the outside."

To their credit, none of them gave even a hint that they suspected she might be chemmed on hallucinogens in addition to being drunk.

"Have you ever heard of Ayorinn's Legacy?"

Luka, Beva, and Adams shook their heads. Morganthur gave no indication, which Seshulla took to mean she probably had, but not in a context she was willing to admit. Seshulla would bet her best handwoven spidersilk carpet that not even Beva, with her galaxy-class interrogation talent, could get anything out of Morganthur she wasn't willing to give.

"Once upon a time…" she stopped and smiled playfully. "That's how all the best stories start."

Beva smiled with good humor. Seshulla allowed herself one sip from her snifter. It was exquisitely breathtaking.

"Maybe twenty-five years ago, there was a legendary, and possibly mythical, forecaster named Ayorinn. The best there's ever been. You must understand that good forecasters do more than predict the future, they can influence it. Ayorinn spent ten years developing a forecast, because he wanted to move the entire galaxy. He knew certain government organizations would do everything they could to suppress it, so he hid it in a series of coded poetic quatrains on timed release. The goal of his forecast was freedom for people with secrets."

Beva reached out and patted Seshulla's hand on the table. "Seshulla, *mon bon ami,* you're two sheets to the wind. Are you sure you want to be telling us all this?"

Seshulla laughed, but it sounded hollow to her ears. "I'd feel worse if I didn't. You're the closest thing I have to friends, and if that isn't a telling commentary on my life, I don't know what is."

She knew only Beva wasn't astounded to be considered a friend. Luka, of the generous heart and insatiable curiosity, took it in stride. Adams was visibly startled. She hadn't spent much time with him directly, but she admired how he'd come into his own after surviving the pharma case, settling in with his family, and helping Beva exceed the return on investment for the Personal Security Division. Unless she missed her guess, his daughter would be joining the "people with secrets" category. Seshulla still didn't have a handle on what Morganthur was thinking, and maybe never would, but believed they had more in common than either of them might imagine.

"Why…" asked Luka. "Oh, I see. Another part of the Ayorinn forecast came out."

There, thought Seshulla, was the brilliant investigator that Leo Balkovsky had sold her on, making those uncanny intuitive leaps.

She tried to smile encouragingly at him, but the weight of what was in the newly unfolded piece of Ayorinn's Legacy made it hard. The gathering storm clouds were dark and deadly. "Yes."

She was grateful he didn't think to ask about how she came by the cryptogon to decode them, or he might guess more than was safe.

"My talent doesn't usually work well for individuals, but for groups, yes. Change is inevitable for us all. Some factions have been trying to prevent it or control it. When they're cornered, they'll be dangerous. You could try burying yourselves on some frontier planet to ride it out, but knowing who you all are, you won't. You can't."

The alcohol was making her maudlin. It was also making her shaky, because it interfered with her carefully tuned wake-sleep cycle. She'd crater soon, and pay for it for the next few days until she got back on schedule. But rare cognac and rare company were worth it.

A single chime went off, then the very old, lovingly tended bell clock rang out thirteen perfectly pitched and timed notes in succession. A tone poem meditation on time slipping away.

When the last bell's harmonics finally faded, she raised her glass to her friends.

"To a prosperous new year."

Beva, Luka, and Jerzi raised their glasses and touched rims. Morganthur watched them all with a slightly bemused expression, as if she'd never seen the ritual before. Seshulla occasionally wondered if the woman had been raised by wolves. She was slightly envious. It would have been much better than being raised in the rigidly proper, obscenely rich, and oppressively stultifying environment of her own youth. It was a good thing her family thought she was long dead.

"La Plata did well this year, thanks in no small part to each of you."

Beva laughed. "It doesn't hurt to have a forecaster at the helm, either." She turned to the others. "Seshulla won't tell you, but she saved this company seven years ago, and the board made her president."

"For my sins," said Seshulla, with a self-deprecating smile.

Everyone smiled at her humor, and relaxed a little.

Luka turned to Jerzi. "I've been meaning to ask. Now that Dhorya and Pico have been here six months, are they missing her family?"

Jerzi shook his head. "Not for a minute, but the family is sure missing Dhorya. Or rather, they're missing her free accountant services, and the chance to meddle. She's happier than I've ever seen her. Pico, too. If I'd known how bad things were…" He shrugged, guilt seeping into his expression.

"Don't kick yourself, *cher*," said Beva. "They're here now, and that's what counts."

Luka nodded. "You can't change the past, only the future." He glanced at Morganthur in silent communication.

"Speaking of the future," said Beva, "our oldest kids are planning a huge party for our thirtieth wedding anniversary next month. It's supposed to be a secret, so I hope you'll let them think it still is when they invite you. Jen and I are practicing looking surprised." She demonstrated, melodramatically gasping and clutching at imaginary pearls. Everyone laughed.

The conversation meandered a bit, and Seshulla let it breeze around her like a drift of butterflies until Luka mentioned that he and Mairwen were looking for a new place to live. One near running trails and that had a flitter pad, since their cases often took them out of town.

Mairwen, whose chair had somehow ended up close to Luka's, slid her hand into his and threaded their fingers together. "He just doesn't want to drive in Etonver ground traffic."

He laughed. "Guilty as charged." He squeezed her fingers playfully. "It's gotten worse. I didn't think that was even possible."

Seshulla was relieved her little party had finally made Mairwen feel comfortable enough to engage, even if it was just with Luka. Beva was right. They were good for each other.

Seshulla smiled. "I had an uncle once who hated traffic jams so much that he bought a mixed-use highrise and moved his business there so his commute choices would be the lifts or the stairs. Of course, it may have been because the province revoked his permit permanently for causing so many accidents. He hated traffic rules, too."

They laughed, as she'd intended, and the others recounted their own traffic horror stories. Everyone who lived in Etonver had them.

She hoped it hadn't been too much of a nudge. Luka had finally begun seriously looking for an assistant, based on the idea seed she'd planted months ago. She could have wished he'd started sooner, but he'd been distracted by falling in love. It was nice to see.

Like most forecasters, she tended to be too obsessed by tomorrow to pay attention to today, and none of her relationships had survived that.

She needed to be slow and careful when dangling threads at smart people like Luka, or they'd see them. When chess pieces became self-aware, they sometimes went their own direction. La Plata had been a good place for Luka to recover from whatever had hurt him so badly, but both he and Mairwen, wildcard that she was, needed to get away from the corporate environment to flourish.

La Plata would perform well in the coming year, barring catastrophes. Beva and Jerzi would grow the Personal Security Division enough to keep the board happy, even when Luka and Mairwen moved on. She'd make sure it was an amicable split, to preserve present alliances. La Plata was a useful tool in furthering bloody Ayorinn's legacy, but she selfishly wanted her friends to be safe from people or organizations that wanted to hurt them.

She was fading fast under the influence of the cognac. She served everyone another round of their selected drinks, then brought out the bag she'd discreetly left behind her desk.

She pulled out twelve ancient coins with round edges and square holes in the center. They had little left of their original engraving, so their value was more sentimental than intrinsic. She stacked them on the table in front of her.

"In pre-flight days on old Earth, there was a tradition of making way for good luck by making resolutions for the coming year. I'm going to be rudely presumptuous and offer some for you."

She carefully slid one coin to Beva, Luka, Adams, and Morganthur, making eye contact with each.

"First. Know who your friends are, and keep them close."

She slid another coin to each of them.

"Second. Have more than one way out of the city and off the planet, and safe landing places for yourselves and anyone you care about."

Her hand twitched uncontrollably, causing her to splash a bit of cognac on the hand-polished wood. She took a deep breath, centering herself, willing the shaking to stop. When it did, she slid the last of her coins to her friends.

"Third. Never, ever trust the fucking Citizen Protection Service."

She hadn't meant that last resolution to be so vehement or pointed, and it went against the unofficial forecaster motto of softly softly, catchee monkey, but she didn't think she was telling them anything they didn't already believe. It felt good to be direct for once.

"And on that happy note," said Beva with a teasing twinkle in her eye, "I offer a toast to good friends."

She raised her glass in invitation, and they all clinked their glasses and drank.

Jerzi held up his stein. "To having places to go."

The glasses clinked again.

Luka raised his glass and gave Seshulla a crooked, slightly knowing smile. "To a good future."

They clinked their glasses one last time.

Luka set his glass down, then drew Mairwen close for a kiss and muttered something to her too quiet for the others to hear. She smiled softly at him, love shining in her eyes, before drawing back. Jerzi smiled, and Beva sighed.

Love between two people, or friends, or for what was right, would help them all survive the coming conflagration.

For the first time what seemed like forever, Seshulla felt hope.

ABOUT THIS BOOK

Thanks for reading *Overload Flux*, and I hope you enjoyed it. This is the first of the Central Galactic Concordance space opera series, and more are out now and coming soon. Book 2, *Minder Rising*, starts a year after the events in *Overload Flux*, with new characters and challenges. Luka's and Mairwen's adventures continue in the novella *Zero Flux*, Book 2.5, about a very cold case. Book 3, *Pico's Crush*, features new and returning characters in a fast-paced adventure on a paradise planet. Book 4, *Jumper's Hope*, has new characters on the run from whoever wants them dead, this time for real.

If you're enjoying the series, please post an online review of this book and the others at your favorite book retailer. Even if it's short and sweet, it really helps. Reviews are what get books noticed and read by others. Think of it as paying forward for the last time someone recommended a book you really liked.

Find out about new releases before anyone else by signing up for my newsletter at bit.ly/CVN-news. I promise not to send photos of my cats or vacations (unless it's somewhere off-planet).

I'd love to know what you think about the story, and what you'd like to see in future books in the series. Visit my website and blog at Author.CarolVanNatta.com and comment or drop me a line, or connect with me on Facebook at "CarolVanNattaAuthor."

I owe a deep debt of gratitude to Karen in Iceland, who patiently helped make Luka's Icelandic accurate and realistic, and to my friends and beta readers Judy, Jill, T3, Ann, John, and Roger, who kindly pointed out myriad ways to improve, well, everything. I am also grateful for the professional editing services provided by Shelley Holloway of Holloway House, and a fantastic cover design by Gene Mollica Studio.

ABOUT THE AUTHOR

Carol Van Natta is a science fiction and fantasy author. She shares her home in Fort Collins, Colorado with a sometime-mad scientist and various cats. Any violations of the laws of physics in her books are the fault of the cats, not the mad scientist.

Sign up for her newsletter at her website, http://Author.CarolVanNatta.com.

BOOKS BY CAROL VAN NATTA

Space Opera
Overload Flux (Central Galactic Concordance, Book 1)
Minder Rising (CGC Book 2)
Zero Flux (CGC Novella 2.5)
Pico's Crush (CGC Book 3)
Jumper's Hope (CGC Book 4)

Fantasy
In Graves Below
Shift of Destiny

Retro Science Fiction Comedy
Hooray for Holopticon (with Ann Harbour)

ORLAND PARK PUBLIC LIBRARY

CPSIA information can be obtained
at www.ICGtesting.com
Printed in the USA
LVOW10s1520100518
576717LV00011B/942/P